MW00323614

# STRANGE
# FOLK

# STRANGE FOLK

A Novel

## ALLI DYER

**ATRIA** BOOKS

NEW YORK · LONDON · TORONTO · SYDNEY · NEW DELHI

An Imprint of Simon & Schuster, LLC
1230 Avenue of the Americas
New York, NY 10020

First Atria Books hardcover edition August 2024

**ATRIA** B O O K S and colophon are trademarks of Simon & Schuster, LLC

Simon & Schuster: Celebrating 100 Years of Publishing in 2024

For information about special discounts for bulk purchases, please contact Simon & Schuster Special Sales at 1-866-506-1949 or business@simonandschuster.com.

The Simon & Schuster Speakers Bureau can bring authors to your live event. For more information or to book an event, contact the Simon & Schuster Speakers Bureau at 1-866-248-3049 or visit our website at www.simonspeakers.com.

Manufactured in the United States of America

1 3 5 7 9 10 8 6 4 2

Library of Congress Cataloging-in-Publication Data
Names: Dyer, Alli, author.
Title: Strange folk : a novel / Alli Dyer.
Description: First Atria Books hardcover edition. | New York : Atria Paperback, 2024.
Identifiers: LCCN 2023038061 (print) | LCCN 2023038062 (ebook) |
ISBN 9781668045770 (hardcover) | ISBN 9781668045787 (paperback) |
ISBN 9781668045794 (ebook)
Subjects: BISAC: FICTION / Thrillers / Psychological | FICTION / Occult & Supernatural | LCGFT: Paranormal fiction. | Novels.
Classification: LCC PS3604.Y44 S77 2024 (print) | LCC PS3604.Y44 (ebook) |
DDC 813/.6--dc23/eng/20231124
LC record available at https://lccn.loc.gov/2023038061
LC ebook record available at https://lccn.loc.gov/2023038062

ISBN 978-1-6680-4577-0
ISBN 978-1-6680-4579-4 (ebook)

For Mama

# STRANGE
# FOLK

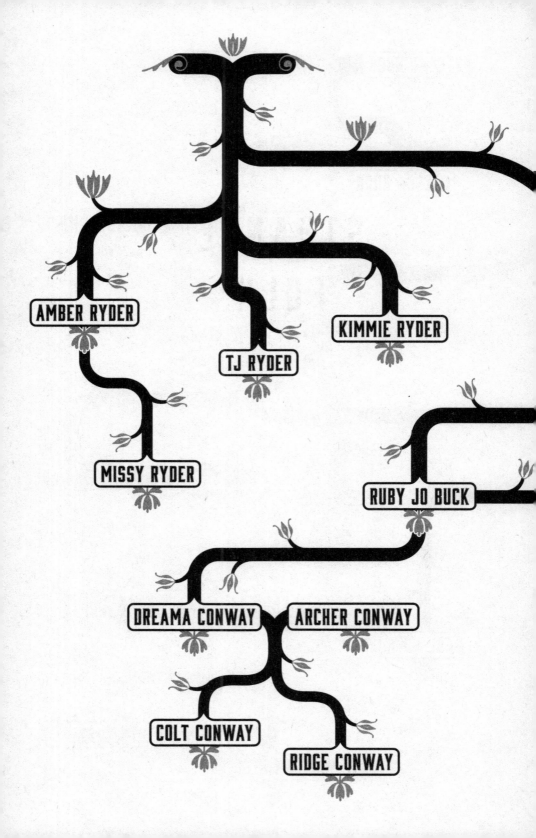

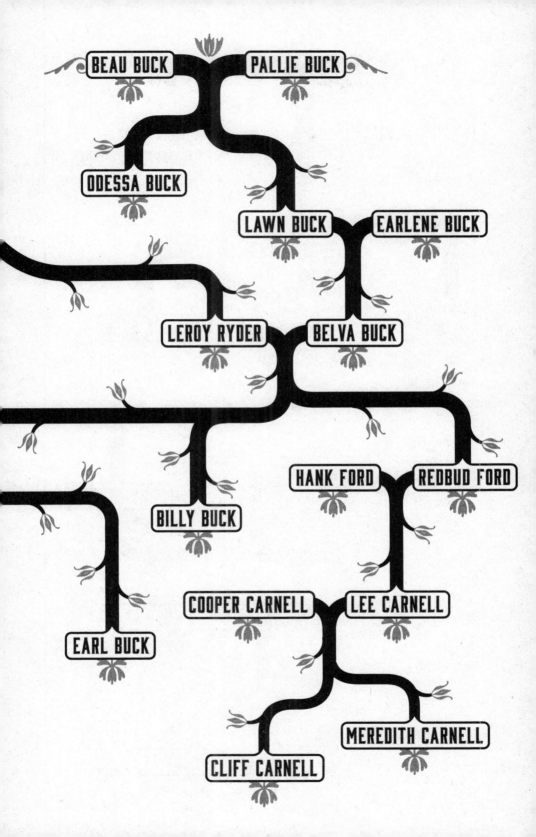

# PROLOGUE

The girl watched from the blackberry bush as the cabin glowed in the falling darkness.

The windows radiated warm voices and the smell of chicken and dumplings. Her belly churned. She hadn't eaten or uttered a word in days.

A dark-haired woman led a small group out of the cabin into the backyard, where a fire blazed. As they gathered around the flames, the woman pulled out a large canning jar filled with a gray powder, and a black leather book.

The girl's breath quickened, and she held it. She was only ten or so feet away, hidden at the dense edge of the woods. They would hear if she made a sound.

The woman took off her shoes and stood in a wide, powerful stance with her bare feet planted firmly in the ground. Her voice was hard and potent as she addressed the group, and the girl leaned in to listen from the shadows. Her pulse skipped when she heard why they had gathered. A secret unfurled inside her like a daddy longlegs stretching its limbs.

The woman started to hum with a strange voice that buzzed in the girl's chest. The others joined in harmony, growing louder, and the buzz spread, vibrating through every inch of the girl's body.

The woman violently shook the jar and passed it to the next person, who repeated the motion. She picked up the black book, and as she read out the words, the wind surged and the clouds rolled in front of the moon so that there was only the fire to illuminate them. The girl was left in thick, solitary darkness at the outer edge.

The woman put the jar into a hole in the ground and buried it with fistfuls of dirt. Then she took out a knife and ran it across her hand, and the girl could feel a phantom sear in her own. She watched as the woman squeezed her palm over the dirt mound and blood trickled down into it.

The woman's speech became a fierce chant, and the others joined in again, flinging the words into the fire so that it jerked and smoked.

Eventually their voices began to slow, and then the hum finally died with one resounding *amen* that the girl whispered to herself. The others fell back into the dirt, laughing maniacally with sweat glistening on their faces.

That was when the girl saw it. A shadow lurking just outside the circle. No one seemed to notice, except for the dark-haired woman, who stared at the shadow, transfixed.

It moved through the circle amidst their giddy, sprawled bodies, but they still did not see it. The girl watched each shiver as it passed. Even from her hiding place, she could feel its chill seeping into her bones.

At the edge of the clearing, the shadow turned back to look at the woman.

Then it disappeared into the dark.

# ONE

## LEE

It was quiet in the car when the road began to climb into the mountains. In the front seat, Meredith's head rested against the seat belt in a sling. Cliff was hunched on his side, making a contorted bed out of the backseat. Lee's mouth tasted like fermented pennies from the coffee she'd gotten in Arkansas early that morning.

As the incline of the highway steepened, a chill crept in through the vents, and the air turned to mist around the car. Lee pressed the back of her hand to the window. It was freezing.

Soon the fog was so thick that she was forced to turn on her headlights and slow to a crawl, hugging the innermost lane to avoid the edge. She wound slowly through the twists of the road and passed large semi-trucks barely creeping along the pavement. Her hands were slick and tightly gripped on the steering wheel, and her foot shook a little on the gas. One swift movement, and she and her children would go careening off the edge.

They were on hour thirty-four of a three-day trek from California, and she was starting to lose it. *Only a few more hours to go.* She tried to put a podcast on, but she couldn't concentrate. Her mind wandered back to the last time she'd been home.

Twenty years ago, she'd been heading in the opposite direction on a bus bound for college, looking out the window at the fog-cloaked valley erasing in front of her and replaying her last moments with Mama outside the bus station. Mama was two months sober and still a little bit beautiful, but Lee could see the cracks forming. She was on the verge of collapse; as soon as Lee was no longer there to watch her, she would fall apart.

At the driver's final call, Mama hugged her suddenly, violently, with ash and gardenia filling Lee's nose. Then she put her lips to Lee's ear and whispered, "If you ever come back here, Opaline, I will skin you alive."

College had not been what Lee expected. Her goal had been only escape, and it had taken every ounce of her to do it. She'd denounced everything she'd known, including her own name. But then she wondered, *What now?* She didn't know how to make friends, didn't know how to approach people and make herself open to them. She had the kind of weirdness that sealed her off from people. A *strangeness.*

She was adrift until she met Cooper with his shaggy blond hair and disheveled Bohemian style that belied his money. He claimed to like her strangeness, but after years of him trying to sand down her edges and of her contorting herself to fit his rich, shiny world, she had lost sight of who she was or where she belonged. She was a mother, and she loved that. But beneath it, she had devolved into something she recognized too well. There was a deep wrongness inside of her that she hadn't escaped.

Lee hadn't planned on ever coming back to Craw Valley. And yet, here she was, running away from a failed marriage and an empty life. Returning to this place because she had nowhere else to go.

The car began to angle downward, and the thick fog receded. In the clear air, the valley revealed itself as a wet, green, sprawling country that became blue mountains in the distance. Lee opened her window and inhaled the sweet chill, her desert-dried skin reanimating with the moisture and her mind clearing of her failures for a brief moment.

She looked out over the mountains and could feel their pull even from here, reeling her in.

At the rush of air, Meredith yawned and sat up, and Cliff stretched in her rearview mirror.

"I dreamt we were in the forest and there was a fire," her son shared sleepily. "Like we were camping, but not. It was me, you, and a bunch of strangers standing around it. You were saying something in this scary voice, and there was this buzzing like a bug in my ear. It was really weird."

Unease slithered down Lee's spine. "Creepy, Iff."

"What about me? Was I there?" Meredith asked.

"No. Just me and Mom."

"That's messed up." Meredith reached into the backseat and swatted his leg. "So what happened next?"

"I don't know. Mom rolled down the window and woke me up."

"I had to. Look at this. Smell it." She gestured out the window at the landscape and inhaled dramatically.

"I think you have car fever," Meredith said.

Cliff kicked Meredith's seat and shrieked, "I've got the fever, too!"

Lee lowered the other windows, and their hair started whipping around their heads. Cliff laughed, and Meredith reluctantly gave up a smile.

"Are you ready?" Lee yelled at them through the thumping current.

They both answered, "Yes!"

"As hard as you can, okay?"

She counted to three, and they leaned their heads out the windows and screamed over the mountains as hard as they could. In Lee's howl was the force of all her anxieties and regrets and love, announcing herself to this godforsaken place.

•   •   •

An hour later, Lee took the familiar exit. She marveled at the cluster of new chain restaurants, the freshly stuccoed Walmart, the dead-stock retailers with parking lots packed to the gills.

As she moved farther away from the highway, the country took over and the strip malls became the thick woods and empty fields she recognized. A string of local businesses sprouted up amidst the green of the pine and the hickory and maple turning gold and crimson—a hamburger stand, a tractor supply, a new Mexican place where the Italian joint had been.

She felt herself entering a familiar groove. A part of her brain that she had tried to repurpose for anything else was now awakening at the scenery she'd passed thousands of times as a child, imprinted on her like a second language. There was the red-and-yellow sign for Hardee's where she had waited for Mama in the hash-brown fumes when she forgot to pick her up. And the small brick façade of the public library where she'd slept the nights Mama had people over who tried to climb into Lee's bed.

A tender pain bubbled up in her chest, and she quickly buried it. She wanted to see the place through new eyes, as an outsider.

"So, is this it? Are we here?" Meredith asked.

"Yep. This is it. The great town of Craw Valley." Her children were quiet as they scanned out the windows. "Don't worry. Six months max, remember? Probably less. Enough time for your dad and I to work out an arrangement." She knew it was ridiculous that she refused to say the word "divorce" to them, but the word was charged and made of a torturous metal when she saw it in her mind. This was not the childhood she'd wanted for them. At least *arrangement* held a tinge of enlightenment.

"I think it's kind of . . . cute."

Lee glanced at Meredith, searching for one eyebrow arched in sarcasm. Her daughter approved of very few things anymore, and none of them were *cute*. But her face was earnest. "You think it's *cute*."

"I mean, it's not trying to be something it's not. It's not trying so hard. Like, 'look at me, look at who I am, buy things from me.'"

"I'll give you that. It's definitely not trying very hard. Iff, what do you think?"

"I kind of like it, too. It makes me think of something red and veined, like when you see an animal ear in the sun."

Lee looked back out the window and marveled at how he was able to capture the world in such a strange and perfect way. "I know what you mean," she agreed.

Cliff saw the world through a different filter; people and places evoked colors or specific images, and he often couldn't distinguish between his imagination and reality. Sometimes he knew things he shouldn't: little predictions for the future, undisclosed facts about people. She had expected it to go away as he got older, but the fantasies only strengthened as he moved closer to adolescence. He had been seen by many doctors and given many diagnoses at her husband's insistence, but they never entirely fit.

They continued down a one-lane road and passed small, neat salt boxes and prefabricated ranch houses. One decaying wood house stood with an abandoned school bus parked out front and a cracked plastic pool piled in the side yard. And then there were no houses, only a narrow, winding road with a succession of dirt and gravel drives receding into a wall of trees on each side, closing them in. Lee felt safe under its canopy, no longer exposed to the sky and the elements as she'd been for the thousands of miles they'd streaked through flat, dry country.

Before she was aware of it, she spotted the crooked oak and hung a right onto a gravel road. Though her hybrid SUV was supposedly made for off-roading, she could hear scraping as she navigated each curve and dip. After a while, the trees gave way to a clearing with a modest cabin in its center, as if raised from the earth itself. Buckets and barrels sat around its perimeter, waiting for rain, and something copper-colored hung from the tree in front at a sinister angle. She parked in the dirt next to a pickup truck, and they emerged stiff-legged from the car.

Lee took a deep breath in. The air was pure rain-watered wetness, and it smelled of trees—the salted bark, the vegetable leaves, the oxygen fumes. She told herself she could appreciate this place like a tourist. No plans to stay long term. Just passing through to soak up the clean air and leer at the deciduous shedding their leaves in a riot of color.

A Black woman came out of the screened porch, and it took Lee a moment to place her. A friend of her mother's, but only in the early years. She was wearing sensible, loose-fitting jeans, and her hair was combed back from a high-cheekboned face with no makeup. She pulled her hands out of her pockets and gestured at them in welcome.

"Hey, darlin'. Do you remember me? Luann?"

"Yes, I think I do. You were Mama's friend."

"Yeah, that's right. It's been a long time." She reached out and shook her hand with both palms wrapped around Lee's. "Belva's out back."

"Sounds good."

Cliff held on to Meredith's sleeve as they warily approached from the other side of the car. They weren't very high on strangers.

"Meredith and Cliff, this is Luann. A friend of the family."

They nodded in greeting, and Meredith pointed to the thing hanging in the tree. "What's that?"

"Oh, yes. We been light on rain for the past week, so Belva split a snake down its middle and hung it in the tree there. Got a good sprinkling this morning before y'all arrived."

Meredith's eyes widened, and Cliff huddled closer to her. Luann took her cue. "You must be tired after your trip. Y'all come on in."

They followed Luann through the porch and then the front door, still painted blue with old iron tools hung above its frame.

The small wood-lined living room was the same as it had always been, with the orange polyester couch and the rag rug fraying at the edges. Carved birds sat perched on shelves looking down at them. The old money jar stood by the door filled with coins and labeled MYRTLE BEACH in faded marker. Lee wondered if Belva ever made it to the ocean.

The most pronounced change was a spread of picture frames on the east wall. As Lee moved closer, she realized it was every Christmas card she'd ever sent. Fifteen photos of Lee and her family in sweaters, lined up in black plastic Walmart frames. It broke her heart a little bit, this preservation of the type of card that people usually threw away when January came around. This grasping at some connection to the granddaughter who had neglected their relationship for decades. She wondered if Belva understood that it had never been about her. It was about this place, and this life. It was hard to hold on to a piece of it when she'd intended to leave it wholly behind.

Before she could dwell on it further, she noticed a hulking man in a worn flannel standing at the counter in the kitchen. He was covering steaks in a marinade with large callused hands studded with thyme flowers, and when he looked up, his eyes sparkled with mirth.

"Shit dog, it's Opaline." As he came around to hug Lee with hands pointed up to protect her shirt, Meredith shot her a look and mouthed *Opaline?*

"Uncle Billy! I'm actually going by 'Lee' now."

"Oh, right, I knew that. I seen the Christmas cards."

Lee's shame was renewed at the mention of them. "I didn't know you'd be here. How are you?"

Billy sighed. "Same old, same old. I couldn't miss meeting the famous Meredith and Cliff." He bent his large frame toward the kids. "Meredith, I'm Billy. I'm sure your mama's never talked about me, so I'll save you the trouble and tell you I'm Redbud's crazy little brother." He eyed the paperback sticking out of her bag. "So you're a reader, huh? What you reading right now?"

Meredith shot Lee another look as if to say *Redbud?* "Oh. Um. I guess I've been reading a lot of Ursula K. Le Guin."

"I don't know her. What does she write?"

"Sci-fi fantasy. She's one of the most important writers in that genre."

Billy whistled. "Can I borrow one? Damn shame I never heard of her."

Meredith visibly softened. "Yeah, sure. I only found out about her on Reddit. It's, like, a crime no one talks about her."

Billy pivoted toward Cliff and studied him for a little bit before asking, "What do you make of this place?"

Cliff's eyes scanned the walls and the people around him with an intent gaze. Lee expected Cliff to shy away from Billy, but he seemed drawn to him. His voice was dreamy as he said, "There are so many colors here."

Billy nodded. "What's my color?"

"You're sorta orangey gold. Like those flowers outside. With the tiny petals."

"Marigold."

"Yeah, like that."

Billy smiled. "This is a special place. Not much like it except for my cabin a little ways down the road. Y'all should come over sometime. I got a mess of animals and other stuff I can show you."

Cliff glittered at the mention of it.

Billy turned back to the steaks and sprinkled salt on them. "Hope y'all like venison."

Meredith and Cliff looked at Lee incredulously.

"Venison is deer, guys."

They both went a little wide-eyed, and Billy guffawed up to the ceiling.

In the silence of her children, Billy kept jabbering on, but Lee couldn't hear him. A vibration was building in the air, and Lee was the only one who could feel it, pulling her toward the back of the house.

She left the kids in the kitchen and traced a path down the hallway. On a side table covered in white lace sat a few framed photographs with candles, a gold necklace, and a packet of chewing tobacco in front of them. One photo was an old glamour shot of an auburn-haired woman with intense, nervous eyes and a red feather boa wrapped dissonantly around her shoulders. It had been so long since she'd seen her aunt Ruby Jo that she had a hard time recognizing her at first. She died when Lee was still in elementary school. Next to her frame was a senior portrait of a fluffy-haired white boy with the grainy overexposure of the early 2000s. It was Ruby Jo's son, her cousin Earl. Lee remembered when her mother called her in the middle of the night years ago. Her words had dissolved in her mouth as she raved, drunk or high or both, about Earl dying in a motorcycle accident. It wasn't until Lee had looked it up online that she learned he'd been running from the police after a drug bust.

The vibration built, rippling through her as she continued down the hallway toward the sunshine spilling from the back windows.

When she stepped out the back door, the buzzing swelled into a primordial harmony.

The real magic of the property was the garden, which stretched from the back door to the woods, as thick with life as you've ever seen a patch of earth. There were rows and rows of vegetables, flowers, herbs, and plants that defied category. Countless stalks loomed and coiled and presented their autumn blooms to the sky with a prescient boldness, and the air fizzed with insects.

Some of her best memories as a child had been in this garden, wandering the rows with her grandmother and learning the names and uses of its wild inhabitants.

In a clearing to the right, an imposing figure clad in cream canvas and a wide, netted headdress stood wreathed in smoke, surrounded by shoulder-high white boxes that buzzed with the sweet, resonant music that had pulled Lee here. She watched for a while as the figure removed trays from the boxes coated in wax and dripping with honey, whispering to the bees.

The figure noticed her standing there and stepped away from the hives, pulling back their headpiece to reveal an older woman. Her hair had become the same shade as her skin, both bleached to a pale, dull pink.

Lee and Belva moved toward one another and embraced tightly. Lee inhaled dandelion heads and Dial soap through the canvas and relaxed against the familiar smells of her grandmother. A fleeting sense of safety washed over her. She hadn't been held like this in so long that she'd forgotten what it could feel like. It was too much too quickly, and the buzz in her chest turned to a warm, sickening ache.

"Hell's bells. I can't believe you're here." Belva scanned her face, and Lee could feel the power of her observation penetrating beneath the skin. She instinctively took a step back.

"Let's go inside. I wanna meet my great-grandbabies."

. . .

After the introductions, Billy finished dinner, and the group gathered around the old oak table. The thick deer steaks were served with soup beans and cabbage cooked soft with bacon, and the food restored and fortified Lee like no meal had done in a long time.

The conversation was relaxed and irreverent, like the times she and the kids had when Cooper was away on business trips and they could be themselves. When Cliff spilled salt on the table, Belva showed them how to throw it from their right hand over their left shoulder to ward off bad luck, and she asked them specific, interesting questions about themselves—not the usual patronizing fodder. When Belva asked Cliff what her color was, he studied her for a moment and whispered, "Green glitter." Belva looked impressed.

It was late by the time they'd cleared the table, and Meredith and Cliff were exhausted. Luann and Belva set them up on cots in a small room used to store Belva's issues of *National Geographic* dating back decades. Lee helped Cliff settle in; she knew it was hard for him to sleep outside of his room back home. He seemed a little uncomfortable as his eyes roved fearfully over the walls, but it was nothing he couldn't handle. He would adapt to its new colors and images.

As Lee went to leave, Meredith sat up on her cot. "Mom, this place is amazing. Your childhood must have been beautiful. Why didn't you tell us?"

Lee closed her eyes and took a deep breath. "I didn't grow up in this house, honey."

"What do you mean? Where did . . . ?"

"My mom raised me. Redbud."

"Oh, so that's who that is. When did she die, again?"

"She's not exactly *dead*."

"What does *that* mean? You for sure told us she was dead."

As terrible as it sounded, it was so much easier to think of her as gone. She wasn't ready to explain this to her children. "We can talk about it later."

"What about our grandpa? Is he still alive, too?"

Lee startled at the mention of her father. It had been a while since she'd thought of him. "I said I don't want to talk about it." Lee could feel the sharp edge of the words on her tongue.

Meredith's skepticism dissolved into hurt, and Lee's chest lurched. This was why she'd kept them separate from this part of her life; it only caused pain. "No, he's been gone for a long time. Get some sleep."

.   .   .

Lee was given the old living room sofa covered in a sheet and a wool afghan. She stayed up watching TV until everyone was asleep, and then she snuck out to the car, pulled a box of wine from the trunk, and sat on the front porch swing sipping from a coffee mug in the dark. She deserved a drink after all that driving.

There was no moon that night, and no lights for miles, so it felt like she was at the back of a cave, hunched over her wine, brooding over the past.

Lee recalled the last time she sat in the porch swing. She was nine years old, and she had just gotten her period. Her mother had dropped her off to be with Belva, and it had been the beginning of something. An initiation into a world of magic. The gift of a black book and an introduction into how she might wield the power of the land around them.

The very fact of *being a witch* wasn't too impressive in Craw Valley; it was well known but rarely acknowledged that some in the community could get rid of warts with the touch of a hand, or blow out the fire in a burn. But the Bucks were notorious for their special talents and ability to perform powerful mountain magic, and Lee was next in their illustrious line.

Then her father died the next morning, and Mama cut them off from Belva, and just like that, her connection was severed. Her access to that world, that power, denied.

Lee now saw the magic for what it really was—a way for people with very few resources to feel they had some control over their hard, chaotic lives. Losing the magic hadn't been a great loss; Lee had found school as another way of seizing power.

But losing Belva had been crushing.

She'd asked her mother over and over why she couldn't see Belva anymore, but Redbud only told her that it wasn't safe and refused to explain further. She told Lee that she was better than this place, and that one day she'd get out. That was what she needed to focus on. Forget Belva, and the magic, and Craw Valley, and even her.

Lee hadn't only lost her father—she lost her mother, too. The woman who was once the vibrant center of her universe collapsed in on herself and went dark; she now floated around the house like a dead star. When Lee needed Belva most, when she was forced to take care of herself and hurt all alone, her mother took Belva away from her.

When Lee was around thirteen and things had gotten really bad with her mother, she snuck over to Belva's cabin one afternoon. She pleaded with Belva to let her stay with her, but Belva drove her back immediately, telling her she couldn't violate her mama's wishes. When Lee asked why, she wouldn't say, but Lee could see tears in her eyes. Belva's mere presence had acted as a balm for her loneliness, but as she disappeared down the road, leaving her alone at that house, Lee felt the despair returning, threatening to pull her under.

Belva still loved her. She was the only person left who loved her. And Mama didn't let her have that love.

She never forgave her for that.

After Lee went off to college, Belva wrote her letters, hoping they could have a relationship now that she was no longer under her mama's roof. She told her if she ever needed anything, she'd be there for her. If she needed a place to stay for the holidays or summer break, she was welcome at the cabin.

Lee didn't respond to a single letter; she'd vowed to cut all ties with Craw Valley and start over, and she couldn't allow herself to get sucked back in. The bond she once shared with Belva felt remote to an eighteen-year-old Lee on her college campus hundreds of miles away. It wasn't worth it.

But when Lee decided to leave Cooper, she needed a place to go. And Belva's cabin was the only place that came to mind. After so long, the cabin would finally be her sanctuary.

A spark came from the corner of the porch, startling Lee. In that brief flash, she could see the large, round outline of Belva. She wondered how long she'd been there. A plume of herbed smoke snaked from her direction, and each time the cherry in her pipe illuminated, Lee could see a little more of her.

"Why didn't you drink at dinner?"

"I know how you feel about it."

"Better than sneaking out here like someone with a problem."

"I'm sorry, Grandma Mama. I know I just sprang this on you. We won't be here for long. Six months, tops."

"Now, don't make it about that. You can stay here forever if you want. I'm trying to talk to you about how *you* are doing." She took another pull from her pipe. "So what happened with the husband?"

"That's not an easy answer."

"I'm sure it ain't, honey."

Lee wasn't ready to expose the specific disappointments of her life to Belva. She decided to change the subject. "How long has Luann lived here?"

"A few years. After her husband died."

Belva had always offered a home to people in need when Lee was growing up, but she'd never known anyone to stay for this long. She'd also noticed there wasn't a bed set up for Luann, but Lee waited for her to say more. It wasn't their custom to pry beyond what people wanted to reveal about themselves, even among family.

"She's a one-of-a-kind lady." Belva smiled at her and took another puff, and Lee knew that was all she would say about it. The smoke smelled almost savory, like standing in a kitchen while chicken and vegetables cooked down into a rich broth. It wound around Lee and cocooned her in its warm safety.

"Did he hurt you? I can help."

"No. I don't need—"

"I'm happy to help. We can keep him from doing any more harm to you."

"I said no." Lee crossed her arms.

Belva ignored her frustration. "Has Meredith gotten her period yet? I'd have thought she would at her age, but I can sense she's not open."

"No. Don't mention it to her. She's sensitive about it. I made a doctor's appointment in California, but we left before we could go."

"No need for doctors. It'll happen when she's ready. You know, you don't seem very open either. I bet you can't even feel it." She brought her foot down on the wood planks. When Lee didn't respond, Belva took a deep breath. "You got any money, child?"

"Not very much. He controlled the money. I wasn't good with it." As Lee said it, she wondered at its logic. It was something she and Cooper had decided years ago, and she'd come to accept it as reality. But she was the one who knew how to live on so little. "There was a prenup. I'll get half of what we made during our marriage, but he mostly volunteered for his family's nonprofit, and I took care of the kids. We essentially lived off his parents and his trust fund. So there's basically nothing that's ours to split." Lee sighed. "I'll fight for the kids' support. But I won't fight the prenup. I don't need his family's money."

"Damn straight. You don't need him or his stuck-up family. We got everything we need right here." Belva brought her foot down on the wood planks again.

"For now, I've got a credit card that we can live on for a bit. I can buy food and things for the kids. I have an interview for a long-term sub job at the high school tomorrow. The eleventh-grade history teacher is going on maternity leave."

"Oh yes, Debbie's daughter. She's had a hard time with it, but she'll deliver soon." Belva put the pipe to her mouth and inhaled, letting out a thick stream of smoke. "If you give me your left sock, I can fix something up to help you get the job—not that you need it, but no harm in it, huh?"

Lee nearly laughed. The contrast between the bland suburban life she'd left behind and this absurd one she'd returned to was hard to believe. "No, thank you. I appreciate it, though."

Belva huffed. "Suit yourself." She looked back toward the house. "They're good kids. Bucks through and through. I thought they might be different, growing up away from the land, but they've got it in them."

Lee wasn't sure how she felt about this. She'd spent most of her adult life trying to prevent them from being anything like the Bucks. She changed the subject.

"Have you seen Mama?" Lee asked.

Belva stared into the darkness beyond the porch. "No."

"Any idea how she's doing?" Lee couldn't help but ask.

"No, honey. I think Billy still checks up on her sometimes. Don't know why he does that to himself." *And I don't know why you'd do it either.* Lee could hear it in the spaces between the words.

Belva didn't need to worry. Lee hadn't spoken to her mother in fifteen years, and she didn't plan to change that now.

There was so much more to say, but the air had cooled. The smoke of Belva's pipe dissipated and left behind a feeling of vulnerability, then exhaustion.

"You want me to draw you a special bath? It'll clean that spirit right up."

Lee shook her head. As much as she yearned for comfort, it was a different thing to open herself up to it.

Belva sighed and went inside, and Lee took another sip.

• • •

It was still dark out when Lee awoke on the porch to the sound of screaming. Through the wine haze, she recognized Cliff's howl.

She stumbled into their makeshift room and found Belva, Luann, and Meredith swatting at the ceiling with brooms and rolled *National Geographic*s as a bat whirled around the fan. All the windows in the room were open, like deep, black portals to the great beyond.

Cliff was curled in a ball on his cot, so Lee wrapped herself around him, like adding clay to a smaller piece of clay. Her heart was equally crazed from waking with half the alcohol curdling in her system and the other half still burning brightly. Soon they were breathing calmly as one.

Luann caught the bat in a fishing net and released it through the window.

Belva asked Meredith why they'd been sleeping with the windows open, and she declared that they'd been shut when they went to sleep.

They asked Cliff if he knew what happened, and he wearily replied that he'd seen a figure cross the room and open the windows. It was too dark for him to see what the figure looked like; it was only a shadow.

This was not new territory for Cliff; he experienced night terrors every few weeks that felt so real they left him sweating and shaking. He always insisted they had, in fact, happened, but Lee and Cooper always reassured him they weren't real. He was safe. Lately, Cliff had stopped fighting to be understood, and she wondered if he held things back from her now, expecting she wouldn't believe him.

But Cliff had found a new audience in Belva. She looked deeply concerned and asked him detailed questions about the figure. When she was satisfied, she hung rosemary above the windows and placed a rabbit's foot under Cliff's mattress. Then she drew a cross over the door with white chalk and bid them goodnight.

Lee lay down with Cliff on the cot and tried to put her arms around him, but he turned away from her toward the wall, not touching, except for one foot wrapped around hers. She stared up at the ceiling, remembering the nights she'd spent in this room before everything fell apart.

"Are you awake?" Meredith whispered.

"Yes."

She was quiet for a moment. "I like it here."

"It's only been four hours. Give it time."

Meredith ignored her. "Belva is so cool. What was she doing with the rosemary and the rabbit's foot?"

"It's just an old mountain superstition."

Meredith paused, and Lee could hear her thinking in the dark. "Why didn't you tell me? About your family?"

"I had a hard time growing up." A bit of that tender pain bubbled up again, and Lee pushed it down. "But I don't like to dwell on it. I left it behind and started over, and I had you and Cliff, and you guys became my family." She paused. "I never meant to keep anything from you. Believe me, none of it is good. You're not missing out."

"Okay." Meredith paused. "I'm sorry it was hard for you."

"That's all right, honey. It was a long time ago."

"I won't make you relive your trauma for me."

"Thanks." Lee looked over at her shadowy outline. "Do you want me to scratch your back?"

"No. I think I can feel it pulling me under."

"Me too. Goodnight."

"Night."

Lee turned back to the ceiling and felt sleep no closer. When Belva put her to bed in this room as a child, they'd always said the same prayer. Lee said it to herself now, praying to lose consciousness.

*Now I lay me down to sleep,*
*I pray the Lord my soul to keep;*
*If I should die before I wake,*
*I pray the Lord my soul to take.*
*Amen.*

# TWO

Lee woke to the pound of steel against wood and the sizzle of cast iron against flame. She felt hollowed and sour, and her damp skin prickled against the wool of the afghan. She'd moved to the couch sometime in the night.

She took a seat at the kitchen table, and Belva put a mug of tea and a plate of fried potatoes in front of her. Through the glazed windows she could see the distorted shapes of Luann splitting wood with an ax as her children looked on from a safe distance.

"Drink this." Belva pointed to the tea.

"I'll just take some Advil."

"This is better. Spicewood. And chew on this." She stuck a piece of bark into the tea like a cinnamon stick. "Willow."

"I'll just swing by the drugstore on the way to the school."

Belva clicked her teeth with her tongue. "Eat the food, at least. You're skinnier than sin." She pulled a buckeye from her pocket. "And carry this with you for the interview. For good luck."

Lee gave her a woozy look.

"Humor an old broad."

Lee begrudgingly took the large nut and stuffed it in her purse.

Luann came in with the kids, their cheeks flushed and eyes shining. Meredith threw a warrior pose in the middle of the room. "Mom, Luann is a total badass. She let me split wood with an *ax*."

Lee imagined her headstrong daughter slicing off a limb with a sharp blade, and she internally cringed. "Iff, did you have fun?"

"Yeah. I didn't want to hold it, though."

"That's all right, bud. Me and Meredith can chop the wood around here." Luann gave his shoulders a squeeze.

Lee searched his face for any signs of last night's disturbance. "Are you still up for school today?"

He paused, but then nodded. "Yeah, I'm fine."

The whistle of a cardinal came from a clock on the wall, signaling that it was seven a.m.

There was a sick blur at the edges of Lee's perception as she tried to focus on her children. She brought her hands down firmly on the table, attempting to clear it. "We need to leave in twenty minutes. I'll get ready."

. . .

Lee pulled up to the brick school and parked among the students' rusting pickups and hand-me-down Corollas like no time had passed. It was a sad, ugly building, but it had been glorious to her as a teenager. Every day spent there had been one step closer to her getting out.

"Is *this* my school or Cliff's?" Meredith said with a slight sneer as they got out of the car.

"Both. The middle school and the high school are in the same building."

"Weird. So this is, like, a public school, right? It looks like it was built in the eighties."

"Yes. A *public school.* I think it was the sixties. Kids used to sneak into the Cold War bomb shelter to smoke when I was here."

At that, Meredith looked slightly impressed.

As they stood there, an incongruous red Tesla SUV pulled up at the drop-off circle in front of them and the driver's window came down, revealing a blonde, tanned woman.

Lee froze.

"Opaline?"

Lee barely recognized her cousin Dreama. She'd dyed her long, stringy, ash-colored hair to a yellow gold threaded with platinum and had her nose shaped into a thin, pert tip. Her face was airbrushed, her left ring finger sagged under an ostentatious diamond ring, and her blouse was a blush silk.

With nowhere to hide, Lee walked slowly over to the window. "Hey, how's it going?"

"What are you doing here? Are you moving back?"

"We're staying for a little while. I'm surprised Grandma Mama didn't tell you."

"Yeah, well, Belva and I aren't close. She doesn't like that my *husband* and I are opening up new businesses around town. But we deserve to have nice places just like anywhere else. You'll appreciate this more than anyone." Her eyes narrowed in on Lee. "We're going to make Craw Valley *the* destination in this area. We'll have cool restaurants, nice neighborhoods, good jobs. My husband is the one who put the shopping center in at Exit 118—you might have passed it. We're building a new subdivision out in Cradleburg right now. You should come see our house; it's *gorgeous*." She smiled. "When we're done with it, people will actually *want* to come here. There's more than enough cheap land for anything they want to build. It's the dream."

The idea intrigued Lee, but she was distracted by Dreama's transformation. She had once been a quiet, sullen teenager who walked quickly in between classes and spoke only to her brother in public. It was hard to reconcile that girl with the magnetic woman in front of her.

Dreama continued in a more somber tone, "Honestly, it's sad. I used to look up to Belva. Now she seems so out of touch. But anyway. Are those your kids? I'd love to meet them."

Lee waved them over and made the introductions as Dreama and her sons stepped out of their car. The two boys were around Meredith's age with neat haircuts; lean, muscular bodies; and perfect teeth.

"This is my older son, Colt. He's the quarterback on the football team. And this is Ridge. A modeling agency in Franklin City just scouted him. You should follow him. @ridgeconway."

Meredith looked at the boys like they were aliens, and Cliff gave Lee the *let's GTFO* look.

Lee politely told them they needed to get going. As they walked to-ward the school, Meredith asked, "*Who* was that?"

"My mother had a sister named Ruby Jo, and that was her daughter. We were close when we were little, but she wasn't a big fan of mine when we were teenagers. Though you wouldn't know it now . . ."

Lee kept her head down as they walked around the building to the school entrance, afraid more people would jump out of the bushes, de-manding to catch up. As she reached for the door handle, a few drops of red fell onto the pavement, flecking her shoes.

She and the kids looked up.

Hanging above the arch was a deer with its neck split and the blood running in tributaries over the door frame.

"Holy shit. That is *gnarly*. Am I going to be sacrificed?" Meredith looked impressed in the way she reserved only for great feats of human ability. Lee wasn't sure what to make of this. Didn't she find it all so . . . *barbaric*?

"I remember this. First day of deer hunting season." She turned to them both. "Don't worry, guys. I'll get us out of here soon."

.   .   .

In the office, she filled out employment forms after a mildly humiliating interview with the vice principal in which she had thankfully gotten the sub position. This wasn't the triumphant return she'd imagined.

She spotted a man in a conspicuous dark purple blazer out of the corner of her eye, pulling papers out of a cubbyhole.

"Mr. Hall?"

The man looked shocked at first, but then quickly recovered, his eyes shining with pleasure.

"Opaline Ford. As I live and breathe."

Lee took him in. Unlike most people from her old life, her feelings about Mr. Hall were uncomplicated. He had been her favorite teacher.

Even after his class ended her sophomore year, she often dropped by his classroom during lunch or after school just to talk. He had moved to Craw Valley from some distant place and gone to college at a fancy school. He helped shape what her future might look like; he gave her hope.

"I'm actually going by Lee now. Lee Carnell."

He gave her the smirk she remembered from his lectures on *Catcher in the Rye*. "Married, then?"

"I was. Or, technically, I am. But it will be past tense soon." She chuckled self-deprecatingly.

He spared her the divorce condolences and said, "I see. Well, if we're reintroducing ourselves, I go by Joseph. Outside the classroom."

"Really? I can't believe you were an average Joe this whole time."

"*Never* Joe. Or Joey. Only Joseph."

Lee laughed and readied herself for the next question. *Why was she here? How had she fallen so far?*

"Would you like to have a coffee? I have a free period."

"Yes. That would be lovely."

The teachers' lounge was empty and smelled of burnt toast. Mr. Hall skipped the ancient, stained coffeemaker and pulled out two mugs, a Tupperware of ground coffee, and a pour-over device.

"I grind it myself every morning." He poured boiling water from a kettle over the grounds. As the coffee diffused into the cups, she told him she had just taken the long-term sub position.

"What lucky children they will be," he commented but didn't pry further.

He had always been this way, allowing her to reveal only what she wanted of herself, to curate the personhood she desired.

Lee was transported back to those afternoons in her junior year. The light had seemed mixed with a different color once school ended. While Lee's vocabulary was impeccable, she couldn't fight the accent she'd imitated since birth. When she voiced a concern that she wouldn't be taken seriously once she finally escaped the town, Mr. Hall offered to help her eradicate it. Once a week, she stood in front of him in the empty classroom and recited Shakespeare over and over, until the round, grassy accent was leached from her voice entirely.

There were times in high school when Mr. Hall seemed like the only person who understood her, and she felt the old urge to unburden herself to him.

"I know you're wondering what I'm doing here," she said. "And honestly, I don't know. When I left Craw Valley, I really thought that I was going to make a nice life. And now I'm back, and I don't have much to show for it. There are my children, but they are their own people. I can't take credit for them. I don't have a home, or a career, or a place to be. I'm not even back at the beginning. I've devolved beyond that, into this thing . . ."

He put a light hand on her shoulder. "Lee. To this day, you remain one of the most gifted students I have ever taught at this school. That kind of ability doesn't just leave a person. It sounds like you've had a hard time of late. But what does literature teach us? Have you already forgotten my class?" He tried to coax a smile from her, but she couldn't dredge one up. "The greatest heroines all go through trying times. Those are the moments we see what they are truly made of. It is how we know they are great."

He'd always been able to make her feel better, even when her home life was a mess and all she had to cling to were the few hours at school when she felt a special light shining inside of her. She wanted to believe this was true, that there was some greatness that would reveal itself now that she'd ended up here. But it was doubtful.

Disgusted with her self-pitying, she studied Mr. Hall. Though she could tell he had aged by the sagging of the skin around his eyes and the airbrush of gray along his temples, he seemed the same man she had taken class from twenty years prior. His core was untarnished by the years of repetition and wrangling and solitude. This must be what it was like to find your place in the world.

Seeing him now, as a real person, she realized their relationship had only ever been about her. What she thought and what she dreamed of. She knew very little about him.

"How did *you* end up in Craw Valley?"

He paused and looked out the window. "When I was in grad school, my girlfriend got pregnant. Her family lived here, and she wanted to be close to them so they could help with the baby. So I graduated, we moved, and I got a teaching job at the high school." He looked back at her. "The baby was stillborn. One morning I woke up, and she was gone. Ours was not a great love story—we were only together because she got pregnant. I should have moved on, but I loved it here. I felt like a Romantic poet or Thoreau by his pond. I imagined myself chasing fair maidens barefoot through the trees and drinking from fresh streams. One can build their own life here without feeling the pressures of the outside."

Lee had never seen her hometown through this filter. Mr. Hall seemed to see everything through gossamer, the town's crumbling school and faded American flags shimmering like gasoline in water. She wondered if Mr. Hall would have thrived on the outside, or if he'd sensed that he would be crushed underfoot.

# THREE

Lee found herself on the porch again that night, hunched over a mug of mystery liquor.

That afternoon after school, she'd found a can of motor oil in the shed to top off her tank, but when she opened the lid, she smelled a sharp, leafy sweetness like dogwood blossoms preserved in acetone. She'd dipped her finger and brought it to her tongue. It was definitely a liquor of some kind, though nothing like the stuff you bought at a store. There was something mercurial about it, the smell and taste shifting from one sip to the next— wild, unfiltered, unregulated. It must have been Luann's. Or Billy's. Belva never drank.

Lee sat in the hot coals of the liquor's strange buzz, her mind glinting gold and purple in the utter darkness. She replayed recent humiliations, picking apart each word. She could still taste Cooper in her back molar, his mouth a little sour from the last argument they had before she left.

He'd wanted to take Cliff to yet another specialist, and she'd finally confessed that she wasn't sure something was wrong with him. Perhaps he was merely not what Cooper had hoped for in a son. She knew this incessant need to discover the root cause of his difference hurt Cliff's feelings and made him retreat into himself, afraid of expressing what he was thinking and feeling for fear it would make Cooper angry. Cliff had once been a vibrant, social creature, but now he only spoke in front of Lee and Meredith, which had spawned new criticism from his father. Suddenly he was too shy. Too quiet. He was a freak no matter what he did. She couldn't watch him be hurt like that any longer.

She couldn't sit there feeling Cooper's silent blame either, this sense that she'd somehow passed it along from her inferior body. Through a toxin absorbed in her womb or a kink in her mountain folk genetics: a protein shaped like a starburst in the chain.

If Lee was honest with herself, sometimes she wondered if she *had* passed something along to her children. When she was younger, she thought that once you got out, you'd be rid of the land's twisting, stultifying effects. But over the years, Lee worried that it was still inside her. This strangeness. And now she had brought her children here. If they stayed too long, they would soak it up as she had and eventually lose themselves. She would have to stay vigilant. She would need to find a way out and not allow the place to suck her back in with its sinking gravity.

All she needed was *money*. That one constant throughout her life. The type of essential physics they neglected to teach in school, each person learning it in their own time.

Her first lesson was at age ten, the summer after the bridge collapse. Ten people had died, including her father and her aunt Ruby Jo. It happened early on a Sunday morning, when most of the cars were on their way to church. Except for her father—she imagined him hungover in his truck with a crease in his cheek from the couch he'd passed out on the night before. They were waiting for a train to pass, the cars backed up along the bridge filled with women in their best dresses and children silently pinching each other in the backseat with their hair still wet from the shower.

The wood buckled in the center, and then both halves sloped down and deposited car after car into the frigid water. The sheriff said her father hit his head on the way down and sat there unconscious as his truck filled to the top. He was still belted in when they found him.

Her lesson was this: one less income that summer. Three months of her ten-year-old self selling vacuums door to door and swooning in the heat while her mother turned to husk.

A shock of light streaked through her reverie as a car pulled up to the front of the house. A figure stepped out with the engine still running and the brights on, so that she could only see its shadowy outline.

"Opaline?"

". . . Yes?"

"It's Otis. I'm here for Belva."

*Otis.*

The outdoor lights came on. Otis turned off the car, and the brights went black. Belva and Luann stepped onto the porch as he came through the screen door with an old man cradled in his arms like a child. Belva hurriedly opened the door and gestured them over to the living room couch already made up for Lee. She propped his head up on the cushion and wrapped him in the afghan while Luann pulled her ax from the wall and slid it under the couch.

Lee watched Otis from the other side of the room as he conferred with Belva. She recognized his collection of lines, and its imprint thrummed deep inside of her. The curve of the nose sloping into the mouth and curling up into the chin. The biceps covered in fine, dark hairs. His hair was longer and more loose without the gel that was popular when they were younger, and he'd grown a beard. But he still maintained his inscrutable calm.

"I'm sorry it's so late. Dad hasn't slept for three days, and the pain is making it hard for him to breathe. He won't take the pills they gave him, and he made me promise not to take him back to the hospital. I didn't know what to do."

Belva reached up and put a firm hand on his shoulder. "You did the right thing. Luann will sit with him while you and Opaline help me in the back."

Lee wondered if it was legal to practice alternative medicine on a man who clearly needed real medical attention. She knew this was part of Belva exercising her folk magic, but she saw it through a new lens now. She had encountered plenty of it on the West Coast. Lee generally believed these methods had as much power as the people believed them to have, but they couldn't treat real, body-destroying illness. The mind could only do so much.

Meredith came out into the living room in her pajamas with her hair askew. "Mom, what's going on?"

Lee put her hands on her shoulders and steered her back into the bedroom. "We're just helping a friend out. Everything is fine. Go back to sleep."

"Why? What are you guys doing?" Meredith shrugged out of her grip and tried to return to the living room, but Belva's sturdy form blocked the doorway.

"Listen to your mama, little girl. I ain't gonna tell you twice."

Meredith paled and quieted in response, and Lee closed the door.

Lee and Otis followed Belva to the back room where she did most of her work. Dried bunches of flowers and herbs hung from the rafters above their heads, and a fireplace stood in the corner, scarred black from frequent use. A large wooden table sat in the middle, covered with candles, piles of fabric scraps, knives, a small scale, plastic funnels. Shelves lined the walls, filled with mismatched jars of colored powders and gleaming oils, knots of hair and pieces of bone. There was a section of dirts labeled in cursive script citing dates and locations around the county, and a line of waters tinted various colors and floating with debris. The room smelled fresh and dried, zest and dust, a scent that contained too much for the brain to process.

Belva began pulling jars down and setting them on the table. She opened one marked "rainwater, thunderstorm" with an unintelligible date, dipped her fingertips, and dabbed her forehead, behind her ears, and at her wrists like perfume. She dabbed Lee and Otis in the same places.

"Opaline, I need fresh mugwort. Can you snip a few stalks? Otis, you go with her." She handed Lee a pair of garden shears and left the room.

Otis followed Lee out to the garden. As they silently walked up and down the rows using their phones as flashlights, she tried to conjure a memory of mugwort. For years, before her father died and her mother cut her off from Belva, she'd spent afternoons with her in the garden, learning the names and powers of the plants. But now she couldn't access that knowledge, as if the effort to erase that life had erased even the tiny, beautiful blooms of it.

She could feel Otis getting impatient. The urgency of his father's pain weighed heavily over them.

"So what are we looking for, exactly? If you describe it, I might be able to help."

"Um . . . it's hard to describe . . . it's been a long time . . ."

"That's a first."

She looked up at him, and there was a smile beneath his concern. "What do you mean by that?"

"You used to have all the answers." He turned to his phone and googled it, holding up an image showing small yellow buds.

Lee made a noise of recognition and searched the garden. At the very edge, she thought she saw dots of yellow against the darkness, and she stepped into the woods. That was the thing about Belva's garden—it didn't really end. The woods were a part of it too, with its offerings covering the mountains for miles.

A memory suddenly resurfaced of an afternoon in early spring when Belva had taken Lee and Dreama on a hike through the woods, pointing out the various plants she used in her remedies. She'd bent over and ruffled her hand over a stalk of flowering yellow. "Mugwort. Dangerous for pregnant women. Good for bad dreams and insomnia, digestion, irregular periods, bad liver." Lee remembered fingering the small blooms and feeling the power they contained.

Finally, Lee saw the plant, snapped off a few stalks, and returned to Otis.

They found Belva looming over a steaming pot in her workshop, her face pink and wet from exertion. She took the stalks, ran her fist down their lengths, and tossed a handful of the flowers into the brew. The smell of hot sauce and lavender thickened in the room, and Lee could feel her body going numb. She looked over at Otis and could see he was feeling something, too. Belva asked her something she couldn't quite make out, and when Lee didn't answer, she ushered both of them outside to get some fresh air.

The chill immediately revived them, and they stood there breathing deeply for a few minutes without talking.

"It's MS." Otis kept staring ahead.

"I'm sorry to hear that."

"I'm still getting used to taking care of him. My sister was doing it for a while, but she started taking from his pill stash and took off."

Lee nodded knowingly. "That's why your dad won't take the drugs for the pain. It makes sense."

He shrugged. "He also hates how it makes him feel—like a corpse, he says, so he might as well be dead. At least the pain is a feeling."

"The hospital can't help him?"

"He got a nasty infection there last time. He always feels worse when he goes there, so we try to avoid it. I still want him to have a choice. It's his body. His life."

Lee had the impulse to reach out and touch him, as if this was something she did often, but then Luann stepped out into the porch light. "We're ready for you."

Inside, Otis picked his father up off the couch like a parent putting a sleeping child to bed. Belva went out the back door, and the rest followed, with Luann holding an oil lantern to light their way. The old man grunted and moaned like a wounded animal in the dark.

When they were children, Otis's father reminded her of a rooster. Thin and sinewy and mean as hell. If you'd had to eat him to survive, he would have been stringy and tough, the small segments of meat spoiled and dried out. Once in middle school, when she and Otis spent most of a tedious, all-day Easter egg hunt talking, she'd overheard him telling his son "not to mingle with that devil woman." At the time, she felt nearly honored by the notion, but she'd also felt the sear of his aversion.

Now he was utterly vulnerable, all of his gristle stripped away until he was nothing but a small, raw creature, like this was at the center of all of our bodies, and what you saw were just layers of covering added over the years. This was the soft, red center of us all. She was bewildered by it.

When they reached the creek, Belva kicked off her shoes and waded in. She motioned for Otis to follow, and he hesitated, looking from her to the water with his brow furrowed.

"Are you sure? What is this going to do?"

"Otis, you can trust me. This will help with his pain." Her voice was calm but forceful, and Lee couldn't imagine disobeying.

Otis attempted to pry his boots off while balancing his father in his arms. As he struggled, Lee kneeled in front of him and unlaced them, feeling the warmth of his feet under the thin leather. She guided each ankle out of its shoe, and they met eyes for a moment before he stepped slowly into the creek. Luann followed Otis into the water, and Belva made the same beckoning gesture at Lee.

She obeyed and waded in, clenching her teeth to block the reaction to the chill. But the water was like a bath ten minutes in—soothing and warm, the temperature of her own skin. She felt her clothes inflate and float, writhing around her like sea plants as she made her way over to them in the waist-high water.

The women surrounded Otis and his father, with Belva by the old man's head. She uncorked a bottle from a floating basket and brought its amber glass to the man's lips. As the liquid flowed down his throat, Lee watched his body and face unclench, and then his arms and legs extended outward until he was entirely unfurled and serene, floating unaided on the surface of the water like a lily. Lee felt herself relax as well, and she watched in amazement as they all instinctively brought their arms out and, starting with Belva, began to float on the surface of the water together.

With the warm water lapping against Lee's ears, there was only gurgling silence and the sky above her. She felt an arm against hers and allowed it to rest there, unwilling to break the spell to find out who it was.

They floated there for a while, until Lee felt a disturbance below the surface. She brought her feet to the muddy bottom, and Otis was standing next to her. Belva motioned to the floating old man, who had fallen asleep with a slight smile on his face. Otis pulled him into his arms, and they filed out with Luann's lantern guiding their way along the path back to the house.

Belva helped Otis wrap the old man in a towel, and they set him down in front of the living room fire to dry and sleep. They all took towels for themselves and sat in old cane chairs around him in a comfortable silence. Lee could still feel the flicker of that wild liquor in her veins, now mixed with an airy, pore-opening high from the creek float. She hovered there, feeling a bit lightheaded, willing the fire to ground her.

She studied Otis across from her, the flames illuminating the line of his jaw, and her chest tightened and heated as it once had.

Lee had spent her adolescence in a state of isolation. She'd mostly preferred it that way, but sometimes the yearning became too much. She would periodically pick a boy on whom to project all of her passionate desires, fueling her vivid imagination. But she was never entirely fulfilled by this. She wanted more, and by senior year of high school, the burn of it was overwhelming.

There was one boy in school. He was tall, handsome, muscular. The shape of his nose and mouth together was both angular and *luscious*. She was convinced this area was the key to attraction, though people could rarely identify it. He sat in the back of the class and rarely spoke, but she knew he got good grades. He liked to sit at lunch away from the others, on a bench out by the football field, and read beautiful, violent books like those of Cormac McCarthy. He had this tranquil confidence that some-times bordered on arrogance. One could never be sure what he thought of them. They were the type of people who should have been friends but had never gotten past each other's introverted natures. They'd bantered a bit through the years. She liked to insult him to see what he would do, but he never took the bait. Otis was impenetrable.

Then one day at school, a few months before graduation, she was so

restless she thought she might leave her skin behind. She followed Otis
to his locker after the last bell and brought her face up to his ear. She
told him to take her to his car in a firm voice, not inviting any questions.
To her surprise, he obeyed. As they walked out to the lot without looking at one another, she'd never felt more calm and assured. She was in
control.

She got into the passenger side of his dark blue Bronco and told him to
drive somewhere private. There was a field behind the high school that had
lain fallow for years, and he pulled to a stop under a tree on the far side.
When they turned toward one another, she hesitated, and in that moment
the dynamic shifted, and he took her face in his hands and kissed her. He
smelled like blueberries with the dust of nature still on them. Opaline
forgot herself entirely in that kiss, something wild and uncontrollable un-
furling inside of her. When he pulled away, she nibbled on his jaw with
unrestrained desire, wanting to devour it whole.

She felt him stiffen, and she pulled back. He seemed bewildered. Not
disgusted. No, it wasn't that. But in that moment, a shame filled her. This
overwhelming desire inside of her had been exposed, and the spell was
broken.

She asked him to take her back to school, and she caught the bus back
home. As she lay in bed that night, she replayed the interaction in her
head. He'd held power over her for those few moments in the car. He'd
taken her to a more raw, vulnerable place than she ever allowed herself to
go. And she wanted more of it.

She had become a master of controlling hunger of all kinds, but her
hunger for him felt mad and untamable as it swelled inside of her, and
she was terrified. She was mere months from leaving this place behind for
good. She had resolved to be untethered when she left, and she wouldn't
let anything hold her down.

The next day, he waited for her after school and reached for her arm
as she walked past. She forced herself to wrench it back and throw him
a contemptuous look before continuing to the bus. Her arm burned from

his touch as she watched him walk forlornly to his car from the dirty bus window.

He kept his distance after that, and she had moments of profound regret, but then they went off to college and it didn't matter anymore. She hadn't seen or spoken to Otis since, but over the years she thought of that kiss whenever she felt particularly ordinary. It had been a strange, transcendent moment, like the experience they had tonight in the creek. She wanted more of that feeling.

Across the room, Otis readied to leave. He asked Belva about payment, and she brought him into the kitchen. Lee watched as he handed over a thin fold of cash in exchange for a small jar of liquid.

As he carried his father through the living room and toward the door, she saw the earnest, sturdy boy she had fantasized about years ago, and it was easy to see why he had intrigued her. He had an element of the unexpected that he kept carefully guarded, and that was a rare trait to find in anyone. But in Otis, it was uniquely alluring.

He caught her staring at him, and they held eye contact for a brief, charged moment. And then he was gone.

# FOUR

## MEREDITH

The woman next to Meredith was losing it.

She held her arms up toward the preacher with pink, tear-soaked cheeks and chanted, "Yes, Jesus. Yes, Jesus." She was under its spell.

And Meredith was *here for it*.

Since they came to Craw Valley a week ago, she had witnessed one strange thing after the other. It had been days since she was bored or felt a haze pulling her under.

Back in California, she awoke every morning to a heavy, dirty cloud hovering above her. They drove through the flinty, sun-parched suburbs to school, and she tried not to pass out from how depressing it was. She liked some of her classes, but most of it was distant and numbing, like a show playing in the background of a room. Even her friends felt a little fake, like they were just going through the motions. Their conversations at school were inert, their texts brief and empty. Everyone was either too sick or lazy or busy with other things to actually hang out on weekends—and what would they have done? Watched a show? Walked around the mall? Made a video? She got bored just imagining it.

But out here, in the middle of nowhere, there were real things happening. And there was an energy. She could feel it at night lying on her cot in Belva's cabin, a light electricity coursing through her that made it hard to sleep. It had been the strongest last night, after those men came over and her mom locked her in her room. She'd barely slept at all.

She should have been exhausted, but she felt the opposite. She was buzzing.

*What is Mom keeping from me?*

Meredith was no stranger to alternative medicine; a friend's mom had dabbled in Reiki back in California and used her daughter's friends as guinea pigs. She'd felt the pricks of something on her table. But it was nothing like what she felt here.

Her mother had always treated her like she was an equal, even when she was very young. She didn't bullshit her. She gave her adult books to read, and they watched the same shows together. To call a mother a best friend was usually pathetic or saccharine, but in this case it was an unvarnished truth. They told each other everything.

But her mother had been keeping secrets. A secret name, and a secret family that she'd told them about only a few weeks ago. And now, something else. Something just beyond Meredith's reach.

They stood up to sing another song, and Cliff flipped to the page in the hymnal indicated on the program. They'd been confused at first, but Cliff had picked it up quickly. As they launched into the song, Meredith sang discordantly, and Cliff shook with silent laughter while he tried to stay in tune. He always tried to do the right thing, even when most only saw the wrong in him. It made her heart hurt.

Meredith could feel eyes on her, and she looked down the row to see Belva giving her a blistering stare. A cold sweat broke along the back of her neck, and she immediately changed her voice to meld with the others.

Soon, the service was over and people started collecting their things and shaking each other's hands. She watched as her mom scooted quickly out of the pew and motioned for them to follow to avoid the swarms of friendly grasping palms.

They filed out of the church in a line past the ancient preacher and the corny youth pastor. When it was Meredith's turn, the old man took her palm and rubbed his finger lightly across her wrist, giving her the chills. His eyes were pink and blue and glistening like raw oysters, and he reminded her of an ancient oracle. She wondered if he could see her future.

They'd barely gone a few feet in the grass out front before they were accosted by Mom's cousin Dreama and a group of women who looked like knock-off versions of her. They were a flock of patterned sundresses and ankle-strapped heels.

"Meredith, honey, would you like to volunteer for our fundraiser in a few weeks?" Dreama asked. "All the young ladies are doing it." She smiled brightly and turned toward Mom. "It's at the new restaurant my husband and I built near Exit 115. It's *beautiful* and the menu is *amazing*. We're in talks with investors to franchise."

Meredith tried not to roll her eyes. "What are you raising money for?"

"We want to build Pastor Jax a new church out near 81. It'll fit thousands and have a school and a bookstore and a little coffee shop. It's just what this community needs. Most people don't want to drive out to this old place, but that kind of church will attract a crowd. I guarantee it."

Meredith and her mother looked at the church behind them with its simple bell tower and white paint wearing thin at the wood. It filled Meredith with the same feeling as Belva's house—it felt undeniably a part of the place, as if raised from the ground like any other tree or rock. There was a tiny waterfall behind it that flowed down from some unseen place in the mountains and turned into a creek that completed the pastoral vibes. She wasn't sure about the Christian God (actually, she was pretty sure it was a fantasy), but one could feel close to nature here, at least. That was one thing she loved about being in Craw Valley.

As the adults continued their conversation, Meredith and Cliff walked away toward the creek on the far side of the lawn. Billy stood on the bank, scanning the water through his sunglasses.

"What are you doing?" she asked.

"Looking for fish. These glasses are polarized, so I can see through the glare into the water." He took them off and gave them to Cliff so he could take a look. "Y'all wanna catch crawdads?"

Cliff looked to Meredith with the sunglasses obscuring his small face.

"You should do it. I'll stand right here and watch."

She thought he would decline, but Cliff nodded and started rolling up his pants legs like Billy. Cliff had always been a curious kid, but she'd seen that punished over and over again, especially by their dad and the people at school, and he'd learned to retreat into himself and explore only within.

But he was slowly opening up to the world again, his curious mind set loose on the landscape of Craw Valley with Billy's steadying presence beside him. She was happy to see it.

As she watched him wade in, she felt a tap on her shoulder. She turned around to find a girl from one of her classes.

*Tiffany Wang.*

Everyone called her by both names as if she were a celebrity. She sat in the back of geometry with an intimidating look on her face, daring anyone to mess with her.

"Hey. You're Meredith, right?"

"Yes."

"What's it like living with *a witch*?"

The word reverberated inside of her. "What are you talking about?"

Tiffany narrowed her eyes. "Don't fuck with me. Everyone knows about your family. You don't have to, like, keep it a secret."

"I really don't know what you're talking about. I thought my mom's family was dead until a few weeks ago."

"Wow. That's messed up." Tiffany paused. "So you haven't noticed anything weird?"

Meredith looked across the church lawn to where her mother was talking to the man from last night.

"I mean, yes. Definitely. But I thought Belva was into energy healing and stuff."

Tiffany smiled mockingly. "This isn't *California*. Belva's a legit witch. Mountain magic and shit. I was hoping you could teach me what she showed you . . . but it sounds like you don't know anything."

Meredith deflated. *Is Tiffany messing with me? Why don't I know any of this?* Anger bloomed at the thought of her mother keeping something so special from her. It was hot and sticky and made her itch.

Tiffany leaned in. "If you want to learn magic, I know a place. The Ryders don't know it like Belva, but they're not uptight either. Anyone is allowed to come, and they let you party." She grabbed Meredith's phone from her hand and typed in her number. "Text me if you ever want to go."

As Tiffany rejoined her family, Meredith noticed Mr. Hall approaching in his purple blazer and polished oxfords. She had him for fifth period English, and she was surprised to find someone like him in Craw Valley. He reminded her of a rare bird she once saw on a field trip to a small zoo. It had preened in its roost, surrounded by the common foal.

"Good morning, Meredith. How did you find the service?"

"It was fine, I guess." Meredith hadn't absorbed a word of the preacher's muddled speech. She'd been too distracted by the spectacle. "What did *you* think?"

"This particular message didn't resonate with me. I struggle with the blind-faith element of Christianity."

"Then why do you come?"

"No other place in town offers a public forum for literary analysis and interpretation. I take what I can get." He winked at her.

Meredith could feel him straining to be clever, and she found it a little off-putting. *What does he care what I think?*

"Did you know I taught your mother?" He looked at her intently.

"Yes, she mentioned it."

"She was one of the most brilliant students I've ever had. So . . . incisive." He paused and smiled. "You remind me of her."

Meredith instinctively warmed at the comparison, but when she tried to imagine this version of her mother, the girl was a stranger.

She heard her name being called from the other side of the lawn where her mom stood with Belva, Luann, and the man from last night, and she excused herself from Mr. Hall. Cliff and Billy came out of the creek and dried their bare feet on the grass as they walked over to join them.

Meredith heard the man ask her mother, "Would you like to grab a drink with me tonight?"

Her mom looked surprised as she replied, "I don't know, I have to be with the kids . . ."

Meredith knew this was an excuse. They could take care of themselves.

"She'll go," Belva said. "We can keep the kids."

"But—" Mom protested.

"She'll meet you at the bar around eight."

The man smiled and nodded, and then he headed for the parking lot, disappearing into the cloud of dust kicked up by the cars leaving.

Meredith caught up to her mother as they walked across the lot. "That's the guy from last night."

"Yes, Otis. We went to high school together."

"What were you guys doing? Everyone was being super sketch, and then I smelled something weird."

They both watched as, a few steps ahead, Belva took out an empty bread bag she'd swiped from the refreshments table and scooped in a bit of dirt from the church lawn.

"Grandma Mama makes homeopathic remedies out of herbs from her garden, and Otis's father needed one."

Meredith narrowed her eyes and searched her mother's face. "Tiffany told me Belva's a *witch*."

"Oh, ha. That's an old rumor."

Meredith's heart sank. She thought when faced with a direct question, her mother would certainly reveal the truth. But she could feel the lie in it. They never lied to each other. They always shared the same reality, criticizing others for the lies they lived.

"It's only a rumor," Meredith repeated.

Her mother nodded. "Yes. She helps people. That's it."

Meredith studied the familiar lines of her mother's face. Then she got into the dusty SUV and slammed the door.

.   .   .

Back at the cabin, the family squatted on stools in the side yard and snapped the ends off beans from the garden into piles for compost.

"Who are the Ryders?" Meredith asked casually. It was better to come at this sideways, judging by her mother's behavior that morning.

"That's Leroy's family," said Belva.

Meredith's eyes lit up. "Who's *Leroy*?"

Belva sighed. "My ex-husband."

"So, like, our great-grandfather?"

"That's the one."

"Where is he now?"

"His body's under six feet of dirt, but I like to think his soul is burning in hell."

"Grandma Mama!" Mom exclaimed as Meredith and Cliff giggled.

"Opaline, they should know where they come from. I know you've done your damnedest to keep that from happening, but they're here now."

Mom stayed quiet, and Belva continued, "Leroy came from a family of moonshiners. Real rough people. But when I met him, he was working at the old plant. He was a real cat daddy, if you know what I mean."

"I have no idea what you mean," Meredith said.

"It means he was good-looking, and he knew it. I fell pretty hard for him. He dated a lot of the girls in the county, but he said I was special."

This was her chance to ask what made Belva special, but Mom cut her off. "Grandma Mama is *very* smart. Her parents made her drop out of school in the fourth grade, but she kept studying on her own. She can identify any plant or bird in this area."

Belva waved her away. "After we got married, things were good for a while," she continued. "I got pregnant real quick with Redbud, then your aunt

Ruby Jo, and then Billy right after that. We were a nice little family. But then Leroy started to change. He got laid off from the plant and started working for his father. They would take these old cars and put secret compartments in the bottom so you could hide the booze if you got stopped by the law or robbed on the back roads. He got hooked on liquor and started drinking all day, every day. He started beating me, and I tried to . . . intervene . . ." Belva made eye contact with Mom, and Meredith recognized the omission.

"But it was no use. So I filed for divorce."

"She was the *first* woman to ever file for divorce in the county," Mom interjected again.

Belva laughed. "At first they weren't sure how to even do it at the courthouse, and I told them that it was probably how they did it when a man filed. They looked at me like I had two heads." She shook her head, and her face lost some of its glint. "Leroy died only a few days after it was done. The family blamed me, said I put a curse on him, but I don't see how they figured that when he drove off the side of a mountain drunk as a skunk and died face down in a creek. Seems like no fault but his." She clucked her tongue in disapproval. "Things ain't been very good with the Ryders since. They don't like me meddling in their business. As long as they don't mess with me, I don't mess with them."

"You are so badass." Meredith was transfixed. "So does Redbud still live here? Why hasn't she come over?" she followed up innocently, avoiding eye contact with her mother.

Belva raised an eyebrow at Mom, but she stayed quiet. "Your grandma is a troubled woman. She has her own kind of life, and we've got ours. Best if we don't mix them."

Meredith wanted nothing more than to meet this mysterious woman, but she knew better than to question Belva. It wasn't that Belva had ever done anything to her that might inspire fear; it was the sense of what she *could* do.

·   ·   ·

Meredith pretended to read in her room while she waited for Mom to leave for the bar and Belva and Luann to lie down for the night. Once the house was quiet and Cliff was asleep, she crept into the back room that her mom had declared off-limits.

The room was warmer than the rest of the house, though Meredith couldn't see a heat source. It was as if an invisible fire raged in the empty black hearth. There was something tantalizing about the rows of jars, despite their hodgepodge, recycled appearance, and she ran her fingers along them, reading the labels. Each unfamiliar word evoked a new intoxicating image—boneset, devil's bit, bloodroot, fleabane. And then there were things she recognized but had never considered as something to be bottled—ant eggs, ditchwater, church dirt, black cat fur.

Next to the shelves was an old table filled with pictures of people in the dreamy, faded tones of decades past. Meredith's gaze snagged on an image of a woman in the garden with her hands on her hips. Even in the stillness, she radiated a powerful force, as if she might step out of the frame. Meredith had to make herself look away.

On the wooden table in the center of the room sat a battered black leather book thick with the edges of inserted pages. The energy surged inside her at the sight of it, and she walked over to the book. She trailed her hand across the unmarked front and opened to the first page. There were handwritten words in a vintage-looking cursive reading:

*Property of Belva Buck*
*"Trespassers will be shot"*

There was nothing else on the page. With shaking hands, Meredith flipped to the next one. The left corner was dated June 17, 1965.

*I am a woman today. And for my first act as a woman, I will make Leroy mine.*
*Granny Rallie showed me this trick with a bit of*

*honey and it worked ok. I saw him looking at me in
church which is more than he's done in the ten years
we've been in school together.*

*But I know it can be stronger.*

*I have a love recipe in my heart, and I think that
if I say it to the bees over and over, day after day,
eventually it will get into their honey. And it will—*

"Find something interesting?"

Meredith shrieked and spun around, her heart beating hard in her chest. Belva stood in the doorway in her polyester housecoat and slippers with a forbidding glare.

"Oh my god, I'm so sorry. I didn't mean to—" She slammed the book shut and faced Belva once again, afraid to make eye contact.

Belva walked over to the book and reopened it to the first page and scanned it, her face curving into slight amusement. "I had a real flair for the dramatic when I was younger." She studied Meredith as if debating something with herself, then she put her fingers under Meredith's chin and forced her to look her in the eyes. "What you want to know, child? There's no need to go snooping around at night." Belva sat down on one of the wooden stools under the table and motioned for Meredith to join her.

Meredith took a deep breath and tried to calm herself. Here was her chance.

"What is this book for? Is it like a diary?"

Belva nodded. "Sort of. But it's more than that. It holds all of the recipes I've written and ones my Granny Pallie taught me when I was about your age." She flipped to the next page with the heading "Love Honey."

*1 handful of cotton*
*2 red clovers*
*A few drops of honeysuckle nectar*
*Dash of nutmeg sugar*

*Put all ingredients inside a copper bee smoker. Light it with a match soaked in rosemary oil and drop it in. Go to a hive you know well at sunrise and say the words while you smoke them:*

*Come to me, my love*
*You will find me in the creek swimming you*
*Or in the kitchen baking you*
*Or in my bed sleeping you*
*I will think only of you*
*And you will think only of me*
*You will be hungry when you eat*
*You will be tired when you sleep*
*Until you come to me*
*My love*

Belva flipped farther into the book, and Meredith saw more pages of recipes with lists of ingredients with instructions and sections of words like poems. She saw drawings of animals and plants, and stacks of old pages in another handwriting that must have been Granny Pallie's. "It's the most precious thing I own, and I usually keep it hidden." She raised an eyebrow. "But I forgot this afternoon. I was coming to put it away when I found you rifling through it."

"Are these recipes . . . spells?"

"I wouldn't call them that. Ain't my word."

Meredith continued to flip through the book. "But it's true, then. You're a witch."

"Like I said, I don't have much use for other people's words. There's the work, and I do it, and there's no point to calling it anything special. Keeps you humble and close to the land. That's what's most important."

"What do you mean?"

"There is power in the land, and when we need it, we can call upon it humbly and respectfully. That is at the core of the work. We must respect and feed the land, so that it may feed us."

Meredith nodded. She had too many questions. "What can the land power do, exactly? Like, what kind of . . . work?"

Belva paused. "It helps us in all ways—with our bodies that move us and the plants that feed us and the weather around us. It helps us love the people who are here, and to stay connected to the people who have moved on. It protects us from people who seek to do us harm. It provides whatever we need, as long as we pay our respects and give back." She stood up and went to a drawer where she pulled out an old wooden pipe. She started packing it from a small baggie in the drawer.

"Can anyone do it?"

She nodded over her pipe. "Yes, I believe anyone *can* do it, in some small way at least. Helps to have a good mind and a strong will, but also a willingness to give yourself over to something greater. Some lack a natural constitution for it, and they struggle. Your aunt Ruby Jo was like that. She went wherever the wind blew her. Always looking in the wrong places for something to make her feel special. Never could get a hang of it."

"Where is she?"

Belva sighed. "She passed years ago." She put a palm to her chest and looked up at the ceiling. "But like I was saying, there are some in our family who are born with special gifts. They're usually related to who we are. Like Billy. He's gentle and wild, so he's real good with animals. Says he can sense what they're thinking and feeling. Or me. I always taken care of people, even when I was a youngin. So, my talent is for healing. Making people feel better and all that." She took a puff from the pipe and coughed huskily.

"Healing is most of the work. Helping people in their time of need. A lot of it you can do on your own. But sometimes, the problem is something bigger. You can't just spread a poultice on it or light a candle. It takes a group of people and some powerful work. You gather at a crossroads, and you enter the spirit world together."

Meredith's eyes widened.

"There are exceptions. Your granny Redbud, for one, was born angrier than a hornet. She loved a good fight. When she started coming into her gift, she told me she could feel the power of the land coursing through her at night." Belva gestured toward the photograph of the mesmerizing woman in the garden.

*Like me*, Meredith thought.

"She had a talent for pulling power straight from the land. Some of the time she didn't even need a gathering to make something big happen. She was a powerful woman."

"What happened to her?"

Belva sighed. "When her husband died, your grandpa, she gave up the work. And then she lost herself."

Meredith waited for her to elaborate, but Belva only stared off into space. "Where is she? Why can't I see her?"

Belva's eyes bored into her. "I told you. It ain't safe. I'm not gonna say it again."

Meredith backed off. "What about Mom? Does she have a gift?"

Belva sighed again. "Red kept your mama away from me after Hank died. She was angry and in a lot of pain, and she had to find somewhere to put it." She looked away. "So I never really got to show Opaline what I know. If she has a gift, it's not something like Red's. It's something more . . . inside. Even when she was little, she liked to keep to herself. She wasn't one of those kids that demand constant minding. I've always respected her for that."

Meredith had loved that her mother kept to herself around everyone but her and Cliff. It made her feel special, like they were the only people worthy of her mother's fierce, vibrant attention.

But it hadn't been real. She had hidden herself and this amazing secret from them just like everyone else.

The thought burned angrily in her chest. Just because her mother hadn't learned the work didn't mean that Meredith couldn't. "What about me? Do *I* have a talent? Can you teach me?"

Belva studied her. "You're not ready yet."

"But I feel ready. I think I can feel it. The power of the land. I'm ready, Grandma Mama. Please."

"When your blood comes, you'll be ready."

Meredith's cheeks burned with shame. "But what if I never bleed? Does that mean I'll never be able to do the work?" Her anger ignited. "What about Billy? Did he have to get his *period*?"

Belva raised an eyebrow. "Watch your tone. Your mama might let you run your mouth, but that ain't gonna fly with me."

Cold sweat broke along the back of her neck again, and Meredith went silent. She looked down at the table.

"The gifts in our family usually come around puberty. It don't have to be a period, but I can sense it'll come for you soon. You gotta be patient."

"But when?"

Belva raised both eyebrows this time. "I said soon. Don't make me repeat myself again. Until then, stay out of this room. If you don't respect the rules, you will never learn our ways."

Meredith shivered and nodded under Belva's intent stare. As she left the room, her gaze briefly lingered on Redbud's powerful, flashing eyes in the picture, wondering what secrets she held.

# FIVE

## Lee

There was technically more than one bar in town, but this was *the bar*.

It had been more a figment of her imagination than a real place to Lee as a kid. She remembered waiting up late when her dad—and then her mom—didn't come home, imagining a large room dominated by a demonic, glowing furnace. But it seemed much less sinister in person, by the dim light of adulthood. Every surface was made of wood, and the walls were covered in mismatched ephemera, like photographs of the Lions Club from 1982 and a stuffed deer head named Big Merle. It was the town's storage unit for sentimental junk.

The *hip* restaurants back in California tried to create a sense of history and culture in the tastefully random placement of artifacts, but the vintage typewriters and the sepia photos purchased at flea markets represented no time or place. They were stand-ins for meaning, the idea of a memory without its nectary weight.

She wondered at her romancing of this place now, and she felt like one of those people that fantasizes about a rural life they could never stomach in reality. She knew better; she'd been gone for too long.

The bar was empty except for a few old men sitting in a back booth with their noses swollen and red. She took a seat at the bar, and a minute later, light blazed through the dark room from the front door. Otis walked toward her with the sun lingering in his outline, and something inside her whispered, *There he is.*

He took the stool beside her and ordered a whiskey neat. She ordered the same.

They had already covered the basic facts of the last twenty years at church—Otis had majored in engineering at the state school a few hours away and now worked for a firm in Cradleburg designing wastewater treatment plants. He had recently moved in with his dad to take care of him. No wife. No kids.

Lee studied the feral smile of a mounted possum above the bar and took a sip. "Have you ever thought about living somewhere else?"

He ran a hand through his hair. "I lived in Atlanta for a semester to intern at a big firm down there. I made friends with the more senior guys. Their lives were centered around going out to eat at expensive restaurants and living in these massive subdivisions of basically mansions with lawns, and I didn't feel a real connection to it. It's a nice place, but I missed being out in nature. Part of me was curious to spend time around city people who supposedly live these more sophisticated lives, but that wasn't the case, for the most part."

"I know what you mean." Lee thought about her urban life. The endless days she spent driving around to shopping centers, buying food and paper and plastic. Some nights, when Cooper was in town, they would go to a restaurant with another couple and eat burrata and Brussels sprouts and steak and get wasted off wine twenty dollars by the glass. Conversation revolved around home renovations, resorts, other restaurants where they could have burrata and wine.

"It's interesting to see you back here," Otis said. "I know how much you wanted to 'get out.'"

Lee nodded. "I wanted to leave so badly for so long." Her grip tightened on the whiskey glass. "And then I got it. And even though I spent years trying to evolve and become a totally different person, I still ended up in a place that felt wrong. In a marriage and a life that felt hollow. So I had to come here. But it's only for a few months. Just until I can figure out my next move. I don't want my kids growing up here."

Taking all of this in, he said, "It's not a perfect place, but it's not all bad."

"Look, I know. I just want more for them." He couldn't understand what she was trying to protect them from. Otis knew pain. His sister's drug problems, his mother's death when they were in high school, his father's meanness. He could understand her in this way, but he didn't seem to feel a wrongness at the center of him.

He put his hand on hers. "I've had friends go through divorces. I know it's hell."

Lee thought back to a few weeks ago, when she found a pair of women's shorts in Cooper's laundry after a business trip. She wore the shorts around the house for a week after, but he didn't notice. She still resented him for turning her into a cliché; at least he could have betrayed her with some poignancy. When she confronted him, he didn't deny it. Instead, he turned it back on her: she had given him no choice; he needed a refuge from her *unhappiness*. It was an umbrella term he used to describe everything that was wrong with Lee—her antisocial behavior, her melancholy, her negativity, her *drinking problem*.

When they first met, Cooper liked the novelty of her strangeness. But once they left the experiment of college and entered his rich, shiny world, things changed between them.

At first she was dazzled by its comfort and security. His parents bought them a beautiful house in a brand-new subdivision, and Lee couldn't believe how clean and untainted it was. The fridge was filled with rows and drawers of gleaming food. The water gushed from the tap every time she swung the handle. For the first time in her life, her jaw unclenched and her shoulders relaxed.

But no matter how hard she tried to fit in with his family and friends, she couldn't shake a feeling of otherness. It was her effort that set her apart, and subtle errors that compounded into a greater difference. It was also her own doing—she insisted on staying other because she deeply disliked these people. There was an essential weakness in them that she couldn't respect.

She thought she and Cooper could hold on to their little life, but he started to see her strangeness through their eyes, and she started to see their weakness in him. He would make comments about her standoffish nature, or mention that she always led with negativity instead of gratitude. On the surface they were benign suggestions for self-improvement, but soon every move she made was criticized, as if there was something inherently wrong with her.

She and Cooper drank in the same quantities, but while he drank every evening and weekend with other people, Lee stayed at home and drank by herself. It was funny, because she'd only started drinking to please Cooper and his friends. She'd associated drinking with poor, ruined people until she left Craw Valley and discovered that people drank everywhere, even and especially the rich. She drank to become one of them, but eventually not even the booze could slide her into place among them.

Despite all of this, they continued to go through the motions. The arrival of Meredith and Cliff made it livable—they were the family she'd always wanted, and she didn't need him anymore. When they were very small, Cooper had connected with them. But as their personalities emerged, the relationships became strained. Even with Meredith, with whom he'd always had a special bond, there was this disconnect. It would be easy to blame it solely on his emotional distance and his suffocating expectations. But there was also something organic that bound Lee and her children together that he wasn't a part of. When she told him she was leaving and taking the children with her, he didn't flinch.

The cheating was only pretense; it was a long time coming.

But Lee couldn't help feeling like a failure. She had tried to find her people and build a new life outside of this town. But she had only brought her children into her strange, small world, and now they were unmoored and dependent upon others. This wasn't the life she'd worked so hard to give them, or that she'd imagined for herself. Sometimes she wondered, *Where is the life I'm supposed to be living?*

She relayed pieces of this to Otis, who nodded intently and didn't try to interject. "That must have been difficult to live with for so long."

Lee knew what he meant, but the sad part was that she'd barely felt it. Not until the cheating had she really woken up to how truly unhappy she'd been.

"Have you ever gotten close?" she asked.

He took a deep breath and stared into the mirror at the back of the bar. "Naw, I've never found the right person."

"No one? Do you date?"

"I've had girlfriends that were very kind and I enjoyed being with them, but it never felt like the kind of connection I'd want in a life partner. I'm not willing to settle for something less than that."

Lee tried conjuring a woman for Otis in her mind. Someone with long, thick hair and a strong jaw.

"Do you remember the field?" he asked, smirking.

"I'm not sure what you mean." She flushed with the memory of their kiss.

"At the time it sort of scared me, because I was afraid of anything I couldn't understand. It made me feel anxious and inadequate. But now, I appreciate that. I wish strange things happened more often." He smiled at her, but Lee just felt ashamed.

"I don't feel like her anymore. I can't imagine doing something so *bold* now."

He didn't leap to reassure her. "I think a lot of people walk around wondering if they've moved backward. We're all trying not to fall apart after a certain age. It's hard enough to maintain the status quo. I think this constant need for moving forward and growing is exhausting."

"But that's all I used to think about. Moving to a new place. Transforming into something better. I don't know what to do or who I am if I'm not pursuing that goal."

They both took a sip from their drinks.

"The truth is, you're *not* her anymore. You're *Lee*." He raised an eyebrow and smiled into his glass. She knocked her shoulder against his.

"*Ha ha*. It was my chance to start over. No one at college knew about my family. I could be anyone I wanted. *Opaline* is a country girl no matter what she does. Lee is ambiguous. I wanted to be ambiguous."

He smiled. "I like Lee. She's . . . not soft. But maybe . . . open. More vulnerable."

"So now I'm a sad, soft woman, huh?"

He ignored her. "You know, I'd wanted to ask you out for a long time before we went to the field. You were this mystery, and I wanted to know what was behind it. I had a feeling it was something special. But you were also a little scary. I thought you'd bite my head off if I asked."

They both laughed. "I *was* a little scary, huh? I used to have so much rage. I know it wasn't approachable, but I miss it."

Suddenly from the back of the bar, a woman drawled, "O-pa-line Ford, ho-ly shit."

Lee turned around, and there was Kimmie Ryder, standing with a pool stick in one hand and her right hip cocked. If there was any indication time had passed, this was it. She had once been smooth-skinned and muscley, but now her face was wrinkled and pocked under heavy foundation and thick black eyeliner. She had the skinny limbs and slightly bloated torso of someone who didn't eat very often but drank liberally; her rhinestone tank top stretched across her middle like it might bust a seam.

Lee, Kimmie, and Dreama had once been an odd trio forced together by family. Whenever things got bad at home for Kimmie, she'd run away and live with Belva for a while before the Ryders dragged her back. The Ryders were somehow related to them, and Lee had always been aware of the simmering feud between their families, but she'd only had a child's vague understanding.

Redbud hadn't explicitly cut her off from Kimmie when her father died, but without Belva to bring them together, they slowly grew apart.

"I heard you were back."

Lee stood up and went in for a hug, and Kimmie picked her up and spun her around. She set her down and made eyes at Otis. "Sorry to *interrupt*."

"That's fine. How you doing, Kimmie?" Otis asked.

"Oh, you know." She signaled for the bartender, and he poured her a shot of tequila. "Needed to pay the power bill, so I came here to wipe the floor with these sorry fucks." She gestured toward the back room where a few bearded men loitered around the pool table. She took the shot and slammed it down. "Hey, O. Let's go out tonight." Kimmie raised an eyebrow at Lee.

"We *are* out."

"*Are we?*" She gestured around at the mostly empty bar. "I know a place. Back holler shit. It'll blow your tits off."

Lee thought of her kids sleeping safely back in Belva's cabin. As essentially the only caregiver for her children, and then her mother before that, life hadn't granted her the luxury of spontaneity. She'd been so careful. So afraid she would get stuck in this town, or later that they would take her new life away from her if she made a wrong move.

But in spite of her efforts, she'd lost it anyway.

She wanted to be bold again, as she'd been with Otis that afternoon they kissed in a field.

She returned to her stool and turned away from Kimmie. "What do you think? Might be fun." She slid her knee between Otis's legs.

"You continue to surprise me." Mirth sparkled in his eyes. "Let's do it."

·  ·  ·

Otis and Lee pulled up to a large clearing deep in the woods with cars and trucks parked in long, disheveled rows. People poured out, calling to one another and carrying six-packs of cheap beer. There was the whole spectrum of young and old, from men with long gray hair to teenage girls clutching each other's arms. They all moved toward a bonfire at the center of the clearing like woodland creatures gathering for a pagan ritual.

Lee had never been to a party like this, never attended a single booze-drenched throwdown in high school. She'd been too terrified.

She had imagined alcohol and drugs were a kind of paralyzing agent that kept you from leaving the house or this town. That's what it'd seemed like with her mom; she got fucked up and then she lay down and didn't get up.

As Lee and Otis moved toward the flames, she noticed a few women loping by like deer and staring her down.

"I think you have a few admirers." Lee raised an eyebrow.

Otis didn't respond and instead shifted his gaze to a group of men and women who were setting up chairs on the far side of the fire and tuning instruments. Lee noticed a small piano placed behind them, and wondered how they'd gotten it up here.

Kimmie approached with a few men, and the crowd seemed to part for them. Lee recognized Kimmie's brother TJ. She remembered the animal magnetism of him, prowling the halls of their high school, tinted further by her vague understanding of a fraught family connection. They were somehow related, but not in any direct way that she could track. She'd fantasized about his lean chest in a white tank top and the freckles along his cheeks and collarbone, aware that there was something taboo in this fantasy.

He'd since filled out into something meaty and menacing, with the perpetually flushed skin of an older man even though he was close to her age. Under one arm he held a small white puppy that was red-eyed and raw like it'd been pulled from its mother too young. TJ stroked its soft skull with his thumb.

He and Otis hugged, and Lee remembered they were friends. TJ took a step back and looked Lee over from head to toe in an exaggerated gesture. "Opaline. Looking good, girl. That real cashmere?"

Lee looked down at her black sweater and flinched. She'd tried to dress more simply since she returned, knowing she'd be mocked if they caught even a whiff of elitism. But she'd been married to a rich man for fifteen years, and all of her clothes were on the higher end.

"Yes, good spot."

"I know about shit. I ain't just an ignorant redneck." He smiled and continued to pet the dog. She studied him more closely and noticed that his jeans looked expensive and the rhinestones in his ears glinted like real diamonds.

"How's your granny doing?" His smile was replaced by a more shifting, unreadable expression.

"She's fine. Why do you ask?"

The smile returned. "It's called manners, Opaline."

A woman cleared her throat across the fire, and their heads turned toward her. She stood in front of the band, ready to sing. Every instrument was made of wood and animal hair, and gut and throat, so that when the rich sound of the bluegrass music began, it seemed at one with the place, a chorus of nature surrounding them with its plucks of trunk and falls of rain and the keening of an animal searching for a mate.

As they listened, she could feel the solidity of Otis's body a few inches from hers, prickling at the edges. Not touching, but sensing one another. They let that feeling hang heavily between them as the music pulled them into its orbit.

After a few songs, the slow and steady rhythm gave way to something harder and grittier. The musicians laid into their instruments as if to destroy them with their playing, and the singer's sweet, luscious voice like fermented fruit turned to a scream.

A few boys made a circle and started crashing into one another to the music, their bones meeting in full force, going horn to horn. Lee watched as Kimmie dove into the cluster of them, flailing, catching one boy on the cheekbone with her fist. He brought his elbow up in response and made her mouth bleed. She laughed at him, spraying red into his face, and they howled together up at the moon.

The music slowed again, turning hypnotic this time, and the moshers' movements slowed with it and became more like a dance. A few girls entered the circle and started moving like nymphs, their arms swaying back and forth.

Otis took an airplane bottle out of his pocket, pulled on it, and handed it to Lee. She took a sip and felt the warmth of his mouth on the rim. She realized it was the same oil can liquor she'd found in the shed, but this stuff tasted fresher. Pure, shifting nectar. It slid like venomous honey down her throat.

She looked closer at the bottle where someone had taken off the label and affixed a sticker with the emblem of a black flower.

She started to ask Otis about it, but he took her hand and pulled her into the fray, and she was pleasantly shocked as he started to dance around the fire with the rest of them. Kimmie swiveled her hips suggestively as she drank from a glass jar with the same black flower. She made eye contact with Lee, challenging her to join.

Lee gave herself over to it. In its breathless plush, it felt as if she and Otis were the only two people, and everything else became a blur around them. They danced without touching, like bees in a mating dance, weaving shapes between them as the music kept time with the rhythm of the blood coursing through their veins.

After a while, he pulled her toward his chest, and they just stood there for a moment breathing together, their skin searing from the flames. He looked down at her, and she held his gaze.

"I need to be . . . closer." He brought his forehead to hers, both damp with the anticipation of it. This need to be skin to skin.

There was something tender about his voice, tinged with just a bit of fear. Lee was surprised she felt no fear herself; it had been so long since she wanted to touch or be touched, but she could feel her body reaching for him. She knew why they called desire *thirst*. She felt the pulse of wanting in her tongue.

She nodded, and he led her away from the fire toward the trees. The air cooled and darkened the farther they went, but the heat still radiated from each of their bodies. Lee felt like a warm jewel, a ruby held in a palm until it's hot to the touch. She thought she could see an emerald hue emanating from him, standing out from the dark blues and purples and blacks.

At some point, she had begun to lead him, and she stopped at a tree deep enough to give them privacy, but not so far away that they'd lost sight of the flames in the distance. Her eyes had adjusted by now, and she could see the charcoal of his features as he brought his face to hers and pushed her gently back against the bark.

She ran her fingers through the silk of his hair and gave consciousness up to her senses. His nose against her cheek, then her mouth inside his, his arms cradled around her back. It was more than flesh meeting flesh. It was their two selves meeting in each point of contact, a bone-deep pleasure billowing from each touch.

When he got on his knees, pulled down her clothes, and slid his tongue down the slit of her, she could feel herself spreading and dislocating, her mind meeting his mouth in each movement.

Suddenly, the beam of a flashlight swept through the trees, and a woman's voice came from behind them. They instinctively pulled apart, and Lee frantically pulled her jeans back over her hips.

The woman was calling for someone, but Lee couldn't make out the name. As the light swept through again, Lee saw that there were other pairs of bodies in the woods around them, blooming in the combination of moonlight and fire glow like an ancient pleasure garden.

She saw a flash of a young girl about Meredith's age, naked to the waist and clutched against a man in a purple blazer with his pants unbuckled and his silver temples glinting in the glare.

In the next sweep of light, the figures were gone. The tree bare.

Lee smelled white ash, wood burned to powder. An owl appeared and perched in the tree above them. It swiveled its head toward her without moving its body and stared into her eyes with its unfeeling ink.

# SIX

**W**hen Lee opened her eyes, everything was blue.

She was a hard gray stone, numb to the touch.

Rain clinked against the roof of the car, its smell mixing with the wool of the seats and the smoked denim of her jacket. The clearing outside the window had turned to a wasteland of old pickup trucks with a pile of wet ash at the center.

Otis was hunched in the driver's seat, breathing rhythmically. The minor imperfections of his face were clear and on display in the somber, cloud-diffused light. She nudged him gently and told him she needed to get back to her kids. He nodded without a word and cleared his throat as he put the car in gear, pulled out of the mud, and curved toward the gravel road.

The night before, she'd been desperate to be with her children after seeing Mr. Hall with the girl, and she'd asked Otis if he could take her home without telling him what she'd seen. They took off in his pickup, but when they got to the old livestock gate, it was padlocked shut. Otis remembered this was the only rule for these parties, established years ago after a girl left drunk one night and drove right off the mountain.

Now it was morning and the gate was open. As they pulled out, Otis silently focused on the road, and Lee sat brooding with one elbow on the door, unraveling everything she knew about Mr. Hall. Reinterpreting every intimate moment, every eloquent line. She thought of how an artist could become a predator. How the silken qualities of a creative mind could slip between the lines.

She thought of Crystal. A girl with frothy blonde hair and a legendary chest who had been in her English class sophomore year. She'd been famous for mauling another girl at lunch the year prior. At first, Lee was baffled by her presence in Mr. Hall's class, but then she read one of her essays in a peer-review exercise. Crystal wrote with a forceful truth that disarmed the reader, shedding all pretense and cutting straight to the marrow. It was the kind of writing that made Lee question the verbose style she'd adopted from the authors she read.

She thought of Mr. Hall scolding Crystal for always wearing a puffy jacket in his class, even at the parched end of spring when the flowers were starting to wilt and brown in their beds. He always insisted she take it off, to show some decorum. Lee had felt herself aligned with him—*punish her, teach her what it means to be a dignified person*. But now it was cast in a different light. He'd wanted her to bare herself to him.

As the world shifted and offered this new lens, it was clear that he treated the girls differently, placing them into categories like characters in novels. There were girls who were smart, stubborn, and bound for greatness, who needed to be nurtured and *preserved* and made into devotees. That was Lee. And then there were girls that were meant to be ravaged, embodiments of fresh, ripe sexuality, existing only for this purpose. Like Crystal, or the young woman she saw in the woods.

Otis slowly drove up Belva's driveway, careful not to displace the gravel. His ease should have been calming, but she was anxious to leave the car and take refuge in the cabin. Her hand was already on the handle as he came to a stop.

"Thank you for taking me home." She saw that his face was guarded, his usual stoicism forced to mask something. She put her hand on his in a hasty attempt at tenderness. None of this was his fault. She hadn't explained the urgency last night, and he hadn't pressed her. He had done everything right.

"Wait a minute. Are you okay?"

"Yes, of course. I'm just tired from last night. Need to sleep." She got out of the car before he could say anything else.

Inside, Luann was cleaning her gun on the kitchen table, and the smell of the oil made Lee want to vomit. She was suddenly painfully aware of her body. The throb in her head, the hollow in her stomach. She wanted to say something about gun safety, but the words escaped her. Lee asked Luann where everyone was, and she told her Belva was setting up at the antique mall and the children were playing in the woods. This filled her with fresh panic, and she went out to look for them.

The rain had turned into a faint drizzle, and tiny water droplets pearled in her hair. The leaves underfoot were an amber mash and the woods were awash in that prehistoric smell—fog, ferns, and mud emitting their fragrances without intervention.

She found Meredith and Cliff hunched over something in a ravine filled with enormous moss-covered stones. At the sound of her footsteps, they looked up toward her. Meredith held something small and furred against her chest as Cliff stroked its head with his finger.

"Can we keep it?"

Lee saw that it was a black barn kitten. "You'll have to ask Belva. You can bring it up to the house for now." Lee took the kitten from Meredith and brought it to her chest. She hadn't felt this ache since she'd moved in with Cooper, and he'd forced her to give up her cat. This was how she'd ended up with so many animals when she was younger.

At first it had driven Mama crazy, and she would make her release them into the woods. But as Mama disconnected from Lee and the rest of the world, she stopped coming into Lee's room or noticing much of anything she did unless it caused her direct, concrete trouble.

In her loneliness, Lee collected a legion of animals in her room, where she left the window open to let them come and go. There were barn kittens and baby mice and tiny raccoons and little possum. They always grew up and eventually left her, but she was okay with that. Sometimes she'd see them in the woods months or years after, and they'd make eye contact, and an understanding would pass between them. It was the type of memory that she questioned now, skeptical of its plausibility. Yet, she could still remember the feeling of falling asleep at night with quivering fur against her cheek.

When they got to the house, she told Cliff to go inside, and she and Meredith sat on the porch with the kitten between them on the swing.

"How are things going? I feel like I haven't talked to you in forever."

Meredith let the kitten sink its tiny fangs into her palm. "Fine."

"Yeah?" Lee wondered if she was in one of her moods. She told herself to give her space. She didn't need to know everything that was happening inside her at all times.

"Yeah, I don't know. I guess I like it here."

Lee had expected her daughter to hate this place as much as she had when she was her age; she'd braced herself for the misery. But this attitude was harder for Lee to grapple with—she didn't *want* Meredith to like it here. She wanted her to stay separate and rarified. Her mean, brilliant teenager who wouldn't settle for less. She'd come to believe that Meredith would finally get it right. She would have the shimmering, successful life. Lee was just a bridge. But *this*. She didn't know how to handle this.

"That's . . . great. I want you to be happy." Lee paused. "I'm going to ask you something, and it's important that you're honest. I promise that nothing you tell me will get you in trouble."

Meredith furrowed her brow. "Okay . . ."

"Has Mr. Hall said or done anything . . . *inappropriate* to you since we got here? I know it's only been a week, but I have to ask."

"What? No. "

"You're sure?"

"Yes! What is going on?"

"I think . . . something happened with another girl. I just need to know for sure that nothing has happened with you."

"I mean, I get a weird vibe from him. Like he's trying to be my friend. Which is fine. Teachers are people, too. But . . . I don't know."

Lee knew what she meant, but she'd welcomed it when she was younger. She'd been so hungry for kinship. "All right, thank you for being honest. Keep this between us for now, okay?"

Meredith nodded.

In the shower, Lee rubbed body wash into her legs and swore she could see new veins spidering up her calves since last night. Her nose and eyes were scarlet in the bathroom mirror, and she tried to bleach them with foundation and a few drops of wild rose water from the bathroom cabinet. She huddled inside of herself, searching for some comfort. But all she could find was sickness.

•   •   •

Peeper's Antique Mall shared a parking lot with a small strip center church, and a giant white cross, easily the tallest thing for miles, stood out in front.

The mall was a large, low-ceilinged warehouse partitioned into small cubicles that people rented out to hawk their wares. There were booths filled with rusted rifles and faded NASCAR memorabilia, poorly painted portraits of strangers long dead, sparkling costume jewelry and hand-painted *live laugh love* signs. Some were neatly arranged, and others looked like a glorified yard sale with the cat hair still stuck to the items.

Lee followed a stream of people moving toward the back of the store where the air was colder and the booths creepier. She passed one with nothing but wide-eyed, catatonic dolls with their hair matted against their heads and their dresses pulled up over their legs, and another with hundreds of ceramic hands reaching up to the heavens. It was the type of stuff that showed up with high price tags in urban boutiques but only went for a few dollars at Peeper's.

Belva's booth was at the very back in a wing that branched off from the rest of the store. It was entirely unadorned. Three large pieces of white pegboard surrounded her so that *she* was the thing on display: an older woman with peach hair sitting in front of a card table covered in a white handkerchief, a few tea candles burned to the metal, and a worn Bible. Next to her chair sat the type of red-and-white cooler famous for its ability to chill many beers at a time and a graying tacklebox. A folded screen stood in one corner like the kind women dressed behind in old movies.

Lee watched as a woman pretended to browse the wares in the booths nearby, and then furtively approached Belva, speaking low. Belva motioned for her to come behind the screen, and there was some brief murmuring before they came back out. Belva unfurled the tacklebox and plucked a string from its compartments of feathers, coins, flannel strips, stones, and animal teeth. The woman raised her shirt, and Belva tied it around her waist. Then Belva told her to visit a cemetery before sunrise, and the woman nodded solemnly.

Lee waited until the woman left and sat in the chair on the other side of the table.

"Ms. Buck, I feel like a corpse this morning. What do you advise?"

Belva raised an eyebrow. "You might try putting down the bottle one of these nights."

Lee was ready for this. "That might help long term, but I'm looking for something more immediate. As in, right now."

Belva sighed. "I'm not sure you deserve it, but I don't like seeing you in pain." She dipped into the cooler and pulled out a vial of a bright green liquid. Lee had only been joking, but she was drawn to the vial now, her mouth watering. She took it from Belva, uncapped it, and shot it back. The taste was of plants picked too young—sweet, raw, and nearly fizzing with life.

She waited for something to happen.

Nothing.

Belva watched her intently, and Lee wondered at her curiosity. She'd probably given this hangover remedy thousands of times.

And then Lee felt it. The smell of wet dust and the hum of the fluorescents and the staleness inside of her receded. In its place, the smell of dewy grass and the silent spill of sunshine and the feeling of a new day beginning spread through her.

Like a phoenix, she was resurrected.

Lee found a discarded chair in a corner and sat next to Belva as more patients came through. After an acne-ridden teen boy left with a bag of stones and some cream, Lee asked Belva why these people didn't just go to the doctor. Belva explained that some in the community didn't have health insurance. She was all they had until the big nonprofit medical vans rolled in at the end of the summer and parked up in the hills for the weekend to deliver free medical care to the mountain folk. People would wait in line for days to have their rotten teeth pulled and their diabetes checked.

And some just believed in her methods. She'd healed them before, and they kept coming back.

Lee eyed the booths around them, making sure no one was within earshot, and pulled the chair closer to Belva. She bowed her head and spoke in the same low voice as her abashed patrons.

"What do you know about Joseph Hall?"

Belva met her gaze. "Why do you ask?"

"I think I saw something last night. With a young girl."

"Tell me more."

Lee told her what she had seen, and Belva was quiet for a moment.

"Did you know the girl?"

"No, I didn't recognize her. But there's no way she was more than fifteen."

Belva closed her eyes. "There were whispers a few years ago, but nothing happened. If he's at it again, he has to be stopped."

"I agree."

"I'll call my people when I get home and see if we can get enough for a gathering. Would you join us? We could really use you. Our numbers aren't like they used to be. Just a bunch of grannies and Billy. Sometimes Kimmie. We need more youngins."

Lee couldn't believe what she was hearing. It was one thing to use the folk magic for healing, but it was another thing to think it could protect the community from a pedophile. "Look, this isn't a joke. He needs to be held accountable. We have to report this to the police."

"Look here, *girl*. I ain't *joking*. Someone filed a complaint with the school a few years back. Got the police involved. He's their best teacher.

*The only one who gives two shits.* No one wants to see it. They got the girl to take it back. It went away. This is what the Bucks do. This is what they've *always* done."

Lee opened her mouth to interject, but Belva cut her off. "Why didn't you go to the po-lice first, huh? You didn't have to come here and report to me."

Lee wondered at that herself. There had been no internal deliberation; she had instinctively come. "I guess I wanted to know it was real. There's a part of me that still doesn't believe it happened."

Belva studied her again. "So you're saying you ain't sure?"

"No . . . no. I'm certain it was him."

"Well, all right, then. It's settled. We'll take care of him tonight."

"I'm going to sit this one out—I wouldn't be of any use to you anyway. I'll tell the principal first thing tomorrow. He'll know what to do."

"You do what you need, darlin'."

# SEVEN

## MEREDITH

**M**eredith woke to the sound of dogs howling and the strange energy surging through her with a strength she'd not yet experienced. She rolled out of bed and opened the small window in their room. Cliff shifted in his sleep. The faintest glow was coming from deeper in the woods, and she could smell smoke on the breeze.

Earlier that evening, she and Cliff listened from their bedroom as cars pulled up and voices receded into the trees. She told him she thought a ritual was happening that night, but she wasn't sure. She'd already shared everything that Belva told her about their family, and Cliff was as excited by it as she was. She thought the things Cliff saw and felt that seemed strange to people were actually some magical sensitivity, and she wanted him to ask Belva about it. But Cliff was still too scared of Belva. She was an incredibly sturdy caregiver, but there was a steely quality that made you think twice before approaching her.

Meredith knew sneaking out to watch the ritual was a risk, but it didn't feel like a choice. She was being pulled into the woods by an invisible force.

She threw on a fleece and sneakers and walked quietly out into the living room. Her mom was passed out in front of the TV with her hand still wrapped around a beige mug. Her breathing was slow and heavy, and she had that dead look that used to scare Cliff when they were little. Cliff would come to Meredith's room with his fists pressed against his chest and ask her to help him check if Mom was still alive. They'd stand a few feet from her bed and watch her throat and chest for movement, too scared to touch her. Their mother only liked to be touched on her terms, and she didn't like to be surprised. She would always wake with a gasp, startled by them looming over her.

Meredith slipped out the back door, stepping carefully at first, and then with more abandon as her eyes adjusted and she saw the path into the woods before her illuminated by moonlight. She followed the glow and its smoke until she could see a fire with people gathered around it. She crouched behind a log at a distance so that she wouldn't be spotted, but she could still feel the vibrations of their voices and the crack of the logs.

It sounded like Luann was speaking, and she watched as she took something out of a bag and buried it in a small hole in the ground. The magic had been a figment to her until now, but here it was, happening in the real world.

A sound came from behind her, but when she wheeled around, there was nothing there.

She watched as Belva held up a taut piece of string, and Mom's cousin Kimmie approached with a pair of scissors and cut it. Belva tied a knot in the string, raised it up to the sky, and then flung it into the fire. She began to chant unintelligible words, and the women began to hum. The buzz of it seemed to penetrate the soil; Meredith could feel it tingling under her feet.

It was similar to the night energy that coursed through her, but this was stronger and fuller. It had definition and character where before it had felt amorphous. It was too intense to be pleasurable, but Meredith was drawn to it nonetheless. It was better than feeling good. It felt like the power of the land Belva had described.

Meredith lay down on the ground and felt the power surging along every inch of her. She allowed it to enter her fully.

It felt like the earth itself was telling her a secret, and she lay there for a long time, not listening or thinking or speaking, only feeling.

And then she was no longer in her body—only floating through some inky expanse.

# EIGHT

## LEE

K immie lay face down and spread-eagled across the porch sofa in the early-morning light. Her white Kmart sneakers were caked in mud and her arms were covered in rows of long thin scrapes pearled with dried blood. Lee kicked the bottom of the couch to try to rouse her, but she didn't stir. A few more kicks did nothing.

As she bent over to shake her shoulder, a stream of water came from behind Lee and soaked the back of Kimmie's head. Kimmie shot up and crouched in a fighting position, staring behind Lee at Belva holding a plastic pitcher.

"What the fuck?"

Belva ignored her and said to Lee, "It ain't pretty, but it's the only way with her. She sleeps like the dead," then walked back into the house.

Kimmie shook her head like a dog and rubbed the water from her eyes, the remnants of mascara bleeding down her face and mixing with the dirt in a marble pattern. She collapsed back on the couch and pulled out a plastic baggie filled with dry brown tobacco and a few squares of white paper and began to roll a thin, frayed cigarette.

"How was the gathering last night?" Lee asked.

"Hell of a time."

"Do you think it worked?"

Kimmie smiled. "Oh, I don't know. I don't much care. Felt good either way." She placed a small filter at the end and started to roll. "Saw you getting close with Otis at the party. He's a real piece. Some of the girls were so pissed. I love that shit."

Lee had a hazy memory of women watching them at the bonfire.

"Has he ever dated any of them?"

"Naw. He doesn't go for the local poon. He likes the imports. Like you." She raised an eyebrow at Lee.

"I grew up here. I'm not exactly foreign."

"Sure you are, hon. Look at you. Listen to you. You weren't from here even when you were."

This was how Lee had long wanted to be perceived, but a need to defend her territory rose up in her like bile. The truth was, Lee hadn't wanted to leave, not at first.

It started out as her mother's wish for her after her father died. They woke up that next morning in Lee's bed, and Mama whispered, "I had a vision of your future. It came to me in a dream." She'd pushed herself up to sitting and forced Lee to look her in her bloodshot eyes. "You're gonna be the brightest, most promising student this town has ever seen, and you're gonna blow all of the colleges away, and when you graduate, you're gonna leave this town and start a new life somewhere else. You promise? To do everything you can to get out?"

Lee was already an exceptional student at nine, so it didn't seem out of the question that she could maybe get into college one day. But she'd never thought about leaving and never coming back. She loved her strange, wild mother; and her equally strange, wild grandmother; and her cousins; and the woods that continually offered something new. She liked Craw Valley, but it seemed important to Mama, so she promised she would.

A few years passed, and her mother didn't get better, but she tried to keep it together. Then she started complaining about her wrists, and she went to the doctor for the pain. He gave her pills so that she could go back to work at the deli counter, but after a while she started calling in sick a few days a week. Eventually they fired her, and she went on disability. During the day, she stayed in her room with the TV on and the door shut. At night, she often went out and didn't return until late or the next day.

Her mother had sunk into some deeper, more wretched place, and Lee would have crawled into it with her, if Mama had let her. But she had shut her out.

So when Lee started high school, her mother's dream for her became Lee's dream. To one day leave this all behind and start a new life. It was the only way she would survive.

Kimmie put the finished cigarette between her teeth, and Lee followed her inside.

Belva was in the kitchen cutting biscuits out of dough with a water glass while Luann fried bacon in the cast iron. Lee could smell last night's woodsmoke still clinging to their hair. They both hummed the same unknowable tune, and their arms moved with the same rhythm. They were a few feet apart from one another, but Lee had the sense that they were touching.

This was an intimacy she'd never seen in her parents' marriage, or her own. She wondered what that felt like, a love allowed to grow and deepen away from the rest of the world, molded into the precise, unique shapes of their desires and needs.

From what she gleaned, they didn't get together until Luann's husband died suddenly years earlier. She wondered if it started before then, or if it blossomed out of this new, free chapter in Luann's life. Belva never had a true partner when Lee was small, but her house was always full of people who needed her help. Lee was glad Belva now had someone who cared for her as much as she cared for them.

Kimmie lit her cigarette with the front-left burner and puffed the cherry to life. Belva waved her arms and told Kimmie to take it outside.

Lee had smelled cigarettes over the years, brief, husky whiffs outside bars and on the beach when she and Cooper went to Europe before they had kids. But it was never the smoke of her childhood, this smoke that lingered in the kitchen now.

It conjured a specter of her mother standing in the same kitchen, holding a cigarette and making them laugh while Belva taught Lee how to make biscuits. It was hard to believe that the three of them had once spent time together so carelessly, like people who belonged together. The image felt distant, like she was watching other people through a window.

Belva announced breakfast was ready, and Lee went to get the children up. They were going to be late for school.

Lee opened the door to their room to find all the windows open, as they'd been the night the bat got in, and a chill swept through her. She was suddenly aware of an unease collecting in her periphery that she'd failed to register until now. It was the same feeling she'd gotten when Cliff broke his arm. She'd been at the grocery store alone, when a sickness filled her without warning. She'd raced home to find Cliff clutching his arm in the backyard while Cooper watched a documentary on full volume in his office. Cliff had been sitting on the windowsill and fallen two stories.

In the bed closest to the door, she could see the outline of Cliff and his tuft of hair poking out of the blanket. She pushed it down gently to expose his head and put a finger under his nose to feel for the slight wind of his breathing.

Across the room, the comforter was violently arranged around Meredith. She crept closer and pulled it back to find only empty space.

. . .

Lee, Cliff, Luann, and Belva strode through the crush of leaves, calling out Meredith's name. Lee wasn't sure how long they'd been looking, but they'd gone deep enough where it looked the same in every direction. The trees appeared fake and flattened like wallpaper. She was still in that breathless moment after receiving traumatic news, when nothing feels real.

One time, Lee, Kimmie, and Dreama had gotten lost in these woods.

In their trio, Kimmie was the wild one, Dreama was the practical one, and Lee fell somewhere in the middle. That day, Lee and Kimmie ran headlong into the woods with Dreama trailing behind, eating blackberries off bushes and laughing at the shapes the trees made in the distance. But then one particular tree looked like a body with its back snapped and its middle bursting forth. The woods seemed to grow darker, and they became aware of the trees surrounding them without distinction, like people in a lifeboat who've just realized they are in the middle of the ocean.

They wandered for a bit, Dreama weeping, Lee squeezing out a few tears for dramatic effect, and Kimmie berating them for being babies, before encountering the thin creek that ran through the neighboring cow farm. Sweet salvation! This would lead them home.

That was the closest she, Kimmie, and Dreama would ever be as they walked home along the creek bed and talked quietly about food in the evening light.

Dreama's mom, Ruby Jo, died in the same bridge collapse that killed Lee's dad a few months later, and afterward, Dreama didn't come around anymore. In her will, Ruby Jo left Dreama and her brother, Earl, in the care of a fellow church member, out of fear that Belva and Redbud's devilish ways would corrupt her children without her around. Ruby Jo had been sliding into religious fanaticism for years at that point, having donated the sale of her house to a new radical church and moving herself, Dreama, and Earl into a room at the Red Roof Inn by the highway. At school after her death, Dreama avoided Lee like the plague and muttered to herself whenever they crossed paths. They both ate lunch alone, each in a different corner of the cafeteria. Lee hiding behind a book, and Dreama hiding behind the long hair her mother never let her cut in the name of the Lord.

A few crisp gunshots punctured the air around them, and Lee gasped.

"Don't worry," Belva said. "That's a few miles off. Probably the Lawsons hunting turkeys. Nothing to worry about."

Cliff clutched Lee's arm. "I think this was in my dream last night. I remember the gunshot, and then Belva saying something about turkeys."

Belva crouched down to his level and looked into his eyes. "What else do you remember?"

He gazed up at the treetops for a moment and then scanned around the woods. "There was a big rock that sort of looked like a rabbit—with the ears." He put two hands on top of his head, and Luann grunted.

"I know that rock. It's over here." She took off, and they followed her, breath scalding their throats. A few feet in, Lee spotted the small boulder and sprinted toward it.

Meredith was curled up behind the rock with her lips nearly blue. There was a smear of blood across the front of her pajama pants. Lee crouched down and put a hand to her forehead, feeling the warmth under the chilled skin. Relief flooded her.

Meredith's eyes fluttered open, and as she took in the sky above her, she looked over at Lee in horror.

"Mom. I'm so sorry."

"What happened? Are you okay? What is this?" She pointed to the blood.

Meredith looked down, and a different kind of horror crossed her face. "I . . . I have no idea." She touched the stain with her fingertips, and they came away wet.

Lee took Meredith by the shoulders and pulled her up to a sitting position. "Meredith. Why are you out here? Tell me what happened." Lee grasped for the right reaction but couldn't find anything solid inside of her. The initial relief had been fleeting, and she'd become pure panic, the cold air whistling down her throat and straight through her, making her lightheaded and frantic.

Meredith's eyes welled with tears, and she looked down at the ground as she spoke. "I wanted to see the magic."

"What else? What else happened?"

"I . . . I don't know! I don't remember anything else. I must have fallen asleep."

Belva crouched down on the other side of Meredith and placed her hands on her in different places. As she asked her questions, Lee noticed vines of dark flowers growing around the trees near them, fanning out on the ground and tangling like pumpkin vines.

Belva smiled slightly, and it brought Lee back into her body.

"My dear, I believe you've started your period."

Meredith was caught between horror and joy, and she returned the same smile. "Oh my god. Wow. Okay." She looked up hopefully at Belva. "Does this mean—"

Belva started to answer, but Lee cut her off. "We can talk at the house. We need to get her warm."

Belva and Lee helped Meredith stand. As they moved to leave the woods, Meredith let out a gasp. Lee followed her eyes to a clearing partly obscured by thickets of those dark flowering vines.

At its center was the pale, naked body of Mr. Hall, splayed out like a star.

# NINE

Belva sat on the sofa with her hand in Luann's as the sheriff asked her questions. She looked out of her element, and for the first time since Lee returned, she noticed an unfamiliar fragility in her grandmother, a bewilderment in her face when Lee had only ever seen complete control.

As the officers came through the back door from the woods, Lee could see them peeking into Belva's workshop and eyeing the jars of hair and animal bone. They'd been there since early that morning when Lee had called them. When Kimmie had heard the cops were coming, she'd disappeared into the woods so quickly that Lee didn't have time to stop her. Lee was the one who lead them to the body.

Mr. Hall's face and body had grayed and hardened to stone. His eyes were closed, and his mouth was slightly open. His limbs were outstretched, as if he'd died in ecstasy, or as if they'd been arranged by someone else after his death. His pale, shriveled penis was visible through thinning hair, and part of it stuck to his inner thigh next to an odd mark. It looked as if something parasitic had burrowed into his leg, and she moved closer to get a better view. The shape was more complex than the circle of a ringworm. The raised pink ridges curved into the shape of a simple flower, like it had been burned into the flesh of his leg.

It was then that the officers asked her to back away so they could do their jobs. She watched as they entered the clearing with their black boots and trampled the dark flowers. They set up equipment, pulled things out of plastic bags, and took pictures with the flash on. Lee imagined the photos of the body: the woods around him flooded with artificial light, all of its magic bleached.

Meredith sat at the kitchen table, staring vacantly ahead. Lee had tried to comfort her, but she'd bristled at her touch and refused all the food and remedies Belva offered her while they waited for the police. They'd decided not to tell them about finding her in the woods. It had been Belva's idea, and Lee hadn't questioned it.

During Lee's interview, she'd considered telling the officer about Mr. Hall and the girl the night of the bonfire. *This is my chance.* But she could tell the officer was suspicious of them, and she knew this could implicate them even more. She didn't know what to do with the information now. There was no safe place to put it.

From the other room came the quiet voice of Cliff as he told Billy something she couldn't make out. Billy had come to the cabin immediately after they found Mr. Hall and helped distract Cliff. Lee had kept both kids out of school and called in sick from her job.

Billy began to laugh deeply, and it rang strangely through the room and out over the driveway as they loaded the covered body into the ambulance. The sun was beginning to set, the woods a silhouette aflame, filling the living room with a harsh light.

"Did you know Joseph Hall?" asked the sheriff.

"Yes, of course. I know everybody." Belva waved him away like this was all ridiculous, but Lee could see it was a hollow performance that obscured something else.

"Was there any reason he would be on your property?"

"No, sir. We weren't close. I don't think he's ever been out here."

"We found evidence of a fire in the clearing where the body was discovered. Can you tell me about that?"

"We use that clearing for social gatherings. I had a few friends over yesterday evening, and we built a fire. Just a bunch of old women jawing and singing a few songs."

"Did you notice anything of note during your . . . gathering?"

"No, nothing at all."

"Look, Belva. You know I got nothing against you. I think you're a good woman, and I appreciate what you did for my son. But I know it wasn't just some women gossiping around a fire. I want the truth."

Belva put one hand up and brought the other to her chest. "I swear."

"Y'all weren't doing some ritual or something on the man and things got out of hand?"

"We don't do rituals on bodies, Randy. Get your head on straight."

He snorted and stood up. "Well, all right. That'll do it for now. I'll need the names of every person who was at your so-called sing-along."

"Whatever you need, Sheriff." Belva stood and shook his hand confidently, but when he turned away, her body slackened, and Luann reached out for her, lowering her to the couch.

Lee followed the sheriff out and stopped him outside the house. "Was he murdered?" she asked.

He looked a bit taken aback. "I can't share the details of an active investigation. You have anything else you want to tell me?"

"No. I told you everything. I just wanted to know. He was my favorite teacher growing up."

The sheriff softened. "Off the record, there's no evidence on the body that he was killed. But we need to do an autopsy. Right now, it looks like the life was clean sucked out of him."

.  .  .

After the police cleared out, Belva put on soup beans and baked a cornbread. They all ate their dinner in different corners of the house.

When Belva left hers on the counter and went out to the woods with a lantern, Lee wanted to stop her, but Luann told her to let her go. She would be safe.

Meredith still refused to eat anything despite Lee's best efforts, and instead remained lying on her bed and looking up at the ceiling as she listened to music.

Billy was showing Cliff how to tie flies for fishing at the kitchen table.

Cliff stroked the piles of bright feathers, the spools of iridescent string, and the pieces of yellow and orange foam. Lee sat down at the table with them and started scratching the inside of Cliff's arm the way he liked it. She'd been so focused on herself since they came to Craw Valley. It was comforting to come back to this space with him.

Cliff looked up at her. "Are you okay? I can see the cloud again."

A few weeks before they left California, Cliff told her he could see a thick cloud hovering around her. It was only then that she became fully aware of how unhappy she was in that house and in the life Cooper had built around them. It had become a part of the atmosphere she inhaled, so that she couldn't see or feel it. But once she did, it couldn't be ignored. This was the magic of her strange little boy.

"I'm okay. It's been a hard day. How are *you*? Are you okay?"

He considered this question for a moment and spoke low so that only she and Billy could hear it. "I saw something last night after Meredith left—out there." He pointed out the window to the woods slowly darkening.

Her stomach dropped. "What was it?"

"I don't know. But I could tell something was moving between the trees. I got really cold when I saw it." Cliff's shoulders shook, and the shiver rippled through Lee as well. When pressed, he didn't say more.

After Cliff went to bed, Lee waited on the porch for Belva to return. She'd snuck more of the liquor from the oil can, careful not to take too much for fear that the real owner would notice. She knew by now that you only needed one drink before you were blurring boundaries.

As it trickled down through her insides, her thoughts became small droplets packed with sediment, dripping one after the other, until they became stalactites.

She saw Mr. Hall's pale, bloated body resting on ash. A brand on his thigh of the same flower she'd seen on the bottle of moonshine Otis shared with her at the bonfire. This body, this man, was a stranger to her, and she didn't mourn him.

Rather, she thought of the man who had been like a father to her for a brief time. A bookish father who lent her novels outside of the curriculum and passed along his refined taste. A supportive father who edited every one of her college essays until they were gleaming with insight. Her own father had been a mere figment at her periphery even when he was alive, and so she mourned the death of this figment that had meant something to her when she really needed it.

It was getting late, and Belva still hadn't come back. Luann might have thought Belva was indestructible, but Lee had seen her brittleness. She went to the spot where she saw Belva enter the woods and moved toward a flicker of light she spotted up the slant of the mountain.

She wished she'd taken her phone with her as she trudged through the thick underbrush. Her body tensed at every small sound, and she got so spooked that she considered turning around.

Eventually the trees parted on a small clearing with a cluster of weathered gravestones and wooden crosses rising up from the ground. Belva leaned against one of the stones with the lantern flickering next to her and a biscuit and a cup of coffee sitting untouched in the grass.

Lee crouched to lean against the stone next to it, but Belva's voice came quick and harsh out of the low light. "Don't sit there. You don't wanna get involved with her."

Lee studied the stone but could only make out a few shallow lines blurring at the edges. "Who was she?"

"My daddy's sister. Mean as a snake."

Lee shifted and leaned against the other side of Belva's stone.

The clearing was situated so that the trees fell away before them, revealing the valley below. A few lights twinkled, but otherwise it was blue and purple with shadow.

Belva took out her pipe, and lit it and Lee let her take a few puffs in silence. The smoke was different this time—thick, cloying, sweet, like a freshly laundered blanket pressed firmly against her nose and mouth. Lee found it hard to form words, though she'd been stewing over what she would say all evening.

Belva spoke first. "We had nothing to do with that man's death. We chanted to keep him from doing harm. Take away his sexual impulses. That's it. This is not our doing."

Lee's words came slowly. "I don't know what to believe. On one hand, I know it's impossible, and on the other, it's a pretty profound coincidence."

"Honey, you overestimate me. I still have the touch when it comes to healing because that's always been my gift. But I can't cast like I used to. I wasn't even sure it would work last night. Like I told you, we don't have the type of energy we need. Not enough youngins."

"Then how do you explain this?"

Belva put her hand on the stone, and her gaze unfocused.

"I knew something bad was coming. At first all I saw was you coming home, and there was a brightness to that. Then the strawberries bloomed outta season. I saw something else would come after and bring suffering, like a shadow to your arrival."

Lee stood up and crossed her arms, looming over Belva. "I can't use that type of information to make decisions for my kids. What I need to know is whether there is a killer in the woods."

"This ain't no TV killer." Belva took a deep drag on her pipe and exhaled, enveloping Lee in another thick cloud. "I've been talking with Granny Pallie out here, and she never heard of such a thing happening before. But she agrees it's from our world. Something from the land, like an angry spirit."

"Who?"

Belva patted the stone. "You know, your great-great-granny Pallie."

"You can speak to her?"

"Not like this"—she gestured between Lee and herself—"us talking right now. But if I come out here and open myself up, usually I can find her. We can sort of send pictures and feelings back and forth, and it feels like talking. She helps me when I don't understand something." She smiled. "It still happens, even when you're older than dirt like me. I've never had much of a talent for the sight beyond a few dreams here and there. And I know how to read the signs in nature. But Pallie was a true seer."

Lee considered all of this. It was hard to parse what was real and what wasn't in this place. But she couldn't deny the reality of a cold body lying in the woods. "It looked like there was a symbol of a flower burned into Mr. Hall's skin. I saw the same symbol on a bottle of moonshine at the party two nights ago. Does that mean anything to you?"

Belva exhaled roughly. "Sounds like a coincidence. I doubt it's got anything to do with his death."

Lee could tell something was amiss. "Are you sure? It feels like it means something—"

Belva cut her off. "I'm sure."

Lee wanted to press further, but it seemed futile. "So you think something is out there that could hurt us?"

"I'm certain of that."

"Cliff said he saw something moving through the trees last night."

"Did he say anything else?"

Lee shook her head.

"Well, whatever it is, I'll keep y'all safe. The house is protected. Our people who built it a hundred years ago used logs from the woods and put protection on them. Mixed yarrow into the concrete, stuff like that. And I'll add a few extras."

"What about when we're not in the house?"

"I'll make protections for you and the kids. This is nothing we can't handle."

Lee thought she saw doubt flicker across Belva's face in the lantern light. She couldn't rely on folk charms to keep her children safe. She needed to find out who was behind this, and she had a feeling it was connected to the black flower.

She looked out at the wall of trees at the edge of the clearing, forcing herself to stare hard without looking away, imagining a creature loping out of it with such speed that it would devour her before she had the chance to run.

But only darkness stared back at her.

# TEN

On her lunch break the next day, Lee pulled up to the neon sign of the dollar store.

The principal had gotten on the announcements in first period and mentioned the untimely death of one of their beloved teachers without going into detail. Students were urged to visit the counseling office if they needed help processing the news. Lee was impressed with the way the school seemed to be acknowledging mental health these days. Her guidance counselor had been an older woman known for her religious conviction and quick judgments.

All through the morning, she'd felt the stares, and her students had behaved suspiciously well and answered her questions in courteous and complete sentences. She wondered if they'd gotten swept up in the rumors and truly thought she was capable of using her evil magic on them. If only they knew how powerless she felt.

Chili ran down her wrists as she took big, juicy bites of her Sonic cheeseburger and studied the store's entrance. When she was little and they were both in a bad mood, Mama would drive them to the dollar store, and they'd pick out the weirdest, most frivolous crap they could find. Their money problems bore down on them at all times, in every purchase at Walmart, every butter sandwich, every sip of Diet Rite. But in these spontaneous visits, money was no longer a construct and life was pure fucking whimsy.

Kimmie worked as a cashier there, and Lee wanted to ask her about the black flower. She'd been drinking from one of the flower-stamped jars at the party, and Lee thought she must know something.

When she was done with her burger, Lee went in and asked at the front if Kimmie was working. They told her she'd quit that morning. Lee wasn't surprised. Kimmie didn't have a consistent phone number, so she would have to reach her another way, maybe later at the cabin if she stopped by to visit Belva.

Lee still had a bit of time, so she took the store row by row, feeling grit under her heels. That morning before school, Belva had salt-and-peppered the soles of their shoes and forced them to give her clippings of their hair, toenails, and warm jars of pee for something she couldn't imagine. She'd wanted to protest, but she saw the calm that settled over Meredith and Cliff when Belva gave them each a bundle of God knows what wrapped in discount catalog paper and tied with red string for hanging around their necks under their clothes. So she'd gone along with it, though she'd refused to eat the tiny blue robin eggs Belva fried up. She had her limits.

The smell of candied pineapple hit her hard as she passed a whole section of the same small, bright yellow candle marked TROPICAL PARADISE, offering transcendence in a plastic jar. Then there were the watered-down cleaning supplies, the pregnancy tests, the weed-detection kits. A young woman passed her wearing a tight hot-pink T-shirt with WI-FI QUEEN across the front.

The real romance was in the candy aisle. She took her time browsing the row, looking for the fruits filled with sugar powder that were her favorite as a kid. Her mother always bought her a sleeve for her birthday and served them in a bowl like fruit salad at breakfast. She gathered a basketful for Meredith and Cliff: candy necklaces like tangy chalk, Pop Rocks, bubble gum shredded to imitate tobacco chew. She willed herself not to think about the mounting balance on her credit card. Her sub paycheck would barely cover gas. But that wasn't the type of thing you considered within the walls of the dollar store.

When she was called to the checkout, she stopped short of the conveyor belt. The cashier was shriveled and cratered underneath the slick blue nylon of her store vest. When she saw Lee, she nearly smiled, but she kept her mouth closed, no doubt hiding a row of mangled teeth. Lee felt her heart begin to pound. Unsure of what she should do, she kept moving forward and stacked the bags of candy on the belt. She watched the woman as she scanned them and touched keys on a pad. Her signature black hair was thin and stringy, hanging limply against her skull where it used to froth around her head in a cloud—Lee had always found her in stores by her hair. Her skin was sallow and pocked where it used to be russet and smooth. Her eyes were dull. *Dirty.*

She finally made eye contact with Lee. "That'll be seven fifty."

"Mama."

"Hey, baby. Thought maybe you didn't recognize me." She smiled again with her lips pressed tightly in a crooked line.

"Of course I did."

"I heard you were in town. Billy told me."

"Just for a little while." Lee wanted to ask her how she was doing, but she didn't want to hear the old lies.

"I tried to come see you, but Mama told me to stay away. From my own daughter and my own grandchildren." She spat.

"I don't think it's a good idea. Not while you're using."

Redbud took Lee by the wrist and pulled her close. "I got the right to see my own kin, Opaline. You can't keep them from me." She had that look of dry electricity about her, like a current running through parched terrain.

Lee became aware of the shoppers waiting behind her, their impatience filling the air like a vapor. This was hardly the arena for a woman to confront her mother after a twenty-year absence. "I have to get back to school. I'm filling in as a teacher right now."

"Left your husband, huh? He cheat on you?"

Lee's chest tightened, but she didn't respond.

"Sounds about right." She let go of Lee's wrist. "All right. Get on now."

Her eyes glazed over as she bagged the candy and gave her the receipt. She motioned for the next customer, and it was as if she'd forgotten Lee was ever there.

Lee walked out of the store, but she barely registered her movements. Her skin radiated white heat, and she couldn't feel her limbs. She got in the car and closed her eyes, waiting for the feeling to pass.

In telling her husband and children that her mother was dead, Redbud had experienced a kind of death in the story Lee told herself about her life. She had held a funeral for her in her mind, and she had let go of all the pain.

But now her mother had risen from the dead, bringing the old emotions back with her.

The last time she'd talked to her was a few weeks after she had Meredith. She remembered standing in the middle of the spotless nursery and speaking low into her phone while she rocked Meredith in a sling against her chest. Redbud had called in a panic, said they turned off her heat and a near-apocalyptic ice storm was coming. Lee could hear the performance in it. Before the drugs, her mother wasn't the type to fluster. She never felt the need to act out her emotions for anyone.

Lee didn't have her grad school stipend any longer. They were now relying on Cooper's trust fund, and she would have had to reveal things about her background she wasn't willing to share. She was starting this brand-new grown-up life with her brand-new baby, and her mother's problems didn't have a place in it. She told her she was sorry, and the next day she got a new phone number.

Redbud had somehow stayed alive through the overdoses and the stints in jail, all reported by Billy in emails that came every few years. But Lee couldn't get over the erosion of her, as if the grains of her were wearing away.

Lee had left her mother alone, and this was what happened. The heavy, stinking guilt traveled from her chest to her stomach, and she thought she might be sick. She rolled down the window and inhaled the fresh air.

She had made the right choice. Redbud had told her to leave and never come back. But if she'd stayed, could she have helped her? If she hadn't cut her off, could she have done something? She had been living in luxury for decades while her mother suffered, poor and alone in this place.

Lee leaned her head back against the headrest and tried to banish the thoughts.

She'd protected herself and her children, and she would continue to do so no matter how much guilt she felt.

.  .  .

When Lee and the kids pulled up at home after school, she asked Cliff to go inside without them. She turned to Meredith in the front seat and stroked her arm.

"How are you doing, honey?"

Meredith pulled out of reach. "Fine."

"Do you want to talk about Mr. Hall? I'm struggling with it, too. You don't have to process it alone."

Meredith exhaled sharply. "Ha. So now you want to share?"

Things had been tense with her daughter, and she'd tried to give her space. But she didn't expect such disdain. "What is that supposed to mean?"

"I know you've been lying to me, Mom. You've been lying to Cliff and me our whole lives. Why should I tell you anything? Why should I trust you?" Her face was reddening, and a few tears escaped down her cheeks.

Lee reached out for her again and settled for the edge of her thigh. "Oh, Ith. I haven't been lying to you. I haven't told you some things because I want to keep you safe, and I want to spare you from my issues with my own family. I want you to have a clean slate."

Meredith sniffed. "But you're also keeping us from the good stuff. You act like this place is so terrible and dangerous, but it's not, Mom."

"Meredith, we just found a dead body in the woods—"

"You don't get it." Meredith got out and slammed the car door, cutting her off. Lee slunk after her in defeat.

Glossy vulture feathers hung over the entrance to the cabin, and they had to step over a line of salt and dirt spread across the threshold.

A new black leather book lay on the counter when they came inside. Lee recognized its simple lines and lustrous cover, though it had been a long time since she'd seen one. Belva came out of the back carrying another black leather book, but this one was bulging with inserted pages, and the leather was stained and warped. She had to hold it with both arms to support its bulk. She avoided Lee's eyes as she hefted the book onto the counter next to the new one. "How was school?"

Cliff shrugged from the table where he nibbled on leftover cornbread.

Meredith stared intensely at the two black books. "Everyone thinks you killed Mr. Hall."

"I know, darlin'. Most folks around here can't find their ass in the dark with both hands." Belva sucked her teeth. "I thought a reminder of your power might help." Belva picked up the new black book and laid her hand on the cover. "This is a very special time in the life of a Buck."

"Grandma Mama, we need to talk about this," Lee interjected.

Meredith thrust her forearm in front of her mother, as if to exclude her from the moment. "Don't listen to her. She doesn't speak for me. I'm ready."

Lee could feel her face heating. She couldn't let Meredith be pulled deeper into this place, to absorb its desolation and allow it to infect her as it had with Lee. She didn't know what connection Belva's work had with Mr. Hall's death, but she couldn't allow Meredith to be exposed to that danger. "I am the mother, and you are the child. Belva, this is not happening. I am not okay with this."

Belva looked crestfallen but unsurprised, and Lee wondered how far she would go. She might have strong beliefs, but there were certain lines that weren't crossed. The ability to make decisions about one's own family was sacred here.

Meredith looked from Belva to Lee, as if she could sense the situation resolving itself without her. "Mom, this is fucked up! I have a right to learn. You can't keep this from me!"

Belva's eyes softened, and her voice went sweet and soothing as she said, "Opaline, her blood came. She's ready whether you like it or not. It will find a way to get out. I'm just proposing that we teach her how to control it."

"I know from personal experience that isn't true. She should be focusing on school and getting into college."

"What if I don't want to go to college? What if I want to learn from Belva and do what she does? You're so narrow-minded, Mom!" Meredith screeched.

"You just like the novelty of this place. It's fun for you because you've never suffered. You don't know what it can be like."

Meredith narrowed her eyes at Lee. "You don't know how I feel about things, or what I've been through. You don't know anything about me."

Lee gritted her teeth against the sting. "Ith, how could you say that?" She reached for her, but Meredith stepped back. "I don't want to fight. I just want to keep you safe."

"I don't see what's so dangerous about it. You should be teaching me to be, like, a curious, open-minded person in touch with their culture, and instead you're acting like the people who live here are backwards and don't matter."

Lee exhaled. "I'm not going to change my mind. This is not a discussion."

Meredith gave her a withering look and then stormed from the room, slamming the bedroom door behind her.

Lee glowered at Belva, but she just turned her back and began pulling things out of the fridge for dinner. "How could you do that without asking me? You had no right."

"She can feel the power in the land. It's her time, and she's ready. Why shouldn't I show her how to use it?"

Lee didn't respond, still waiting for some kind of apology.

Instead, Belva turned around with real pain in her eyes. "I don't know why it bothers you so much. Your mama went through her own shit, and that's why she kept you from the work, and from me. But what is *your* problem with it? What did I ever do to you? Why'd you come back here if you think you're so much better than all this?"

*What did I ever do to you?*

Lee thought of that day when she was thirteen and Belva had driven her back after she'd snuck out to her cabin. As her truck disappeared out of sight, it dawned on Lee that no one was going to save them. She was all alone in that house, haunted by the drug-addicted ghost of her mother. She'd never felt so powerless or insignificant. She didn't want to *be* anymore. She just wanted it to be over.

She found some of her mother's pills carefully hidden in a jar of coffee grounds in the kitchen. There were maybe enough to do it—she was still skinny then. She hadn't figured out how to feed herself yet, and she mostly lived off toast and jelly. She considered her other options—a bottle of dollar-store glass cleaner, a kitchen knife, her father's old pistol. It all seemed too gruesome. It was the action itself that ultimately kept her from doing it. If she could have drifted off into nothingness, she would have done it.

The urge to undo her existence lingered long after she'd decided never to try, in little flashes when she felt particularly worthless or alone. It changed when she had Meredith. It terrified her to imagine leaving her alone in the world. But that wasn't the same as wanting to be alive.

None of this was Belva's fault. But part of Lee was angry that Belva hadn't stepped in and rescued her, Redbud's wishes be damned.

"Why didn't you let me stay here? Why didn't you take me in?"

She said it without context, but Belva's eyes were knowing as her face paled. "Oh, hon. I thought I was doing the right thing."

"You were so hell-bent on respecting Mama's wishes back then, even though you knew it was bad. And now, when I'm asking for you to respect mine, you ignore them?"

Belva looked as fragile as she had after they found the body, wobbling on her feet and dropping into the closest chair. Lee regretted having brought it up. "Shit, I'm sorry."

Belva's face went steely again. "Don't you dare apologize to me. I'm the one who's sorry. You're right—I shouldn't have left you there." She softened. "I was afraid of what would happen to your mama if she was all by her lonesome—but that was too much to put on you."

Lee understood. She remembered those final moments before she'd gotten on the bus for college, scared of what would happen to her mother when she was gone.

Belva continued. "I learned my lesson, which is why I'm pushing you on Meredith. You think you're keeping her safe, but you're just putting her in more danger. We don't know what's out there." She closed her eyes, composing herself. "I still don't understand why you came back if you don't want them to know where they come from."

The question remained: *Why did I come here?* It had been her only option. This place was a safe haven. But no matter how she rationalized it, the answer never seemed entirely true. If she was being honest with herself, it had felt outside of her conscious mind. The only way she could think to describe it was that she'd been *called.*

"I came back because I thought we'd be safe here. That's how I remembered it feeling when I was little. It's why I came to you when things got bad with Mama."

"I'm sure that's some of it. But there's more to it than that. The time has come, Opaline. I gotta pass on what I know. There's no one else. Ruby Jo is dead. Your mama is a lost cause. Dreama is a pod person. It's gotta be you, and when she's ready, Meredith."

"What are you talking about? I don't know anything about your work."

"I'm not saying you're ready for it. But it don't change the fact that it's gotta be you."

"But, Grandma Mama, I don't know if I even believe in this stuff."

Belva raised her eyebrows and closed her mouth. She didn't respond.

Lee rushed to add, "I mean, I respect that it makes you feel like you have power and control. Who doesn't want that? I'd love to feel like I have some control—everything seems to be falling apart around me."

Belva's mouth curved into an injured smile as she shook her head. "Don't you talk down to me. I know you been to school and seen a lot of things, but there's still a lot you don't know." Belva turned her back and quietly resumed chopping.

Lee went out to the porch to get some air and found Kimmie curled up on the swing, smoking a cigarette, like a barn cat stealing a bit of comfort.

"Sorry you had to hear that."

Kimmie laughed. "That's nothing. If it was my family, y'all'd still be rolling around on the floor."

Lee smiled at the absurdity of the image. "I've been looking for you all day."

"Well, here I am."

"They said you quit the dollar store."

"Yeah, the manager was pissing me off, so I picked up a shift at Walmart. I bounce back and forth depending on who's being a bigger dick that day."

Lee sat down next to her and pulled out a water bottle from beneath the swing, where she'd stashed the last drips of moonshine from the oil can. She took a small sip and let it coat the pain of the day in a rainbow syrup.

"You didn't tell me you worked with Redbud."

Kimmie sucked her teeth. "Sorry, girl. She don't come in much, and she barely talks at work. Didn't seem worth mentioning."

"How is she doing?"

Kimmie raised an eyebrow. "You ask her yourself. I got enough family shit. I'm not getting in the middle of yours."

"Okay, fine." Lee took another small sip. "The other night, at the party. I saw you drinking from a jar with a black flower on it. Where'd you get it from?"

Kimmie frowned. "Why you wanna know?"

Lee thought about mentioning Mr. Hall, but something told her to keep it close to the chest. "Just curious."

"I'd keep your curiosity to yourself if I were you."

"But that black flower is so distinctive. What does it mean?"

Kimmie reached out and grabbed Lee's wrist hard. "I'm serious. I wouldn't be asking questions about that. Ain't no good coming from it. Do you hear me?"

Lee nodded, and Kimmie released her. They sat in tense silence for a bit, and then Kimmie went inside.

*Who or what is she protecting?* Lee remembered Kimmie disappearing as soon as she'd heard the word "police." She didn't want to think she was capable of being involved in a murder, especially one that someone was trying to pin on Belva. But Lee had been gone for a long time. And there'd always been that wildness in Kimmie. You could never predict what form it would take.

Lee checked her phone. Otis hadn't texted since he'd dropped her off after the party. He would probably wait for her to make the next move after the way she'd behaved.

She tapped on his name, typed an apology, and asked when he was free to get together again. She wanted to see him, but she had another motive. He was her only other link to the black flower. She needed to find out what he knew.

# ELEVEN

## MEREDITH

This time, Meredith left through the window.

She flashed her phone light twice into the night-darkened trees, and a double flash answered somewhere off to the left. She dashed toward it, dodging sticks and dry leaves and praying that Belva didn't have a psychic tripwire for sneaking out.

A few feet into the woods, a hand grabbed her arm and another came over her mouth to muffle her scream. She could see Tiffany's smile gleaming in the half moonlight as she removed her hands.

"Follow me," she whispered.

Meredith nodded, and they set off through the trees. When they passed the clearing where she'd spotted Mr. Hall's body, a shiver went through her at the image of his pale, splayed form. It still haunted her that she'd slept so close to a dead body. Was she there, asleep, when he was killed? Did the killer see her? She scanned the edges of the clearing, imagining the killer lurking out there, watching them. Mom and Belva had told her not to go in the woods until they knew what happened to Mr. Hall, and she briefly regretted ignoring their warning.

"Are you sure we're safe out here?"

Tiffany looked at Meredith for a moment, as if reconsidering her invitation. "Um, yeah. What are you afraid of? Bigfoot?" She laughed. "I forget you're such a city girl."

Meredith tried to laugh it off, but the humiliation was sour. "Mr. Hall was killed in these woods. Doesn't that freak you out?"

"Why should it? Belva's got no beef with me." Tiffany looked back the way they came, as if searching for her in the trees. "I'm glad she put him down. He was a mega creep."

Meredith balked. "Belva didn't kill Mr. Hall."

"You sure about that?"

"I think I would know." Her delivery was firm, but she felt a seed of doubt take root.

Ten minutes into their walk, Tiffany stopped and pulled out two pillowcases from her backpack and handed one to Meredith. "Price of admission is one pillowcase of the black flowers that grow on the Buck property." Tiffany pointed to the thick, twisting vines sprouted with dark wildflowers that seemed to grow all over Belva's land. She plucked a bud from a vine and put it in the pillowcase, and Meredith did the same. It was difficult separating the flowers from their stalks, and more than once she came away with a slit in her fingertip. Both of their hands were bloodied by the time they were finished, and she watched as Tiffany wiped hers on a tree branch.

"Offering for the tree spirits."

Meredith couldn't tell what was real and what was play here, and perhaps that was why she liked it. She painted her own red streak across the bark.

Tiffany continued into the woods, and Meredith followed.

"When we get there, just follow my lead, okay? They're cool, but you gotta be careful. They can get kind of paranoid if they think you're gonna rat. So don't look like a rat."

Meredith tried to catch her eye to see if she was kidding, but Tiffany's face was serious in the moonlight. "Okay. Got it." A sense of danger was building around this night, and there was something wonderful about it. A night wind whipped against her cheeks, and she felt high with the possibilities. Tonight she would do magic.

When they finally arrived, they entered a clearing illuminated by a small fire and the front lights of what looked like a trailer-type house. People were scattered around the fire and in clusters in the shadows. On the far side, a group of men sat on couches in the grass. Trap played from a vintage car's glowing sound system off to the right, and as Tiffany led Meredith over to the couches, the bass pulsing in her like the land's energy below, she felt they were descending into the spirit world.

The men looked the girls over as they stood there clutching their pillowcases. They were maybe in their twenties, and they reminded her of the boys who played drums and slept in the grass on the Venice boardwalk. One of them was particularly beautiful; he had golden dreads; sleepy, hooded eyes; and this beautiful, angular nose over plump lips. He looked like a Greek demigod masquerading as a stoner. Meredith made eye contact with him, and he licked his bottom lip.

"We brought some flowers," Tiffany said to an older man in a gray plush recliner.

"That was mighty nice of you, girls." He motioned to one of the men on the couch, and he took the pillowcases from them. "Ain't you gonna introduce your friend?"

"This is Meredith." Tiffany nudged her forward.

The man reached out for her hand, and she let him take it. His palm was rough in hers.

"Nice to meet you, Meredith. I'm TJ." He ran his fingers over her smooth skin. "You Opaline's kid, ain't you?" He let go of her hand and made a show of studying her. "I can see it. You's a Buck woman. Ain't no denying it."

Meredith wondered what he saw, and if it had to do with the magic. "Yes. That's me."

"I'll try not to hold it against you." His expression was playful, but there was something else beneath it. They made eye contact, and fear slithered into her belly. "You angels run along now. Have fun."

Tiffany pulled Meredith away toward the fire, where they sat in front of it with their hips touching. The stoner god approached and offered them a mason jar filled with a clear liquid and stamped with a black flower. Tiffany said yes and thanked him, but when she extended her hand for it, he pulled it out of reach.

"Y'all wanna go on a night hike? We can drink moonshine under the moon." He smiled as if this was clever. Meredith felt Tiffany tense next to her, and she waited for her to respond. Her instinct was hell no, but what if this was how you learned about the magic? Maybe it had to happen in the woods, under the moon. Maybe this beautiful boy was a practitioner. She thought, *This is what real magic is, out in the real world.* It wasn't the spooky depictions of witchery you saw on television or read about in books. These were real people, with real power. She felt herself evolving right there, her notion of the world expanding to a more nuanced version of itself. She would go wherever she needed to go.

Meredith nodded, and he said, "All right, then." He helped her up to standing, but Tiffany remained on the ground, avoiding eye contact with the boy. "S'all right. She don't have to come. It can be just you and me."

As he led her away from the fire toward the trees, a sharp voice came from behind them.

"Get your hands off her."

Meredith turned to find a tall, sturdy woman with tangled black hair silhouetted imposingly against the fire.

The boy immediately dropped her hand and backed away. "No problem, ma'am. I'm gone." He walked quickly back to the security of the couches.

The woman approached Meredith slowly, her face coming into focus with each step. The hollows in her cheeks, her wrinkles, and finally her hazel eyes, ones that reminded Meredith of her own, came into relief. "Redbud."

"Meredith."

Redbud smoothed a hand over Meredith's hair and then lightly cupped her cheek. "Why were you following that boy? I know you're smarter than that."

"I thought he would teach me magic. Tiffany said I could learn here—that's the only reason I came."

"That boy has nothing to teach you, honey. I guarantee that." Redbud studied her and then crouched down and put her palm to the ground. "Do you feel it?"

Meredith thought she might cry. Finally, someone who would talk to her about it like a real person. "Yes. I feel it. It's like this surge of energy coming up through the land. It courses through me at night and I can't sleep."

An intense, unreadable expression passed over Redbud's face. "You feel it now?"

Meredith turned inward and assessed. "It's not very strong here. It's much stronger back at the cabin."

Redbud smiled crookedly, as if her hard, craggy face had forgotten how. "You remind me of myself when I started to feel it." She guided Meredith over to a pair of lawn chairs and motioned for her to sit. "Has Belva showed you anything? Have you been learning from her?"

*Oh god*, Meredith thought. *Please don't let this ruin my chance.* "No. She wanted to, but my mom wouldn't let her. She thinks it's dangerous."

Redbud smiled again. "Your mama was always so smart." Meredith thought she looked a little sad then, but she pulled herself back together. "That's good, though. I know it don't seem like it, but Belva *is* dangerous. You don't want to be learning from her."

Meredith was surprised to hear this, but it didn't seem impossible. She couldn't deny the fear that she sometimes felt around her. She'd never experienced people who could be both tender and threatening before she came to Craw Valley.

"You've been given a powerful gift, darlin'. It's important you learn how to use it right."

"Will you teach me? I'll be careful. I'll do whatever you say."

Redbud was solemn. "Yes, I'll teach you. But it's gotta be our secret." Her eyes pierced Meredith's. "All right?"

Meredith's breath shallowed. "I won't tell anyone. I promise."

Redbud nodded, and she pulled one of the stamped glass jars from underneath the chair. She handed it to Meredith and instructed her to take a small sip. "For anointing," she explained. "To keep you safe from the spirits while passing through their realm."

Meredith let a bit trickle into her mouth, careful not to take too much. It tasted like nail polish remover, scalding her throat with its cold fire. She choked, and Redbud handed her another jar. "Don't worry, this is water. Drink." Meredith chugged it.

When she was done, Redbud led her over to the fire, and they both sat down. Tiffany was still there. Someone had given her a jar, and she was drinking from it. When their eyes met, it felt like Tiffany was looking through her at something else.

"Do you have a black book? Like Belva?"

Redbud bristled. "No. I don't need a book. I got it all up here." She pointed to her head and smirked. "You and I don't need books or anybody else to do our work."

Redbud told her to lie down in the grass, and she obeyed. It was like the night she'd watched Belva's ritual; she could feel the energy surging up from the land. But it wasn't the same; it didn't feel like it was speaking to her. It just radiated without form. "It feels . . . different. Is it this land? Is there something wrong with it?"

"No, baby." Redbud lay down next to her. "It'll do that now that you're learning to use it." She took a deep breath. "Now, I want you to focus on that energy and imagine directing it into your hands. Pull it out of the earth and store the energy in your palms."

Meredith imagined it as a sort of fog made of light. She channeled it into two gaseous tentacles on either side of her and directed them to penetrate her hands. After a few seconds, she could feel warmth in her palms, and she brought them up in front of her face. They glowed gold against the night sky. She had a distant notion that she should be exclaiming and

freaking out, but she was adrift in some current, unable to form the expressions.

"Now sit up and find that boy from before." Redbud's voice flowed
along the current with her, like an oracle chanting in her brain.

Meredith obeyed and scanned around the fire. There he was, across
the flames.

Redbud's voice came from right behind her ear. "That boy thought he
could take advantage of you."

Meredith stared hard at the boy, and the rage was stoked, heating her
hands to a nearly painful temperature.

"But he has no idea how powerful you are. How much stronger you are
than him."

The rage burned higher. She flexed her fingers in and out at her sides.

"Make him regret ever thinking he could take you. Make him regret
the day he met you."

Meredith extended her hands toward him and imagined the energy
leaving her palms like snakes. They moved like twisting neon through the
darkness over the fire and wrapped around the boy's head. She saw sparks,
and her breath caught in her throat. *Oh god, what have I done? What if he
gets really hurt?*

But then she noticed he didn't seem to be reacting. "There's something
wrong. I don't think it's working."

Redbud took her by the shoulder. "Look—his head is starting to get
hot. He's sweating." They watched him scratch at his dreads as a sheen of
new sweat glistened along his forehead. "You're still learning, so it ain't
very strong. But you did that. You made that happen."

Meredith felt the remaining energy travel from her palms to her middle, and it pulsed there like static electricity waiting to strike. It was real.
It was actually fucking real. And she could do it. She could use magic.

The people in the lot started to move toward the fire and encircle them.
Redbud stood and reached for Meredith's hand to pull her up. "It's time
for bed, kid. You okay to get home?"

"But I want to stay. I won't tell anyone anything. I promise. Please let me stay," she pleaded.

Redbud shook her head. "This ain't for you, honey. Not yet. But keep coming to see me, and I'll teach you, okay? I'm here most nights."

Meredith didn't protest. She could sense it was futile, just like with Belva or her mother. They were more alike than any of them knew. She searched around the circle for Tiffany, but she was nowhere to be found. "My friend—I need to find her."

"Don't worry. I'll look out for her. Run along now."

Though they'd only just met, Meredith felt she could trust Redbud. There was something strong and direct about her; she didn't have to wade through subtext to find the truth. She didn't understand what Belva and Mom were so worried about—Redbud was amazing.

At this thought, Meredith felt the rage rise up anew. Her mother had kept her from this all of her life; it was only now that she'd taken things into her own hands that she was discovering the magic and the family that she'd been missing.

But she tried to push these thoughts away—she wanted to revel in this night. She wouldn't let her mother ruin this, too.

As Meredith walked home through the trees, she noticed how her filter on the world had changed. There were slightly different colors, different smells, an altered feeling. The darkness radiated gem-like hues, and she could smell each part of the forest down to the sweet, earthy beetle shells and musky tree nuts. She felt grounded with a good dirt—the best, most-fertile soil. Solid, clear, awake. Rooted to the earth. The opposite of her old, hazy self.

It wasn't like Cliff's visions.

No.

It was the sense that one era had ended and a new one had begun. And she would never be the same again.

# TWELVE

## LEE

As Lee crested the peak, the dense trees receded into rock and open sky. She could hear Otis close behind her, his breath steady and strong where hers was short and ragged.

They scrambled up a large limestone rock jutting out over the edge of the mountain, known by locals as Giant's Tooth, and sat down at the top. The air up there was thin and violent, and they huddled together and looked out over the scenery in awe. She wished she could dissolve into the moment and give herself over to the majesty of the view. But she couldn't let go of the feeling that somewhere in the miles of ancient trees surrounding them, Mr. Hall's killer was watching.

"I'm glad you could take off early on a Wednesday."

He smiled. "Me too. Teacher hours seem pretty great. Done by three p.m., the rest of the day yours."

She raised an eyebrow. "I have to be at work by seven, and it's basically hell, but I see your point."

Otis pulled two bottles of brown glass out of his backpack and uncapped them with a simple silver opener. He handed one to Lee.

"What's this?" she asked.

He smiled. "My beer. I put basil in this batch. Tastes a little like pizza, but it's not bad."

Lee took a sip. The herbal bite reminded her of soap, but there was a raw sweetness that made it almost enjoyable.

"And . . . honey?"

"I'm impressed. Belva helped me with the recipe. Gave me some of her honey."

Lee took another sip and let the bubbles linger on her tongue.

She wondered if Otis knew Belva's honey was a love potion of sorts. There were those who had fallen for one another under its influence, others who had rekindled stale marriages, and still others who had merely experienced the greatest sex of their lives. For a moment, Lee imagined dipping her finger in a pot of the honey, spreading it on Otis's lips, and licking it off.

She put her hand on his thigh and let it slide between his legs. He made eye contact with a trace of surprise in his gaze, then cupped her face and kissed her deeply. She pulled him on top of her as she leaned back onto the rock. The world around them receded, and it surprised her how quickly she wanted him inside of her, the need coursing through her without ceremony.

It wasn't that she'd lost her sexual desire. It had never left. But for years it had been relegated to a fantasy compartment of her brain, disconnected from Cooper or any other person.

In these moments with Otis, Lee felt the desire rising to the surface, this craving to be touched by something solid and outside of herself.

A strong gust ripped over them, cooling her feverish skin, and they broke apart. Lee looked around and saw a family of four approaching from below. The kids had already broken away and were climbing the steep walls of the boulder behind theirs. She pushed away from Otis and sat up, chuckling softly as she pointed at the kids. He smiled with flushed cheeks. She'd nearly forgotten why she asked to see him and was grateful for the cold, sobering air beating against her face.

"Do you have something stronger? Maybe some of that liquor from the party?" She hoped she sounded casual, or a bit fiendish at worst, but not someone with an ulterior motive.

"Naw, that's only for . . . certain occasions."

"Where'd you get it? I've never had anything like it."

"Oh, a friend gave it to me. It's one of his hobbies."

"Which friend? I'd love to buy some."

His expression changed. "I don't know. He can be pretty paranoid. It's illegal, and he could get arrested if it got out."

"I promise I won't tell anyone." She hoped she wasn't pushing too hard, but he was being more guarded than she'd anticipated.

He looked at her skeptically before relaxing again. "It's TJ. He makes it."

Lee remembered how people had treated him with reverence at the bonfire. "Oh, cool. Do I just text him, or how does it work?"

"He doesn't do phones. You have to look out for the signal at the turn-off to his place. If you see it, they're open for business. If not, don't go up there."

"That's intense."

"He just doesn't want to get caught. He could go to jail for a few jars of craft liquor."

"Okay, okay, I get it."

Lee dropped it then. She was pretty sure TJ wasn't some country hip-ster resurrecting outmoded artisanal practices, but whatever else the black flower entailed seemed outside of Otis's purview. She would go to TJ's under the guise of buying moonshine and gather more information. She could sense she was getting closer.

Lee took a sip of her beer. "I'm sorry again about the other morning. I wasn't trying to be cold. I was tired and hungover and . . . it's still strange being back."

Otis set his beer down and looked into her eyes. "Hey, it's fine. Don't worry about it. How are you holding up?"

"I'm fine." Lee wanted to tell him about Mr. Hall and the black flower and the strange connections that seemed to radiate out from it, but she couldn't without revealing her suspicions about his friend and exposing her family. There was something undeniable between them, but she couldn't trust him yet. "I'm worried about Meredith. She was there when we found his body, and she won't talk to me about it. Things have been strained between us since we got here. We used to be so close, and now she fights me on everything." She had never felt this much distance from her daughter, and it was unnerving. "I see my kids assimilating here and finding joy, and I'm mystified by it, because this isn't what I wanted for them. They don't see that they're taking a step backwards. But then I wonder if I'm just jealous that they're able to touch the world in a way I never have."

They had once been a trio that shared their own strange world, but her children were growing beyond the confines of that world and finding belonging here. Lee didn't know where she fit in this new life.

"Like I said, it's not so bad here."

She gave him a look, and he let it go.

"Things hit you harder when you're a kid. When my mom died, I didn't want to be around anyone. Everything they said made me want to scream." Otis reached out and put his hand on Lee's. "But you're there for her, which is what counts. She'll come to you when she's ready."

Lee leaned against his shoulder. "I remember when she passed away senior year. I thought, I wish my mom would die. Then at least she'd have some peace and I'd be really alone and not in this limbo state where she was there but not there. It was a terrible thought, and I felt evil for having it." She paused. "Not to make it about me. God, I'm sorry."

He wrapped his hand around hers and pulled her closer to him against the wind. "When my sister OD'd the first time, I kept imagining her waking up in the hospital with this new lease on life and wanting to get clean. Something about seeing the other side and realizing she didn't want to die anymore." He chuckled. "But when she woke up, she told me she wished they'd let her die. She started using again as soon as they let her out." He looked out over the valley with the mountains rising beyond it. "I'm sure your mama wished she was dead, too. That disease is torture. It's hard to watch the people you love in pain like that. You wanted a bit of mercy for her."

Lee never talked about Redbud with anyone. It was easier to hold it inside and avoid exposing its complexities to others' misunderstanding and judgment.

But Otis was different. He was open and thoughtful in a way she'd never encountered, and she trusted him with this one piece of her strangeness.

"It was more than that."

She told him how her mother's disability and other assistance had covered her pain pill prescription, paid the scant utilities, bought some food. But anything else Lee needed, like shampoo or college application fees, she had to figure out for herself. The prospect of plunging fries into oil or working the cash register as the dull hours ticked by seemed torturous, though she knew if she said this to anyone, they would accuse her of "smelling her own piss," as if ambition was a character flaw. They thought someone like her should be grateful for whatever she was offered.

It was Mr. Hall who introduced her to Beau, a man who lived in Cradleburg and built solid wood furniture that was popular on the craft fair circuit. He needed an assistant. In the months leading up to the deadline for her college applications, Lee saved every dollar Beau paid her and stored the cash in a wooden box she'd made herself. By Thanksgiving, she had completed all the forms and written the essays. She only needed to slip the cash inside and seal the envelopes. That evening, after Lee ate tater tots alone at the kitchen counter for Thanksgiving lunch, she went to her box for the cash, and it was gone. Not a single bill left.

Lee could still remember it vividly. An old black-and-white movie was playing on the TV in her mother's bedroom when she went to confront her. She was under the covers, and Lee could only see the black frizz of her hair poking out from the top. The room was even more sour than usual, and there was a sweet tang where there was normally an earthy body odor. She got closer and saw that vomit stained the edge of the sheet and was dripping down onto the floor. She pulled the covers back, and her mother's face was already turning violet. She put her finger up to her nose and felt nothing. She called Billy, who called a friend who was a paramedic. While she waited and stared at her mother's body, she did not try to save her life, even though she'd learned CPR in health class. Underneath the panic and fear, she felt a bit of relief. Maybe now things would finally change. Maybe now her mama would find some peace.

As Lee finished her story, her chest tightened and her stomach churned.

"It wasn't your job to save her," he said.

"I know."

"We can't save them."

Her voice wavered. "I know."

When she used to get upset, Cooper would pull her into him and crush her face against his chest, smothering the feeling out of her. At first she'd thought, *This is love. This is the force of love.* But, eventually, she realized that it was a denial of her feelings. A straitjacket. Later, he wouldn't touch her at all; her sadness, which had once been complex and exciting to him, was now a moral failing, exposing an inability to embrace life.

Otis brought his hands up and smoothed them over her hair, trailing his thumbs down her cheeks. It was just the right amount of pressure; she felt comforted but not smothered. She laid her hands on his chest, and he wrapped his arms securely around her. She swelled with the need to kiss him.

The noise of the family behind them broke the spell, and Otis stood and offered her a hand. They climbed down from the rock and followed the trail back the way they came in a comfortable, contemplative silence.

At the trailhead, his car was parked on the far side of the lot underneath a thicket of tall pines. It had rained that morning, and there was only one other car in the lot. They got into the car, and it was mossy inside from the moisture.

Before he could turn the ignition, she straddled him in the front seat. He buried his face in her chest as she held him against her by the back of his neck.

Otis was all quiet, storming intelligence, meeting her in each touch. It was deliberate, solid, tender. She felt seen and stripped to her desires, so there was no hiding. Just as it had twenty years ago, the passion inside of her was unleashed as a bewildering, carnal force. But this time he was ready to receive it, and she wasn't afraid to let it take her under.

The moment had its own momentum that she gave herself over to, sliding her shorts down with desperate hands as he unzipped his pants and brought her down on top of him. Relief filled her. As they moved, they created their own weather in the car, the windows becoming opaque with fog and shielding them from the rest of the world.

# THIRTEEN

That Friday night, the stadium lights were the brightest thing for miles, casting everything around them into thick, forceful shadow as Lee, Billy, and Cliff sat in the stands.

Lee had asked Meredith to join, but she'd refused. Since their fight a few days ago, she spent most of her time out of the house with friends, and when Lee tried to talk to her, she shut down completely. Lee had never exerted control over her daughter; they'd lived in such easy, honest coexistence that she didn't need to. It would have been an insult. And now that she had, something had changed between them. They were no longer living in the same reality. But safe boundaries meant she cared; she wished her mother had given a single damn when she was younger.

She'd made no progress on the mystery of the black flower. She'd driven by the address Otis gave her every afternoon and evening the last few days, but there was no sign of the Grim Reaper Halloween statue that signaled TJ was open for business. She wondered if Otis had deliberately thrown her off course, but she didn't want to think that could be true. She was afraid to go up there uninvited; her only option was to get Kimmie to take her to TJ somehow. She would figure out a way.

She nudged Billy's arm with her elbow. "I saw Mama a few days ago."

"Where?"

"At the dollar store." Lee paused. "She said you told her we were in town and that Belva wouldn't let her come around."

"She asked me if you were here, and I didn't lie to her. She got the notion into her head somehow."

"Has she really tried to see us?"

"Yeah, I asked Mama for her, and she said, 'Not on her life.'"

Lee didn't like that Belva had made a decision on her behalf and then kept it from her, but it was exactly what she would have done. "She did the right thing. I can't let the kids be around her."

Billy was uncommonly quiet and avoided eye contact.

"Do you not agree?"

"I hear what you're saying, but I don't like how Mama treats Red. She got all this compassion for other people, but not a drop for her own daughter."

Lee considered this. She admired Billy's empathy, but he hadn't lived with this version of Redbud. He couldn't understand that cutting her off was survival. Even if the guilt sometimes reared its ugly head, she knew this was true.

The intercom cracked above them, and Lee traced it to the high school principal, who stood on a flimsy platform in front of the bleachers.

"Ladies and gentlemen, thank you for coming out tonight to cheer on our Craw Valley Buzzards!"

As people half-heartedly cheered, Lee leaned over and asked Billy, "The 'Buzzards'? Didn't it used to be the 'Indians' or something disrespectful like that?"

"A few years ago, they got pressure from the reservation to change it. They let the students decide, and I guess they thought it'd be a good joke if we were the 'Buzzards.'"

"The carcass eaters. I don't hate it."

"I like it, too," Cliff added. "Vultures are beautiful."

Billy smiled. "I hear you. Those red heads and pretty black feathers? Cleaning up what no one else wants? Buzzards are done dirty."

The principal took on a somber tone in the background, and Lee tuned back in.

"Many of you have heard by now of Mr. Hall's tragic passing. He was one of the greatest teachers Craw Valley has ever had, and he'll be greatly missed. We dedicate tonight's game to him. As he liked to say, 'These might be boys, but when they step onto this field, they become gladiators.'

I know he's looking down on us from Heaven right now. Make him proud, Buzzards!"

The crowd cheered, and Lee wondered if any of them knew the truth about Mr. Hall. They must, and yet here they were, clapping for him like a fallen hero. An old couple next to them gawked at Lee and her family, and she knew what they were thinking. *Murderers.*

Lee decided this was the perfect time to visit the snack bar. As she made her way down the metal stairs with Cliff beside her, she could feel hundreds of eyes following them. A kid in a black-feathered vulture costume pretended to fly along the sidelines, cawing in an ominous key.

Standing before the concrete cube, she introduced Cliff to all the familiar foods: the nacho cheese that was only a thick, salty suggestion of cheese; the watery slush puppies; the hot dogs. He had a particular passion for processed foods that amused her; he'd eaten healthy, expensive food since birth, and all he wanted was the junk she'd grown up eating. His eyes widened at the Little Debbies with their smooth plastic frosting, and she let him pick one.

As they walked away, eager to enjoy their treats, they crossed paths with Dreama. She wore an oversized CVHS jersey with her son's number over slim jeans and large diamond hoops in her ears. As the jewels glinted in the stadium lights, Lee couldn't help but be mesmerized by them.

"Hey, family. How are y'all holding up?"

"We're fine."

"I was so sorry to hear about Mr. Hall." She lowered her voice and put a hand up to the side of her mouth. "It must have been terrible for the children to see. Talk about *trauma.*"

"It was scary for all of us."

Dreama leaned in close to Lee, and an expensive ginger-and-tobacco scent wafted from beneath her clothes. "If y'all don't feel safe up there, you're always welcome at our house. Our basement has two guest bedrooms and its own kitchen."

"Oh, thanks. That's very kind. But I can't leave Belva and Luann up there by themselves."

Dreama raised an eyebrow. "Belva's the one you gotta get away from. She is *dangerous*. I've suspected it for a while, and this just proves it."

Lee looked down at Cliff, who was scowling at Dreama. She told him to return to the seats without her, and she turned back to Dreama. "There is no way she killed Mr. Hall. You know her. She's *your grandmother*."

"I *do* know her. The real her. That's how I know she's behind this. I should have warned you earlier, but I thought you would have seen it."

"All I've seen is a woman who actually cares about people. She might be a bit eccentric, but her intentions are always in the right place."

Dreama gave her a pitying smile. "I know it's hard to believe. She was magical when we were kids. But it's the truth." She patted Lee's arm. "If you change your mind, my offer stands."

Dreama walked past Lee and into the bleachers, where she took a seat in the front row next to her husband. He was from the Northeast somewhere, and he and Dreama had met at a real estate conference in DC. There was something untouchable about him. He seemed to glide through the community without actually engaging with it, like a prince visiting the commoners in his kingdom. They made eye contact briefly, and he broke into a wide, toothy smile. The vacancy behind his eyes gave her the chills.

Lee spotted Cliff standing at the chain-link fence and walked over to him. He was staring across the field at the trees that bordered it on one side. She searched for something of note, but all she saw was a dark wall in the shadow of the lights.

"What are you looking at?"

"It's here," he said softly.

"What's here?"

"The thing I saw in the woods. It's watching us over there."

"Where?" Lee searched again, but she still couldn't see anything.

"I can't see it, but I can feel it."

Lee exhaled. She had been down this road before. She and Cooper were forced to switch Cliff's room with the playroom because he was convinced it was haunted.

She told him it would be okay and tried to lead him back toward the seats, but he resisted.

"We need to leave. Now."

She rubbed his back and reminded him to breathe, but he recoiled from her touch. "Mom. Stop. We have to go. Please just listen to me." The last few words came out as a yell, and heads turned from the game to them. Lee met eyes with Billy, and he quickly left the stands and joined them. She told him Cliff wanted to leave, and he said that's probably what they should do.

. . .

That night, after Lee put a calmed Cliff to sleep and Kimmie came over for a nightcap, they lay on their backs in the garden, looking up at the stars and passing a bottle of cheap whiskey back and forth. Once Kimmie was soft and giddy, she wouldn't say no to an adventure.

As Lee waited for the alcohol to trickle through their systems, she could feel it taking her to a grim place, and she longed for the elation of the moonshine. Lee had appreciated alcohol for many reasons over the years, but it had never provided such a direct path to transcendence as the moonshine. It created magic where there was none.

Kimmie passed her the bottle, and she took another tiny sip. She needed to be cogent to pull this off.

"You know what would be good right now?" Lee asked.

"A chicken pot pie and a hard dick?"

"Jesus. No. Well, maybe the pie. And maybe the dick." Lee and Kimmie giggled. "But that's not what I'm talking about."

"What, then?"

Lee took a deep breath. "I want some of that moonshine."

Kimmie sighed. "I want some, too . . . Today was too damn boring for my taste. I need to get a little weird."

"God, me too."

Kimmie shifted on her side to face Lee and bared her teeth in a sly smile. "I know where we can get it."

"Where?"

"My brother's place."

Lee sobered. Here was her chance. She couldn't sound too eager. "Let's go, then."

Kimmie's brow furrowed as she played it out in her mind. "I should go and bring it back. You can wait here."

"What? No. I want to come."

"It's not a good idea."

"It will be fun . . ."

Kimmie was quiet for a bit, and then in a whispered threat, "If you come, you gotta do everything I say. I mean it, girl. I tell you to shit, and you squat."

"Yes, ma'am. I promise." Lee pulled herself to standing, and the land swiveled slightly on its axis. "Can you drive?" She looked over, and Kimmie seemed to be steadying herself as well.

"Naw. We don't need wheels, though. I know a trail."

Lee followed Kimmie to the ritual clearing where three trails jutted from it in different directions. Belva had told Lee as a kid that the clearing lay at the crossroads of two paths, and she must never take the path headed west. She'd imagined vague horrors at its end, and it scared her enough to never attempt it. Now, Kimmie stepped onto the westward trail, and Lee followed. As they ventured farther, the path faded underfoot, but Kimmie was confident as she strode on. If anything was a creature of this place, it was her.

They walked for a while with the only sound their footsteps crunching through leaves. Lee listened for anything sinister beneath it as the image of a creature darting out of the woods ran once again through her mind.

Then Kimmie picked up speed in front of her, and Lee matched it as if pulled along in her jet stream. They both ran through the trees with the liquor burning like gasoline in their chests. She could keep moving all night if she needed to.

After a while, Lee noticed the dark around them was slowly leaching into gray. The trees parted, and they entered a clearing with a pale blue mobile home with new additions jutting out from both sides. Parked in front was what looked like a souped-up black Ford Coupe with a low bottom.

People milled about the lot, but she had a hard time seeing their faces under their hoodies and through the shadow cast by a small fire burning in the center. This gathering had a much different feel than the party she'd attended with Otis. She saw one group huddled in the shadow of a shed, and when Lee met the eyes of one of the men, she could see dirt clouding his gaze. He reminded her of her mother's old friends who used to linger in their living room for days on end.

On the far side of the clearing, TJ and a couple men sprawled on living room furniture in the grass. One of them called to Kimmie, and she dragged Lee over with her.

TJ sat in a gray La-Z-Boy like a redneck lord. "O-pa-line Ford." He gestured to an old polyester sofa in a brown floral print, and she sat down next to a kid in his late teens or early twenties. He had blond dreads and smelled like stale bong water, and his eyelids were slitted against the firelight.

"Nice place you have here," Lee said.

"Ma left it to me when she passed, and I kept a lot of her things. Some of this shit is built to last, you know? A lot of this new stuff is cheap shit." The arm of the recliner gave slightly as TJ brought his fist down, and he looked satisfied by the demonstration. Lee noticed the expensive watch glinting from his wrist. "Kimmie said y'all been hanging out again." He paused and took a drink of a Monster energy in the chair's cup holder. He hadn't looked at Kimmie since they'd walked over, and he continued to talk as if she wasn't there. "I love her cause she's my sister, but that bitch is crazy."

Kimmie grunted but didn't speak. Lee had never seen her this quiet. She wanted to defend her, but Kimmie gave her a look. She'd promised to follow her lead.

There was a silence then. Not necessarily awkward, but more of a standoff to see who would speak first.

"So what can I do for you?" he asked.

Kimmie cut in. "We're here to party."

TJ still refused to look at her, but he nodded in acknowledgment. "Well, all right then. Let's get fucked up." He motioned to a man standing near the trailer, who went inside and came out holding two small flower-stamped canning jars filled with a clear liquid. A fresh black flower lay in the bottom of one with a sinister nonchalance that mesmerized Lee.

As Kimmie reached for the jars, Lee and TJ met eyes, and she saw something ancient and animal staring back at her. A deep cunning, and an indifference that ran cold through her veins.

Before Lee could explore further, Kimmie took her hand and led her forcefully over to the fire. They sat down on the grass, and Kimmie took the first sip of the jar with the black flower in the bottom. She didn't break eye contact with Lee as she let the liquid flow into her mouth for a long, luxurious moment. Then she passed it to her.

Lee pretended to sip, but she only let a little go down her throat. It no longer burned like it did the first time. Now it tasted almost smooth, like drinking from a hot spring.

She covertly studied the people around her, looking for some indication of why they were there. Was it just a place to buy drugs and get fucked up, or was there something else happening beneath the surface? Where had Mr. Hall fit in a place like this? She couldn't imagine him sitting here in his blazer, making pretentious quips.

The jar quickly drained between them, with Kimmie drinking most of it, until only the soaked flower lay at the bottom. Kimmie reached in with her fingers and brought it to Lee's face with mischief glistering in her eyes. She tickled the tip of her nose and trailed it down. Without thinking, Lee closed her eyes and parted her lips. She felt it fill her mouth like a soft spider. The petals were jellied and lush as she bit softly and chewed.

The taste was an overwhelming version of the liquor itself. A phantasm of undiluted shifting flavors: honey, leaves, bubblegum, ash, blood. When she finally swallowed, she lay back on the ground with the force of it.

Her skin tingled like something was coming up through her pores. Thin roots sprouted from every inch of skin that touched the grass: the back of her head, her shoulder blades, her thighs. They probed into the dirt and snaked their way down, farther into the earth, branching and spreading below her. She could feel the roots glowing. An electricity crackled through her, and she knew it was the power of the land. They were connected.

She sensed the groundwater flowing below as it fed the wells of the houses tucked into the mountains. When she focused on the water itself, she could access the memories it held, of every living thing that ever made a home on this land. A dinosaur lapping from a creek with its long tongue. A prehistoric woman peering down into its reflective surface and seeing herself staring back.

She could sense the coal, the natural gas, the zinc, the marble, nestled like treasure deep within the clay and stone.

She could feel the trees and their individual natures. They were not all calm and stoic. One tree longed to bend toward the tree next to it and merge limbs for eternity. She could feel its bark straining, moving so gradually the average human couldn't detect it. But through the roots, its yearning and stretching filled her with a delicious sadness that brought tears to her eyes.

She could feel her roots entwining with those of Belva's garden plants and beyond, swaying and asleep in the night breeze, dreaming of the sun. She could sense the fungi huddled in their dark corners, radiating mystery.

And then there was a rustling and a scrape in her perception. A chorus of them. The birds and the squirrels and the possums and the raccoons and the foxes and the deer and the bears and all the little hands and hooves and claws scraping against the earth. The sheer number of them and all the life they contained nearly overwhelmed her. She tried to direct her focus toward something more manageable.

She turned her head to watch a doe and three fawns emerge from the trees to her right and move toward the clearing. Their glossy fur was cream and almond in the bonfire light, and they had the most mesmerizing eyes. She had the feeling she could speak to them if she liked, and they would understand her.

As they came closer, hair sprouted from their heads, their faces flattened, and their backs arched up and straight, transforming them into people.

But not just any people.

There was Redbud's black hair, and Tiffany Wang's sneer, and the curves of the girl Lee had seen with Mr. Hall at the bonfire. And behind them in her oversized sweatshirt was Meredith.

Lee tried to discern if this was hallucination or reality, but there was no dividing line between the liquor and her own faculties. The entire world was a smear of sickening rainbow.

She became aware of a tiny rumble. She heard the scrape of wings against insect bodies, the burrowing of beetles, the slide of a centipede through the leaves. The ground roiled around her, and she felt the tiny creatures slowly moving up her sides to cover her body. She tried to stand up and shake them off, but the roots held her to the ground. She was lashed to the earth like a sacrifice. As she struggled to get free, panic rising inside of her, she felt the roots pulling her deeper until she was submerged in the soil and its churning insects. It was taking her, finally. The land was pulling her under.

Her mother's voice whistled through the darkness.

"Opaline. Listen, goddammit. Follow my voice. Follow my voice, baby."

Lee reached toward the voice, and then something was pulling her up to the surface and bringing her back into the light. Relief washed through her. She relaxed, allowing the roots to release their grip and slink up and back into her skin. She felt she could move again, and sat up. Meredith and Redbud were crouched over her with Kimmie looking guilty next to them. Tiffany and the girl stood farther away, watching her.

"Mom, are you okay?" Meredith asked.

Lee tried to shrug it off. "Yes. I'm fine." She ignored her mother's presence and attempted to arrange her face into something she hoped resembled stern. "What are you doing here?"

There was no shame or apology in Meredith's face when she spoke. She was radiant with discovery. "Mamaw led us on a midnight hike to search for spirits. I saw the ghost of a crow."

Redbud smirked at Lee.

*Mamaw?* "What is happening? Am I in a dream?"

"No, honey, you're just drunk off your ass."

Shame filled Lee, and she thought she might vomit. She turned away from them and hunched over in the grass, attempting to right herself. Meredith tried to touch her, but Lee held up a hand. It felt like her eyes were being squeezed into ovals.

Lee pulled Kimmie down and whispered, "What the fuck did you give me?"

"Shit, I'm sorry. I thought you'd have a good time, like maybe you needed it. It always makes me feel more connected."

Lee could still feel the land pulsing beneath her, reminding her of a time when she felt connected to the life held within it. You were never alone with this link. You could still feel lonely, but there was always something to reach out and touch, and it would touch you back.

The land had been silent since her return, but now she could feel its touch . . .

Lee searched for the urgent thought she'd had just a minute ago. It was right there . . .

"Who is that girl? The one with Meredith and Tiffany."

Kimmie looked over at the group. "Oh, that's my niece Missy. Her mama lit out of town a few years ago and left her with us."

"Why don't I recognize her from school?"

"She don't go much. I try to make her, but TJ lets her do whatever she wants."

It took a beat, but the realization had weight and color once it strained through her altered consciousness. *TJ must have seen Mr. Hall with Missy that night.* The world dipped. *He killed him. He's the murderer.*

Lee watched through blurred lenses as the milling bodies organized themselves into a circle around the fire and passed a jar of the liquor around. They gulped hungrily from the jar, and afterwards, the desperation faded from their faces.

Redbud took a place at what seemed like the head of it. She stood with her eyes closed and palms facing out by her sides. She was all dull, unreflecting surfaces in the firelight, and her hair clung lifelessly to her skull. When she opened her eyes, they were thickly dusted, like pollen on an old truck hood.

Meredith took a spot next to Redbud and mimicked her motions. In their doubled images, Lee could see the resemblance between them. There was the dark hair and their tall, sturdy bodies, but it was more than that. Meredith had her chaos, her defiance. Redbud was her mangled twin.

Lee pulled herself up to a wobbling stand. "Get the fuck away from her." She walked up to them and wrenched Meredith away. "Are you okay? Did she make you drink the moonshine?"

"What the fuck, Mom. I'm fine." Meredith fought Lee's grip, but she just gripped harder, feeling the bones of Meredith's arm under her fingers.

"We are leaving."

Redbud glowered at Lee. "You got no right to keep her from me. She's my flesh and blood."

"I have every right. She's my daughter. *You* are a stranger. I'm protecting her like a mother should. You wouldn't know about that."

Hurt wrinkled Redbud's face, but it was quickly replaced by rage. "You're putting her in danger and you don't even know it. *I'm* the one protecting her."

Lee knew this look in her mother's eyes. The paranoia hovering like mist above a chasm. The only way to save yourself was to turn back. Otherwise you'd fall toward the center of a deep, hopeless nothing with her.

Lee turned to leave the way they came and stumbled a bit, still unsteady on her feet from the flower's effects. The husked voice came from behind her.

"Look at you. You ain't no better mother than I am. You act like you so much better than me, but you ain't *no different.*"

Lee felt the acid in her throat, and the sickness spread through her. The world dipped again.

Lee went to leave with a new urgency, but this time TJ and a few of his men blocked their path. She noticed he was wearing a dark purple blazer. Had he been wearing that before, or was Lee still hallucinating? She cursed herself for putting them in this position. She needed to be clearheaded to get them out of this.

"Where you going, Opaline?"

"I need to get Meredith home." She moved to go around him, and he stepped with her.

"Stay a little longer. The fun is just getting started."

New panic was breaking through the moonshine haze. She imagined running at him and using her speed and weight to throw him off so Meredith could get away. She saw Kimmie off to the side and gestured toward her. "Help me."

Kimmie hesitated, and Lee saw that she was on her own. Her mind cleared. She had to get Meredith out of here. Her body steeled itself as she turned to TJ.

"You know, it's only a matter of time before they figure it out."

"Figure what out?"

"Who killed Joseph Hall."

His smirk dropped, and he crossed the grass so that their faces were very close to one another. When he spoke, it felt like he was breathing into her mouth. "I remember how smart you were. Big fucking genius who don't give two fucks about anyone. This"—he gestured between them with his dirty nails—"is not very smart."

Lee stood her ground, not moving a muscle. TJ eventually relaxed, and a dangerous smile curled his mouth. "You just like your grandma. Always putting her nose where it don't belong."

When she moved to leave once more, he didn't get in her way. Meredith no longer struggled as Lee walked toward the trees with her arm still in her grip. She forced herself to keep looking ahead.

When they were finally enshrouded in darkness and Lee could look back, there was no one. They were alone. She started to shiver, and her body slackened. She went to her knees and tried to catch her breath. Meredith pulled her up and let her lean her weight on her as they made their way back to the cabin. Lee worried they'd get lost without Kimmie to guide them down the unfamiliar trail, but as they went along, she realized that Meredith knew the way. This was not the first time she spent time with those people.

When Lee glimpsed Meredith's face in a slash of moonlight, she saw her again. It was Redbud staring back.

# FOURTEEN

I know who killed Mr. Hall."

Lee and Belva sat hunched in old metal chairs against the shed, out of earshot of the house. She had woken her up as soon as they returned.

Lee told her about going to the Ryder property, discovering who Missy was, and finding Meredith there with Redbud.

"Why the hell would you go up there?" Belva asked.

Lee told her what she'd been up to, and Belva paused for a long time, ruminating. She pulled out a pipe from her jacket pocket and began to puff thoughtfully. The smoke curled around Lee and cleared her head.

"I had a feeling you'd gotten hooked on that stuff," Belva said.

"I'm not *hooked*. I just like the taste and the feel of it. I haven't even drank that much."

"I can tell you're half gone right now. You can barely focus on me."

Lee's vision was still a bit blurred, but she thought she was holding it together. She knew it was time to confront the drinking. How could she not after tonight? But she would deal with it herself, when things calmed down. "That's not the issue here. Why would TJ dump the body in your woods?"

Belva's complexion grayed, and Lee caught another glimpse of her fragility. "I bet he wanted me to get blamed for it. All the old shit's coming back to bite me in the ass."

"What do you mean?"

Belva began to tell Lee the real story of her first love.

*Leroy Ryder.*

In those first years after her love charm worked its magic, their love was easy, and he respected her work. But after he was laid off at the plant, he began to resent it and the ecstasy it provided. She'd tried to include him in the gatherings before, but he failed to feel the power of the land. Just as she healed everyone else around her, she wanted to find a cure for his melancholy.

She knew of a flower that grew in the clearing where she performed her rituals. It was the darkest green, so dark that it appeared black to most. She'd never seen it anywhere else, nor could she ever identify it using her numerous botany books. Her grandmother believed it grew out of the ashes of their words and intentions, that their work seeded and fertilized the blooms. If anything could offer transcendence in digestible form, it would be this.

Belva began to experiment—dried and powdered, steeped and brewed. Eventually, she distilled it into a liquor. The first time he drank it, they spent all night dancing and talking around the fire. He could experience the power of the land without actually wielding it, like a simulation that allowed him a little window into her sacred realm. They were able to connect on a level she hadn't thought possible.

But then he asked for more, and more. She told him it was only meant for certain occasions and in small quantities, but she found him stealing from her stash early in the morning when he thought she was asleep. He became defensive, then resentful. He started working for his family, running moonshine deliveries through the mountains. Prohibition had been over for decades, but people still liked the cheap, powerful burn and getting one over on the law. When the batch she'd made ran out and she refused to make more, he stole a pillowcase of the flowers and brought it to his family's property to make their own.

The drinking became constant, and he started to beat Belva and terrorize Redbud, Ruby Jo, and Billy, swooning between euphoria, depression, and paranoia. When she tried to help him, he'd fight her like she was a demon. She wrote recipes and brewed concoctions, but their effects were no match for his sickness. She felt responsible, so she hung on for a while, but eventually it got too dangerous for the kids. That was when she marched over to the courthouse and filed for divorce. She didn't ask for anything, and he didn't put up much of a fight. He was rarely coherent enough for sustained objections.

A few days after it was finalized, Leroy was found face down in a creek. His car with the false bottom was overturned next to him, with broken bottles scattered around it. It's said that the families who lived downriver from the crash and relied on the fish hallucinated for days afterwards.

The Ryders naturally blamed Belva, the ex-wife who happened to be a bona fide witch, despite her pointing out that alcoholism and driving were often a lethal mix. But they were too afraid to actually retaliate. If she was capable of murder, what else could she do to them? What grew out of it was a cold rivalry. Over the years, she'd looked the other way on their drug business, and in return they'd let her go about her work without intervention.

Lee took Belva's hand. "I'm sorry I went up there. I didn't mean to cross a line. But if you've been living in peace, why'd they dump the body here?"

Belva inhaled deeply on the pipe and exhaled the fragrant smoke. "About eight months ago, Kimmie told me she was pregnant. She'd hid it from her family, but she was really starting to show. She wanted to give birth but didn't want to keep it. She wanted it to have a nice life, away from her brother. It was a boy."

Lee thought about the way Kimmie acted with total abandon, hurling her body into any situation as if it didn't need protection. She had seen it as wildness, but now she saw it also as someone coping with loss.

"She wanted to stay with me until he was born, and for me to find a home that would take good care of him. I said yes, and she hid out with me, and I made sure she ate well and didn't use or drink, and she made them think she ran off for a bit. I found a good family I'd treated out in Scarwell. I delivered Kimmie's baby right here in the garden, and we handed him over." Belva gazed at a spot a few feet away, where the grass was particularly thick.

"Kimmie returned home as if nothing happened, but I wondered if TJ'd somehow find out. We can be damn sure he has."

Everything pointed to TJ, but Lee still didn't have all the answers she needed to situate it in her mind.

"Do you think Kimmie was involved? Do you think she knew it was TJ?"

Belva sighed. "I'm sure she didn't have a hand in it. I know she seems rough, but she's gentle at her core. She mighta known after. If she kept quiet, it was only because she was scared to talk. We can trust her."

Lee nodded. "Then what I can't understand is why Mr. Hall had the black flower branded on his thigh."

"Maybe they were marking their kill. Who knows what them animals get up to."

"And why didn't you tell me this story when I mentioned the flower after they found his body?"

"I was ashamed. Didn't want you to think less of me." She took a deep breath. "Leroy ain't the only one who's gotten hooked on the moonshine over the years. Your aunt Ruby Jo got into it when a local preacher started using it to give his followers visions of God. Ruby didn't have the touch for the work, and I think she always felt left out. So she went looking for another way to feel something higher than herself." She paused. "I really didn't think it had anything to do with Mr. Hall's death. I'm sorry for keeping it from you."

"That's okay. But I still think there's something else there, with the black flower. It looked like Mama was performing a spell last night. You said there was magic tied up in it."

"I know it's hard to believe, but I ain't always right, honey. I don't know what you saw, but I guarantee you Redbud ain't casting. She was just there to buy drugs."

"How do you know? We should ask Meredith again. Maybe you can get her to talk." Lee had already asked her about Redbud and TJ and what she had witnessed, and she'd refused to tell her anything.

"*I* know. And I warned you about Meredith. You kept her from it, and she found another way."

Lee knew there was truth in this. "Fine. What are we going to do about TJ?"

"We take care of him."

"How?"

"Opaline, I swear to God. When are you gonna start believing in the power of this land?"

Lee didn't respond. She *wanted* to believe in it, and to feel its real power coursing through her. Not just some moonshine acid trip.

"*We* are gonna bind him from doing any more harm," Belva continued.

"Are you sure that will work?"

Belva huffed. "If you and Meredith join, I think it will."

"Not Meredith. I'll do it, but not her."

"You're making a mistake. Who knows what Red's been teaching her. At least let me show her the right way."

"I'm not ready to make that call."

"Opaline. You're denying her the power of her birthright. The same thing happened with you, and look what happened."

"Drop it. Please."

Belva sighed. "You're as stubborn as your mother. Well, all right. But do me a favor—don't drink tonight. We need everyone sober."

"Okay. No problem."

*What the hell am I doing?*

. . .

That evening, the air was unnaturally warm. The dark flowers surrounded Lee as she walked to the clearing, their petals thick and veined. When the moonlight caught them at the right angle, they shimmered with sentience.

Lee took a sip from a bottle of iced tea spiked with just enough moonshine to keep her level. Belva didn't have to know.

When Lee was very small and would often stay over at Belva's, she would watch from the window as twenty or thirty people filed into the woods for a gathering. Now there were only a handful who came. Lee recognized some of Belva's group from the church—Linda from the high school and Beverly, the owner of a local restaurant. They sat in camping chairs gossiping quietly as if it was any community function, though Lee could sense hesitation in their postures and expressions. The group was even smaller than the last ritual; the Mr. Hall rumors must have scared the rest off.

Lee was surprised to see Kimmie standing quietly next to Billy. She took a spot next to her and whispered, "What are you doing here?"

"TJ didn't kill Joe."

Lee tried to protest, but Kimmie stopped her. "I swear he didn't. He's done a lot of bad shit, but not this."

"Then why are you here?"

"If Belva's gonna bind him from doing more harm, I want to help." She sighed. "I know it's hard to believe, but there's some good under there. Maybe this'll give him a chance to turn things around."

Lee tried to respond, but Belva clapped her hands, and they went silent. "Let's get started."

The others pushed back their chairs and stood up. They brought their arms to their sides with palms faced out and closed their eyes. Lee repeated the motion, but she kept her eyes half open so she could watch.

Luann was the first to speak. "We offer thanks to the land for lending its power to us tonight. We acknowledge that before our Scotch-Irish ancestors stole this land, our Cherokee ancestors lived on it, honored it, and drew from its power." She spoke with a deep, reverent rhythm, like a pastor delivering a sermon.

She and Belva brought out a Walmart bag and pulled a bag of Cheetos and a container of neon frosted cookies from it. They dumped them into a small hole and filled it with dirt and patted it firm. Two black cans of Monster energy drink were popped and poured over it, and they listened to it sizzle in the soil. Luann offered these treats to the spirits of the land for allowing them to practice the work on their turf.

Then Belva spoke. "We gather to draw from this sacred land. These mountains that existed before the dinosaurs. These valleys that stood calm and silent for millennia. We draw from it so that we may ease suffering. Nothing more or less." Her voice took on an edge. "TJ Ryder is selling poison to our people. He is committing murder. He is terrorizing this community."

She paused, allowing the words to sink in. Lee saw Kimmie scowling next to her.

"We can't let this happen any longer. Tonight, we call upon the land to aid us in binding him from doing harm. May he never take the life of another as long as the power exists in these hills."

In the center next to the fire, a large straight branch was staked into the ground with another small hole in the dirt beneath it. Luann moved toward it with her tool belt slung low around her waist.

"Kimmie, bring forth TJ's artifact."

Kimmie pulled a small comb from her pocket and brought it to Luann in the center. She pried the hairs from the tines, put them in the hole, and filled it in with dirt.

Luann handed Kimmie a small knife, and she dug its sharp point into the wood. She carved vigorously, her biceps bulging in the firelight. When she stepped away, a crude "TJ" emblazoned the branch.

"Now, bring forth your offerings," Luann instructed.

Belva leaned over to Lee and whispered, "Each of us brought something belonging to a loved one who was hurt by TJ. Billy brought something for you, too. We'll use these to bind him."

Beverly pulled a wad of cloth from her purse and handed it to Luann before returning to her spot. Luann allowed it to unfurl into what looked like strips of a man's white T-shirt tied end to end and nailed one end to the top of the branch so that it hung down like a ribbon on a maypole. One after the other, they stepped forward with their offerings. An old ace bandage. A fishing line. Strips of a baby blanket.

When it was Billy's turn, he pulled out two purple vintage chiffon scarves tied together, and then two more in yellow that he handed to Lee. They were her mother's favorite accessories; she used to tie one around her neck like a choker. Lee put her nose to it and inhaled a dusty trace of her mother's gardenia perfume.

After Billy gave his to Luann, Lee stepped up and handed her scarf chain over. She felt awkward knowing everyone was watching her. She saw that in a true ritual, every movement had significance, so that the power of it built with each gesture.

Hers was the last, and as the nail was driven in, Belva began to hum, and the others joined in. Lee hummed softly at first, afraid of creating the wrong frequency, but soon, as the sound built and melded, the humming became like a cocoon that enveloped Lee, and she couldn't distinguish her voice from the rest.

Belva spoke again with a voice more savage. "My daughter used to be a marvel."

Everyone grabbed the loose end of their offering and held it taut in front of them. Then they began to move in a circle, weaving in and out of one another slowly. Lee focused on following Billy.

"She was the greatest thing I ever created. I couldn't wait to see what she would become. But then she got hooked on the poison. All that greatness became dust. She's nothing now!" The last line was an angry wail in Belva's throat.

The weaving quickened, and Lee strained to keep up.

"A man lay dead in this very clearing, slain by the hands of this man. How many more have died?"

Beverly wailed about her son-in-law who would never hold his baby girl.

Linda howled about her nephew who would never graduate from high school and take his football scholarship. The sound and pain of their voices echoed up and out of the clearing.

The weaving picked up even more speed, and the hum became a shriek around Lee. Their shadows were thick and hulking against the tree trunks that surrounded them. Some gnashed their teeth and spit at the wood, and others tore at their hair, flinging strands into the fire that burned nutty and golden for a flash. Kimmie jumped into the center, squatted over the filled-in hole, and peed while she screeched up at the moon.

Lee watched it all as a spectator. She didn't feel their fury. For a moment, she felt the presence of someone behind her, watching from behind the trees. But when she turned around, there was nothing there.

"Opaline! Tell us your suffering!"

Lee found herself back in her mother's bedroom, staring at her body as the life leaked out of it. How could she capture everything that had happened to her mother and the tortured, shifting, sometimes shameful way she felt through most of it? That she still felt? Her voice caught in her throat as she tried to find the words. Her tongue was thick in her mouth, and whatever shred of harmony she'd felt moments before slipped away. As she hesitated, she felt the energy dip.

Belva launched back in, screaming, "SCREW HIM!" and the circle answered, "SCREW HIM!" They went back and forth for a few choruses until the pace slowed and the hum died.

Linda collapsed onto the ground, laughing hysterically, and then Beverly did the same, until all except for Lee were sprawled and giggling with heaving chests and wet eyes gleaming in the firelight. They'd braided most of the fabric so that the branch was wrapped in a crosshatch pattern with the loose ends peeking out of the bottom.

Belva pulled a large container from her bag and set it down on the ground, revealing a platter of rolls stuffed with sliced ham and mayonnaise. The others pulled out containers as well, of fried chicken and macaroni salad and liters of off-brand cola. They descended upon the food, starved and giddy and using only their hands. A euphoric Kimmie leaned against Billy, holding a chicken wing with her cheeks covered in grease.

Lee sat back and watched them, declining all offers of food and drink. The emptiness inside of her didn't burn with hunger; it just sat there, cold and lonely. She hadn't felt any power coursing through her.

Maybe there was something wrong with her.

Or maybe it hadn't worked.

Or, maybe, it wasn't real.

As she marinated in her disappointment, something swept through the firelight behind Belva and Kimmie. So quick and subtle that no one else in the circle noticed, and Lee dismissed it as a trick of the fire.

It was only a shadow.

# FIFTEEN

## MEREDITH

As Meredith crept through the darkness around the clearing, the energy of the land rose up through her feet and met her fury, becoming molten. She worried the leaves would catch fire.

That morning, she had listened from her hiding place as Belva told her mother about the moonshine and the way it could simulate magic. A thought that had been forming deep inside of her for a while floated to the surface and ignited. She had waited all day, her insides blistering, for the moment when the adults would take the path for the ritual and leave her and Cliff alone.

It was not long before she arrived at TJ's. There was no fire this time, and there were fewer people milling about than usual. She moved toward the group congregated around the couches, but as she got closer, her steps slowed.

Redbud was laid out on one of them with her eyes closed. Her skin was dry and corpse-like in the low light of the trailer's porch bulbs. Tiffany lay next to her in the same position, looking angelic in her motionlessness. Meredith noticed the curves of a flower freshly burned into the inside of her thigh, and her breath caught. Mom described the same flower on Mr. Hall's body to Belva.

She ran toward them, but TJ stood up and held her back. "Hey, Mer, we weren't expecting you. What you doing here?"

"What's wrong with them? Are they okay?" She jerked from his grasp, but he just gripped harder and pressed his dirty nails into her flesh.

"This ain't a good time. Why don't you go on home."

Meredith fought harder, and he released her. She moved to go around him, and he moved with her. He tried to put his hands on her again, and she took a step back. "Don't touch me."

He put his hands up and chuckled. "No one's trying to touch you. I told you to get. Now, *get*." He stepped toward her with his full weight. He thought he could scare her like one of his pups.

"I'm not going anywhere until I see that Redbud and Tiffany are okay." She could feel the heat flowing up through her sneakers again and meeting at her middle, where her anger and power collected. She imagined it moving up her shoulders, down her arms, and into her hands like Redbud had taught her. She thought of how much she wanted to hurt him for threatening her, and for whatever he'd done to her grandmother and Tiffany.

Her hands heated until the pain became too great. Then she stretched out her arms and unleashed it on him. She braced for some extreme reaction: his face contorted in pain, or his body writhing in the grass.

But he only stood there smiling at her. "Look here, y'all, we got ourselves a real witch." Laughter came from every direction, and Meredith realized she was surrounded by TJ's boys. Fear sparked and spread through her. She stared hard at Redbud's blank face, willing her to wake up, but she remained still as stone.

She tried the spell again, and again it failed. Her fear gave off a different heat than her fury; it warmed and prickled in her cheeks. The laughter ceased, and in their silence, they closed in on her. A boy grabbed her from behind by the shoulders and another dove for her legs. She jerked her body as they lifted her off the ground, and their laughter rose again with her resistance.

She had thought this would never happen to her now that she had this gift, and so the pain cut deeper when she felt the absence of her power, her body no longer hers to control.

Redbud's sallow face loomed into view with a look of demonic possession. "Junior, put her down, *now*." The boys froze and turned to TJ, who looked between Meredith and Redbud. After a moment, he nodded, and they dropped her on the ground. She quickly stood up and stepped away from the group. She knew she should run, but she couldn't leave Tiffany.

Redbud collapsed on the couch and tipped her head back. Meredith approached cautiously, watching the boys as she moved toward Tiffany. When it was clear they wouldn't jump her, she went to her and felt for a pulse at her neck. Her heart beat softly beneath her smooth, warm skin, and Meredith exhaled. She shook her gently, but she didn't wake up.

"What's wrong with her? Is she sick?"

When Redbud didn't respond, Meredith slapped her arm and yelled a guttural "hey" like Mom sometimes did to stop their fighting. Redbud's eyelids fluttered open, and she looked dreamily over at Meredith. There was no life behind her eyes, only dirty vapor. Meredith repeated her question.

"Nothing wrong with her. She's feeling better than anyone should feel . . ."

"What did she take? Should I take her to the hospital?"

"No, no, she'll be fine . . ."

It was like trying to talk to a small child. Redbud was a wisp of consciousness, floating there, barely existing. Meredith didn't recognize this person.

She had imagined this confrontation fueled by anger, but there were tears in her eyes as she asked, "Did you really teach me magic, or was it just fake?"

Redbud blinked back into being for a moment, becoming solid as her brow dipped. "Oh, honey . . ."

"Do I even have a gift? Do you? Or was it all just make-believe?" The tears slipped down her cheeks as the idea was given air and took its first breath.

"You don't want it . . ."

"Is it real or not?"

"I was protecting you . . ."

Meredith's shoulders slumped. "I'm so tired of people protecting me. I just want the truth."

"You don't understand, baby. It'll ruin your life."

"And I'm so tired of people telling me I don't understand, as if that justifies their lies."

"Please, just trust me, okay?"

"Why would I trust you? You've lied to me since the moment we met. You told me you'd take care of Tiffany, and now look at her—"

"I promise I'll be better. I'll tell you everything. I'm gonna get clean for you and Cliff."

"I don't believe a single word you say. Mom and Belva were right. You're poison. I wish I never met you."

Redbud's face contorted, and she whispered, "Please . . ."

Meredith immediately regretted the force of it, but part of her was glad to see she'd drawn blood. Tiffany stirred, and Meredith asked if she could take her home. She nodded sleepily, and Meredith pulled her up to standing.

Redbud tried to help, but Meredith pushed her arm away. "Don't."

As she and Tiffany turned toward the woods, Redbud wrapped her arms tightly around Meredith. She pleaded "Please don't leave" in her ear with dry, putrid breath. Meredith tried to shake her off, but she wouldn't let go.

"I promise I'll be better. Don't give up on me . . ."

Meredith continued to struggle, and a sick, sad anger built in her chest. She had thought there was magic here with Redbud, and instead there were only lies and disease and rot. The feeling continued to build, until the pressure released and the world went black for a moment.

When she refocused, Redbud was on the ground unconscious.

Meredith stared down at her, horrified. With panic coursing through her, she took Tiffany's hand, and they stumbled into the woods.

After she helped Tiffany get home, she climbed quietly back into her room. When she collapsed onto the cot, her hip hit against something hard, and she winced. Beneath the comforter she found Belva's black book. She pulled it out, and for the first time since she'd learned of this magical tradition, she was frightened by what lay behind its cover. She put it back and crawled into bed with Cliff and lay against him with their backs pressed together. Neither of them liked to be held, but she wanted to feel someone there.

"Did you know?" Meredith whispered in the dark.

"Know what?"

"That Redbud lied to me. That she's sick."

"Mom and Grandma Mama told us to stay away from her."

"I know. I mean, did you *see* it?"

"No."

Her shoulder blades started to shake against Cliff's, and he reached back and grabbed her hand. The mourning of what she'd lost burned through her, and as it receded, she felt a soft cooling enter her hand through his and travel along her veins, relaxing her body. She took a few deep breaths and wiped her face on the blanket.

"I think something bad is going to happen." His voice was delicate and wispy like spider silk.

"Something bad *did* happen. Multiple bads."

"This will be worse."

Meredith could feel the panic returning. "What? What could be worse?"

"I don't know. I can't see any shape around it. But it gives me this scary feeling."

Meredith was silent.

"What should we do?" he asked.

"I don't know." Meredith squeezed his hand. "But no matter what happens, we will take care of each other."

"How?"

"We'll find a way."

"Okay."

"Do you believe me?"

"Yes." Cliff pressed harder against her back, and Meredith wrapped the blanket tighter around them, sealing them off from the rest of the world.

# SIXTEEN

## LEE

The morning mist still carried the smell of fire as Lee sat drinking weak coffee and clutching her knees in an old hunting jacket on the porch. The empty feeling from last night lingered along with the smoke.

In the cold light of morning, it was hard for her to believe that she had relied on folk magic to bring a murderer, with a clear grudge against her family, to justice. This place had gotten inside of her, and she'd started to believe they might have some power in this fucked-up world. She had lost her goddamn mind.

She was so distracted that she didn't hear the truck pull up. Belva got out and came toward the house with her dress splattered in blood. Lee rushed to meet her.

"Morning."

"What happened? Are you okay?"

"Yeah, why?" Lee pointed at her dress, and Belva looked down at it. "Oh, that's nothing. You know Debbie's daughter, the teacher? She had her baby about an hour ago. Both are healthy."

"Oh. That's nice." Lee thought back to the night before. "When did you leave?"

"I got the call right after you went to bed." Belva looked completely drained. She was unsteady on her feet, and Lee caught her as she stumbled. Belva gripped Lee's hand tightly as she led her carefully into the house.

Kimmie was passed out on the couch with her mouth open, and she didn't stir as they came in. Lee helped Belva ease into an armchair. As she fixed her a hot cup of coffee and a biscuit with dandelion jelly, Belva watched her.

"I was proud of you for joining last night."

Lee didn't want to argue with her while she was weak. She nodded and gave her a perfunctory smile. "Do you think it worked?"

"It was strong. I could feel it."

Lee nodded and didn't press further. She wouldn't allow this type of magical thinking to guide her decisions any longer. She needed to know that her children and the rest of the family were safe. They couldn't live here without that certainty, and she couldn't leave knowing that Belva and the rest were in danger.

Belva coughed jaggedly into her hand. "Hey, I want to give you something." She gestured toward a small baggie on the counter as another coughing fit came on, and Lee handed it to her.

Belva opened it and pulled out a black-streaked gold necklace with a large round locket dappled with age spots. Her hands shook slightly as she held it up to Lee. "This was Granny Pallie's. It ain't worth nothing, but it's got history. I want you to have it. It's usually passed down to the next in line who's got the gift. You're ready for it now." Belva smiled weakly at Lee, and though Lee was sure she hadn't inherited any gift, she couldn't help but take it from her. She slipped it over her head and hid it beneath her sweater.

"Thank you, Grandma Mama. It's beautiful. I'll keep it close."

Belva patted her hand and leaned back against the chair with her eyes closed.

Lee shook Kimmie's shoulder until she started showing signs of life. She leaned over and whispered in her ear, "Meet me in the back room. I need to talk to you." Then Lee went to find Billy, who'd crashed in some corner of the house.

When they were all in the back room, Lee shut the door and turned to them. "Kimmie, I noticed TJ wearing a purple blazer two nights ago. Do you remember seeing that?" Lee couldn't be sure if it'd been real or not given her state at the time.

Kimmie wiped the crust from her eyes and scowled. "Why?"

"That blazer belonged to Mr. Hall. I want to turn TJ in to the police, but I need real evidence. They won't believe half of what I have to tell them."

Kimmie exhaled. "I told you, he didn't kill Joe Hall. And even if he did, we don't do cops around here. We can take care of our own problems."

"She's right, Lee," Billy interjected.

"I know you don't want to believe it, but he killed him. And he threatened our family. I can't just let that go. And I can't rely on some folk ritual to take care of it. This is my only option. Please. Help me protect our family."

Kimmie took a rolled cigarette from behind her ear and lit it. She smoked for a bit, staring off into space. "I don't remember a purple coat."

"Bullshit." She tried to catch Kimmie's eye. "We have to go up there and check. Maybe there will be other evidence. The police will have to take it seriously."

"Have you lost your mind? TJ will shoot you on sight."

Billy put a hand on Lee's shoulder. "Listen to her. If you wanna bring the law down on him, there's a charm we could work. All we need is a bit of police station dirt, some snuff, a sprinkle of pepper. Kimmie can bury it on the property."

"Like hell I will—"

"I told you I can't count on folk magic to take care of this. We need to do something real. We can't just stand by and wait for a handful of dirt to take care of our problems."

Billy went to say something but decided against it, shaking his head.

Lee turned back to Kimmie. "Do you know when the property might be empty today?"

Kimmie was quiet a beat as she blew smoke into the sunshine through the window screen. "You ain't letting this go, huh?"

Lee nodded. "I can't."

Kimmie exhaled loudly. "There's a flea market in Franklin City. Everyone's going. They'll probably leave in the afternoon and come back late."

Lee went to speak, but Kimmie cut her off. "To be crystal fucking clear, we are not going there on some mission to bring my brother to the law." She pointed at Lee. "You are gonna see there's no blazer, and then you're gonna leave it alone."

Lee agreed and turned back to Billy, "Will you come with us?" She didn't want to go up there without reinforcements.

He eyed her. "I assume we ain't telling Mama about this."

"She wouldn't understand. She thinks she's taken care of it. And she's not feeling well. I don't want to worry her."

He put his hands on his hips and shook his head again. "All right."

·   ·   ·

The sun was sinking toward the ridge by the time they made it to the property.

It looked different in the light, but it was no less sinister. The sunshine imbued the uncut grass and the flowering weeds with a stark, frenzied quality, and the silence that buzzed around the trailer and the various storage sheds seemed sentient. Lee felt the prickle of being stalked at a close distance.

"Are you sure no one's here?"

Kimmie gave her a look and didn't respond.

Lee shook off the feeling as she opened the flimsy metal door to the trailer and stepped inside. Kimmie led them to TJ's bedroom where the traces of him—designer clothes with the tags still on, small bottles of expensive skincare, a stack of books with titles like *How to Give Zero Fucks and Get Rich*—gave off thick fumes of his presence. Her hands shook and her body tingled as they searched through his closet, his drawers, and under his bed, but there was no sign of the purple blazer. There were, however, a lot of guns. Lee's pulse quickened at the sight of their gleaming barrels. Billy tsked when he saw one leaned against the corner of the closet. "Boy needs to get a safe."

They continued on to Missy's room in the new addition jutting off the end. The room was meticulously decorated in purples and greens, and there was a brand-new MacBook resting on the desk. As they rifled through every drawer and shoebox, Lee thought of a time not long ago when Meredith had slept in a room like this, and Lee had felt closer to her than anyone she'd ever known. Now Meredith refused to talk to Lee about anything, and sometimes she felt like a stranger.

They found no trace of Mr. Hall—not a single handwritten note or signed gift. No purple blazer. Nothing they could use.

They went back out into the hall, where Kimmie stood with her arms folded. "That prove it for you? There ain't nothing here."

Lee shook her head. "I'd like to check outside."

There were storage sheds all over the property, so they split up and rooted through them as the sun descended further. Lee's shed was pitch black inside, and she had to pull out her phone light. The dirty plastic dog bowls and rusted farm equipment pocked with spider sacs were horror-tinged in the heavy silence; at any moment, TJ and his boys could come roaring up the driveway.

They met back up in the darkness just out of range of the trailer's automatic lights.

"Where else can we look? We haven't found any moonshine or anything illegal. There's got to be another place where he keeps things."

"And if we go there and you see all the stuff and no blazer, that will be the end of it? I mean it, the end."

Lee hesitated, and then nodded. "Yes."

Kimmie scanned up the ridge. "He's got a little place up there where they make the moonshine. That's where he keeps most of the drugs and other shit. I can show you the way, but it'll be darker than a dog's asshole with no moon."

Billy pointed to his headlamp. "We can use this. "

.   .   .

They were like coal miners making their way through a narrow passage. The light from the headlamp made the dark around them more absolute, becoming flat and impenetrable on either side. The only evidence of creatures around them was the buzz of their wings and the scrape of their limbs against the brush. Lee might have been more terrified were it not for Billy's tall, wide figure in front of her, guiding her deeper into the woods. A burly beacon in the dark.

Her mind wandered to the night of the party when she'd led Otis into the trees. She imagined his arm materializing out of the darkness and pulling her into it. He would lay her down on a bed of pine needles and slowly unbutton her dress and unhook the front clasp of her bra, exposing her to the elements. He would gently stroke her front, starting at her neck and making his way down. She would lay there shivering until he took off his clothes and used his body's heat to warm the length of her.

A hoarse scream came from somewhere in front of them, and Billy stopped. Lee froze. The scream came again and again, the short repetition of it mad and desperate. She whispered as softly as she could. "Billy, is someone hurt?" But he didn't respond or turn around.

She cautiously joined him and Kimmie at the front, and she saw a bobcat in Billy's lamp light, staring them down as a humanlike wail came from the cat's mouth.

Billy moved slowly toward the animal with his arm outstretched as Lee pleaded for him to come back. When he reached it and offered his hand up to smell, the animal froze with its teeth bared. Lee imagined it mauling him and then moving on to her.

But then the animal rubbed its cheek against his palm like a housecat, and Lee heard a low rumbling. The creature was purring. He gave it love for a few minutes until the cat got tired of it and loped out of sight.

He let out a breath and chuckled low to himself. "She was just lonely."

They kept on walking for a little while before Billy stopped once again. Lee figured they'd finally reached the place, and she came up beside them to look.

It took her a moment to make sense of the pale man lying contorted in the leaves. There were freckles sprinkled over his cheeks and across his collarbone like a faun's speckles. An imprint of a flower was burned into his bicep with the petals ridged in pink.

Even in cold, stiff death, TJ still had that animal magnetism.

Kimmie crouched down and placed a small hand on his chest. Lee reached out to console her, but she pulled violently away and stood up. She paced and ran her fingers through her hair as her face contorted with fury.

Kimmie walked over to the body again and gazed down for a while as if she was memorizing its lines. Then she took off running into the woods, the small figure of her swallowed up by the trees.

A howl came up in the distance like an animal wounded, alone, keening for her pack.

# SEVENTEEN

They hung in the cold, fluorescent limbo of three a.m. in the police station waiting room.

Lee was bent over in her chair with her face in her hands, attempting to find darkness in them. She wished to lose consciousness, if only for a few minutes. Her mouth was sore for a drink.

They had questioned Lee and Billy first, and then Kimmie, after they'd found her curled up in TJ's bed. Lee had tried to be as vague as possible, though she wasn't sure she'd pulled it off. They had nothing to hide, and yet, there was much that could be misinterpreted. She thought of Belva coming home that morning with blood streaked down her front. Lee had been so sure that TJ was responsible for the murder. Now she wasn't sure what to believe.

The sheriff seemed to know quite a bit about what was done and who had been at the gathering the night before, and Lee assumed one of Belva's ladies had talked.

They had also found what looked like a hex bag on TJ. Billy tried to explain that it was probably one TJ made himself to ward off the police. He had one just like it on him at that very moment; never left home without it. But this seemed to only confirm their suspicion that it was the work of their family.

Billy paced the room; they'd taken Belva to question an hour before, and they were still back there. An officer walked by, and Billy blocked his path.

"What's taking so long?"

"We'll bring her to you when we're done." The man tried to move around him, but Billy stepped forward and allowed himself to expand. He could be a large man when he wanted to be.

"What exactly do y'all think happened?"

"I'm not at liberty to discuss the case with you, sir."

"Look, we were happy to help y'all out, but I know my rights. She ain't answering any more questions without a lawyer."

"Sir, she ain't a minor. She's the one who got to ask for a lawyer. I'll bring her back to you when we're done."

Billy's hands curled into fists, and the air charged around them. The officer paled and began to back away slowly with his hand poised above his gun.

Lee knew Billy to be gentle and empathetic to the point of supernatural, but he was also a creature of the mountains with his own rules for how to live. He would protect himself and his family no matter the cost.

Kimmie's voice came from the corner where she'd sat silently since they arrived. "Calm yourself, Billy. We don't want no trouble."

Billy lowered his shoulders and backed away a few steps.

"If you can't control yourself, sir, I'm gonna have to lock you up," said the officer.

"Don't push it, Tyler." Kimmie's voice was rough and lifeless. Lee had never seen her like this, even when things were bad when they were kids. She went over to try to comfort her, but Kimmie pushed her hard, and she fell back onto the linoleum.

"Don't fucking touch me. It's cause of you that we're here, and my own brother is dead." She spit on the floor near Lee's hand.

"I didn't have anything to do with his death."

"Then who was it, huh?"

Kimmie stared into her eyes, and Lee saw the hurt she usually kept hidden. "I was happy when you came back. I thought maybe it could be like when we were kids again. But I wish you'd stayed away. Everything's gone to shit."

Something inside Lee tightened painfully.

Kimmie stalked up to the officer at the desk. "Can I go?"

"Yes, the detective on the case will call you when there's an update."

"Fantastic." She left the room without looking at Lee.

They continued to wait, until a commotion came from the back room where they were holding Belva. Billy looked toward it and then back at Lee. Without speaking, she stood up, and they rushed toward it, ignoring the calls to stop from the officer.

Belva was sprawled on the floor of the interrogation room with her eyes roving in their sockets. Lee knelt down and held her gaze, and she'd never seen such raw helplessness. Belva tried to speak, but her mouth slanted and no sound came out. The left half of her face was melting down as if her features might slide off onto the government linoleum.

An officer pulled Lee away and started taking Belva's vitals. Lee tried to maintain eye contact to let her know she was still there, but then Belva's eyelids drooped, and she lost consciousness. It was excruciating to watch the slow movements of the procedure as Lee imagined Belva's mind dissolving inside her skull, each glorious thread of her becoming syrup.

More officers came in with a stretcher and loaded her onto it. Lee tried to keep one hand on Belva as they rushed her out the front door, but they pulled ahead of her, and she was left running after them into the parking lot.

.  .  .

Belva was a deflated, gray-skinned stranger in the hospital bed. Lee had never seen her in an environment so removed from nature, and she worried the tangle of wires and machines might be the opposite of what she needed. But there was no alternative. If they took her off the machines, she could die.

Belva didn't seem like the type who *could* die. If anything, Lee imagined her disappearing into the woods one day to become one of the trees.

Luann sat in a chair next to the bed, holding Belva's limp, waxy hand and reciting Bible verses under her breath. When Meredith had seen Belva in the hospital bed, she'd taken on the same vacant expression she'd had after finding Mr. Hall, and Cliff had gotten upset and embarrassed, so Billy had taken them back to the cabin. Lee wanted to be with them, but she couldn't leave Belva. She and Billy would switch shifts in a few hours.

Dreama leaned against the window holding a Styrofoam cup of coffee. "Lee, look at this." She pointed out the window where Lee saw birds of different kinds perched on the windowsill and peering into the glass, as if trying to find a way in. When she got closer, she saw more lining the roofline and hovering just outside. Hundreds of them.

Lee stepped away from the glass and started pacing. "Where is the doctor? It's been hours. Shouldn't they be doing something?"

Dreama reached out and tried to steady her. "Hey. Look at me. She has the best doctor in this place. I made sure of it. He'll be here soon, and we'll know more. Until then, just try to stay calm."

Dreama had been an authoritative, grounding presence since she arrived, and Lee was grateful she'd come, despite her problems with Belva.

Preferring to stay in motion, Lee went to the nurse's station to see if she could speak to someone about the doctor's status. A woman with brilliant red hair and aging skin looked up and answered, "What's your name, honey?"

"Lee—uh—Ford." She'd started using her maiden name again, but it still sounded weird.

"For Redbud Ford?"

"Um, no. For Belva. Buck."

"Okay, got it. The doctor is in surgery right now, but he should be done in a few hours. He'll come see her then." Lee processed this and attempted to smother the rising panic. They would be waiting for a while before anyone told them a goddamn thing.

"Is Redbud Ford *here*?"

"You family?"

"Yes. I'm her daughter."

"Well then, yes. She's just down the hall."

"What happened to her?"

"She walked out into traffic at that new intersection near the Walmart. Most of the cars stopped, but one wasn't paying attention and nicked her side. She's lucky to be alive."

Lee asked for the room number and made her way down the hall. She found Redbud sleeping in a hospital bed, looking dead to the world. She sat quietly in a chair and peeked over to the other side of the room where a person lay covered head to toe in a blanket. She wondered what they looked like.

"He's been covered this whole time. I still don't know what's under there." Her mother's eyes remained closed.

"What happened to you?"

"Oh, honey, it was crazy." She finally looked at Lee. "I was trying to cross the street, and I thought the sign said walk, but it musta been broke, because then all the cars went, and I got trapped in the intersection. I swear I'm gonna sue the county. They're lucky it was old broke-down me that no one cares about. What if it'd been a child—"

"Mama. I'm going to leave if you aren't honest with me."

"But I'm telling the truth! That traffic light almost killed me!"

"All right. Hope you feel better." Lee got up to leave, but Redbud's spotted arm darted out from the blanket and gripped Lee's wrist.

"Fine! Shit. You always were a tough old bitch."

Lee waited. She had heard so many lies over the years. Each story encrusted with its own specific details. A disability check lost in the mail, probably in a dirty puddle somewhere after the storm they just had. A broken refrigerator with wires chewed through by rebellious adolescent raccoons. She was always in a constant state of needing money, and by money, the drugs that the money would buy her. When Lee finally changed her number, she'd done it out of self-preservation.

"I've been trying to get clean for you and the kids. I just needed something to hold me over until I could get into detox. But TJ wasn't around. One of his boys told me he fucking *died* and wouldn't float me. Then I was all fucked up and starting to feel real bad, so I walked out in front of those cars." She avoided making eye contact with Lee.

"Worst case, I'd die, and it would be a fucking relief. And best case, I'd wind up here with my little button." Redbud held up a plastic device with a button connected to a morphine drip and pressed it with a dramatic flourish. She lay back on the bed and closed her eyes for a moment, nestling into the crinkle of paper pillowcases.

"Mama. What were you doing with Meredith at the Ryders'? Did you go back to the work?"

"No. I gave her a little moonshine to make her think she was learning. I figured she'd eventually get tired of it and move on to something else. I was protecting her, like I protected you from it."

Lee narrowed her eyes at this rewriting of history. She hadn't protected her from anything. "You gave my fifteen-year-old moonshine?"

"It was only a little bit. Just enough so she'd get the effects."

Lee swallowed her anger. She knew better than to argue with her mother's twisted logic. She took a pad of paper and a pen from a side table and drew the black flower symbol. She held it up in front of her face. "What is this? I know it's on the moonshine bottles, but what else? I know it's bigger than that."

Redbud squinted at the paper. "I don't know what you're talking about. That's all it is. TJ called it branding. Like he needed anything fancy to sell that shit."

Maybe she was right. Maybe it meant nothing at all, and Lee was chasing a backwoods conspiracy that wasn't real. But then who killed TJ and Mr. Hall? What was she missing?

Redbud propped herself up on her elbows and looked at Lee hopefully. "Did you bring the children with you? Can I see them? I still haven't met your boy."

"No."

"Just for a minute, huh? I'll be good. I promise."

"Mama."

For a moment, Lee imagined her mother running through the trees, strong and beguiling, followed by a shrieking Meredith and Cliff. She would never have been conventional, but she would have inspired them.

Lee studied the real version of her mother in the hospital bed, frail and eroded, but somehow still alive. Beneath the ruin, she could still see the old her. A streak of her beautiful, powerful mother glinted in the hospital fluorescents. Maybe Redbud didn't deserve her guilt. But Lee couldn't deny that she cared for her any longer.

"Let me help you. I know people from college who are therapists now. I bet they can get you into a nice rehab somewhere. Let's do it for real this time. You don't have to do it on your own."

Her mother's face twisted into a scowl. "I don't need your fucking help," she hissed. "You can't just disappear and never call me or ask me how I'm doing and then come here and tell me how to live my fucking life. You don't know shit about me or my life. You didn't care when I was so broke I nearly froze to death. You didn't care when I was arrested and all I needed was just one person to say I was half decent. You changed your phone number like I was some stalker and not the woman who gave you life." Her hair was nearly standing on end.

Lee tensed and filled with adrenaline in response to her mother's rising energy, like when she was a kid. "*You* are the one who told me to leave and never come back, and *you* are the one who made life here so hard that I'd never want to." Lee took a deep breath. "But for some reason I can't fathom, I still want to help you. Let me help you."

"You don't wanna *help* me. You wanna ship me off to get rid of your own guilt. These 'therapists' you talk about are professional drug dealers paid by the drug companies and the government to keep me poor and stupid so they can do God knows what when no one is looking. These therapists are crazier than I ever been." Redbud threw herself back down on the bed and turned her head away from Lee.

Lee's glimpse of her old mother vanished, and now she only saw the woman who had made her life hell. She'd fallen into the trap once again, and she scolded herself for being so stupid.

And yet, despite everything, Lee still couldn't be mad at her in the way she wanted. She knew her mother was a deeply sick person.

And there was nothing she could do about it.

"Nice talk, Mama." Lee got up and wrenched her arm away when her mother grabbed for it again. "Stay away from my kids." She kept her head down and refused to make eye contact as she left the room.

In the hallway, she imagined her mother's outstretched arms still hanging there, mouth gaping, fingers grasping for anything to fill her.

# EIGHTEEN

The stars were out when Lee knocked on Otis's front door.

She stood there for a few minutes, but no one answered. Low music was coming from the back, and she walked around the side of the house to a large wooden shed with an open front.

Otis was bent over a slab of wood with a large sander gripped in his hands, and his body moved back and forth over it as a thrashing metal played low. His hair was slicked back and his white T-shirt was translucent with sweat. She stood there, watching the ropes and bulges of his arms flex with each stroke.

He looked up, startled. Lee entered the shed and took a pair of goggles neatly hooked on the wall and a piece of sandpaper from the pile on the table. She moved around the slab to what looked like a chair leg and started to delicately sand it.

Once Meredith and Cliff had entered school, Lee had returned to woodworking. It never grew beyond making pieces for the house and neighbors, but it gave her a small escape from her life with Cooper. Moving her body over the wood provided a distraction, and a release, from all that she kept carefully contained.

Otis turned off the music, and they both worked in silence for a while, except for the rhythmic scraping of them wearing down the wood grain by grain.

Finally, she set the paper down and pulled the goggles from her head.

"Belva had a stroke." She gritted her teeth, attempting to hold it together.

Otis took off his own goggles and disarmed himself of his sander. He came around the wood and pulled her toward him gently. Her inner resolve collapsed at his touch, and she finally let herself become undone.

"For years, I acted like she was already dead. I let my family think she was so we wouldn't have to come here. Now she's actually dying, and I'm pissed because I love her, but also because I *need* her. It's so selfish."

Belva was the only person who could help her figure out what was happening, and now she was all but lost to them. But Lee's hopelessness extended beyond a grappling with her relationship with Belva or the mystery behind the murders. Her understanding of herself and the life she'd built had entirely unraveled, and there was nothing that could help her make sense of it or weave it back together. The reality of it came in a wave, like a tide of polluted water washing over her, and the tears finally came.

He held her against him and let her cry into his shirt until she felt empty and bruised. When she quieted, he asked if she wanted some water, and she followed him inside.

She'd never been inside his house before, and it smelled like his scalp and the folds of his shirts. The kitchen was clean with dishes drying on a towel next to the sink. He took a glass out of a cabinet that contained a jar of the moonshine. Her heart leapt at the sight of it, and she noticed him watching her.

"I don't think that's a good idea for tonight."

"I agree." She had taken a few sips from her own jar before she got out of her car. She knew she needed to stop, but this didn't feel like the right night to do it.

The small space of the kitchen brought them closer together, sealing them in. Lee wanted to be against his body again, but as she moved toward him, he took a step back.

"Let's go for a walk."

They went out the back door and walked by the strawberry field, still warm and dry from the day's sun. Summer had ended months ago, but they were somehow still on the vine, soft and darkly ripe. Lee remembered Belva saying the strawberries had bloomed out of season.

She pulled one from a plant and put it in her mouth. The sugars were on the very cusp of fermentation, the last curve of life before plunging off the side.

They walked into a large thicket of trees, tamer than Belva's woods, with well-treaded paths. The moon was just bright enough and the neighbors just close enough that they could see in front of them.

"Did you hear about TJ?"

A shadow passed over his features. "Yes."

"I'm so sorry. I know you were friends."

Lee could barely see his expression, but she sensed a shift in mood, the air sparking.

"What?"

"They're saying Belva killed him. And that you might've been involved."

"Who's *they*?"

"My friends. Family. Anyone I've talked to in the last twelve hours."

"And what about you? What do you think?"

"I'm more interested in what you think."

"So you actually think we killed someone?"

He took a deep breath and looked into the trees. "I get the feeling there are things happening that I'm not aware of or don't understand. First, we see Mr. Hall and a girl in the woods. Two days later, he's found dead. On Belva's land. Then, you ask me about TJ. A few days later, he's also found dead."

"You saw Mr. Hall that night?"

"Yeah, of course. It was hard to miss him."

"Why didn't you say something?"

"It seemed like you didn't want to talk about it."

Lee was quiet for a beat. Coming here was a mistake. "I didn't kill *anyone*. And Belva didn't either."

"Then what's going on?"

"I honestly don't have an answer."

For a moment, the only sounds were their breathing and the hiss of the woods around them.

"Did you put a *spell* on him . . . or curse him?" Otis finally asked.

"Did you know TJ was *dealing*?" She deflected.

"He's always done that. He used to sell weed in high school. I don't mess around with that stuff."

"How could you be friends with him, then?"

He stopped and looked at her, and in the moonlight, she watched an anger move through him, his face barely recognizable.

"What if that was the only way TJ knew how to support his family? He is not the one who got everyone hooked on painkillers. That was doctors and drug companies. TJ is not the enemy."

"But—"

"It's not up to me to pass judgment on others around here. I appreciate what Belva has done for my father, but she doesn't get to decide who is right and wrong in this town. I understand when people say they're tired of that."

"Wait—"

"That always bothered me about you in high school. You acted like we were all hillbilly idiots, as if you had the right to decide what had value. You thought because I was quiet and read books that somehow I was better, that it meant I might be worth something. And you still threw me away."

"Otis, I'm sorry, you have it wrong . . ." Lee tasted the falseness of the words. There was truth in what he was saying; Meredith had screamed this at her.

"You act like this place isn't good enough to live in, that you can't wait to leave."

Lee found her voice. "Just because I want better for my children doesn't make me a bad person. That's what we should all be striving for."

He grunted in frustration. "Look, it's not really about that." He ran a hand through his hair. "You still haven't answered my question. Did y'all put a curse on TJ?"

Lee wanted to trust him, but this was bigger than the two of them. It seemed like any explanation she gave would make him even more suspicious that she and Belva were behind it. She couldn't put her family at risk.

When Lee didn't answer, he said, "TJ was one of my best friends. And now he's dead, and it seems like you were involved. I'm giving you a chance to set the record straight but you won't be honest with me."

He waited for her to defend herself, but she remained silent.

"I thought you'd changed. But it's still hard to get close to you. I'm not sure if you see me as a person sometimes. If you did, you'd have come here tonight knowing I'd be upset about TJ. But instead you came here seeking comfort for yourself." He paused, then said, "I'm sorry to hear about your grandma. I can see that you need someone right now. But it can't be me."

This thing between them had been unexpected. She hadn't taken the time or space to contemplate it, and so it had never quite taken shape. But now, whatever it had been was disintegrating and turning to ash on the wind.

She wanted to touch him one more time, to feel her self meeting his in their skin. Perhaps she could still find him there. But as she reached for his hand, he took a step back from her.

They didn't speak after that.

# NINETEEN

## MEREDITH

A crash startled Meredith awake. She rolled over and checked her phone. *3:45 a.m.*

Across the room, Cliff stirred but remained asleep. Meredith groaned and heaved herself out of bed. Lights blazed in the hallway, and she had to shield her eyes. Another crash came, and she staggered zombielike to the back of the house.

Garbage bags lined the entryway leading to Billy's old bedroom that was now used for storage. She opened the door and was confronted by a wall of boxes. She entered a small opening to the right and crept along the narrow pathway, following the sound of her mother swearing. Stacks of newspapers, heaps of pots, and piles of baby clothes loomed on either side. An old porcelain clown leered at her with one eye as she passed.

She found her mother hunched over a shattered lamp in the corner. "Mom?"

She spun around and put a hand to her chest. "God, you scared me." Her eyes were bloodshot and her hair was messy in a way Meredith had never seen before. Mom was annoyingly meticulous about her appearance.

"Have you been up all night?"

"I don't know. What time is it? I think I lost my phone." She put her hands on her hips and surveyed the room. "But look at this! Doesn't it already look so much better?"

Meredith looked around. The room was still a nightmare. "Maybe you should take a break."

Her mother had barely slept in the four days since Belva was taken to the hospital.

Back in California, when her mother was upset, she would always throw herself into a project, like building a wooden table for the back patio or redoing the guest bathroom with thousands of hand-stamped gold feathers. But this was on another level. Meredith was still angry at her mother, but her concern was stronger.

"I'm so close, though. I don't want to stop now. I'm in the zone." Mom pulled a stack of old school lunch trays from somewhere and showed them to Meredith. "Aren't these cool? We could use these." She looked rabid beneath the room's bare bulb, and her breath had the cheap perfume scent of the moonshine Redbud had given Meredith.

"Yeah, sure." Meredith picked up a photo album balanced on a tower of paint cans and opened it. Two teenagers with milky skin and feathered hair held a baby between them and looked at the camera with proud half smiles. "Is this you with Redbud and your dad?"

Mom put down the trays and snatched the album out of her hands. "Yes." She set it down on another pile and picked up a box cutter. Meredith watched as she opened a new box and started pulling out empty Coke bottles and lining them up on a chest of drawers.

"Fine. I'm going back to bed."

She didn't respond.

·   ·   ·

In the morning, Meredith and Cliff sat down to an elaborate breakfast of cinnamon rolls, sausage, and some kind of frittata. She begged her mother to sit down for a moment and eat with them, and she begrudgingly obliged. As Mom sat there, no longer in motion, she visibly sank. She stared at the food absentmindedly but didn't take a bite.

"Why don't we go to the pumpkin patch today? Tiffany said everyone goes this time of year." Meredith could hear the forced cheer in her voice.

When Mom didn't respond, Meredith caught Cliff's eye across the room and gestured for him to back her up. He nodded and said "Mom, the pumpkin patch sounds really fun. I want to go" in a voice sweetened with corn syrup. Meredith gave him a look, convinced that Mom would call bullshit, but instead she looked up from the food and smiled weakly.

"All right, if that's what you want."

. . .

Meredith stroked the smooth ridges of the pumpkin and grabbed hold of its spongy stalk, feeling it give slightly in her fist. She turned it over and found the other side had rotted right through. A spider crawled out of it as if the mold was taking animal form.

She rolled it away and stood up to survey the barren hills dotted with orange and parched green. Without trees to shade her, the sun was metallic in its intensity.

Cliff called to her from down the hill, and she made her way over to him. Mom stood a few feet away looking dazedly out over the farm to some distant point, and she didn't respond to Cliff's calls.

"What a fine specimen." Meredith fingered the pumpkin's stalk still rooted to the earth. "Doesn't look like they've cut her loose yet."

Cliff gently nudged her shoulder aside. "I'll take care of it." He pulled the knife that Billy gave him from his pocket and carefully cut the stem.

Meredith corralled Mom, and they carried the pumpkin to a truck idling nearby with a flatbed trailer stacked with hay bales and covered on all sides by bright orange banners advertising Home Depot. Every other bale was spray-painted orange, and it tinged the goat-shitted farm air with sweet chemical fumes. The driver, who looked about fourteen, turned the truck on, and EDM blasted from the sound system, sending a rumble through the bales. They winced at the sun as they rambled slowly through the rows of pumpkins back to the festival grounds.

Her mom perked up briefly as they searched for kettle corn in the food stall area, but they found nothing but tents selling TGI Friday's boneless wings and Red Robin cheeseburgers with onion straws poking out of the sides like claws. People stared at them from the food lines and picnic tables, some with unabashed fear and others with a curiosity reserved for car crashes. When they sat down at one of the tables, the small family next to them quickly got up and moved to another table.

As they sat eating popcorn shrimp, a man in a farmer costume came up to Cliff and handed him a smiling yellow Walmart balloon. Meredith compared this man with his painfully blue overalls, inexplicable neck scarf, and hole-worn hat with the actual farmers that sat chewing at the tables around them.

"To be honest, I was expecting something more . . . quaint. Some of the *aesthetic* choices have harshed the pastoral vibes." Meredith grimaced at her mom from across the table as she dipped a shrimp into a creamy orange sauce.

"It wasn't like this when I was a kid. We would get apple cider and kettle corn and Mama would give me a quarter for the 'world's largest cow' tent. There was something about enormous animals that spoke to me."

Meredith raised an eyebrow. "That sounds like animal abuse."

"You're probably right." Mom deflated again, and Meredith regretted her sarcasm. She searched around the festival for an appealing activity. "Look, Cliff, they have a corn maze."

He contemplated its entrance to their left. Stretched across a wall of bales at the front was a banner advertising "Conway Development" with a close-up picture of Dreama and her husband flashing veneers and subtle spray tans.

Cliff's eyes lit up. "Will you guys go with me?"

"Sure." Meredith looked at her mom, whose gaze had unfocused again. "Mom?"

"What?"

"Will you do the corn maze with us?"

She looked over at the wall of corn. "Oh. That's okay, honey. I'm a little tired. Text me when you get out."

Meredith and Cliff declined the paper map offered at the front entrance showing the maze in the shape of a black cat, convinced it would be cheating. At first, they took it at a wild run and allowed themselves to get lost. She missed being with Cliff like this; they used to spend hours playing make-believe together, but now everything had to be so real all the time. Meredith inhaled the sweet hay fumes, forgetting the weight of the last few days, and just let go.

When they'd penetrated deep into the maze and found themselves all alone, they decided it was time to make their way back. Cliff wanted to use their "powers" to find the way, so they both closed their eyes and tried to focus on the land beneath them, listening for where they should go. Meredith wasn't sure this was how it worked, but it was fun regardless. She hadn't tried to use her gift since the night she hurt Redbud.

As she half-heartedly attempted to connect with the land, she heard Cliff gasp, and she opened her eyes. He was staring at something behind her with the look he had after a night terror, when he still felt the demon in the room. A chill swept down her neck and back, and she shivered in the autumn heat.

Before she could turn around, the world shifted to black.

# TWENTY

## LEE

Lee bought a triple of hot honey whiskey from the Wild Turkey stand and prayed for it to send her to a warm place where she could pretend to be alive and well for her kids.

She hadn't felt like this since the first untethered months of college. She'd wandered from dorm to hall to library, afraid she might float away. She'd heard it described as a heaviness, but for her, it was a weightlessness that made her nearly immaterial, a state so close to nonexistence that she could almost feel its relief. The only things that saved her were the hours of classes and schoolwork.

As the liquor filled her with a warm, tethering weight, she roamed and observed the people going from booth to booth.

*Is the killer here?*

She wished they had gone somewhere more quiet and uncrowded, but there was a comfort in the presence of so many witnesses, even if they were the gawking, judgmental kind.

She heard her name being called and saw Dreama waving to her.

"Hey, how is she doing?"

"No change."

"Her brain is still healing. I'm sure she'll come out of it."

Lee's chest seized at the image of Belva's brain dissolved to syrup, and another wave rolled over her. She wanted to think of the Belva she'd known, and not the one lying in the hospital bed. "Do you remember when she used to bring us to the festival?"

Dreama smiled. "Yeah, she'd make us volunteer for the kettle corn booth with her. I still have burns from that thing." She held up her forearm and showed Lee a faded pink slash.

"But then Mama and Aunt Ruby would come at night, and we'd do the corn maze." Redbud and Ruby Jo became children again when they entered the maze, running through its narrow corridors in the dark and shrieking whenever they came upon some other lost soul. She and Dreama always held hands so they wouldn't be scared. It had been one of Lee's favorite times of the year, like a holiday that came right before Halloween.

Dreama gave Lee a genuine smile, and she caught a glimpse of the girl she'd once known. "Yeah, I remember."

Suddenly a wail came from the direction of the maze that filled Lee's body with adrenaline. *Cliff.*

By the time she and Dreama got to the entrance, a crowd had formed with some of the parents looking frantic but doing nothing. Another wail came. This time with a ripple in it that was pure horror.

*Fuck this.*

Lee charged into the maze and ran in the direction of the screams. The paths had emptied so that Lee was alone as she raced through its turns, sweating and crying out every time she hit a dead-end. The penetrating sun had dimmed to an evening intensity that revealed every aspect of the narrow passages in flat, terrifying detail. A few times she felt something, not behind her, but beside or above her, looming just out of sight.

She heard heavy breathing behind a wall of corn and pushed the thick stalks aside, forcing her way through and scraping her arms. She stumbled over something on the other side and came to her knees in the next row. It was the small body of Cliff curled against the maze wall and breathing heavily. She spoke low into his ear, and he looked up to verify her identity with his knife blade clutched in his small hand. He reached out for her and buried his face against her collarbone.

They breathed together for a while until he'd calmed.

"Where's Meredith?" Lee asked.

He looked up at her, stricken. "Something took her."

Lee's breath caught. "What do you mean?"

"It took her."

"*It?*"

"The thing I warned you about."

"What thing?"

"I see it everywhere. I don't know what it is. It's like, a shadow."

The shadow again. She had never seen Cliff so preoccupied with one image—first, the night they arrived. Then, the night of Mr. Hall's murder, at the stadium, and now here. She took a deep breath. "Where'd it take her?"

Cliff grimaced like he might cry. "I didn't see. I don't know. Just away."

"Okay. Let's check to see if she's at the front, and if she's not there, we'll look for her."

He nodded, and they quickly exited the maze with a discarded map.

The spectators had grown in number at the entrance. As Lee and Cliff made their way through the crowd, they took a few steps back and gawked, as if seeing them confirmed all their suspicions about the Buck family. Lee searched their faces for Meredith's, but she didn't see her.

Lee took out her phone and called her. No answer. Lee texted her, attempting not to sound too frantic if it turned out she'd allowed paranoia to take over her judgment. She could almost imagine Meredith talking to Tiffany by the photobooth and rolling her eyes at her mother's hysteria. But this vision seemed made of a fool's sunshine. The sun had dipped behind the mountains in the distance; they were in the shadows.

.   .   .

The night sky rolled in waves made by hundreds of small roving flashlight beams.

All around her, people were attempting to find her daughter.

Lee was standing in the middle of it, shaking. It felt like she was having a seizure in slow motion, her mind stuck on an image of Meredith disappearing into the woods with the hunched, greasy shadow of a man.

The sheriff waved his hand in her face again and gave her a concerned but frustrated look. "Opaline. Stay with me. We gotta get through these questions."

He asked her about every move Meredith had made at the festival, her mental state, the situation at home.

"We'll search as long as the volunteers and my officers last."

She could tell by his expression that he thought any sort of manual search was futile. This was a performance the whole town was taking part in. When people disappeared, it was because someone wanted them to stay hidden.

Lee found Billy and Cliff sitting on a log off to the side. She crouched down in front of Cliff, who sat with his arms folded in a tight knot across his chest. He had been shy with the sheriff and vague in his answers. He knew something had taken Meredith, but he couldn't give a description.

"Iff. I know you're scared. I'm scared, too. But I need your help. I need you to tell me what you saw in the maze."

"I didn't see his face."

"So it's a him now?"

"I guess. The sheriff said it was probably a him."

"Do you remember anything else about him? Face, hair, clothes, height?"

He took a deep breath and looked her in the eye. "I didn't see his face. Or hair. Or clothes. I think he was tall—"

"That's all you noticed?" He had fear in his eyes, and she realized she was clutching his arms too hard. She released them, revealing red marks on his skin.

He fought back tears. "I wish I could tell you. He was like a shadow. I couldn't see anything."

"And you *saw* him take Meredith?"

"No. He sorta appeared in front of us. He was just standing there. And then I felt really cold and I blacked out. I don't remember anything until you found me. But I know he took her." The tears began to fall. "You don't believe me."

Lee reached out and pulled him into her. She whispered "I believe you, I believe you" into his ear as he continued to sob.

He pulled away again and looked up at her. "Mom, I can't feel her. Or see her. It's like she's really *gone*." He started to cry again, and Lee's stomach dropped. She told herself it didn't mean anything; he was just upset.

When he'd quieted down, she gestured Billy off to the side where she could keep Cliff in sight.

"I need you to take him home with you."

"Okay. You coming later? I got plenty of room."

"No. I have to figure out what's going on so I can find Meredith."

Lee watched Cliff sitting on the log. A night breeze ruffled the curled ends of his hair as he fought to keep a calm, smooth face.

"Don't let Cliff go to school. Or anywhere. Just keep him at your cabin. Can you do that? Can you take off work?"

"Yeah, I can do that. It's no problem. We'll lay low."

"Thanks." She took a deep breath. "Is it possible Belva killed TJ? Could this be retribution for his death?"

"There's no way in hell."

"But what if they think she did?"

"No one connected to TJ has the sense to pull something off like this."

Lee looked back at the maze where the flashlights still strobed. She thought of how much Redbud had wanted to see Meredith, and the relationship they'd struck up behind her back. "What if Mama took her? Maybe she had help from someone." Kidnapping sounded extreme even for Redbud, but she couldn't rule it out.

Billy shook his head. "Red wouldn't do that."

"Either way, she was at that gathering at TJ's. She might know something. Do you know where she is?" When Lee went back four days ago to check on her mother, she was already gone. The nurse told her they'd realized she was a dope fiend and cut her off. They'd tried to get her into a detox center, but she'd checked out instead.

"She's at home."

"How is she doing?"

"Not good. She's on day four of detox."

Lee nodded. She'd seen it before, and it wasn't pretty. "Take care of my boy for me?"

"I will. Go see Red."

# TWENTY-ONE

The land around the old white house felt like a different country. The trees had been cleared out for crops decades ago, and now it stood in a dry expanse, the night wind gusting uninhibited against her front.

Even after twenty years, she still felt exposed here.

The screen door lay propped against the side of the house, creating an open maw at the front. The main door, a cracked version of Belva's blue, was ajar. She knocked against it and called out so as not to startle anyone. Her mother had once split open a possum's head with a frying pan when it came through the cat flap uninvited.

No one answered, so she pushed the door in and walked inside.

It was dark except for a new hole in the roof that allowed moonlight to pour through to the cratered and molded floorboards beneath. It still smelled like the gunpowder sting of cigarettes. The living room was filled with stained mattresses on the floor, and the walls that had once been white were a pale yellow and streaked with different stains. On one wall, an enormous black flower was burned into the plaster.

She flipped the light switch on the wall. Nothing happened.

Belva had inherited this house from an uncle, and when Redbud and Hank had a baby and got married, she gave it to them. But she'd never put it in their name. It was the only thing Redbud couldn't sell for drugs, and so she'd hung on to it all these years.

Lee's old bedroom was nearly empty except for a pile of papers and books in the corner. They were the only pieces of her childhood her mom and her friends hadn't taken. Things that weren't of value to anyone but Lee. Stacks of her high school essays, the word-processed pages now torn and smudged. Envelopes of college acceptances and her SAT results and financial aid information. At the bottom of all this paper that had meant so much to her was a black leather book. She opened it and found her name written in her own childish handwriting. It was filled with blank pages.

Lee found her mother's door closed. No one answered her knock, but she could feel her presence behind the door like a child hiding under a bed.

The room was bare except for a large mattress lying on the floor against the wall. Redbud was laid out on the bed under a yellow polyester coverlet with her thin hair fanned out from her face on a single pillow. She radiated the feverish, sweaty saintliness of the newly sober, illuminated by the moonlight coming through the bald window above her head.

"Mama."

"Hey, baby," she croaked.

"Where is Meredith?"

"How would I know? You're her mama." Redbud picked up a pack of cigarettes from the floor and sat up against the wall, trying to light one with a shaking hand.

Lee slapped it out of her fist, and the lighter went skidding across the floorboards. "Look at me. Meredith is missing, and I think you know where she is. So you better fucking tell me right now. I don't want any of your bullshit."

"She's missing? Oh god . . ." Redbud paled to an even lighter shade and fell back against the wall.

"Where is she?" Lee shouted.

Redbud's pained expression turned to a scowl. "Why don't you ask Belva where she is, huh? Since y'all are so close now."

"Belva is in the hospital. She had a stroke."

Redbud closed her eyes and pressed her lips together. "Oh, Mama," she said in a soft voice.

"Cliff saw someone take Meredith in the corn maze at the pumpkin patch. We don't have a description—he only saw a tall shadow."

Redbud opened her eyes and looked at Lee with newly heightened awareness. Her features became more defined, as if she was finally coming into focus.

"Two men have died. Joseph Hall and TJ Ryder, which you know about. People think Belva did it. And now Meredith is missing—" Lee started shaking again but willed herself to keep going. "And I think it has something to do with this, but I don't know how." Lee pulled the drawing of the black flower symbol from her back pocket and held it up to her again. "What does this mean? And before you start lying, there's one about three feet tall burned into your living room wall."

"Oh, baby, it ain't what you think."

"And what do I think?"

"This flower got very little to do with those bodies and Meredith." She paused. "Did you know you can't use the power of the land when you're under the influence? You gotta have a clear head. Ready to receive."

Lee wanted to choke her. "Can you just tell me what it means? Be honest and direct for once in your fucking life?"

Redbud sighed. "The flower is just a little thing I made up. After I stopped doing the work, I got kinda homesick for it. I missed the gatherings and being with people and doing something that felt special." She looked down. "I also found out if you drank some of that moonshine, you wouldn't feel so sick between fixes. It let you have a little breather, and when I was drinking it, it almost felt like I could connect with the land again. So I started having a bunch of people over like TJ and other people in town who were into the booze, or we'd go over to TJ's, and we'd make a little fire like at Belva's, and we'd get all fucked up and play witch. The brand was my idea. Thought it would make it more real for them. Didn't hurt that much when you were flying so high. But it sure as shit hurt when you came down. Or at least that's what it looked like." She paused. "There was no way in hell I was letting them burn something into *my* skin."

"Is this what I saw the other night? You made Meredith a part of this group?" Lee processed this. "Did you *brand* her?"

"How dare you ask me that. Of course not." Redbud huffed. "I didn't let anyone mess with her. I already told you, I was protecting her."

"But did this group kill Mr. Hall and TJ? Do they have Meredith?"

"No, honey, that's what I'm trying to tell you. TJ got a little carried away with it, started using that silly flower everywhere like some kinda logo. But it's nothing but a bunch of addicts and weirdos who like to get together and pretend to be witches. Your Mr. Hall loved it. He thought he was in *Macbeth* or some shit."

Even as Lee wanted to ask more questions, she needed to keep her on track. "So if they don't have Meredith, where is she? Who took her?"

Redbud was silent for a moment. "I ain't been sober in a long time, and I thought maybe my gifts had dried up." She dropped her cigarette butt into a jar of water on the floor. "They can change as you get older. You lose the ability to pull the energy from the land, but you can still guide it if a youngin is there to pull it." She coughed into her fist. "I might have held on to my gifts for longer if I'd taken better care of myself. But I can still do one thing." She pushed her sleeves up her arms. "Do you remember when we used to pass memories back and forth when you were little?"

It sounded vaguely familiar, but she couldn't be sure. "Sort of."

Redbud stretched her hand out toward Lee. "Gimme your arm."

Lee obeyed without thinking and reached out to feel her touch. Redbud took her wrist and turned it over to expose the tender, veined inside. She pressed her thumb to its center.

Lee watched as Redbud's intent face began to pulse with Lee's own heartbeat, and then the walls and the floor were beating, the room dissolving around her with each pulse until she lost all sense of self.

# TWENTY-TWO

## Redbud

Redbud pierced the flesh of the left boot with a nail, driving it raggedly through the thick toe and then richly through the sole. When the nail hit wood, she wrapped both palms around the handle of the hammer and put all her dread into it, securing the boot firmly to the floor. She repeated the same process with the right.

Opaline watched from above where she lay across the bed with a book propped against the pillow. Redbud replaced the tattered bed skirt and hid the boots from view.

"Are you gonna lay around like that all day?"

Her daughter stretched out further and allowed her head, then her limbs, then her whole body to curl off the edge of the bed onto the floor, collapsing in a heap.

"Graceful." Redbud waited for signs of life. "I have a late shift tonight. I want you to call me when Daddy gets home. Luann says they end at five today."

Opaline stayed motionless on the floor.

"I am asking you a question, which requires acknowledgment and some kinda response."

Opaline flipped on her back and held her middle. "Request acknowledged. Response affirmative."

Redbud smiled to herself. "I made some chicken and dumplings for tonight."

"Acknowledged and appreciated."

"I aims to please."

Opaline still lay there, holding her stomach.

"Are you feeling okay?"

"It feels like snakes are wrestling inside my belly." She clutched her stomach tighter and groaned.

"You need some chamomile syrup?"

"I took some. It's not a big deal. I shall live to see another day." She pantomimed putting on a brave face.

"My fearless little girl." Redbud gazed out the window and saw that it was raining in the stark autumn sunshine. "Looks like the devil is beating his wife again."

She threw her navy-blue apron with WADE's embroidered on the front over her arm, dropped a buckeye nut in her pocket from the bowl by the door, and got into a maroon station wagon idling in the dirt in front of the house. She lit a cigarette for Beverly in the driver's seat, and one for herself, and they took off with a manicured hand dangling out the window on each side.

• • •

At seven p.m., Redbud wiped the ham juice from her hands and picked up the wall telephone at the deli. Opaline answered on the second ring and told her he wasn't there. Redbud fingered the buckeye in her pocket, running her thumb first over its smooth edges, then grinding it over the rough patch at the top.

Half an hour later, she arrived back at home. She called out with false joy as she came through the door, hoping to hear a deep, gravelly reply. Instead, she heard her daughter's cries.

"Mama!"

Redbud ran to their only bathroom and threw open the door. Opaline was huddled in the bathtub with her legs up to her chest and her arms wrapped around her knees. A curl of red snaked from underneath her.

"Did you cut yourself?"

"No. Unless I cut my you-know-what."

"Oh, honey." Redbud's heart snagged. She wasn't ready for this yet. She got to her knees and kneeled next to the tub. "You're okay. This is normal. It's your time of the month."

"This is *normal?*"

"It's a part of your baby-making machinery. When you bleed, your body is telling you you're not pregnant."

Opaline's grimace deepened. *"Pregnant?"*

"Not that you need to worry about being pregnant, but that's what it means."

"Okay . . ." Opaline thought about it for a minute. "So how do we get it to stop?"

"You can't make it stop. It's gotta flow until it's done. It'll be over in a few days or so."

Redbud could see her daughter's marvelous brain burning through all that this implied.

"Do I use a Band-Aid to keep it from bleeding into my pants?"

"God, no. Well, not exactly." She opened the cabinet under the sink and took out a box. "These are pads. You pull off the paper on the back and stick it in your underwear like this." She pulled one out and demonstrated using Opaline's underwear from the floor.

Opaline watched with mild interest while her wheels still turned. "Is it gonna happen again?"

"I'm afraid so, baby. Every month."

*"Every month* for the rest of my life?"

"No, it'll stop in your fifties or somewhere around there."

"So, for one week every month for the next forty years of my life, I have to walk around bleeding into a little diaper?"

"I'm afraid so. It's not that bad once you get used to it."

Opaline scoffed.

"It ain't all bad. You'll get your black book now."

Her sullen expression brightened.

Redbud eyed the small, naked body of her daughter, still crouched in the bath gone cold. "Your tummy still hurting?"

"Yes." But she didn't seem to register it. Her eyes were distant and glowing, no doubt imagining what she would put in her black book.

"All right. Dry off and get into your jammies, and I'll make you a black cohosh tea. It'll fix you right up."

.   .   .

At two a.m., Redbud awoke on the couch with a jelly jar of bourbon in her hand. A truck with no muffler rumbled outside the windows, illuminating the house. She turned on the lamp as Hank came through the door. She expected him to be drunk, but his eyes were clear. He smirked to himself as if recalling a fond memory.

A cloud of something sweet hovered around him—honey, lemon, peppermint—and just the smallest hint of salted blood. It reminded her of the mixture she put in the cornbread she made when the weather turned warm in April and all she wanted was for Hank to chase her around the house.

He went to the kitchen for a glass of water without a word or glance in her direction. She followed and wrapped her arms around his chest from behind in the dim light. He recoiled from her touch as if burned. When she forced him to look at her, his eyes were filled with an indifference reserved for strangers. He mumbled he was tired and walked out of the kitchen. She could hear him humming in the bathroom as he brushed his teeth.

Redbud took his truck keys from the counter and went out to the car. She opened the driver's side and felt around under the seat. In between the carpet fuzz and the empty bottles, her fingers curled around something thin and smooth. She pulled it out and held it up to the dim bulb. A turkey bone.

Redbud snapped the bone in half and threw the pieces into the grass.

On the passenger seat, shining in the overhead light, she found a long, curling auburn hair. Nothing like Redbud or Opaline's coal-black locks. She plucked it from the fabric and walked it to the house where she put it in an old peanut butter jar and hid it in the laundry room.

She went to the bedroom, where Hank was already snoring peacefully and checked under the bed. The boots were still there, bolted to the floor. She tiptoed out to Opaline's room and crawled in next to her. Redbud lay there for a long while and allowed the hollow calm inside her to fill with that sick, heartbroke dread. She stayed perfectly still, afraid it would seep out and into Opaline if she moved even a muscle.

·   ·   ·

The next morning, Redbud called Belva.

"Mama, I need Opaline to stay with you tonight."

"That's fine. What's going on?"

"Hank and I need some time to ourselves."

"That sounds *ro-mantic*."

"Oh, you know Hank. He's a goddamn dreamboat. Also, Opaline got her period."

"Well praise be. I knew it. I have everything ready. I dreamt about it two nights ago."

"Why didn't you warn me?"

"I called and left a message, but you never called me back."

Redbud knew she was right. She'd been so preoccupied with Hank lately that she'd barely thought of anything else. "All right. We'll come by before supper."

Around three p.m., Redbud and Opaline arrived on foot at Belva's cabin. They let themselves into the small hot kitchen smelling of burnt butter and the herbed dust thrown around by the old box fan in the corner. Redbud noticed a fresh black leather-bound book sitting on the counter.

Belva stepped out of the back with her apron on, and Opaline gave her a full-armed hug with an earnestness she reserved solely for Belva.

"Rascal."

"Grandma Mama."

"I hear you've undergone the first big change of life. Congratulations."

"Thank you. I feel like I'm in a horror movie."

Belva and Redbud laughed. "It ain't all bad, honey." She picked up the new black book and set it in front of her. "This is yours to write down all of your weird thoughts and ideas and recipes and anything else you want." She opened it to the first page. "Go ahead and write your name in it."

Redbud moved to leave the kitchen, but Belva caught her by the arm. "Aren't you gonna stay for a bit? I thought we would show her together." She smiled hopefully at her daughter.

Redbud wanted to be there for this, but she had too much to prepare for later. She couldn't spare another moment. "I know, I'm sorry, Mama. I got stuff I need to do. We can show her tomorrow when you drop her off, okay?"

Belva nodded and patted her arm before turning her attention back to Opaline.

Redbud swallowed her guilt and left them to their work, taking a basket from the pile beside the door out to the garden.

She moved up and down its rows, plucking petals and berries with the swiftness of intention. With one eye trained on the house, she snapped a thorn from a dark tangle that looked dead until you got up close and saw that its decay was mere camouflage. The plant's gray limbs were as lush as any of the verdant vines that surrounded it.

When she was done, she laid a cheesecloth over the top of the basket and went back inside to where Belva and Opaline had moved to the workshop. Redbud kissed the top of her daughter's head and told her to have fun, but she was engrossed in reading an entry from Belva's black book and she only nodded in response.

As Redbud left the property, she spotted a buzzard looming overhead, and she smiled to herself; her work would be successful tonight.

. . .

The old hunting cabin sat glowing in the trees with a pile of trucks and rusty sedans parked in front. They arrived in their various forms: Beverly in her nylon dress and dollar-store pearls, Luann still in her jeans from laying down highway asphalt, Billy in his Carhartt and flannel. Only Redbud, who greeted them as they came into the cabin, seemed to know how to truly dress for the occasion, with her midnight-blue sweater and lipstick the color of the blood that pulsed in her cheeks.

Belva and the other elders were absent from the small group. Only fresh faces shone in the moonlight as they stepped into the cabin.

Inside, the modest kitchen was covered in casserole trays and pitchers of tea. A pot of chicken and dumplings bubbled on the stove. The cabin, usually given to odors of sweat, cedar, and carcasses of hunts past, now yielded to the perfume and cigarette smoke and prepared food smell of the gathering.

Eventually the flurry of arrival began to subside, and Redbud led them out to the backyard, where a fire blazed. They dragged chairs out from the house and laid down blankets in the dirt while they murmured in low voices and gathered around the flames.

Once they were settled, Redbud pulled out a red suitcase, placed both hands on the bronze clasps, and released them. Inside the musty, satin-lined interior was a large glass canning jar filled with one auburn hair curled in a layer of gray powder and a black leather book. She pulled both out and set them on the ground in front of her. Then she took off her shoes and stood in a wide, powerful stance with her bare feet planted firmly on the ground.

When she looked up, all conversation ceased and all eyes turned to her.

"Welcome, y'all. I appreciate you coming out here tonight, and keeping it quiet. We are doing something a little special this time, and I wanted only my true-blues to join."

She nodded at them and took a deep breath.

"My husband is a handsome man. He likes to drink. I know where that leads."

There were murmurs of agreement.

"But lately, I have noticed a change. This is no one-night fling. He may think it's love, but I can smell meddling from a mile off. Someone has put a love charm on my husband."

Redbud scanned their faces, looking for an indication that she might be among them, but she only found devoted eyes.

"And I want him back."

Redbud opened the black book to a page marked by a single black ribbon.

"I will not stand by while a woman draws from the power to break my family apart."

Luann called out an "amen," and Billy hollered a "hell yeah."

"I do not know who this woman is, and I do not care to know. I only seek to banish her from our life."

Redbud started to hum, and every person joined in harmony, growing louder.

She shook the jar vigorously and passed it to the next woman, who shook it hard and passed it to the next. She picked up the black book and read out the words written there. She allowed the intention of it to fill her completely; this keening need to find the diseased limb and cut it off at the root.

The wind picked up and clouds rolled in front of the moon, so that there was only the fire to guide them.

When the jar returned to her, she crouched over a small hole and laid the jar in it. Then she replaced the dirt and patted it down.

She took out her pocketknife and dug its blade into her palm. She squeezed her hand over the dirt mound and blood streamed down into it. She felt no pain. Only the sear of power gliding through her.

Redbud's speech became a chant, and the rest joined in, flinging the words into the fire so that it jerked and smoked.

"*I want to* cut *Hank's whore out of my life. I want to* cut *Hank's whore out of my life.*"

Eventually, their voices began to slow, and then the hum finally died with one resounding *amen*. They fell back into the dirt, laughing hysterically, sweat-dewed, like women who have finally, gloriously come.

In the thick of their joy, Redbud noticed what seemed like a shadow lurking just outside the group. Though it had no discernible face, it was inexplicably familiar. It seemed to be studying her.

She scanned the faces of those around her, but no one registered its presence. The shadow moved fluidly through the gathering, giving them chills as it sliced a path between them. When it brushed against Redbud, a cold like snowmelt took the breath from her lungs.

At the edge of the clearing, the shadow looked back at Redbud once again before disappearing into the dark.

It did not feel like a farewell.

The group was giddy and starving as they filed into the cabin, and they dove into the meats and casseroles and cobblers without decorum. Luann lugged in a large jug filled with hard apple cider and filled any glass thrust her way. They leaned shoulder to shoulder and put their arms around one another with the unabashed familiarity of children. Once they were stuffed, they cleaned the backyard and cabin together, as one organism.

Redbud and Beverly were the last to leave. As they thanked Billy for letting them use his place, Redbud suddenly felt faint. She leaned against the front railing and tried to steady herself, but the world blurred and tilted further. Billy helped her to Beverly's car, and she collapsed onto the seat and lost consciousness.

· · ·

The next morning, Redbud woke to a knock at the door. Beverly must have brought her inside and put her to bed. She got up unsteadily, threw on her old robe, and went to the door, expecting to see Belva with Opaline in tow.

It was the sheriff, Billy, and Belva. No Opaline. They told her to sit down.

The bridge out by Bell's Fork had collapsed that morning. There'd been a whole line of cars backed up from the train crossing, waiting for it to pass. They found both Hank and her sister Ruby Jo in the water. They were in the same car.

The news detonated inside Redbud like a nuclear bomb. Everything suspended in time as ash. She saw the shadow from the ritual before her, moving off into the night to perform its mission of cutting Hank's mistress out of her life. *Ruby Jo.*

The guilt of it couldn't be felt then; it only whistled through her like a poisonous gas hovering over land that had already been obliterated. There was nothing for it to attack. But there would be, once the shock wore off.

Belva's thick arms encircled her, and Redbud recoiled. Here was the woman from whom she'd learned all of this. This evil gift that sent the man she loved and her own sister to their deaths.

She would never let that happen to Opaline. She would grow up without this curse.

Redbud asked Belva to leave her house and never come back, but Belva was undeterred; she thought it was only the grief talking. She did not know of the vow Redbud had just made to herself and her daughter. Opaline would avoid obliteration. She would be able to choose her path.

.    .    .

That night, after Redbud was certain everyone was asleep, she took the red suitcase and walked to the fire pit away from the house. Billy had built a fire that evening, and there was still a hint of pink in the coals. She poked it a bit, and the coals began to glow more fiercely. She took the black book out of the suitcase and tore a sheet out of the back, balled it up, and watched it catch fire. She placed one palm on the cover of the book and felt all that it contained.

When she was ready, she set it in front of the fire and pushed it into the flames.

# TWENTY-THREE

## LEE

L ee returned to herself.

At first, all she could feel was the warm thumb on her pulse, but then the bare room rose up around her, and there was her mother's older, ashen face, studying her closely. Lee tried to speak, but she didn't have the words. Part of her was still caught in that memory and unable to process what she just witnessed.

"Lee, can you hear me?"

Lee strained to speak again, but nothing came out. She nodded her head.

"Good. Don't force it. It'll take you a moment to straighten out." Redbud helped Lee sit up so that she was leaning against the wall next to her. "I know it don't mean anything now, but I never meant for anyone to get hurt. I thought the hex would run the lady out of town, and things would go back to normal." She scratched at her arms. "Did you see the shadow at the gathering?"

Lee nodded.

"It made that bridge collapse so that Hank and his mistress would get killed." Her voice cracked, and she struggled to continue. "Ruby Jo. He was sleeping with my own sister, and I had no idea. I didn't even know Ruby Jo could make a love charm. It was awful of them, but I never wanted anyone to die." Her face crumpled.

"That *thing* is still out there somewhere. It's been tormenting me since the day I made it. It takes my desires and twists them until they bleed."

Lee looked at her, bewildered.

"Ever since that night at Billy's cabin, when I want something real bad, it'll happen in the most terrible way."

Lee saw Cliff in front of her, telling her about the figure he saw in their bedroom the night the bat got in, and out the window the night of Mr. Hall's murder, and in the woods at the edge of the stadium. Telling her in the dusky light of the maze that a shadow had taken Meredith.

Lee finally found her voice. "You wanted Meredith for yourself."

"Yes."

"And TJ?"

"I wanted to get clean so bad. But while he was around, it was hard. He's been the only one who will sell to me for a while. I owe a lot of money to people."

"And Mr. Hall?"

"TJ told me about him getting caught at a party with his niece. I was scared for Meredith." She seemed like she wanted to say more, but she stopped.

"And?"

"And I wanted to hurt Belva for keeping me from y'all. Make you scared of her. I think that's why it dumped the body in her woods."

"Does Belva know you made the bridge collapse? Does she know about the shadow?"

"She knows that I abused the work and that something ugly came out of it. But we've never talked about it. I didn't give her the chance. If she had been there that night, maybe things would have been different. I was real full of myself back then. Didn't even give an offering to the spirits. I performed it in secret, because I knew she would have stopped me. The work didn't fit the crime. No one was there to guide the power, and it got all twisted." She looked off to the side, contemplating another life, then shook it off. "It don't matter now. Can't change the past. I kept you away from her and all that power, so you would never make the same mistakes."

Lee put her hand over her mother's frail and shaking one.

"I wanted to die after Hank and Ruby Jo did. The guilt was in every part of me. I imagined vomiting myself up and leaving nothing behind. The only time I didn't feel that way was on my pain pills—"

"I know the rest." Lee pulled her hand away and attempted to assimilate this information into her new reality, overriding every memory. But she didn't have time to process this now. Her daughter was in danger. "You have to help me find Meredith. Where would this thing take her?"

"I—I have no idea."

Lee took her mother roughly by the shoulders. "Think. Fucking think about it for a second. Where?"

Redbud's eyes shone with tears. It was a defense mechanism she had used often when Lee was a kid and she forced her to take responsibility. "I'm sorry . . . I don't know . . ."

"That's not good enough!" Lee hit the bed with her fist. "Can't you use magic?"

Redbud's voice was shaky as she said, "I tried a few years back. There was this doctor who was still prescribing pain pills even though we knew they were dangerous by then. I wanted him to feel the real pain, the shit caused by this stuff." Her eyes dried as she recounted the memory.

"The next week, his teenage daughter died of an accidental overdose. Her first time." She gripped Lee's wrists hard. "I knew it was the shadow. I had to find it before it hurt more people. I checked into a treatment center with my last credit card. When I was clean, I wrote my first spell in years, calling the bastard back to me so I could get rid of him. I convinced some of the women in my group therapy to meet me out back one night. I stole some matches and built a little fire and told the girls what to do. I said the spell, but the power didn't come, and the shadow didn't either." She looked at her hands. "I can't do it no more."

Lee stood up and paced the room. "But you were in a rehab with junkies who'd never done magic before. Of course it didn't work. We just need to do it the right way."

"You're not listening. I'm telling you: I can't."

Lee had forgotten how fatalist this version of her mother could be. "What if we re-created the exact spell you performed to create it?"

"Honey, I don't remember most of the words, and my book is gone. What you saw is all I have."

Lee recalled the way the words were muffled by the hum in the memory. "But I need you to do this. We have to find her. Why can't you just get your shit together and figure it out?"

"I'm sorry. I wish I could."

"Fine. *I'll* figure it out. Show me again." Lee thrust her hand out. Redbud stared at it, then shakily pressed her thumb to her wrist.

•   •   •

There was an unfamiliar car in the driveway when Lee pulled up to Belva's cabin around three a.m. A faceless, shiny rental with out-of-state plates and tinted windows that she strained to peer through in the darkness. She sat in her car as the oxygen depleted and wondered what she should do. Then the door opened, and she saw how thoroughly fucked she was.

Cooper stood in front of her car with his hands in his pockets, and she took a moment to look him over with inches of steel between them. When she'd asked the police to inform him about Meredith, she knew his arrival was inevitable. But it was still jarring to see him.

She got out and walked to the cabin without acknowledging him, and he followed her.

"Lee. What the fuck."

"Can I help you?"

He closed the gap quickly, getting just close enough that he could reach out and grab her if he wanted to.

"Don't fuck with me, Lee. My daughter is missing, and I demand to know what is going on."

The fear of what he thought of her that had at first excited her, and then made her feel trapped and worthless, began to worm its way inside of her again. But this time it only emboldened her. Without sleep or food, her system now ran on pure fear. She shoveled it into her furnace, and the flames licked higher.

"Ask the police."

"I just came from the station, and they clearly have no idea what they're doing."

Lee exhaled and looked out over the night-covered mountains, contemplating her next move. Their arguments had always been exercises in strategy; some days, they had been her only mental stimulation. She flipped through the possibilities in her mind and landed on *the bare truth*. "There is a shadow creature loose in the mountains, and we think it snatched her in the corn maze. If you'll leave me alone, I can figure out how to get her back." She turned toward the house, and he lunged at her, wrenching her arm back so that she was facing him.

"You are a fucking *freak*. The biggest regret of my life is letting our children anywhere near you. You've screwed them up and turned them against me, and now my daughter is probably lying in a ditch somewhere."

Lee pulled her arm out of his grasp. "I don't have to listen to you anymore."

He continued to charge ahead, refusing to acknowledge her words. "Where's Cliff? I want to talk to him about what he saw."

"He saw a shadow monster. And he's at my uncle's cabin, where he'll be safe."

"I'm not going to let my son stay with some redneck Trumper in the middle of the woods where another hillbilly psychopath can kidnap him. Give me the address. I'm taking him to my hotel in Cradleburg."

"I don't have to do what you say."

"I have a lawyer filing with the court right now for custody. And I hired a private investigator to find Meredith."

"You'll take my children over my cold, dead body. Now get off my property." She left him standing in the driveway as she went into the house and locked the door. She leaned back against it and sank to the floor. There were footsteps on the old porch floorboards and then hard bangs on the door that she could feel through the wood against her skull. She left her head there, closing her eyes to feel the pain all the way to her teeth. Then, the banging stopped. She heard a car start, and then the motor sound receded into the distance.

The adrenaline dissipated, and she was left shaking in a cold sweat. She sat against the door and looked around at the empty house. In this new solitude, she could behave with a brazenness that she hadn't known since she was a child, left alone for hours or days while her mom was elsewhere. Even in the long stretches she'd spent alone in her life with Cooper, she'd always felt him watching her. She crawled over to her suitcase, unearthed the moonshine jar from beneath her clothes, and took a few shaky sips on the floor.

When she'd descended to that warm place, she took out the notes she'd made in her empty black book. It was a list of every detail her mother remembered from the ritual. The jar had been filled with an assortment of plants, dried scotch bonnet, powdered spider, a single bullet. She pondered if one of Ruby Jo's hairs would be essential to the mixture. She wasn't sure how she would procure one. There were also fragments of phrases that would need to be made into a spell somehow. She felt perched at the beginning of a new subject in school, a feeling she used to love. But this was different than history or philosophy; she couldn't discern how the pieces fit together. Her inability to understand it made her sick.

·   ·   ·

She walked the rows of the garden, looking for each plant she'd watched her mother pluck. That part of her memory was more clear, and she felt somewhat confident she could re-create the herbal mixture from the jar as long as the plants were still there.

The alternating heat waves and cold snaps had left the plants drooping and weary. Lee imagined the garden withering to a dry tangle without

Belva to care for it. A fresh wave of grief washed over her, and she could feel the shaking coming back. Her body wasn't large enough to hold the panic over her daughter and the grief for her grandmother. She needed to focus on her mission; it would somehow save them all.

She found the sinister gray plant coiled up close to the ground like a snake waiting to strike. It looked like it hadn't been tended to in years, but it had somehow persisted of its own will. When she snapped a stalk with the garden shears, a strawberry oil dripped from the stump.

And then there was Belva's black book. It was her only source of information about writing spells with Belva in limbo and her mother of no use. She needed it to finish the spell, but after an hour of searching, she still hadn't found it.

Lee closed her eyes and tried to remember that day from her own perspective, now forever altered by her mother's memory. Belva's black book had been on the counter along with Lee's new one when her mother dropped her off.

Belva had run through a history of the Buck bloodline, stretching back to the Cherokee who lived in these mountains and discovered the power of the land in its plants and trees, creating rituals to honor and harness it. The Scotch-Irish arrived, and then Africans were kidnapped and brought here against their will, and they came with their own beliefs and rituals and they had babies together, and the traditions mingled, becoming folk medicine and charms. While some Cherokee still lived in the mountains, most were forcibly driven out in the genocide perpetrated by the government. Belva said they had lost a direct connection to these ancestral cultures, but they lived on in what they practiced.

Their descendants became healers, delivering babies and alleviating pain and disease. And in the late hours, when something was out of balance in the community and couldn't be fixed by daylight, the Bucks and their friends would meet in the trees and perform rituals under the moon.

Lee was the newest member of this line. She would inherit everything

Belva and Redbud knew, and she would grow up to be powerful like her mother.

Belva then flipped through her black book and showed Lee that you could take inspiration from anywhere to craft a recipe—what she called a spell. There were diary entries and poems she'd written when she first fell in love with Leroy, and she'd used them to create a love recipe.

They went outside to her hives, and Lee watched as Belva whispered her love charm to the bees as she tended to them. The bees' buzz softened and synchronized until it was like a full-throated sigh enveloping Lee. At Belva's urging, she reached out and swept her finger across a raw, dripping honeycomb and licked it. She had yet to be in love, so all she tasted was her grandmother's first: a young Leroy walking toward her in waist-high grass with sunshine brightening his outline. Belva explained that these love-drunk bees fed only on the blossoms of her garden, passing the land's energy back and forth between them. It was the secret to the strength of her potions.

Then they came back inside, and it was time to make dinner. They cleaned up all the plant clippings, Lee put her new book by the front door so she wouldn't forget it, and . . . Belva showed her how to create a hiding place for her book so that it would be safe.

Lee strained to remember as she retraced their steps into Belva's bedroom. She'd already searched every inch of the room, including a wooden trunk that continued to pulse with significance in her mind but had only contained a pile of itchy afghans.

She opened it again and shook each blanket out to make sure the book wasn't hiding in the folds. As she gazed at the bottom of the trunk, part of it came back to her. A flash of Belva joking that Leroy had taught her one useful thing: how to hide booze from the po-lice.

She ran her palm over the smooth wood of the bottom and noticed a slight hole in the perimeter where the wood didn't quite meet at the seam. She put her pinkie finger into the hole, hooked it, and pulled up. It didn't move. She pulled harder and more desperately until it finally released.

She pried the entire piece up to reveal a false bottom compartment like a moonshine hollow in a Ford Coupe.

But it was empty, with only dust collecting in a perfect square around where a book used to sit. Lee swore loudly and threw the wood against the wall.

Without cleaning up the room, she walked back out into the hallway and found herself face-to-face with the door to Meredith and Cliff's room. She imagined them behind it, sleeping or ignoring her, and for a moment she enjoyed the feeling of them being safe in such a small, confined space. She opened the door, and the warmth dropped out of her.

The cots stood empty, with Cliff's blanket lying flat and tucked around the edges. Meredith's blanket was balled up and half hanging onto the floor. Lee lay down on her bed and pulled the blanket up to her chest. She leaned her head to the side and inhaled the cotton of the pillowcase. It still had the mothball-and-butter smell of Belva's house, but there was a bit of Meredith poking through: a mix of cheap shampoo and the cornflake scent she'd had since she was a toddler.

Lee instinctively reached her arm over the side of the cot and felt underneath for the book Meredith had been reading. She felt a stack of smaller books perched on top of something large and smooth and too heavy to pick up with one hand. Lee knelt down in front of the cot and pried the heavy object from underneath the pile. It was Belva's black book.

They had kept this secret from her, and no one was there to absorb her disapproval.

With her chest aching, she picked up the book, turned on the golden light of the lamp, and began to read.

# TWENTY-FOUR

**W**ell I'll be damned." Lee heard Luann suck on a cigarette through the phone.

"I know."

"I had no idea it went that far. I knew something bad happened at Billy's cabin that night . . . but I didn't know this."

"I've been working on piecing the spell back together. Do you remember any of the words from that night?"

Luann exhaled hard through the phone. "Damn. I wish I could, honey, but that was thirty years ago. All I remember was being at Billy's and this weird kind of feeling but that's it. I'm sorry."

"That's okay. Mama's coming to stay with me. I don't want her to relapse. Who knows how that would affect whatever has Meredith."

"You can put her in our room. I'm gonna keep staying with my friend so I can be closer to Belva."

"Thanks. I think I've got the jar mix right, at least. Once I figure out the words, we should be ready. We'll need some people to join."

"You'll need *a lot* of people. As many as we can convince to do it. It's gonna be tough."

"What about Belva's ladies? They'll come, right?"

"I don't know, darlin'. You ain't Belva, and people are spooked after the murders. Beverly only ever came so she could be in people's business. I don't think you can count on her. Maybe Linda. But everyone knows Belva is in the hospital, and not one of them has called me to see how she is."

"What about all the people Belva has helped over the years?"

Luann sucked her teeth. "It ain't that easy. When she's treating their

shingles, she's a saint. But when folks need someone to blame for something they don't understand, she becomes a witch."

Lee hoped this wasn't entirely true. She couldn't do this on her own.
"God, I wish she was here. I miss her."

"Me, too."

"How is she doing?"

"I can still feel her there, but she's weak. She doesn't do well when
she spends this much time away from the land. It's why we never go
anywhere. She just gets irritated and mean and who wants to deal with
that?"

Imagining a pissed-off Belva just brought the loss more into focus. The
wave threatened to overtake her once more. "What if we never get to talk
again? What if this is it?" She regretted saying it out loud, like she was
calling it into being.

"I have a hard time believing this is how it all ends."

Lee could hear the bone-deep exhaustion in Luann's voice. "How are
*you* doing?"

"Oh. I'm fine. You don't worry about us. Just find your girl."

"Okay. Can I count on you to come, when it's ready?"

"I'll be there. And I'll see who else I can corral. I've got some favors I
can call in."

Lee hung up and checked her phone to see if Kimmie had texted back
from her latest number. All of Lee's voicemails and texts explaining what
really happened to TJ had gone unanswered.

There was nothing from Kimmie, but there were three voicemails from
Cooper and one from his lawyer. She listened to the first from Cooper.
His PI had dug up rumors that Lee was involved in a string of occult murders. His delivery was smug, and she deleted it and the next two without
listening. The one from his lawyer was curt. They were calling an emer-
gency custody hearing regarding the safety of Radcliff Carnell, and she
was required to be in court at nine a.m. Monday morning. It took her a

moment to remember what day it was; everything had been a blur since Meredith was taken. It was Sunday.

She wondered at the consequences of pretending none of these people existed, at least until she got her daughter back. Once that happened, she could face everything else. But there wasn't space inside of her right then.

.    .    .

Reading Belva's black book was one of the most intimate things Lee had ever done, like taking a step inside Belva's internal landscape and walking around. It was comforting to imagine a younger Belva writing in the book, muscled and glowing with health like a girl on a butter box.

Lee remembered that many of the early spells were ones passed down through the family. Belva learned them from her grandmother Pallie, who learned them from hers, and so on. They were simple, ancient remedies for universal problems. Lee imagined generations of people suffering from the same pain and conjuring remedies from the land to ease it. This legacy felt like the missing piece of something she'd been subconsciously searching for, though whether she could access it was still unclear.

As she flipped through the pages, new spells cropped up—ones that Belva invented herself. Mixed in with these spells were diary entries and observations about the weather and the nature around her. Lee could see the evolution of a new spell through the diary entries that served as inspiration, then the need arising, and the formation of it through notes about plants and ideas for wording. Finally, there was the spell itself, which Belva liked to enshrine on its own page. The spoken words of a spell took many forms—they could be like poems, or stories, or sometimes they were merely Bible verses. Belva's spells were more intricate and imaginative than the older ones, and sometimes they used more modern materials like Dr Pepper and pantyhose that she had lying around. This was a cornerstone of the work—you could make magic with whatever you had, no matter how meager.

*I want to* cut *Hank's whore out of my life. I want to* cut *Hank's whore out of my life.*

Redbud had said it over and over in the ritual in her memory. But that was all she could remember of the spell. The rest was just marshmallow noise drowned out by the hum. Judging from Belva's spells, Lee believed Redbud had told her love story with Hank, and she had a feeling that it was partly this potent expression of heartbreak that had formed the shadow. The creature was an extension of Redbud, carrying out her most painful, shame-filled desires and feeding off the suffering that it created.

Lee would put out a little plate of pain for it, like a slab of ground chicken parts for a barn cat.

Lee heard her mother slam something against the counter and swear loudly in the kitchen. She'd showed up a few hours ago and hadn't stopped fidgeting since she got there. Lee walked out to find her hunched over the cutting board with her finger in her mouth. She'd been resistant at first to the notion of staying at the cabin, but she'd settled in quickly. She'd been born here, right in the garden like Kimmie's baby, and she'd been raised within its walls.

"What are you doing?"

"I'm trying to make lunch but these damn knives are duller than a bag of hammers."

Redbud had gone through the worst of the detox, but the effects lingered in the dark circles under her eyes, her bloodless face, her petulant mood. Lee remembered her withdrawal stages well; she'd tried to get clean a few times when Lee was in high school.

Lee led Redbud into the bathroom and ran her shaking finger under the cold water. She dried it and applied a few dabs from a jar marked "for cuts" she found in the cabinet and wrapped a small bandage around it. Time melted as she once again became the teenager who took care of her mother. There was more comfort than anger in it this time.

Redbud avoided Lee's eyes as she patched her up. "I used to cut Billy's hair in here, and then he would do my makeup. He liked experimenting with the colors and using the brushes. He said it was like painting."

"Sounds like you remember more than you think, Mama."

Redbud acted like she hadn't heard her. She was lost in a past life.

"There's something I need your help with. I need to know more about you and Daddy. The important emotional moments, from beginning to end, that capture the arc of your story. I need it for the spell."

Redbud's expression went from dreamy to bitter, and she pulled her finger out of Lee's hand. "I've done a lot to forget about those things."

"But Ma—"

"Look, you know I want to help. But I've told you. I don't got it."

"What if you show me your memories? It might be easier that way."

"I can't show you anything that ain't there." She left the bathroom, and Lee followed her out.

"Meredith's life is at stake here. Every moment that goes by is another one that she's in danger. I need you to help me for once in your goddamn life."

"Don't you think I would if I could? It kills me that Meredith is out there somewhere, and I had something to do with it. I'd do anything to bring her back." Redbud searched around her purse and pulled a pack of cigarettes from it.

Lee took a deep breath. "What if we go somewhere you used to spend time together? Does that ever trigger memories? Like just now with the bathroom and Billy?"

"It won't work. I got too many bad memories from those places now. *That's* what I remember." Redbud went into Belva and Luann's room and shut the door behind her.

Lee took stock of what she had: Mama's story of how they first met in high school and a handful of early memories from before things started to break down.

Lee's parents were the first people to show her the woods and the magic of wandering through them without a plan. Her father would help her find rocks that looked like rough jewels, and her mother would show her things like how to drink the nectar from a honeysuckle bud.

When the sun dipped below the tree line, Redbud would gather her hair up in a fat scrunchie and put a Fleetwood Mac record on. Lee would sit on the kitchen counter, and Redbud would throw something together from the fridge with a sway in her hips. She never had a lot to work with, and she wasn't the best cook, but she was resourceful. Macaroni and cheese laid between slices of bread like tuna salad. Pancakes dotted with the vegetables from Belva's garden. Daddy would swoop in from work and swivel his hips to the final track before disappearing to the bar, or a friend's. After Lee was asleep, Redbud would do her work, and Lee only ever caught glimpses of it. A flicker of candlelight. A whiff of burnt hair. This was how she remembered it, at least. She didn't have a sibling to tell her she was wrong. She was young enough that she didn't notice whatever stood in the periphery, waiting to pull them under.

When she looked at pictures of them in the album Lee found in Belva's storage room, she realized how young they were; her mother was only sixteen when she had her. He was eighteen. Their skin was so luminous that it washed out the pictures, the light blinding the viewer. Daddy had the kind of face that was so beautiful you couldn't help but stare at it. Even when it was glazed from drinking or contorted with anger, you kept gawking to behold the tragedy of his features. You couldn't look away.

Mama wasn't *beautiful* in that easy way. She had a beauty that couldn't be caught in a static image. It wasn't her mouth that you admired, but the way it spread after telling her own joke. The sweep of her arms when she was commanding a room. The narrowing of her olive eyes when she was about to take someone down.

It didn't feel like very much, but there was genuine emotion and love in these memories. She hoped it would be enough joy to show the loss. She had plenty of memories of the falling apart.

Scarcity was a part of the tradition. You made do with what you had.

# TWENTY-FIVE

That evening, Lee went looking for more people to join the ritual.

Dreama's new restaurant looked like a hipster Cracker Barrel. The deep front porch was outfitted with rocking chairs and mid-century modern side tables, and "Ruby Jo's Homeplace" blazed in neon above the entrance in slick hot pink. Inside, the open, high-ceilinged room had a rustic wood-burning fireplace, and the walls were filled with illuminated canning jars and quilts in brightly colored modern geometric designs.

A pretty young woman wearing a low-cut prairie dress with puff sleeves stood behind a wooden table at the front affixed with iPads on stands.

"I'm here for the church fundraiser." Lee showed her the ticket confirmation on her phone.

"Amazing. I'll take you to our private gathering place."

They snaked their way through the dining room to a separate room in the back where a blue banner with WELCOME ALTITUDES hung. The fundraiser invitation said they were rebranding the church, and research showed that people responded to a name that spoke to the way church could help you maximize yourself and *ascend* as opposed to the idea of worship.

A bar station and a buffet were set up along the wall to the right, and people were talking in clusters with drinks in their hands. A small chalkboard propped up next to the bartender advertised a "moonshine mojito" and a "crawdad tempura."

She looked around the room, attempting to seem inviting and pleasant. Instead, she was met with furtive stares. The partygoers whispered to one another and instinctively inched farther away from where she stood. A few eyed the exit. Lee's plan had been to mingle and recruit a few new friends to join a gathering in the middle of the night on a piece of land where a body had been found. But now she saw the fantasy of it. She'd been living outside of reality since Meredith was taken.

She downshifted to Plan B and searched for Dreama in the clusters. Her clones huddled in the corner whispering, but Lee didn't see her among them. Lee felt a hand on her arm, and it was Belva's friend Beverly looking mournfully up at her.

"I was so sorry to hear about Belva and your daughter, honey."

"Thanks. I'm surprised to see you here. I thought you were in favor of keeping the old church."

"I am, I am. But I had to see this place for myself. My restaurant hasn't been doing very well. Everyone wants to come here now. I have to admit it's pretty, though I don't care much for the food." She dipped a spoon into a purple syrup covering what looked like steak and pulled it up, allowing it to drip back down on the plate. "Have you heard Dreama and her husband are gonna franchise—"

Lee cut her off. "Have you heard from Luann? We're having a gathering, and we need all the help we can get. It's to find my daughter—"

"I heard from her. Honey, you know I want to help, but my husband won't let me. I got called in to the police station last time. Can't risk it."

"You know that's all bullshit. I need you. What if *your* daughter went missing?"

"I'm so sorry." Beverly took a few steps away from Lee and set her plate down on one of the high-top tables. "I gotta get going. Give Belva and Luann my love."

As Lee watched her walk away, Dreama came out of a door toward the back of the room carrying a signed football helmet. She put it on a table and leaned down to write on a piece of paper. Lee came up behind her and put a hand on her shoulder.

"Dreama."

She whirled around with a smile plastered to her face that fell as she registered Lee. "Honey, what are you doing here? I didn't expect you to come after everything that's happened . . ."

"I need to talk to you. It's important."

"What's going on? Did they find her?"

"No. But I know how we can get her back."

"So there was a break in the case?"

"No, not with the police. We're going to perform a spell, and I need as many people as I can get. I was hoping you could come and bring your friends. I don't know many people here."

Dreama gave her a pitying look. "Oh, honey. I can't imagine how hard this has been. I'd lose my mind too if something happened to my kids."

"I'm serious. This is going to work. I can feel it."

Dreama glanced around and ushered Lee over to an empty corner of the room. She lowered her voice. "I want to help you, I really do, but I can't do *this*. Do you know how many years it's taken for people to forget who I used to be? I've made a whole new life without any of that stuff in it."

"But this is my daughter's life we're talking about. This is bigger than that."

"If I thought it would do something, I would do it, okay? This is just the stress talking. Why don't you stay at my house, and I can take care of you and Cliff while you wait for news?"

"Fuck that, I need to get my daughter back."

Dreama's mouth flattened. She took a deep breath, closed her eyes, and reopened them with a resolute expression. "I've tried hard to support you and rebuild our relationship since you got back, but it's clear you're not interested in healthy boundaries and mutual respect." She brought her hands together in front of her chest. "I hope the police find Meredith very soon. I will pray for you." She walked away to rejoin the party.

Despair threatened to pull Lee under.

On her way out of the restaurant, she stopped at the bathroom. As she washed her hands in the spotless farmhouse sink, she smelled something familiar and brought her soap-coated hands up to her nose. Sage, and something she'd thought was whiskey but had never been certain. It was Belva's hand soap recipe, though this version was sweeter and sudsier. An inhale of Belva's version always gave her a sense of calm clarity. But whatever Dreama had added to it had neutralized the effect. She felt nothing but dread as she inhaled.

•   •   •

It was dark by the time Lee returned to the cabin. She'd lost another day.

As she paced around the kitchen, it felt like her insides were overheating. She tore off her sweater and the shirt underneath it. She sank to the cold kitchen floor in her bra and closed her eyes, willing it to pass. She heard her mother's footsteps, and the thought of her concern, the richness of it on her tongue, made her want to vomit. She ran her fingers through her sweat-damp roots and tried to empty her mind and close off her senses.

Eventually, the nausea receded, and she opened her eyes. She avoided her mother's gaze as she stood up and walked to the suitcase across the room and pulled out the jar.

Redbud's voice came from behind her. "You gotta be sober for the spell to work."

"I won't drink tomorrow."

Redbud came around to face her. "It's gotta be now. Pour it out." She hadn't seen her mother this clearly defined in a long time.

"I still need it to finish the spell. I'll use it tonight, and then I won't drink tomorrow." The liquor was the only thing that connected Lee to the power of the land, even if it was just a simulation. She couldn't make it happen on her own.

"You don't need it, honey."

Lee ignored her and opened the jar. Redbud grabbed her wrist. "You wanted me to help, right? Well this is me helping." Redbud's righteous expression, the pity of the sober to the addict, made Lee want to punch her in the face. She refused to switch roles with her.

"You've been sober for what, a couple days?"

"I been using long enough to know when someone is lying to themselves. *I'll do it tomorrow. Just one more, and then I'm done.* I know all the tricks in the book, baby. Now stop being stubborn and pour it out."

Lee pulled away, went to the kitchen sink, and smashed the jar against the side, where the glass splintered and cut into her arms.

"I'm not fucking like you," Lee spat at Redbud.

She didn't flinch. "No shit."

Lee deflated, knowing the decision had been made. She wouldn't be drinking tonight. There was a relief in that, but also a terror. There were already so many factors working against her, and now she wouldn't have this one thing that made her feel calm and inspired. It seemed reckless to rely on her own faculties when there was so much on the line.

Redbud told Lee to sit down, and she obeyed.

"I wish I could do more for you. Mama tried every remedy to get me to stop using and drinking. One time she made me eat boiled minnows."

Lee gagged at the image.

"But this disease is too powerful. This is the only way I know how to get through it." Redbud dropped a carton of cookie dough ice cream on the table, pulled off the top, and stuck two spoons in like stakes. Lee took one bite, and then another. She dug the spoon in up to the handle and unearthed massive hunks. The sweet, cold solid of it filled her like nothing else.

Redbud did the same, and they hunched over the carton together in the low kitchen light, a mother and daughter eating ice cream to soothe their troubles.

# TWENTY-SIX

Lee came up for air late the next morning. She had worked all night in a shaking, sweating, sugar-fueled trance, crafting the spell and making sure each element would be ready. She had even found an old jar of Ruby Jo's hair stuffed in the back of Belva's stores.

They would perform the ritual that evening at sundown, life or limb.

But as the sun sliced through the room and the high wore off, she became aware of her sticky, sour mouth, the tremors in her hands, and the dread pooling in her gut like blood.

*It's not enough. It's not going to work.*

She checked her phone. There was a voicemail from a little after nine a.m. She listened to the lawyer's clipped voice saying that Cooper would be taking temporary custody of Cliff after she failed to show up in court that morning. She looked at her phone screen. It was after ten.

Gravel plunked against the sides of her car as she flew down the road to Billy's with her fists white-knuckled at the wheel.

Billy's cabin was more simple than Belva's. It was only one small box with cement steps leading up to the door, but it evoked the same feeling of being raised directly from the ground, no different from the trees and boulders that surrounded it.

She pounded furiously on the door.

No answer.

She wrapped her jacket sleeve around her fist and rubbed the dust from the window.

No one inside.

Billy's truck was in the driveway, but it was possible he'd been taken away by the police. She knew there was nothing he wouldn't do to protect his family.

She called out their names, but the trees were only still and creaking in response. She began to shake harder and tried to stave off the panic.

She walked around the property and searched for some sign of them. Billy's chickens cooed from their small wooden house and his band of hunting dogs sat on haunches next to it with their ears perked. Something was wrong.

Lee heard a low howl coming from the trees. She froze and waited, listening. When she heard it again, she charged in the direction of the sound. As she ran blindly through the woods, the howl came again, and she traced it to a small deer stand up in the trees.

Lee howled back, and Cliff's face appeared over the side of the platform. The sight of him made tears spring to her eyes. He climbed down, and she wrapped him in her arms.

Billy climbed down after him. "An officer rolled up here a bit ago with a few fancy boys. Your husband and his law-yer, I'm assuming."

"What did you tell them? How did they let you keep Cliff?"

"I didn't tell them shit. I got a camera rigged up at the turnoff. We had about five to get gone."

Lee had never been so proud of her family's ability to evade the law.

"Not that they could have gotten into the house. I got enough protections against cops to choke a police horse."

She let go of Cliff and wrapped her arms around Billy. "Thank you."

Billy's expression turned serious. "How's the search going?"

"I've been putting together this spell to get Meredith back, but I don't have enough people. I don't know what to do. Everyone is scared of us now."

"You know you can count on me."

"Thank you. I just wish we had more."

"What about me?" Cliff said next to her.

"Iff, I don't think—"

Billy laid his hand on her shoulder. "I know you want to protect him. But he's strong, and he's connected to the land. He could help."

Lee saw Cliff leaping foot to foot in the trees with Meredith. She couldn't deny he was a part of this place. But he also scared easily. What if he panicked in the middle of the ritual? Or what if it worked and the shadow creature came and took him, too? She couldn't lose him. They might as well take her then.

"I don't know what's going to happen. It could get really scary. You might see the thing you saw in the maze—"

Cliff cut her off. "That's okay. I want to do it."

Lee was taken aback by this new steel in him. "Are you sure you're not scared? It would make sense if you were."

His expression hardened, and he hit the tree in frustration. "Mom. You're not listening. I can do this. I want to get her back. Please let me help."

Lee studied her son. She'd dismissed him when he warned her about the shadow and discounted his version of reality, even as she acted like the only person who truly understood him. He was capable and powerful, and perhaps the safest place for him was with her, and the rest of his family who loved him, while they tried to get his sister back. If he could help, she couldn't say no.

•   •   •

That evening, Lee waited on the porch to see who would show. As the sunset deepened before her, soaking up the last of the sunlight so that the clouds hung heavy with pink, she finally heard the sound of a car coming up the gravel. Linda stepped heavily out of a sedan, and Lee craned her neck to look for other women in the backseat.

"Sorry, hon. It's just me. Everyone else is too chickenshit."

Lee put her arms around Linda and felt how solid she was in comparison. "Thank you for coming."

Linda gently pushed her away and patted her on the back. "Of course, hon. I don't scare easy."

A familiar jeep pulled up next to the sedan. She'd called and left a voicemail on Otis's phone but hadn't heard back. She knew he didn't want to see her anymore, but she didn't care. She needed him.

He walked up to her with his hands in the pockets of his jeans and his shoulders hunched.

"You came."

"Of course I did."

They didn't move toward one another, but she could feel whatever was between them filling the space. It hadn't disintegrated; it was still there. Lee yearned to touch him, but she controlled herself.

Linda looked from Lee to Otis, then put her arm through his and pointed them toward the pathway to the clearing. Lee was left alone and anxiously peering down the driveway.

She'd nearly given up when another car came slowly up the road. Dreama stepped from the Tesla and took a deep breath, looking around at the cabin and the woods.

"I don't think this place has changed in twenty years."

"Dreama. I wasn't expecting you."

"I know. But I couldn't leave you hanging. Not with a child missing. If you think this is going to work, I want to help."

"Thank you. This means so much to—"

"I know, I know. Let's not make a big deal out of it."

"Okay." Lee grabbed a lantern from the porch and snaked her arm through Dreama's like they were kids again, disappearing into the woods for an adventure.

The sun had nearly set when they arrived at the clearing. The circle of faces were amber and primitive, their features hooded and hooked in the flame and shadow of the fire.

Luann and Linda had arranged everyone into position. Otis looked uncomfortable, but he maintained his usual stoicism in the face of it. Next to him, Cliff watched Redbud with a curious, intent gaze. They had met only a few hours ago, and she seemed to fascinate him, as if he couldn't easily discern her essence. Redbud stood anxious and rattling, and Billy gripped her hand tightly from the other side. This would be her first real gathering in thirty years.

Lee felt the absence of Belva as if the world was permanently altered by it. A cosmic, elemental shift in the nature that surrounded them. She felt a crude stand-in as she took Belva's usual spot at the head of the group.

She pushed away the grief as Luann began with the land acknowledgment. She pulled lobes of chicken thigh and small quail breasts from a bag and placed them in a hole and covered them with dirt. She then took a jug of whiskey and a jar of honey and poured them into the ground. The froth soaked into the dark soil. She offered thanks and nourishment to the land and its spirits for allowing them to pull from its power and practice freely there.

Lee sounded weak in comparison as she came in with her part. "We have gathered to summon a shadow that has haunted us for thirty years." She hesitated, worried it sounded too forced. It didn't have the easy, earnest solemnity of Belva's delivery, or the confidence of her mother's. She made eye contact with Otis across the circle, and he wordlessly urged her on.

"Tonight, we ask the shadow to return to us, and to return my daughter, Meredith."

Lee released the clasps of Redbud's old suitcase and pulled out a glass jar filled with gray powder and one auburn hair.

She hummed low and frail at first, and then stronger as the others joined in. The sound began to weave its cocoon around them.

Leaves thrashed in the distance somewhere behind Lee, like a large animal was moving through the brush. The humming broke off, and everyone looked toward the darkness. Lee saw Billy's hands moving toward his bag while his eyes stayed on the direction of the sound, and she realized he must have brought a gun. Redbud moved her body in front of Cliff's.

Kimmie stepped cursing into the firelight with leaves tangled in her hair and dirt on her knees. "Sorry I'm late, y'all. As you were." She took a spot next to Lee and motioned to Dreama to scoot down. Lee caught Kimmie's eye to see if she was okay. It was clear from her half smile that she was not, but her eyes pleaded with Lee to go ahead.

Lee resumed her humming, trying to find the thread of it again. Then everyone joined in, and the cocoon formed more quickly this time, their throats well-oiled and now accustomed to its work. Cliff's hum was a high and sweet flutter, like a hummingbird flitting over their heads, sprinkling shimmer.

Lee shook the jar and watched the powder coat the glass. She then passed the jar to Kimmie, who vigorously shook it and passed it to Dreama. Lee took her own black book from the suitcase and turned to the spell she had written.

She recounted her parents meeting and falling in love with the stories she had heard and witnessed. She put everything she had into the delivery, as if the force of her voice might imbue it with more power.

The jar was returned to her, and she put it in another small hole and buried it, attempting to make her movements reverent.

She slid a knife across her palm, and the blood dripped onto the dark earth mound. She closed her eyes and waited for electricity to pass through her, what she imagined power felt like.

But all she felt was the pain searing her palm and the warmth and connection of the humming cocoon. As she continued the spell, she glanced across the circle at Luann and Linda, who were giving each other concerned looks.

The power wasn't flowing. It wasn't working.

Lee cast about frantically for a solution. She was out of her element. It had taken everything she had to get to this point. Why had she ever thought she could pull this off? The shame that squatted inside of her, ready to be summoned at any moment, awoke and started to expand, threatening to fill every inch of her.

Then she saw her mother. While she'd been scared in the lead-up to the ritual, Redbud now stood firmly on bare feet, her black hair radiating from her skull, the triple-noted hum coming from her the most sonorous and vibrant of the group. She was truly in her element. This was where she belonged.

Lee held her black book out to Redbud and asked her to read. Maybe if she told her own story, it would have more charge to it. It was empty for Lee to recount someone else's pain. Redbud hesitated, and Lee pushed the book forcefully into her arms. She wouldn't let her off the hook this time.

Redbud finally conceded. She settled into the moment and began to read in a small voice. Her confidence built with every word. The birds in the trees wailed, the wind picked up, and the air charged around them like the moment before a lightning strike.

Redbud started to recount the moment when she first discovered her husband's infidelity, and her voice wavered. She dropped the book and went to her knees with her face in her hands. The hum grew softer and the momentum slowed. The wind died and the woods went quiet.

This wasn't working. Lee had to try something else.

She closed her eyes and focused on her feet planted in the earth. She couldn't wield the power that glowed like ore beneath its surface. She could only open herself to it.

She took a deep breath, and against all instinct, let go of her tight control, surrendering to the wild unknown.

Her feet tingled. Then something began to work its way out of the bottoms of them, sprouting painlessly from the skin. The little roots furtively probed into the soil. She could sense them like spindly limbs as they moved farther down into the ground, branching deeper and deeper. Then they stopped.

There was only stillness for a few beats. And then, something. A heat flowing up from the roots. A prickling along the edges of her body. A sensation was building inside of her, the energy of it strengthening with each moment. The force of it like panic as the pressure became combustible.

And then there was only radiant, searing pain coursing through every inch of her. Every cell screaming.

She wanted to escape it somehow, to wrench her feet up and run away from this place.

Instead, she crouched inside herself and put her back to the pain. She told herself to focus.

*Don't flee. Don't reject it. Listen to it. Use it.*

She strained against its onslaught and searched for a path or a shape in the pain.

And then there was the flicker of an outline.

Someone was there. She could taste their pain in her mouth. Shotgun sulfur and strawberry jam.

It was a woman. Dark Buck hair. Olive-gold eyes. Lee was transported to the cabin's kitchen, where she saw the woman mixing cornmeal and water. It was like when Lee had inhabited her mother's memory—she hung there bodiless in the room, watching the scene unfold and sensing the thoughts and emotions of the woman.

As the woman sprinkled St. John's wort into the mush, a sharp crack came from the root cellar. She rushed to the hallway where her children stood hovering over the trapdoor. She told them to go to their room. She lifted the old wood by the iron handle and moved slowly down the ladder. Rotted eggs and dark, sweet strawberries filled her nose before she could make out anything in the dim. Her husband lay in a heap on the floor with a gun next to him. Most of his head was gone and two shades of red pooled around him. A dark, syrupy blood and the brighter red of strawberry jam dripped down from the shattered jars behind him. Fruit and flesh mixed in the puddle without distinction. As she was accustomed to do, she bypassed sorrow and filled with fury.

The cabin disappeared, and then there was something else. A campfire and fresh snow.

A man, woman, and child wrapped in thick blankets and furs hiked up a steep mountainside in light snow. The child stumbled, and the man pulled him onto his back. They came upon a cave carved out of the rock face and huddled inside. They smelled the smoke snaking up from the valley below and listened to the faint gunfire. The snow started to fall more thickly, and its steady pattern was hypnotic, lulling them to sleep as they leaned against one another for warmth with the child between them like their tiny beating heart. Hours later, the man came to. It was dark out and the temperature had plunged. He could see tiny icicles hanging from his eyelashes. When he stood to stretch his legs and warm his blood, the child slumped forward into the snow. The man put a hand on the child's back to pull him up and recoiled. He was hard and cold like a block of ice. The woman woke and shook the boy and wrapped him against her skin inside her blanket, but the man knew it was no use. The man and the woman met blistered eyes across the cave, and their rage ignited.

And then there were more and more people.

Generations of pain surged through Lee like a stimulant bubbling through her veins, activating a vein of fury inside her she hadn't felt in its full force since she was a teenager. A fury for her father's drinking and his death, and her mother's addiction and her loneliness, and the years of feeling trapped and freakish in her life with Cooper. It reached far beyond mere anger. It was the strangeness inside of her, her family's strangeness, lit up and aflame. It unfurled her, and she felt herself rising up, buoyed by its power.

She heard someone gasp and a chill overtook her like a cold plunge. She felt her being sink back down to the earth. When she opened her eyes, she saw only dense, writhing black. The shadow from her mother's memory stood looming a few inches from her face, and the breath left her body.

She felt a small circle of heat against her chest, and she realized it was Pallie's locket. When the shadow reached out and tried to touch her, it stopped just short of her flesh, like there was a force field surrounding her.

In her periphery, she saw Redbud look up from her hands and stare at the thing, transfixed. She rose from her knees without breaking eye contact with the creature. She walked into the center, and the creature moved away from Lee and followed her, so that Redbud was now face-to-face with it. She brought her arm up, and it mimicked the movement with its smooth, inscrutable limb. She brought her other arm up, and it mimicked this gesture as well. She asked it what it wanted, and it only hovered there in silence.

All humming had ceased, and Lee suddenly felt bare. Vulnerable. This creature could do anything to them.

Lee tried to put her body between Redbud and the shadow again, but her mother gently pushed her aside. Lee could feel her mother's fear attempting to undo her, and she realized they were all linked. She didn't feel everyone with the same strength, but she could undeniably feel them. Billy's tightly coiled readiness to attack, Luann's grounding solidity, Kimmie's sorrow-tinged defiance, Otis's awe, Cliff's small glittering soul. Through the act of the ritual, they'd become one.

Redbud held her ground. She put her hand up again, and the shadow mirrored it, but this time she pressed her hand forward. Her palm met its palm in the space between them, touching the boundary of its form.

The night dissolved around Lee and was replaced with sunshine.

Lee saw a young girl of about ten with Redbud's sober, flashing eyes standing at the end of the gravel driveway, watching her grandma cross the road to the mailbox on the other side. When she was halfway across, a car came roaring around the bend and ran right through her grandma without stopping. The impact launched her into the air and brought her down hard against the asphalt. Redbud ran and crouched over her. There was blood running from both nostrils and her mouth was filled with it. Redbud looked at the car that had come to a screeching halt a few yards away. A wobbly high-heeled leg emerged from the car, and a head of disheveled curls and bleeding eye makeup turned to look at them before closing the door and speeding away. Redbud held her grandma in her tiny arms and rocked her in the middle of the road.

Then there was chaos swirling around her. Someone took her cold, stiff grandma away, and the sheriff appeared in front of her. Redbud told him it was the judge's wife who'd done it. He frowned and told her she must have been mistaken.

Then Lee was back in the woods at night, but the faces that surrounded her were young girls in pajamas. Redbud stood confidently in a white nightgown with her hair unbraided and loose around her shoulders. It couldn't be more than a few months later. Instead of a fire, small candles burned at the center, and each girl gripped a flashlight, some scared and others caught up in the game of it. Redbud held up an off-brand Barbie by both legs over her head. She spoke of the judge's wife and her drunk driving that led to the death of her grandma. Then she took the doll by the torso and pulled her right leg forward. She snipped it off at the thigh with a pair of garden shears.

Then it was day, and Redbud was at the farmer's market with Belva. She watched as a woman in nurse scrubs helped the judge's wife out of the backseat of a car into a wheelchair. Her right leg hung lifelessly down. A woman whispered to Belva that she woke up one day and couldn't feel her right leg. The doctors had tried everything, but nothing worked. Belva wondered why they hadn't called her. Redbud made searing eye contact with the judge's wife across the square, who shivered and turned away.

The scene changed again. Redbud strutted down the halls of the school with firm, purposeful steps. She rounded a corner and came upon a boy poking Ruby Jo in her thick, soft stomach and muttering in a low voice as she cowered against the wall in tears. Redbud let out a harsh, guttural "hey," and the boy pulled his hand back and froze. Ruby Jo slid away and stood behind Redbud. She commanded him to turn around and look her in the eyes. He did it seemingly against his will, quaking, his face bloodless. She told him that if he touched her sister again, he would lose his hands. Permanently.

As Redbud chanted under her breath, the boy looked down at his palms and frantically examined them as if searching for some sort of pain. Tears trickled down his face as he sank to his knees and thrust his hands between his legs to try to curb the agony. He was still yelling "My hands are on fire" as she walked back down the hall, arm in arm with Ruby Jo.

Lee was again thrust into a different scene. Redbud crouched behind a bookshelf with Billy and Ruby Jo. There was a crash in the kitchen, and Redbud peered through the slats. Belva was talking in a low voice with her hands up, as if calming a bobcat. Leroy appeared from behind the counter on all fours, his hair wild, crawling closer to Belva as she slowly stepped back. He raised up on his feet and growled at her. He called her a demon and accused her of entering him and making him drink. He told her the only way to stop his drinking was to get rid of the demon. His left hand came up, and Redbud saw he was clutching a meat cleaver. She pulled a row of books down from the shelf, startling Leroy and turning his attention toward her. In that brief moment, Belva pounced on him and wrestled the knife away from his hand, kicking it across the floor.

Redbud picked it up, and she, Billy, and Ruby Jo ran out the door and into the woods, where they buried it. She lit a candle from her pocket, and they held hands over the dirt, whispering to themselves, "And he went down alive into the grave, with everything he owned; the earth closed over him, and he perished, and was gone from the community." Billy took out his pocketknife, and they each slashed their palms. They brought their three hands together over the new mound of dirt, squeezing until they burned, and the blood ran down their wrists and into the dark soil.

Then, Leroy was lugging a suitcase into an old Ford Coupe with a low bottom. Belva stood on the porch with her arms crossed and both eyes purple and yellowed. Redbud and little Billy stood at her side with the same resolute posture, and Ruby Jo cowered behind them. A pile of belongings sat on the grass. When Leroy was done loading the car, he stormed back to the house and attempted to go up the steps to the porch, but something invisible blocked him. He charged at it again and again until he gave up. He shouted at Belva and pointed at the children. He said that she couldn't hide from him in the house forever. He threatened to find her, and his children, wherever they went, before driving away, weaving in a crazed pattern.

It shifted again: Redbud stepped from a car on top of a high ridge. She looked down and saw a white bedsheet covering something on the bank of a small creek. The black Ford Coupe sat overturned in the water with brown and clear glass bottles smashed against the rocks and floating downstream. Belva knelt down and shielded Redbud's face from the scene with a hug. But Redbud was calm and collected over her shoulder, those eyes flashing and her mouth betraying the tiniest smile.

And then they were in a memory that had become so familiar to Lee over the past few days that it was like coming home. The nailing of the boots, Lee's period, the gathering, the sheriff showing up on their doorstep. Once again, those pivotal hours unfolded before her.

After Redbud thrust her black book into the fire, Lee saw something she hadn't registered before: a glimpse of a person in one of the white house's windows, watching Redbud. It was a nine-year-old Lee, a witness to something so consequential that she had forgotten it completely.

The flashes of memory gained speed as they moved through the years of the shadow's independent reign. It prowled the hills outside of Redbud's body and tormented her with her basest desires made real.

There Redbud was, a few years later. Her wrists had started hurting from grinding the deli hunks against the blade, and she asked the town doctor if he had anything for the pain that would let her keep working. Redbud had abandoned Belva's remedies along with the rest of the magic. He gave her a sample for a new kind of pill.

She took a few back at home and started cleaning. Thirty minutes later, she walked outside. The grass was cool and soft against her bare feet. The sunshine was warm and sparkling. She lay down on the ground, and for the first time since she killed her husband, she could feel the power of the earth rising from below and entering her. Her body floated up into the light, lifted by power, transcending all pain and torturous thought.

She was herself again.

Lee tried to look away from the next images, various scenes of taking drugs and the things she did to pay for them. The stints in jail. Then she heard a moan ripping through the flashes, and she was thrust back into the clearing.

Redbud was on her knees in front of the shadow, tearing at her hair, spit flying as she wailed. She curled on the ground and sobbed. Lee could feel her energy draining. She was losing herself to the shadow.

Lee crouched next to her and instinctively put her thumb to Redbud's wrist, reversing the stream of memories and pouring her own in like water.

A few months before Lee left for college, Redbud stopped drinking and taking pills. She woke up every morning and made a simple breakfast. She cleaned. She got a part-time job at the library. She bought Lee a new comforter from Target, a splurge, for her dorm bed. And some evenings, when the clouds pulsed with heat lightning, she and Lee would sit on the porch and talk until they passed out.

In late August, Redbud drove her to the bus station, and it wasn't what Lee had imagined. A big part of her was itching with the need to escape with both middle fingers up. But there was this tender sliver that felt she was leaving something behind. Redbud hugged her hard and told her to never come back, and Lee could feel the love in it. She wanted Lee to have a better life, no matter the cost. Lee pulled away first and gave her a perfunctory smile before boarding the bus. But as they drove away, the bus moving out of sight, Lee broke down, her own love for her mother burning inside of her.

Redbud opened shining eyes and got to her feet. She stepped toward the looming shadow so that they were almost touching and stared into the void of its face. Then she opened her arms and took one final step toward it, wrapping herself around its middle. At first it seemed solid, like she was hugging a statue. But then she gradually began to sink into it. The shadow slowly engulfed her arms, her torso, her legs. The wind picked up around them, and Redbud looked at Lee with eyes filled with love and regret, before her head disappeared entirely into the shadow and the fire was snuffed out, plunging them into darkness.

# TWENTY-SEVEN

Lee stood watch on the porch with Cliff's sleeping body slumped warmly against her. He'd insisted on staying up until Meredith returned.

Out of the endless, tumbling darkness, they had all reached for the sudden light of Billy's headlamp to ground themselves. He had trained the beam on the center of the group where Redbud crouched on her hands and knees. She was alone; the shadow had disappeared. When Redbud looked up at them in the thin shaft of light, Lee could see an inky depth had returned to her eyes. Lee pulled her up to standing by her arm, and her firm, looming pose recalled the stance of the shadow. The connection lingered between Lee and Redbud, weakening by the moment, but she could feel the shadow's anger and appetite pulsing from her.

Redbud and her shadow had been reunited. She would no longer be tormented by her rage and shame made external, out of her control, prowling the hills to torture her. She had accepted it as part of herself.

Redbud had told Lee in a voice like metal scraping stone that she knew where to find Meredith. Lee had tried to follow her into the trees, but she commanded her to stay.

So now she waited for her to bring Meredith home. She refused to consider that it hadn't worked.

The only part of Lee that moved was her mind as it went about accepting and integrating all that had happened over the past weeks. She now recognized that like most mountain folk, she possessed a vein of fierce, magical energy inside her that could take many forms—rage, or a stubborn intelligence, or a thick gray melancholy. It was part inheritance, part product of all that she'd survived. It wasn't a rotted wrongness at the center of her.

Over the years with Cooper, she'd become mostly melancholy. The other parts had no place in her new life, and she'd suppressed them until she could no longer feel their presence.

But they'd always been there, waiting for her.

All night, she had been tricked by rustlings in the woods that never yielded any figure. But now, as she heard something new, she could make out slivers of glowing skin, and she allowed herself to hope.

Her mother came through the trees alone, her black hair dull in the moonlight, and it filled Lee with rage. She wanted to claw her open, looking for the shadow inside.

Then another figure emerged behind her. She was thin and smudged with dirt, but Lee knew her. She leapt from the porch and wrapped herself around Meredith and sobbed into her tangled hair. Cliff's small body clung to her on the other side, and Meredith silently relaxed in their arms and allowed her legs to go limp.

Redbud led the three of them into the house, where they cocooned Meredith in blankets and fed her hot herbal tea and as much food as she could stomach. She didn't speak a word. Lee then helped her into a warm bath and washed her hair like she was a small child again, rinsing the soap with a cup. Leaves and burs and a few bugs floated in the murky water.

Lee put her to bed in Belva's room and got in, careful not to clutch at her. Meredith fell asleep almost instantly, and Lee lay there listening to her slow, shallow breathing. She hadn't slept since Meredith was taken, and her limbs began to relax into the bed, one by one. She always kept most of her stress in her jaw, perpetually clenched, biting down hard to get through it. She felt it start to slacken as her head sank deeper into the pillow, falling through its cotton, falling into nothingness.

She was safe.

# TWENTY-EIGHT

**W**hen Lee woke, Meredith was gone.

She staggered, dizzy and heart pumping in yesterday's clothes, to the kitchen where she saw Meredith, Cliff, Kimmie, Billy, and Redbud huddled together in front of the window. Lee wedged herself between them.

Cooper stood in the front grass looking up at the house in a daze. His blond hair was boyish in the morning sun. There was something about this setting that made him look even weaker than she'd seen him when they were together. She went outside to meet him.

"Coop?"

"Lee. What happened to you? You look . . ."

Lee studied her reflection in the window and saw her soil-streaked clothes; the tangled nest of her hair; her larger, thicker, more powerful body. Black fire ash was smudged around her eyes and across her cheekbones. She looked down at him without answering, and he seemed to cower slightly.

"Last night you texted Meredith came back?"

"Yes, she's here."

"Can I see her?"

"Sure."

"I . . . I can't seem to get inside the house." He looked unnerved as he contemplated the air in front of him. He was not used to confronting barriers.

She took his hand and led him forward. She could feel him gliding through some thickness in the air around the house, like pulling him through butter. He looked around in wonder for a moment, but by the time they made their way through the door, the mask was back up.

He greeted the kids formally, and they gave him dutiful hugs. He studied Meredith, who seemed thinner than usual but who now looked less like a woodland wraith with her body washed and her hair combed out. She was still quiet, but she assured him multiple times that she was fine.

Lee introduced Cooper to her family, and he was awkward in his attempt to seem personable and folksy. They smirked at each other, amused by his slow, simplified pseudo-hick speech.

Cooper sat with them for a few minutes, but Lee could tell he was uncomfortable. He didn't like to be in someone else's domain; he couldn't stomach being the outsider. He made an excuse to leave and asked the kids if they wanted to come by his hotel that afternoon. He couldn't wait to make his escape, even though he'd spent weeks away from them.

She walked Cooper out to his car.

"So, what's the story? She just disappeared in a maze and returned a few days later with no explanation?"

"That about sums it up."

"You're seriously not going to tell me what happened."

Lee didn't respond.

He exhaled and put his hands on his hips. "I have my lawyer working on the divorce papers."

"Fine."

"I'm not giving up the custody case. The kids are in danger here, and I can't have it. There should be another hearing in a couple of days."

Lee felt her newfound fury rippling in the depths of her like a predator moving beneath the surface of a creek.

"If you and the kids come back to California, you can stay with them at the house while we work everything out. And then you can take your settlement and live somewhere safe that I approve. But not here, with these people."

She refused to respond, and her silence enraged him. "You must see the logic here. Meredith nearly died, Lee. You are endangering their lives. You can't be trusted to make decisions for them."

"What would you know about making decisions as a parent? You don't care about them. You just don't want to look bad." She moved closer to him so that their noses were nearly touching. "I warned you what will happen if you try to take my children. I will gut you like a trout, and we will eat you for dinner."

He took a step back.

"You said it yourself. These people are dangerous. Why would you want to cross us?"

He grimaced. "I can't believe I married you. Biggest mistake of my life. You'll be hearing from my lawyer." He scurried to his rental car and got in before Lee could respond.

*You do that. See what happens.*

.   .   .

She hadn't returned to the field behind the high school since the day she'd forced Otis to kiss her. It had lain overgrown and unused for decades, the dewy weeds coming to her waist as she got out of the car. It smelled honeyed in the bright morning fog. A vinyl sign stood at the entrance, designating it as a future site of Conway Development. It would probably be a Hampton Inn by the time she visited again. She looked out over its expanse and enjoyed its ability to just be.

She heard his jeep burrowing through the foliage behind her, but she didn't turn around. Then Otis was next to her with his hand close to hers, but not touching. He looked out with her and waited for her to speak.

"I'm sorry about what happened to TJ. I never wanted him to die. I only wanted to protect people from him."

"I know. I asked my sister, and apparently he'd been selling to her for years. I didn't want to see it, but I knew he was into some bad stuff." He ran his hand through his hair and clicked his tongue. "Sometimes I get so hell-bent on seeing what other people don't that I miss what's obvious. Not that he deserved to die, but I understand he could be dangerous."

"I want you to know that you're a very real, very valuable person to me. I'm sorry I made you feel like you weren't."

He smiled slightly. "You can't *make* me feel anything. That's my own stuff, too."

She moved closer, but they still didn't touch. She could feel the energy pooling between them.

"So, that shadow thing I saw at the ritual. That's what killed TJ?"

"Yes."

"I'm still having a hard time believing it. I've always been more into . . . rationality."

"Me too." She sobered. "It kept me from seeing what was right in front of me. Cliff warned me about the shadow the first night we arrived, and I didn't believe him."

"You had no way of knowing. I wouldn't have believed it either."

"But I should have kept my mind open to him. It's something I want to work on." She ruffled her hand over the tall grass.

"So what's next?"

"Cooper's trying to pressure me into going back to California. But he doesn't get to make those decisions for us anymore. I have to think about what's best for the kids."

He nodded.

"Coming back wasn't what I expected. I didn't think this place would get *inside* of us like it has." She smiled at her own naivete. "Objectively, terrible things have happened. But each of us has also found something special here. It's hard for me to wrap my head around it when I've spent so many years rejecting this place and trying to give them a better, more elegant childhood."

Otis turned his face back to the field, bristling in the sun-shot mist like a scene in a novel, and they both took it in. There was elegance here.

He finally bridged the gap between them and pulled her gently to his chest. They gazed at one another.

"I'm not gonna pretend I have any say over whether you stay or go." He pushed her hair behind her ear. "When I'm with you, life feels like more. It feels like the best, most satisfying version of itself. And I hope we get a chance to explore that."

She pulled his head down to hers and kissed him, and a natural euphoria surged through her. This was the first time she'd kissed him sober. She wanted him, but she didn't need him to fill her like she'd felt since she got here. It was clean-burning transcendence that lifted her up, even if only for a fleeting moment.

She wanted to say something to him in return, but words failed her. She felt Granny Pallie's locket against her chest, and she instinctively pulled it off over her head and put it over his. She tucked it inside his soft sweater. "For you."

"It's still warm." He smiled down at her, and they kissed again.

"The sheriff wants to conduct an investigation into Meredith's kidnapper, so we have to stay for at least a little while. But we all know where that road will lead."

Meredith had opened up later that morning to the police when they were called. She described being taken by a figure in the maze, then waking up alone in a cave deep in the woods. When she tried to leave, it felt as if there was an invisible barrier keeping her inside. The cave had been relatively warm, and water poured from an opening in the rock that she drank when she was thirsty. She ate mushrooms that Belva taught her to forage, and that kept the hunger at bay. The figure never returned, and eventually she found a way out.

*Did you see the kidnapper's face?* the sheriff asked.

*No,* she responded. *Only their shadow.*

A paramedic had done an exam, but Lee was told to take her for a follow-up with a doctor to see if she'd contracted parasites. Lee imagined what Belva would say to that. *The only parasites are the doctors trying to charge thousands for a few minutes of looking and a blood test.*

Lee and Otis stood there for a while holding each other, and then she released him. She needed to pick up the kids from Cooper's hotel.

When she checked her phone in the car, she had a text from Billy.

*Come to the hospital ASAP.*

# TWENTY-NINE

Lee took her children's hands and squeezed them as they got closer to Belva's hospital room, preparing them for what they might see.

A crash came from the room up ahead, followed by a metal tray skidding into the hallway. An older woman in scrubs came out with her hands thrown up and cursing in defeat. Lee ran to the room.

Belva sat on the bed with her face red and fierce and her arms held down by two orderlies on either side. Her breathing apparatus was around her neck, and her skin bled where the tubes had been torn from their veins. Billy stood in the corner with his arms crossed, looking amused, while Luann fluttered around the nurses attempting to calm her.

When Belva saw Lee, her eyes went darker.

"YOU! Did you put me in this death trap? Goddammit, lemme out or I'm gonna slap both your eyes into one!" Belva balled her hands into fists and struggled harder as a jolt of energy moved through her.

Cliff came from behind Lee and laid his small hand on Belva's ankle. He looked into her eyes with his gentle face, and Belva became solely focused on him as if in a trance. Her muscles relaxed, and the red adrenaline drained from her. She looked around and took a calmer stock of the situation. Lee could see the pure misery in her expression.

Lee pulled one of the nurses aside and made eye contact. "Excuse me, can she go home?"

"The doctor wants her to stay for monitoring . . ."

"I mean legally, can she leave?"

"Well, technically, yes, of course. We can't keep her against her will. But it would be very risky—"

"We understand. If you give us the paperwork, we can get out of your hair."

The nurse looked around at the jars of water in the corner, the dirt scattered on the floor, the iron and dogwood bark that Luann had brought from the cabin crowding the nightstand. She stared at them as if they were nuts, the ones that couldn't be helped. The kind of strange folk you had to give up on.

. . .

Kimmie and Dreama were a two-woman welcome committee when they arrived home with Belva. Kimmie wrapped her in a tight hug that nearly crushed her. Belva told her she was sorry about TJ, and Kimmie nodded and went misty-eyed and hugged her again. Dreama greeted Belva stiffly and handed her a tasteful bouquet of store-bought flowers. An odd gift, given the profusion of plants that surrounded them. Belva seemed amused but grateful for her presence.

Billy found a large wheelbarrow in the shed, and Lee laid some pillows down in the bottom. It wasn't glamorous, but it moved. He and Lee pushed Belva around the land in it, one on each side to fight its natural cockeye, as she cooed to her bees and fingered the petals of her garden. A cloud of birds followed and fluttered in the air above them, and Meredith and Cliff ran around trying to touch them. Seeing Belva awake had re-animated Meredith, and Lee was relieved to see it.

Redbud came out of the house and stood a few feet away, waiting for permission to get closer. Belva beckoned with her one good arm, and Redbud walked furtively over. Belva seemed to be growing stronger, even in the few minutes since she'd returned to the land, and she was able to get to her feet with some help. She put her hands on Redbud's forearms to steady herself and looked into her eyes.

"Baby Red. I—" Belva tried to get more out, but her voice failed her. Tears filled her eyes.

Redbud took Belva in her arms and let her rest her full weight on her shoulders. She whispered "I'm sorry, Mama. I'm so sorry" into her ear before her own voice gave out. They both stood there leaning against one another and soaking the shoulders of their sweatshirts.

Billy brought a chair over from the shed and helped Belva sit down. She took Redbud's hand in hers and looked her straight in the eye.

"Red. I've been pure chickenshit all these years. I shoulda tried harder to help you. I let my own anger get in the way, and I gave up too easy. I've been an ignorant bitch, and I'll regret it for the rest of my life."

"No, Mama. I'm sorry for blaming you. I was so ashamed. I didn't want you to see me like that. I couldn't face seeing what I'd become in your eyes. I was the one who stayed away."

Belva gripped her hand harder. "You got nothing to be ashamed about. When I look at you, I see a woman tougher than nails who's been through the shitstorm and come out the other end."

Redbud brought her hand up to cover her teeth and smiled into her palm. Belva reached over and pulled her hand down. "You don't gotta hide from me, girl." She turned more serious. "Even though I wasn't there, I still protected you. From afar."

Redbud wiped another tear and chuckled, showing the gaps between her teeth. "I know. Every time I almost died and came back to life, I knew it was you. I wanted you to stop so I could just be done with it. But now I'm glad you did."

Belva put her arms around her, and they held each other again for a while.

Lee watched from a respectful distance. She was glad Belva and Redbud were reconnecting. She didn't begrudge them that. But she'd been through this before.

She'd exchanged tearful hugs with her mother while she spouted sober epiphanies. She'd felt the glow of a new era dawning, where she could have her mother back and they could pick up right where they left off. But it never lasted. She'd always relapse, and then it was that much more painful to live with the other version. The one who acted as if she didn't exist.

Redbud had accepted her shadow, and Lee wanted to believe that this time, things would be different. But she couldn't ignore the bone-deep instinct warning her not to fall into the trap again.

Dreama and Kimmie started bringing out the food, and they set up a makeshift picnic in the garden around Belva's chair, where Meredith and Cliff clustered around her.

Once everyone had their plates, Dreama sat down next to Lee on a blanket off to the side.

"I'm surprised you came," Lee said. "I mean, I'm happy you're here. Just . . . surprised."

Dreama brought her face up to the sunshine and closed her eyes. "I've been away too long. I'd forgotten what it was like to be around people who've known you for a long time. It's kind of nice."

Kimmie came over and lay down on the other side of Lee, allowing the sun to warm her skin as well. She pulled her flask out of her bra and handed it to Lee, who took it without thinking. Lee could feel the liquid sloshing lushly inside. She handed it back.

"Oh, thanks, but I'm trying to stay clearheaded right now."

"How's that working out for you?" she quipped.

"Pretty damn well."

Kimmie looked at her sideways with her hand shading her face. "Okay, girl. Look at you. I'm inspired." She slipped the flask back in her bra without taking a sip.

"So have you decided? Are you going back to California?" Dreama asked. "I wouldn't blame you."

Lee watched from across the garden as her kids told Belva stories with animated hand gestures, their faces unguarded.

She had asked Meredith and Cliff what they wanted to do. It wasn't just her decision. For too much of her own childhood, she'd been at the mercy of an adult's bad decisions. They deserved to have a say over their own lives.

They both immediately said that they loved it here. *Even after what happened*, Meredith insisted unprompted. This place felt like home.

"I think we're going to stay. For now. Cooper's putting up a fight, but there's no way I'm going to let him take my kids, or tell us where we can live."

Kimmie smiled and pulled Lee into a tight hug against her soft chest. "You's one of us now . . ." she said in a creepy voice as if they'd brainwashed her into becoming another murdering hill person.

Lee laughed. "I wouldn't go that far."

"Have you thought about where you might live long term?" Dreama had gone into Realtor mode.

"We'll stay with Belva for now. I won't have any money until the divorce goes through. We'll take it one step at a time and see where we end up."

"Well, when the time comes, there are some great houses left in the new Cradleburg development. Easy to get around the zoning if you want the kids to go to CVHS."

"Thanks, Dreama, I'll think about it."

"I bet Otis will be happy . . ." Kimmie said, baiting her.

"Actually, it's what the kids wanted—"

Kimmie slapped Lee's arm. "I can't believe you got a man already."

Lee was quiet and awkward, willing this part of the conversation to be over. She wasn't making this decision for him. This was about Lee and her children building a new life on their own terms.

The three women settled back into a comfortable silence and watched the family play and relax in the garden, recalling a time decades ago when they spent Sunday afternoons together whiling away the time. Lee noticed an owl sitting on a branch above them. It reminded her of the one she saw the night she discovered Mr. Hall and the girl. But the bird was serene in the afternoon light.

.    .    .

As Lee hugged the turns into town, the sun set in front of her and turned the scenery into a flat black silhouette. She put the window down and let the crisp air toss around her hair and beat against her cheeks. She pressed her foot a little harder against the gas, and her insides surged with it.

Lee texted Otis that she was there and waited outside of his door. When he didn't answer immediately, she tried the knob and found it unlocked.

She stepped inside and was drawn into the kitchen, where a pot roast sat in the oven emitting rich odors. A few candles stood unlit in their silver holders on the kitchen table made up with place mats and old-fashioned crystal wineglasses. The back door was ajar, and she wondered if this was the game. She had the feeling since she arrived that she was being pulled by an invisible string.

She opened the back door, and the sunset was in full bloom on the horizon. Otis was lying in the strawberry field, watching it with his arms spread wide. Lee went to join him and kneeled into the thick clusters next to him.

His eyes were closed, and his mouth was slightly open as if in mid-speech. His was a stillness that she'd never seen in him before, even at his most stoic. The sweet, overripe smell of the strawberries began to rot in her nose and mouth, and she saw that he was covered with their deep red. She shook his shoulder, but he did not rouse. She could feel through his thin white T-shirt that he was still warm but cooling by the minute, like soil as the sun went down.

She shook him harder, and his neck slumped to the side. His cheek smeared with rotten jam. She put her fingers to his neck and felt for a pulse, but she couldn't find it.

She studied his face, trying to will it back to movement with her memories of its animation. The way he smirked when he was genuinely amused by something. His look of determination when working with his body. The way he had looked at her in the field. She projected all of this onto him, but these spectral faces quickly evaporated, leaving the same absolute stillness.

As if the life had been sucked out of him.

# THIRTY

The room felt like it was at the bottom of everything, buried deep beneath where people lived and where the soil grew life. Way down, deep down, underneath it all.

The curtains were drawn against the morning light, and Lee sat on the floor against the wall. She had been reduced to her most primitive self, crouching in the dark to protect her children from unknown predators. This was all she knew; everything else was sitting far above her on the plane of the living, where nothing made sense.

Meredith stirred from her cot and rolled over to face Lee. "Did you sleep at all?"

Lee shook her head. Cliff moved at the sound of his sister's voice and sat up with his hair cowlicked in the back. He always looked so young in the mornings.

"Guys, I need to talk to you about something. I've thought very deeply about it, and I've considered every facet, and . . . we are going back to California to live with your dad."

"What?" Meredith snapped.

"It won't be permanent. We're still getting a divorce. But we can't stay here, and it's our best option."

"But you said we could stay. That *we* could have a say over our own lives."

"Yes, I did, but things have changed. You know that."

Lee expected to hear more of Meredith's protests, but it was Cliff's voice that came next. "Mom, please don't make us go back there. Please, let us stay here."

Her heart broke a little for how desperate he sounded, but she wouldn't allow that to get in the way. "I can't keep you safe here." Meredith tried to interrupt, but Lee cut her off. "This isn't a discussion. I've made my decision. We'll leave as soon as possible, maybe tomorrow if I can get all of our ducks in a row. Until then, you are not to leave this room except for the bathroom and meals."

Meredith stood up and crouched in front of Lee. "I know you're scared. But we finally have a family, and a place that is right for us, even in spite of everything. What about *their* safety? We can't leave them."

"You'll see them again. But right now, I have to focus on you. You are more important to me than anyone else."

Meredith stood up and crossed her arms. "I refuse. You will have to physically remove me from this house."

"That can be arranged."

Meredith scowled and stormed to the door, but Lee yelled for her to stop. "What did I tell you? You are not to leave this room."

Meredith turned around with tears running down her cheeks. "Fine. Then *you* leave. I don't want to be anywhere near you."

Lee softened her gaze to show her she was doing this out of love. But Meredith kept her eyes on the floor as she went back to her cot. Lee went over to Cliff and tried to smooth his hair down, but he ducked her touch and turned away from her to face the wall.

Lee left the room and collapsed outside the door. A figure entered the hallway, and her body tensed. Then hazel eyes pierced through the low light, and she sat back against the wall as her mother joined her on the floor.

"The sheriff called. They want you to come in again. They got more questions."

"I don't have anything else to say."

"I understand, honey. But you don't want them hunting you down."

Lee had recounted the story so many times to the sheriff, that it clearly wasn't a formality. They were trying to catch her in a lie that would expose her involvement in his attack.

And in a way, she did feel responsible. It was undeniable that Otis's attack and the death of those men were connected to her in some way. But she had no idea how. They'd been wrong at every turn, and now Otis was paying the price.

Redbud didn't push it. "You should probably get ready for the hospital. We gotta leave in a bit."

Lee felt a force building in her chest. "I don't think I can go. I can't see him like that again."

Redbud looked mournfully at her. "I'm so sorry, baby." Redbud reached for her, but Lee pulled away. This wasn't her way back into a real relationship. Lee wouldn't let her sneak in while she was vulnerable. She had to keep her guard up.

"Don't apologize. Your shadow didn't hurt Otis. Or kill those men. There's something else out there."

"I know." She paused, choosing her words carefully. "I think you should go and see him. Remember, he ain't dead yet."

Redbud put her hand on Lee's, and she wanted to pull away again, but she was tired. The force pushed up to her throat and the tears ran down her cheeks and her shoulders shook from the power of it. She felt like she was vomiting air, the breath leaving her and not being replenished.

Redbud rubbed her back and told her that they always persisted, even in the hardest times. Lee flinched from the tenderness of her touch, and her mouth filled with salt when she tried to respond. This wasn't a comforting sentiment. They always persisted, yes, but what were they left with? What was the point of hanging on when life could be so relentless?

Redbud put her thumb to Lee's wrist. She clung to her own consciousness, terrified of leaving her children alone. Redbud whispered to let go. She would protect them. Lee continued to resist, but the pull of the memory was strong. She was so tired.

Lee fell for a while before landing in a bright place. It was her mother's room at the white house. Redbud was in flannel pajamas holding a baby cocooned in a blanket. When the baby opened its eyes, Lee could see herself staring back. Redbud and the baby held eye contact for a long time before her eyes slowly closed again. There was a sweet, soothing mood in the room. It reminded her of late afternoons in early spring when the light was a mix of winter's silver and spring's pale gold and a slight breeze blew through the window screens.

Lee could feel it dissolving around her, but she wasn't willing to go back yet. She sensed that she had gained some control, that this wasn't merely her mother showing her a memory. Perhaps Lee could experience her mother's other memories. She imagined she could explore her memory bank like Belva's storage room with its stacks of unorganized boxes.

The image grew more vivid, until she suddenly realized she was standing in an actual room surrounded by boxes. She was inside of her mother's mind. She went to the closest box and attempted to pry it open, but the tape was strong. Another box looked older and decaying, and she went to open that one.

A teenage Redbud came through a door in one of the walls and fixed her gaze on Lee. She politely asked her to leave with a smooth, undented voice and flashing eyes. Lee couldn't help but be terrified of her. Young Redbud took her hand, led her to another door, and gently pushed her through.

Lee opened her eyes. She was back in the dark hallway. Redbud had released her wrist and was studying her with an appraising look. "Opaline, you are more powerful than you think. In a lotta ways. Remember that." She patted her knee and got up with some trouble.

Lee pulled herself up as well and moved toward the light of the living room. It was time to go aboveground.

·   ·   ·

The hospital waiting room was filled with people Lee vaguely recognized from church. They huddled in clusters, clutching Styrofoam cups and speaking in low voices. A woman with the energy of an unmarried aunt asked Lee to write her name down on a list; they could only go in a few at a time.

While Lee waited for her turn, Dreama approached with a few friends trailing behind.

"I'm so sorry about Otis. I'm praying he'll pull through." She hugged Lee tightly, and Lee relaxed against her for a moment. There was something comforting and solid about Dreama; she'd been there when she'd needed her these last few days.

Dreama's friends fluttered behind her in agreement as all of them remembered their old crushes on Otis. As Lee pulled away, Dreama kept hold of her hands and squeezed them. Lee noticed the softness of her skin and imagined her rubbing expensive creams into it. As she focused on this, she could feel that there was a pathway open to her. She could enter the internal world of this woman as she had earlier with her mother.

She carefully stepped in, and she was instantly met with a barrage of images like someone feverishly scrolling through a feed. Dreama's husband's disappointed face. Columns of numbers she couldn't decipher. A fight with one of her sons. And then, a flash of a fire. Lee strained to see more, but she was forcefully thrown out of wherever she had been.

Dreama's face came into focus again. She had pulled her hand back and was leaning away from Lee. She looked unnerved for a moment before regaining her composure.

"Let's have a girls' night tonight. Come over after the kids are asleep. We'll drink all the wine." Lee nodded but didn't think she would go. She needed to stay close and alert to protect her children. She'd only felt comfortable coming to the hospital knowing Billy, Redbud, Kimmie, and their collective firearms were guarding them.

Dreama turned to go, and the women fluttered after her.

Eventually, it was Lee's turn to visit Otis. She asked Belva and Luann to wait outside for her.

It was hard to see him through the tangle of tubes and wires. One would think the presence of so much electricity and machine whirring

would make him seem more animated, but he still had that absolute stillness underneath it all.

The doctors weren't sure if he would ever wake up.

She wanted to touch him, but she was afraid if she did, she'd feel
only empty flesh, the space inside him hollowed and the wind whistling
through like a cold cavern. The guilt was like a thick web in her throat.

It was her fault he had ended up here. The people that surrounded
her had done nothing but suffer since she'd returned. Something more
dangerous than her mother's shadow followed her, and Otis was its latest
victim.

She wasn't sure how he'd survived when the others had died. Perhaps
because she had found him so soon after he was attacked. It seemed a
small consolation when his life still hung in the balance.

She finally reached out to touch his hand. It was warmer than it had
been in the field. But when she searched for him in his touch, she was met
with the bottomless void she'd feared. Like the person she knew was too
distant to sense—or he was gone entirely.

As she stroked his hand, she could feel again that there was a pathway
open.

She tentatively stepped in, and the room dissolved around her.

.   .   .

It was dark, and a wind whistled through her, brisk and uninhibited. It was
the absolute blackness of a cave without light, and she was afraid to take a
step in any direction for fear of what she might encounter.

But there was something. A familiar vibration in the ground buzzing
through the soles of her shoes. It was coming from behind her.

She took small, slow steps toward it, and after a while, her eyes began
to adjust to the dark.

It felt like she'd been walking for hours when she finally saw a light up
ahead. At first it was only a small white square, but as it grew, it gained

more detail, and then she was running, because there was Otis in the middle of it, surrounded by sunshine and elegant dew-tipped weeds, like a painting hanging in a void.

It was the field behind the high school, but not.

He sat at a large wooden table set with crystal goblets and dinner plates and a roast glistening on a platter in the center. Enormous bees flew lazily around him from the weight of their thick, plush bodies. She tested the grass with her toe and found the ground solid. She stepped in, and when she looked back at the tunnel, it was gone.

She squinted in the brightness and was at a loss for words at the sudden life of Otis in front of her.

"Would you like to sit down?" He smiled as if he'd been waiting for her.

"Uh—are you okay? How are you feeling?"

He looked confused. "I'm fine. How are *you*?"

*He doesn't know.*

*Should I tell him?* She wondered if there was some trick to this, like not waking up a sleepwalker. What if she told him and she only made it worse? His mind had put him in this beautiful, peaceful place for a reason.

"I'm . . . great. It's just been a weird day." She sat down and put her napkin in her lap. He poured her a glass of white wine, and she hesitated. Was it drinking if it happened inside Otis's mind? Would it extinguish her connection to the land's power, ejecting her from this place? Or was this some sort of loophole? She'd love nothing more than to feel that first tangy sip sliding down her throat. She eyed it suspiciously and put off the decision for a bit.

He put his hand on hers, and there it was, the pulse of self she'd been looking for in the hospital room. This wasn't some figment of a mind shutting down; this was the flicker of life inside him. He was still here.

"What's the last thing you remember from . . . before I came?"

He was quiet for a moment, and then his brow furrowed. "I . . . I don't know. I know who I am, and I know who you are. But everything else is sort of fuzzy. Like a mist with these different colored patches. I can't make out anything solid in it." He looked worried, and the scene around them started to fuzz at the edges. She had done something wrong. This was taxing his brain while it was trying to heal; it was why they were here, in the sweetness and light. *Keep it light, Lee. Don't hurt him any more than you already have.*

She stood up, pulled him toward her, and brought him down into the weeds. She nuzzled against his chest, letting the desire flow unchecked. Their clothes evaporated like dew, and then they were moving against one another like tall grass. The sensation was lighter than the body; it floated on the surface and ignited at the edges with a delicate pleasure.

When it was over, they lay on their backs in the grass, and he trailed his fingers up and down her arm.

"Are you hungry?"

"Starving."

Lee stood up and surveyed the untouched dinner he had prepared. The roast was dotted with pearl onions, carrots, potatoes. They sat down with their naked butts against the wood of the chairs, and he served her a large hunk of the meat. She hungrily speared an onion but stopped short of putting it into her mouth. There was a bit of color on it. Rings of olive and gold surrounding a black circle. She touched it with her fingertip and found it slick and spongy.

It was an eyeball.

She looked closer at the pot roast dish, and she saw tufts of hair, fingers with the nails polished, the curve of an ear. She looked at Otis and pointed, and he spit out the meat onto his plate. He bent over and started dry-heaving into the grass.

When she glanced around, wondering who had switched their roast for this nightmare, she saw that the trees had gotten closer. With each passing moment, they seemed to be closing in. And then, without transition, the trees were just there, surrounding them. They were in the woods now, the light dimmed by the dense canopy. The table had vanished.

There was a rustling behind them, and Lee could feel another presence. She turned around and saw the shadows of the trees sticking out at odd angles in a crosshatch of darkness. There was a contour of intelligence in the darkness, like the curve of an opposable thumb.

Otis grabbed her hand, and they took off, running naked through the trees. He was radiant with fear, the adrenaline glowing moon-like in the veins of his face. She had never seen him so disarmed, like a little boy running for his life, the vulnerability right at the surface. As they ran, she searched for somewhere to hide. She could feel its presence growing closer.

Then a man's distant, craggy voice came from behind her.

"She's at it again! Get that devil woman outta here!"

Lee looked back and saw Otis's father pointing a skeletal finger at her from his wheelchair. The woods were replaced by beige walls, tile floor, slick green chairs. She looked in front of her again, searching for Otis running through the trees, but he was back in the hospital bed. His heart monitor manically beeped, and the lines on its interface formed spikes above his lifeless gray body.

A few nurses dashed into the room and pushed Lee and Otis's father out the door into the hallway.

"What'd you do to him this time?" he demanded.

Her head was light from traveling between worlds, and she leaned against the flesh-colored wall.

He cast about for anyone who might be nearby and raised his voice again. "I want this devil woman thrown out! She ain't welcome!"

Shame pooled inside Lee as the crowd stared at her from the waiting area.

Belva moved past Lee and knelt down in front of Otis's father in his chair. When she put a hand on his arm, he pulled it away and refused to look at her. She kept speaking in a low voice that no one else could hear, and after a while, he seemed to soften a bit. He suddenly grasped her hand, and she put hers on top of his. His eyes were wet. She offered him a Styrofoam cup, and he allowed her to pour a little of the liquid into his mouth. His shoulders relaxed, and his eyelids drooped, and Belva wheeled his chair back to the waiting area.

Conversations resumed at a lower rumble, but they all watched as the sheriff walked up to Lee in the hallway.

"I got to ask you a few more questions, Opaline."

She took a deep breath. "Fine. Let's get it over with."

He pulled a plastic bag out of his pocket and held it up to her. Inside was Pallie's gold locket.

"Do you recognize this item?"

She answered on pure impulse. "No, sir."

He narrowed his eyes at her. "You sure?"

Here was her chance to correct her lie. "No. I've never seen it in my life."

He was quiet for a moment. "There was some hair in the locket along with a bit of dried plant debris and some *toenail* clippings." He paused. "We tested the hair against the DNA sample you supplied when Joseph Hall's body was found. It's a match. This is your hair, Opaline."

Lee looked over at Belva, who was watching them covertly from farther down the hall.

"Where did you find it?"

"The EMTs had to take it off Otis when they resuscitated him at the scene."

"I don't know how my hair got in there. I've never seen it before. I promise."

He studied her face and worked something in his mouth with his tongue. "All right. That will be it for now. Don't leave town."

Belva and Luann silently joined Lee as she walked down the hallway, through the spectators in the waiting room, and out the front doors of the hospital. In the safe space of her car, Lee was succinct. "What the hell is going on? Why was *my* hair in that locket?"

Belva shot back. "I put it in for your protection. I didn't know you were gonna give it away. It's a family heirloom for God's sake."

"Fuck. I look so suspicious now."

"Honey, don't you see? That locket is what saved his life."

Lee remembered the way it had protected her during the ritual, and her hand grasped at the empty space on her chest.

She told Belva and Luann what she'd seen inside of Otis. If they didn't find out who was behind this, she worried Otis would eventually stop running and that thing would overtake him. "Do you have any ideas?"

Luann shook her head, and Belva looked frail and confused. "I don't know. I've used all my methods. I never really had the sight, and I make do. But lately, it's like someone's thrown a sheet over the future. There's nothing but blank space."

·   ·   ·

That night, Lee couldn't sleep. She wandered the house, studying the pictures of relatives. In a corner of the living room was Belva's altar to Granny Pallie with its white lace and candy dish. In the framed picture, she sat in a rocking chair on a porch, and the folksiness seemed almost staged. Lee recognized her as the woman from her vision during the shadow ritual, the one who found her husband with his head blown off in the root cellar.

Lee spotted strawberry candies in the dish and promptly replaced them with butterscotch from Belva's sweet stash. Then she lit the candle next to the frame and closed her eyes.

"Granny Pallie. Please help me see who attacked Otis and killed those men. Show me who or what is behind this." She tried to open herself as she had for the shadow ritual, but nothing came.

She repeated the request a few times, but she heard no answer. She waited and hoped for a sign. But there was only the silence of a sleeping house.

She went out to the porch swing for some cool air. The rocking of the swing slowly lulled her into a calm, comfortable place, and she mercifully dropped away.

· · ·

Lee came to on the porch and saw a woman sitting in the chair across from her in the dark. This version of Pallie was a bit older, but her hair was still black against her wrinkled face. Lee recognized the fury burning in her olive eyes.

"Opaline." Pallie studied her. "Belva was right. You *are* special."

Lee was skeptical. "In what way?"

"You are what we call an observer, my child. You will never have a gift for casting. But you can stare into the depths of others and observe." Pallie studied her again with the same penetrating glance she knew from Belva. Lee shook it off.

"Who or what is behind it all? What am I missing?"

The old woman stood up and walked out into the grass, and Lee followed. The wind picked up and gusted through them, and Pallie opened her mouth to it. When it died down, she closed her mouth and lightly smacked her lips. "It tastes like your mother's work. Powerful. Vengeful. No respect for the land and its spirits. Like a gun barrel forced into the mouth."

"But Mama can't pull from the land anymore, and she's been reunited with her shadow. How could it be her?"

Pallie found a patch of dirt in the grass and squatted over it like a child. She pulled a pouch from somewhere in her skirt and poured a handful of dried corn kernels into her palm. She closed her eyes and shook the corn like dice, then she tossed them onto the ground. She bent over and peered at where they had fallen.

"What are you doing?"

"I'm reading the pattern."

Lee bent over and tried to look for meaning in the shapes made by the scattered kernels. "What do you see?" she asked.

"I see . . . hm. I see what Belva means. There is something blocking us. Powerful work."

"You can't see *anything*? Maybe you need to try another method."

"No, the corn don't lie."

"Can't you just try, though?"

Pallie suddenly looked very tired, and the edges of her blurred. "Hush, child. I ain't God. Just an old lady who needs a nap." She smiled at Lee. "You don't need me, honey. Use your gift. There are more secrets left to find."

.  .  .

Lee woke with a start on the porch, but this time she was alone.

The house was still and quiet as she crept back in. Redbud was asleep on the couch. She usually looked like a corpse when she slept, but tonight she twitched back and forth, and little sounds dripped from her mouth.

Lee sat down at her hip and took her arm in her lap. She began to stroke it, and as she did, the boundary between this reality and the one inside of Redbud became permeable. Lee checked around the room before stepping in once more.

She was immediately dropped into her mother's bedroom in the white house. The air was thick, and the images were distorted like in a dream. The sound of a hammer beamed slowly toward her from a figure crouched on the floor, like a submarine signal moving through water. It was her mother again, nailing those goddamn boots to the floor. After all of this, she was still fixated on this memory. Even in the fallout of accepting her shadow back inside of herself and presumably beginning to heal, she still dreamed of this stretch of hours.

Lee let the memory roll dreamily through, until it was once again the night after her father died. Redbud rolled carefully out of Lee's bed and walked on the balls of her feet out of the room. She grabbed the red suitcase still sitting by the door from the night before and went out through the back, careful not to make a sound. She was wearing only a thin T-shirt and underwear with no shoes. The cold wind whipped through her, and the overgrown grass poked through the skin of her feet.

The coals were still glowing from the fire Billy had made for them to stare silently into that evening. She poked and blew on them and added kindling. The fire was reborn, rising from the ashes of itself, and she watched it grow higher. When she was satisfied, she released the clasps on the suitcase and took out her black book. She put her hand on it, and there was a long pause where she closed her eyes and tried to read the contents with her fingers through the leather. She hesitated. Then she set it down at the edge of the fire and pushed it into the hot center.

Redbud turned toward the house as if she'd heard a sound and walked briskly back in. Lee looked for her young self standing in the window as she'd seen during the shadow ritual, but this time, with the moon pulsing high above, Lee saw that it wasn't her. The figure was in her mother's bedroom, not Lee's, and it was too tall to be her. For a moment, she wondered if it was her father's ghost. But as she peered harder, she saw that it was a slightly older girl with a sullen face. Lee realized with a jolt that the girl had been erased from this entire sequence. A person who had been there that night and since forgotten.

It was Dreama.

# THIRTY-ONE

C andles lit the way as Lee followed Dreama deeper into the house. She reached into her pocket and fingered the bundle of tinctures she'd taken from Belva's workshop.

The first floor was one cavernous room with clusters of furniture delineating different spaces. Wide-planked wooden floors stretched out beneath her feet, and white shiplap covered the walls under floating shelves.

Lee had been in this house before. She'd *lived* in this house. Its copies existed everywhere in the country, miles of the same house stretching out into the parched horizon. For a moment, she half expected Cooper to come through the front door and ask what was for dinner.

They stopped in the kitchen, where Dreama opened a low door and pulled a bottle of chilled wine with the barest rinse of pink. She put out two glasses with enormous delicate glass bowls on thin stems and poured them three-fourths of the way full. Lee imagined crushing hers in her hand.

"This place . . ."

Dreama smirked. "I know, right? Brad flew Rebecca Tate from HGTV in to oversee the design. For an extra fee, you can pick from a few design options she put together, and we have a crew come in and place all the furniture and decorations before you move in."

Lee pretended to take a sip of the wine, even as her mouth instinctively moved toward it like an infant reaching for a nipple.

Dreama took a sip of hers and angled her body toward Lee across the marble island. "I am so sorry about what happened to Otis. I really am. I can't imagine how hard it's been."

Lee reached out and put her hands on Dreama's. "Thank you for say-

ing that. And thank you for being such a source of support these last few
weeks. I don't think I could have made it through without you."

There was that soft, permeable, well-moisturized skin. Once more,
Lee stepped into Dreama's internal world and again, she was assaulted by
images: the development's McMansions, a large stucco church, a series of
middle-aged male faces with their freshly shaved stubble and dented features. She strained to pass through this feed of surface concerns to whatever lay beyond it; she needed to travel deeper into Dreama's mind.

On the other side, she found a long motel walkway with a door at
the very end. It was outlined in a flaring yellow-pink, and smoke seeped
from the bottom. As Lee walked toward it, she looked to her left over the
railing. There was a cloudy sky and bare gray mountains in the distance.
To her right, shouts and bangs came from behind scuffed doors. When
she got to the smoking door at the end, she remembered her school fire
training and tested the rusty metal doorknob. It was cold. She opened it
and found a riot of flames in the middle of a room. It gave off an icy heat
that felt like the last flaring tingles of frostbite spreading through her body.
She winced, and the room disappeared.

Dreama's face came into focus again. She had pulled her hand back and
was leaning away from Lee. She looked at her curiously, then shrugged
it off.

"What's next for you guys? I wouldn't blame you if you wanted to leave
and never come back."

"We're going back to California. Cooper and I are still done, but we
can't stay here. Not after everything that's happened."

Dreama smiled. "I'm so happy that you're getting out again. I know
you're miserable here. You deserve to have a nice life."

"Thank you for saying that." Lee allowed herself to crumble a bit. She
became a pitiful, wounded bird across the island. Dreama came around
and put her arms around Lee. Through the press of her skin, Lee again
entered Dreama's internal world, this time running down the walkway
for the door with more speed and intention. She flung open the door and

steeled herself against the cold burn of the fire. She forced herself to focus on the room around it. It wasn't your average cheap motel room. A counter spanned the room, with cabinets above and below, and it had the same clean, trendy style as Dreama's house. Its blank cream pulsed with significance. Something important was inside this room.

Lee furiously opened cabinets and drawers, but they were all empty. She opened the final drawer at the very end of the counter and glimpsed a black book. But before she could investigate further, she was forced out, and Lee found herself back in Dreama's kitchen.

Lee asked if she could have something to eat. Dreama, looking a little bewildered, went to the fridge and pulled out containers of food. When she wasn't looking, Lee reached into her pocket for a mugwort tincture and poured a few drops into Dreama's wine.

As Lee munched on fancy cheeses and farro with arugula, Dreama finished her rosé. Her speech became slurred and her ideas disjointed. She put her face down on the cold marble and wrapped her arms around her head. Lee called out Dreama's name, then slammed her hand on the counter next to her ear and waited. Nothing. She was dead to the world.

Lee took quick, careful steps through the house and searched for the room she had seen in Dreama's mind. Upstairs, she found only tasteful bedrooms with their own bathrooms and not a bud vase or throw pillow out of place.

She remembered the basement she'd been offered as a refuge and found the stairwell. There was a wooden bar, a pool table, a screening room with a large screen and leather chairs. Faceless guest bedrooms that were nothing like the room she'd seen.

The basement opened up to the backyard, and she saw a small structure sitting on the other side. As she ran across the lawn, she could feel the slick, artificial bulk of the grass.

Inside the guesthouse, the walls were covered in mirrors. A Pilates machine sat imposingly on one side, and a boxing bag and a beige dummy torso sat erect on the other. In the middle, two exercise bikes stood side by side in front of a projector screen. There was a shower room and a small kitchen filled with bottled water and protein milks. And that was the extent of it. She was met with a beige wall in the final closet: the end of the line.

Lee realized that the room could be anywhere; it seemed like they had enough money to own houses all over the country. Or maybe it wasn't even real, just a construct of Dreama's mind.

She took another look around the room and remembered the search for Belva's black book and the false bottom. She wondered if Dreama had been given the same tutorial.

Lee studied the smooth expanse of wood floor. It reminded her of Belva's trunk at home. That solid wood meant to trick those not curious enough to prod further and look for the unexpected in a flat gray world. It required the kind of shameless, clawing persistence for which Bucks were notorious.

She got to her knees and began to crawl slowly around the edge of the room, running her hand along the wooden boards of the floor. They'd been seamlessly placed, so that when she came across a small gap, it was easy to spot. She put her thumb through it and lifted it. The board came loose, and she pulled up the boards surrounding it until a small trapdoor was exposed with a flat handle that could be pulled out.

The door was heavy as she lifted it. The first rung of a ladder was visible in the hole with nothing but darkness below. She shined her phone light down and saw the rungs continued until they hit a cement floor.

Lee climbed down the ladder's thin iron planks in the dark. It was cold as a root cellar, and all she could see was the deep-red glow from the illuminated cell phone in her jacket pocket. When she made it to the bottom, light suddenly flooded the space.

It was the room.

Lee began to open the cabinets, and this time they weren't empty. They were filled with neatly labeled plastic jars of herbs, powders, dirt, and hair arranged on bamboo tiers, bottles of tinctures and waters in rotating storage, and tools in stackable containers. In a glass-doored fridge, she saw fresh black flowers cooling on a shelf. It was the West Elm version of Belva's back-room apothecary.

She opened the far drawer, and a black leather book sat in its center on a paisley-patterned liner. The cover was charred and torn at the corners, but when Lee opened it, the pages were only singed at the edges, with all of its contents still intact. In her mother's handwriting, she read the first entry dated May 13, 1980, which described in vivid detail what it first felt like to wield the power of the land. She flipped through and found page after page of spells. So many more than in Belva's book, which was heavier on natural observations with drawings of birds and plants, like something out of Darwin's notebook.

A noise suddenly came from above, and she saw Dreama's face hovering over the entrance like a demented moon.

Lee put down the book, startled. She waited for her to speak, but Dreama only hovered there, silent. Her face was drained of all the cheer and goodwill Lee had noticed in this new Dreama. The angry, judgmental teenager Lee remembered was restored.

"Dreama. I'm sorry about snooping. Let's just talk about this. I'll come up there." Lee moved toward the ladder.

Dreama's face remained cold and impassive. "Stay where you are."

Lee started up one rung.

"I told you not to move."

Cold sweat beaded on the back of her neck. She wished she'd found something sharp.

"What's going on?"

"Don't play dumb. Let's be honest with each other now."

"Fine." Lee paused, attempting to collect herself. "What is all of this down here? Why do you have my mama's black book? I thought you hated this stuff."

Dreama rolled it over in her mind. "I never said I hated it. I've found my own *private* uses for it."

"Did you use it to kill those men? Did you try to kill Otis?"

Dreama narrowed her eyes at Lee. "I've had a hard time figuring you out since you got back. You're *arrogant*, but you have no self-esteem. You detest this place, but you can't seem to leave."

The half logic of her words had a nightmare feel to it. "Please just tell me. Did you try to kill him? Was it you this whole time?"

Dreama sank back into quiet observation.

"Why did you do it? For what possible reason?"

Dreama smiled. "It was all for you, Lee. I did it for you."

"I don't know what you're talking about." Lee was done trying to get answers from her. "Dreama. Let me the fuck out of here."

"I don't think so. I need time to think." She paused, relishing the moment. "Good night."

Dreama's face disappeared, and the door came down over the opening with a bang.

# THIRTY-TWO

"I can't sleep," Meredith said into the dark.

"Me neither," Cliff answered.

"Let's see if there's any food."

They crept into the living room and found Belva and Luann holding hands on the couch as a game show played on TV.

Belva smiled when she saw them. "I can't sleep either. I'll cook us up a little something." She shuffled slowly to the kitchen and started to take ingredients out of the cupboard. Luann tried to take over, but she swatted her away. "I'm not an invalid. Go sit down."

Luann didn't fight her, and she joined the kids at the table. They watched Belva pour milk into a saucepan. While it heated, she pulled herbs from various baggies and pots and placed them on a square of thin fabric. Then she tied it into a bundle and placed it in the pot of milk.

"What was Mom like when she was little?" Meredith asked.

Belva paused with her spoon in the air. "She was real curious and smart, same as you. Like I told you before, she was always inside herself. Even before her daddy died, she lived on the inside. Made me wonder what was going on in there sometimes."

"So she kept things from you?"

Belva shook her head. "That's not how I see it—she has her own world in there, and it's no one's but hers. We're all born with it, but some of us don't really take advantage, do we? We do all our living on the outside."

Belva set mugs of a steaming milky broth in front of each of them and sat down with her own. Meredith blew on it and took a sip. It was a rich, buttery cream spiced with smoky herb and bitter floral. The warmth of it spread through her like a towel wrapped after a cold bath. Tears filled her eyes, and she looked up at Belva and Luann. "I don't want to leave."

Belva sighed and put her hand on Meredith's. "Oh, honey. I don't want you to leave either." Cliff sniffled next to her, and Belva reached over and ruffled his hair.

"I know it's tough, but your mama's trying to do right by you," Luann offered.

Meredith scoffed.

"Your mama had it real hard after your granddaddy died. Growing up all alone in that house with your sick grandma. She did so well in school that we thought it must not be so bad. But we were fools. She was just surviving." Luann paused. "I understand why she didn't want to come back, and why she wants something better for y'all."

Belva frowned. "She's right. I let your mama down when she was little. She is a survivor. That's why she's taking y'all away."

Meredith took this in. She had fallen so deeply into the groove of being angry with her mother and analyzing her every fault that she had lost sight of the truth at the center of it. Her mom had suffered. Her irritating vigilance wasn't a personality defect, but a way of ensuring that they would never experience what she had. This had allowed Meredith to grow up without fear, and in that fearlessness, she could see things her mother couldn't. "I think the hardest thing about leaving is that there's still so much I don't know about the work. I don't know what's real and what's fake, and now I'll never know."

Meredith had tried to use the power of the land to leave the cave after the shadow brought her there, but nothing happened. It was like the land had died, or at least gone silent, beneath her. She'd thought she had this amazing gift, but when she really needed it, she was powerless. At TJ's, when the boys grabbed her, and then at the cave. For two days, she had waited, cold and helpless and hungry because she couldn't save herself.

Belva studied her. "Your mama still at Dreama's?"

Meredith nodded.

"Well, we still got tonight, don't we?" Belva got up with some effort and started down the hallway. "Come on now."

They followed her out into the garden to a place where two rows met in an X. She and Luann took off their shoes and flexed their toes in the grass, and Meredith and Cliff did the same. The blades were soft and cool against her bare skin.

"Close your eyes and concentrate on the land under your feet."

Meredith and Cliff obeyed.

"Now imagine every person who has walked this land before you."

Images of faces streamed through Meredith's mind, and she tried to slow them down, so that she could focus on each one—what they thought and felt, what they feared, what they loved. They were a part of her—she was made of the tiny bits of what they'd once been, and she wanted to feel each bit.

"And every creature that traveled over this land or made its home here."

Her mind was again a blur of images, of every animal she'd encountered— the tiny barn kitten with its bat fangs, the deer standing elegantly in the morning mist, the bees buzzing over the blooms, the snakes slithering beneath the grass. The amount of life that had existed over time, the density of memory in this one spot, it was overwhelming. It contained too much for her to process.

"And before that, when these mountains stood quiet for millions of years, with nothing to carve out its treasure or poison its air and water. It served no purpose; it only existed."

The chaos in Meredith quieted, and a calm descended over her. She imagined herself a small tree standing silently on a hillside, looking out on a sun-drenched valley.

"Now I want you to imagine roots growing out of your feet into the land."

Meredith could feel them slithering out of the bottoms and gently probing the ground. They softly burrowed into the soil and snaked down, and she felt rooted, as if she was that ancient tree. Her roots grew warm, and the glorious heat traveled up her trunk into her middle.

This time, instead of focusing on how she might wield the energy, she only stood there and experienced it. She was a small, quiet part of the land's sweeping, ancient expanse.

"I can feel them!" Cliff exclaimed.

Meredith opened her eyes, and she saw Cliff standing there with his strange light shining brightly in the night.

She looked over at Luann, whose face was content, and then over at Belva, who was watching her.

They locked eyes, and Belva whispered, "*This* is real."

# THIRTY-THREE

## LEE

Lee crouched a few inches from a small space heater in a camouflage hunting jacket, eating a Snickers and reading Redbud's black book.

Though the room was antiseptically tidy, the cabinets and drawers were brimming with things. Stacks of cheap cotton clothing, three of the same appliance, a box of a hundred fine-tipped Sharpies. Lee had done the same thing in her former life with Cooper; she'd kept a hoard of food in the fridge and things stashed in cabinets all over the house. He'd accused her of many things: consumer addiction, a lack of respect for his family, an ignorance toward money that felt like a euphemism for *white trash*. It had filled her with such shame that she'd invented new hiding places and shopped only when he was out of town. He'd never known a creature's scarcity; you stored nuts away for the leaner times. It was the only way to survive.

She'd found a drawer, the only messy one in the entire place, stuffed with empty candy bar wrappers and cookie sleeves and potato chip bags. There'd been a fresh Snickers shoved toward the back. Seeing Dreama's hoard and binge drawer had coerced her into feeling an empathy she didn't want to feel.

Every so often, she checked her phone, even though she knew it would offer the same information. *No service.*

She imagined what was happening to her children out there, unprotected. She wanted to scream, but she'd already done plenty of that to no avail. No one could hear her.

She had made her way through half of her mother's black book, and she'd yet to find a charm she could use to escape. She'd learned how to take revenge in myriad exquisite ways. To call a straying lover back by nailing his boots to the floor under the bed. That setting fire to a string the length of a man's cock could render him impotent. But there was nothing that showed her how to climb out of this hole.

She finally came upon the spell that created the shadow. She read through it and compared her slipshod version to the real thing. She hadn't done a terrible job, though nothing could compare to the force of a spell written in the thick of it.

She turned to a blank page, and then the handwriting changed.

*Dreama.*

The entries became thick-lined and filled with rage, her pencil grinding into the skin of the pages. Lee had a hard time following their meaning. They were like the rants of one possessed.

Then the entries became neater and more focused. She'd created spells that altered and enhanced her physical appearance, something Lee had never seen in either Belva's or Redbud's pages. She'd concocted love and commitment recipes that she used on her husband. She'd written charms that elevated her persuasive powers in business and guarded against unforeseen disasters.

There were no spells that sucked the life out of a body.

Lee wondered if she'd gathered people for this work. She imagined Dreama's flock of imitators raising their manicured hands around a fire. It didn't track. *Was it possible she did all of this by herself? How?*

Lee flipped back to Dreama's earlier entries and attempted to parse meaning from them. She realized that some were spells she had written for use on her adopted parents, the Shorts, a couple of zealots that Lee hadn't known very well. The man was obsessively clean. He made them scrub every surface with bleach, and sometimes he would insist they wash their hands with it. Their skin rubbed off in sheets. One time, he forced her brother Earl to gargle with bleach and water after telling him to fuck off, and his throat burned for weeks.

The woman was prone to bouts of paranoia, and she would sometimes lock them in the closet to "keep them safe." They would sit in there for hours whispering in the dark. Dreama had written a charm that she and Earl said together with their small hands against the door until the lock flicked open.

Lee climbed the ladder with Dreama's words in her head and put her hands up to the trapdoor. She whispered them and pressed up with her arms, but it didn't give.

She said them over and over in a more forceful voice, pressing her palms harder and harder into the metal.

But it didn't budge.

She tried again, this time focusing on all of the years she'd felt trapped in the life she and Cooper built, and before that in the life her mother built in this town. She felt the familiar panic rise through her chest and the certainty of its power as she chanted the words.

But the door still didn't move. She banged on it hard with her fists and screamed. The sound scraped against her raw throat.

The laws of this work still evaded her. She knew she wasn't a gifted caster, but was she incapable of even this child's charm? Had Dreama added a protection to this room? There was still so much she didn't know.

The panic made her lightheaded, and she suddenly swooned from the top rung and gripped the ladder hard to keep from falling. She slowly lowered herself to the floor. She'd only had chocolate to eat, and she was still acclimating to not drinking, but this felt different. It reminded her of when she, Kimmie, and Dreama had passed each other out one evening in elementary school.

She looked around. It didn't seem like the room had any ventilation. She wondered if she was losing oxygen, and she imagined herself slowly asphyxiating. She sank to the floor and lay down on her side, focusing on taking shallow breaths and attempting to conserve the remaining air. She thought of when she was a child, and she wanted nothing more than to drift away. A hidden part of Lee, unlocked by the delirium, felt that it could be so much easier to just pass into nothingness.

But a larger part of her, the one that had been fed and fortified over the last few weeks, not only refused to abandon her children but refused to abandon her own existence. There was still so much left for her to discover. She was a universe within a person. She contained warm creeks and mountain ranges veined with a chaotic rock that, once ignited, could radiate fury and intelligence. And there was a whole world out there, filled with people that each held their own fascinating universe to explore.

She wanted to live.

As she lost consciousness and the room faded to black, this desire sparkled inside of her.

# THIRTY-FOUR

## MEREDITH

Meredith woke to Cliff standing above her like a pale ghost.
"Jesus, what?"

"Something's wrong with Mom."

Meredith looked in the corner and saw for the first morning since she'd found Otis that Mom wasn't in the room with them.

"Where is she?" For some reason, they were whispering.

"I don't know. She was in my dream. It was dark, and she was really scared."

"Are you sure it wasn't just a dream?"

Cliff nodded gravely, and Meredith shivered in the morning chill. "Okay."

It was cold in the house as Meredith and Cliff searched each room for their mother. Meredith tiptoed past Redbud sleeping in the back room and checked the garden. She usually relished the wet chill of this place so early in the day, the breath of it entering her and filling her with inexplicable vitality. But today she only felt it as fresh fear.

After finding nothing, they finally crept into Belva's room and came over to her side of the bed. Meredith was afraid to touch her, and as she considered the best approach, a voice came.

"Y'all got something to say?" Belva's eyes remained closed, and it seemed the voice came from somewhere else in the room. Luann stirred next to her.

"Mom is gone."

Belva's eyes opened. "You check the house? The woods? Maybe she's out for a walk."

"Her car is gone, too."

"Welp, maybe she stayed over at Dreama's."

"Cliff thinks she's in trouble. He had a dream."

Belva heaved herself up. "Tell me about it."

Meredith loved this about Belva. She didn't dismiss what everyone else did.

Cliff spoke up in a small voice. "It was dark, like I couldn't see anything, but I could feel that Mom was there, and she was really hurt and scared."

Belva slowly got out of bed and shuffled over to the window. She opened it and thrust her head out with her mouth slightly open. A stiff breeze blew through the room and down the collar of Meredith's shirt. She shivered.

Belva turned back to them, and Meredith saw fear in her hard face. "I think you're right, Cliffie. Your mama's in trouble."

·   ·   ·

They came from the trees on their hands and knees, crouching behind thick pine to watch Dreama's enormous house. The windows were opaque with early-morning sun, so they couldn't see whether anyone was home. Belva breathed heavily and leaned against a tree trunk while Redbud gave her water; the half-mile walk through the woods had done her in.

"Cliff, you're the smallest. I need you to sneak along the edge of the trees and see if any cars are in the driveway."

Cliff nodded and crept through the trees until they thinned and eventually stopped at the front edge of the property. He was still for a while as he searched the area and listened for life nearby.

From the woods, Meredith heard a door slam shut, followed by the clacking of heels against stone. Dreama's Tesla pulled into the street and drove away. Cliff ran back to them, solemn but giddy. "I saw Mom's car in the garage when it opened. No other cars. Dreama just left."

Belva patted him on the shoulder. "Good work." She took another heaving breath. "Y'all, I gotta save my energy for the walk back. Get me when you found her." Belva wiped sweat from her forehead and gestured them onward. Luann declared she would stay with her.

Redbud, Meredith, and Cliff ran toward the house with their backs arched low. They snuck along the edge until they found an unlocked back door and entered a room with a pool table, bar, overstuffed couches, and the largest TV Meredith had seen in a while.

They fanned out in the house and took different floors. Meredith wound her way through the pristine bedrooms of the upstairs. She rolled her eyes at Dreama's closet, which reminded her of the closets in their old neighborhood where the designer shoes were put in glass cabinets like museum artifacts. There was no sign of her mother.

The three of them met back up on the main floor in the kitchen. They hadn't found Mom either.

Redbud took a large bowl out of a cabinet and started filling it with water from the sink. "I got an idea."

When the bowl was filled, she set it in front of Cliff on the marble island. "Belva told me you have the sight. That true?"

Cliff looked nervous. "I don't know."

"She show you how to scry?"

He shook his head.

"That's okay." She gestured for him to get closer to the bowl. "All you gotta do is look into the water, think about your mama, and tell us what you see."

Cliff shyly leaned over the bowl and stared down into the water. After a few seconds, he looked up at them, stricken. "I can't see anything." His chest started to rise and fall rapidly, and Meredith reached out and grabbed his shoulder, attempting to ground him.

"Hey. Look at me," Redbud instructed.

Cliff turned his head toward her. The hard, weathered angles of her face softened. "I want you to take a deep breath with me, okay?" They inhaled together for a few beats, and then slowly exhaled. They did this two more times, and Meredith could feel him relaxing under her hand.

"Now. Look back into the water, and don't force it. Just allow yourself to let go and see, like you usually do. Let it come to you."

Cliff bent back over and gazed down into the water. A glaze came over his eyes that Meredith recognized, like he was looking beyond this dimension into the next.

"She's somewhere very dark, like I saw in my dream. It smells musty, like a basement. And it's cold." He looked up at them. "She's really weak. I think there's something really wrong with her."

"Must be a cellar of some kind. Somewhere underground."

Meredith went to the window and looked out on the backyard where she saw the small building they'd passed on their way in from the woods. She pointed it out to Redbud.

They decided to split up and search for an entrance. Redbud took the basement, and Meredith and Cliff headed for the guesthouse.

They frantically searched the place for some kind of secret door, though she wasn't sure what that would look like in a house like this. Her only frame of reference were bookshelves masquerading as doors in gothic stories.

She and Cliff opened the last door and found a closet stacked with cases of exercise powders, including one that contained deer velvet. This was Dreama's husband's own witchy stash, though he probably wouldn't have seen it that way. They knocked on the walls like they did in the movies, listening for hollow sounds.

She started to panic in earnest as she walked back to the center of the main room, having found nothing. Her thoughts were fragmenting, feverish. She took a few deep breaths like Redbud had instructed Cliff.

She calmed. She saw Cliff standing there, looking to her for their next move.

"I want you to close your eyes and try to feel or *see* Mom. Whatever you want to call it. You might be able to if she's close."

Cliff did as he was told and stood there for a while. Meredith didn't breathe.

"I think I can feel something." He started to move, and she followed behind him as he took slow, steady steps around the room. When he'd made it to the opposite side, he stopped and took a step back. "It's stronger here, but . . ." He took a step to the side, doubled back, and then took a step in the other direction. He stopped and opened his eyes. "Here. It's strongest here. But it's getting weaker."

Meredith crouched down and frantically clawed at the floorboards, looking for some place to pry them up. When she finally found the hole, she split her thumb bringing it up and spilled blood on the sunken handle of the door.

It was dark in the opening. Meredith called down into the hole but received no answer. She turned around and climbed down the rungs quickly, nearly slipping on her way down. She hit the floor after only a few steps and the light activated, revealing her mother's body on the floor.

She was pale and cool to the touch, and she didn't stir when Meredith shook her. She tried picking her up and putting her over her shoulder to bring her up the ladder, but she was far too heavy. With each second that passed, Meredith became more panicked and incredulous at how she'd gone this long without knowing the basic methods of saving someone's life.

The light above her shifted, and she saw Redbud coming down the ladder. She instructed Meredith to hold the bottom half of her mother's body while Redbud pulled the top half up the ladder in front of her. It was rough going, but they eventually made it up with Cliff's help.

Up above, Redbud checked Mom's pulse and breathing as Cliff looked on in horror. She pressed her palms on Mom's chest as she whispered an incantation that Meredith couldn't quite hear. Then she put her mouth to Mom's and filled her with breath. She did this a few times with tears in her eyes as Meredith stood at a distance and Cliff stroked Mom's lifeless hand. There was no response.

Meredith thought of how cruel she'd been to her mother since they'd come to Craw Valley. She was supposed to be the one who saw the truth of her, the glorious strangeness and the strength beneath what others misunderstood and overlooked, and love her for it. Instead, she had resented and rejected her like everyone else.

She'd wanted to punish her for lying and for keeping the magic from her, and to have the freedom to change and evolve without her mother's constant protection.

And now it all felt ridiculous.

Meredith steeled herself and knelt next to Mom's body opposite Redbud. She took her hands and nodded at her to continue the incantation.

*"Then the Lord God formed man of dust from the ground, and breathed into his nostrils the breath of life,*

*Breathed into his nostrils the breath of life.*

*Breathed into his nostrils the breath of life . . ."*

As Redbud spoke, Meredith closed her eyes and quieted her mind. She visualized the roots snaking down and accessing the power in the land as Belva had shown her, and soon she could feel it flowing through her hands into Redbud's.

She visualized her mother alive. She watched as a younger version of her ran around the yard with her and Cliff until she was sweat-soaked and gasping for breath. She imagined her calming, and her fresh, pink lungs filling and emptying perfectly once again.

Redbud was shouting now.

Meredith opened her eyes, and her mother lay there wild-eyed and wheezing for air. They sat there, suspended, as her breathing steadied.

"Oh, thank god," she rasped. "I didn't want to die."

They all laughed, and then Meredith sobbed into her mother's neck, something she hadn't done since she was too young to remember such things. Mom weakly clutched her shoulders. In her touch, she could feel her mother's love flooding her, warm and light like the heat had been turned on inside her body. This love *knew* her, and this knowing was a comfort that was truly freeing. She tried to send her own love back and gripped her tightly to make the transfer.

"I'm sorry I've been such an asshole," Meredith said, pulling back.

Mom reached up and wiped a tear from Meredith's cheek as she struggled to catch her breath.

"Oh, honey, it runs in the family. You get that honest," Redbud quipped.

Lee chuckled hoarsely, and Cliff giggled, but Meredith didn't join in. "I'm serious. I'm sorry I didn't try to understand. I feel like I betrayed you."

Mom put a shaky hand on Meredith's arm. "No, I'm sorry. I shouldn't have kept it from you. You were right to fight for it—look at how powerful you are." She paused and took a deep breath. "No matter what happens between us, we will always have this." She gripped her harder. "I will never leave you."

Meredith carefully wrapped her arms around her this time, and in the shared space, she felt their worlds joining once again—not into the small, protected world that only they and Cliff had occupied, but into a new, open one that encompassed everything they'd discovered.

"We gotta move," Redbud said, reminding them that they were still in Dreama's guesthouse. Meredith and Redbud helped Mom up on either side, and they slowly walked her toward the door.

"Wait! We need to get Mama's black book. It's still down there," Mom cried.

"I got it." Cliff disappeared down the hole, and a few seconds later he was back, clutching the large book to his chest.

Belva seemed to regain her strength when she saw Mom hanging between them, and she got up, leaning on Luann for support. As they disappeared slowly into the woods, a fierce wind whipped against Meredith's ears and blew through the trees, creating a rushing sound as thousands of branches rubbed together. When she opened her mouth, she could taste metal and blood. She looked back as the sound cascaded over the mountain and thundered like an invisible giant barreling through the woods, heading straight for them.

# THIRTY-FIVE

## LEE

A sliver of moon looked down on the clearing where four women stood with palms facing out at midnight.

There was no fire or bundle of herbs or wooden stake.

Only flesh and bone and blood.

Four generations of blood that rose and fell with each woman like the sawtooth silhouette of a mountain range, until they now stood here, ready to face their demons.

They listened to the snap and tread of someone coming down the path. Her hair glinted like stolen jewelry in the moonlight as she came into view.

Cliff saw that she'd come for the black book tonight. Now he was safely tucked away in the cabin with Billy, Kimmie, and Luann.

Dreama stepped carefully into the clearing and stopped at a distance like a bobcat studying its prey. That cold fire blazed in her eyes, and all cheerful pretense had been dropped.

There would be no more camouflage. They would lay themselves bare before the woods and its spirits tonight.

Dreama's attention settled on Lee, who held the charred black book to her chest. "I'm here to take back what's mine."

"It's not yours. It never was." Lee held it tighter to her chest.

"It was abandoned and I gave it a new home. I used it far better than she ever did."

Lee moved to slice back, but Belva put a hand on her arm. She'd promised she would let Belva try mercy first.

"Why, Dreama?" Belva asked.

Dreama didn't turn toward Belva; instead, she fixed her gaze on Redbud.

"You *killed* my mother. The only person who ever gave a damn about me." She took a deep breath. "I thought about hurting you for years. I would daydream about it when things were bad at the Shorts. It gave me something to work toward. When I was finally ready, I followed you to that motel we used to live at. I watched you go into one of the rooms, and I saw you were torturing yourself far better than I ever could. It didn't feel right." She pulled her gaze from Redbud and paced in front of them.

"I realized I'd been focusing on the wrong thing. I should have been investing in *myself*. So that's what I did. I turned myself into someone worth a damn who could make Craw Valley a better place." She smiled.

"I knew I'd have to get rid of people like Belva and her gatherings. It was all too public. It's fine to use local superstitions as a bit of color, to set up a tour during Halloween or open a gift shop. But you can't actually *practice* it out in the open. It looks backwards to outsiders. I had time on my side. Belva is old, and there was no one for her to pass on the tradition to. Redbud had destroyed herself, Billy's a hermit, and you were gone. When she died, her work would die with it."

She gestured at Lee. "But then you showed up out of nowhere. The last thing I planned for. I thought, Dreama, keep yourself together, she'll only be here a little while. She hates this place. But then I dreamt of a future where you and your children would stay and continue the tradition.

"I had to discredit the work and scare you off, Lee. I had to make people think Belva was killing the targets of her spells. I couldn't risk you taking over for her and getting in my way. And I'd been planning to get rid of those bastards. We couldn't have a pedophile in our school. The scandal would ruin us. And TJ had it coming. He's the one who got my brother into dealing. People don't want to move to a place with a drug problem.

"When Meredith went missing, I thought damn, she'll never leave now. I tried my own ways of finding her, but they didn't work. And then you figured it out, Lee. Turned out Auntie Red still had a few tricks. I thought, this will be the nail in the coffin." Dreama's face went hard again.

"You were going to leave. No one else had to get hurt. But then Otis tells you he loves you or whatever he said and it all went to hell. I never thought you'd throw so much away over a man. Especially after what happened with your mama. Men are a means to an end, and anyone who acts otherwise is gonna end up sad and alone." She now fixed her gaze on all of them. "I can't let y'all get in the way of what I've started here."

Redbud stepped forward as if to touch Dreama. "Honey, I'm sorry about your mama. I didn't know it was her who was messing around with Hank. I didn't want *anyone* to die. It was a big mistake, and I've paid for it."

"It's not about that anymore. This is about the future."

Belva stepped forward as well. "Dreama, we're family. We can help you."

"Don't talk to me about family. You abandoned me and Earl when Mama died. Let us live with those awful people. My brother would still be alive if it weren't for you."

"But those were your mother's wishes. I was trying to respect her."

"You know Mama was half crazy from that church and the moonshine by then. You should have fought for me. But you didn't. Because you didn't think I was special."

Belva inhaled to protest, but this time Lee put a hand on her arm. She had allowed them to reason with Dreama out of their own guilt, and it hadn't worked.

There would be no mercy for her tonight.

"Look, Dreama. You hurt an innocent man. You're dangerous, and we can't allow you to continue your work."

"I'm not scared of you."

Meredith stepped forward, completing the line. A pendant of wood blackened by lightning hung around her neck. The four women joined hands. "So be it."

They closed their eyes and began to hum. The roundness of it was spiked at the edges, like a cocoon made out of razor wire.

Redbud opened her eyes, and they were inky with the desire to protect those she loved. "The woman who stands before us has used the power of the land to harm our community."

Redbud's voice was a gutting blade, and the women gritted their teeth against it. Meredith dug her heels deeper into the earth, and a glow built under the surface of her skin.

"She has killed two men and hurt a third. She has disgraced the Buck name. And she works every day to transform the land and the community so that she may wield its power only for herself."

Meredith was nearly shimmering now, the power of the land drawing up through her and traveling through their hands like an electric current. Lee felt the primordial tingle in every cell.

Redbud chanted, "Blow out her light." And the others responded louder and with more force, "Blow out her light!"

Redbud screamed, "BLOW OUT HER LIGHT!" and the others responded, "BLOW OUT HER LIGHT!" and then they were all screaming as one. "BLOW OUT HER LIGHT!"

Dreama's amusement was replaced by apprehension. She drew inward, and her face was cold when she resurfaced.

Belva had told them the binding wouldn't last forever, but it would allow them to get close enough to sever her connection to the land's power permanently.

"This ain't a fight you can win now, darlin'. Let's work this out," Belva said.

"You've always underestimated me." Dreama turned toward the dark wall of woods to her left. A piece of the darkness broke from the murk and loped toward them.

The shadow looked like a copy of the one Redbud created all those years ago, but more Dreama-like in its essence. It came to a stop next to Dreama and loomed next to her with its flat, blank head turned toward the four women. It seemed to be under her control, with a form more solid than Redbud's, like a nightmare set with gelatin, firm and horrifying.

Dreama nodded her head at the women, and the shadow lumbered toward them.

Belva met it in stride and pulled a handful of black powder from her pocket. A mix of Pallie's grave dirt, gunpowder, and dried snake.

Belva chanted, "Even though I walk through the darkest valley, I will fear no evil, for you are with me." She blew the grit into its face. A thick cloud formed around the creature. When it cleared, it was on its knees with its head down.

But after a moment, it started to rise again. It put a hand to Belva's face, and she went down in a heap on the grass.

Meredith lurched forward to defend Belva. She took the creature by the shoulders, and as she made contact, a shot of leftover energy pulsed from her hands into the murky depths of it, illuminating its form like the sky during a thunderstorm. It hunched over and tried to regain its balance. Meredith placed her hands firmly on its back and delivered an even brighter light pulse, which brought it to the ground. As she crouched down to deliver a third blow, the thing twisted around and met her hands with its own. Darkness passed through Meredith; she flickered in the night like a lightbulb. Lee felt it blink through her as well, and she lost consciousness.

When she came to, Lee was on her back on the ground, still clutching the black book. She saw Meredith lying still a few feet away. She tried to reach for her, but she could barely move.

On her other side, the creature advanced on Redbud, who stood firm and strong before it. She reached out and grabbed its arm as if to share a memory, and Lee wondered what memory she would show. Maybe it would be powerful enough to remind Dreama of her humanity. The creature seemed intrigued at first, and its body went still in her grasp as if a moment from long ago played in its mind. But then the reverie passed, and the creature wrenched its arm out of Redbud's grasp. She had no other defenses, and it swiftly struck her down.

Meredith stirred, but she struggled to get up. The creature loped over to her and kneeled next to her body. It leaned down to put its mouth over hers as Lee imagined it had done to Otis.

At the same time, Dreama walked over to Lee and attempted to pry the black book from her grasp. Filled with sudden adrenaline, Lee reached out and grabbed Dreama's arm.

.    .    .

The land that stretched before Lee was unyieldingly flat and filled with dead trees twisted into unnatural poses. The ground was only empty, mole-colored dust. It was the type of gray day she remembered from childhood where the world felt lifeless. It was contagious, filling her with a heavy inertia. It was hard to move and hard to care about moving.

There was a small yellow house in the distance, and she willed herself to walk to it, propelled only by her stubborn will. As she got closer, she saw that its paint was graying, the roof sagged, and the window glass was shattered. Lee hadn't been to Ruby Jo's house since she was a child, but she still remembered it. Back then it was well-maintained and fastidiously clean. Ruby Jo was always in the kitchen, having inherited Belva's cooking skills, if not her more magical leanings.

Lee stepped inside the house. The plaster was flaking off the walls, and the furniture was covered in mold and dust. There were gaps in the floorboards that Lee had to step over in order to get to Dreama's old room. Inside, a ten-year-old Dreama crouched around a small fire that seemed to blaze without catching the rest of the house. Her palms were held up to it as if to warm them. When she saw Lee, her face went fierce and animalistic.

"What are you doing here?"

Lee studied the bony creature. "You know why I'm here."

Dreama bared her small teeth. "Well you ain't welcome."

Lee felt Dreama's psychic force attempting to eject her from her internal world. Lee's body began to rise and become immaterial, but she dug in her heels. Dreama was weaker now, and Lee had honed her gift.

Dreama grunted and turned back toward the fire.

"It's time to put it out."

"No!" Dreama put herself between Lee and the flames and hunched over it like a mother protecting her young.

"It's the only way to keep you from doing more harm. You'll still be a person. You'll still be able to do anything a person can do."

"That ain't nearly enough," she spat.

"If you keep going this way, you're going to lose yourself completely. Let's put it out while you're still here."

Dreama stood and stared at Lee. "I see what you're playing at. You want to be the only Buck witch in town. Well, no fucking way. It's time for you to leave."

She attempted to eject Lee again, this time with more force, but Lee was able to hang on.

Dreama cried out in frustration and charged at Lee like a wild animal. Lee caught her at the forearms and held her away from her as she flailed. Through her rough, bony limbs, she sensed yet another opening. Something deeper and more secret, like a portal to the center of the earth.

She didn't step in so much as *descend*.

She sank into a place so dense that it was like hovering in the middle of a peach pit. The force surrounding her was strong and familiar, but hard to place at first for its ubiquitous, smothering power. She had never felt emotion with such density, inhaling its most concentrated chemical, right in the atomic middle of its surge. It was pure, uncut *shame*.

And then, there was a memory materializing around Lee.

Dreama lay on a sofa bed in their room at the Red Roof Inn. She could hear the thud of the bed against the wall of the locked bedroom.

After a while, the banging stopped, and she heard a deep voice. Uncle Hank.

At first her mom had snuck him in late at night when she thought Dreama and Earl were asleep. But now, she didn't seem to care if they knew or not. He came at all hours—early in the morning, or at lunchtime, or after dinner. Mama could be obsessive about the things she loved; at one time, she had been obsessed with Dreama and Earl. The force of her attention had almost been too much. Then she'd moved on to God, the church, and the moonshine they served like communion. And then, when Hank started attending the services with her, it became all about Hank. Her world revolved around him; Dreama wasn't sure she knew they were there most of the time.

Through the wall, she heard Mama say, "Let's just run away."

"You mean for the weekend?" he asked.

"No, I mean forever. No kids or wives. No bills. Just you and me. Living the lives we always wanted, far away from this town."

They were quiet for a bit. "Okay. Let's do it," he agreed.

"Really? You would?"

"I'd follow you anywhere, girl." There was giggling, and then her mother was shrieking like he was tickling her.

"I don't wanna wait."

"I don't wanna wait neither."

"Tomorrow, then."

"Tomorrow."

Dreama couldn't listen to any more. She put on her shoes and sweater and ran along the road and through the woods to Uncle Billy's cabin. He let her stay there when she couldn't stand to be in her mother's orbit.

As she got closer, she heard voices. Billy was out of town on a fishing trip; no one should've been there.

From behind a thicket of trees, she watched as Aunt Red, Billy, and a few women she recognized gathered around a fire in the back and began to perform a ritual. She listened to Red as she described her husband's cheating and her intention to banish his mistress from their lives.

Red was talking about her mother. And she had no idea. No one knew but Dreama.

She watched, mesmerized, as the ritual unfolded and the group became wild and vengeful in the flames. She knew Grandma Mama and Red did such things, but her mother had forbidden her from learning the work herself. Red, in particular, was a sight to behold. No wonder her mother was so jealous. She may have figured out a few love charms, but she had none of her sister's power.

When it was over, Dreama saw the shadow lurking at the edge of the woods, and she could tell that Red saw it, too. The chill of death drifted into her lungs and snatched away the air. It would take vengeance against Hank's mistress, her mother. And Dreama welcomed it.

The next morning, Dreama pretended to be asleep when Hank and her mom snuck out of the motel room clutching their suitcases. It wasn't until hours later, the sun already starting to set, when Grandma Mama picked Dreama and Earl up in her truck and took them to Red's house.

By the yellow light of the kitchen, Grandma Mama told them that their mama and uncle Hank had died in a bridge collapse. She said their mama was with God now, but it didn't make it any easier. She knew it was shit luck, and she was sorry for it. She opened her arms, and Earl went to her. But Dreama didn't want to be touched or consoled. She couldn't feel anything. Not her body, or her own mind, or the solid things around her. If someone touched her, the feeling might come flooding back in.

Dreama rose from the table and walked down the hall toward Red's room, where they'd said she could sleep for the night. She passed the open doorway of Opaline's room, where she and Red lay spooned against one another, and Dreama's chest lurched. The feeling was starting to prickle back into her body. She forced herself to turn away and continue down the hall.

Dreama lay down in her clothes on the large bed and felt small and wretched in its expanse. It was her fault. If she had warned them, or stopped Red, Mama would have been saved.

She had *killed* her mother, and now there was no going back. It would never be undone. She and Earl would never see her again.

The prickling increased until it was a deep, searing pain. She lay still and allowed it to burn her inch by inch. She wanted it to turn her to ash. She hoped that in the morning, she would not wake up, because she would no longer exist.

When the pain had nothing left to burn and all that remained was the shame, it compacted into a dense pit at the center of her.

In the nighttime silence of the house, she heard faint footsteps on the hardwood, and then a screen door carefully opened and shut. She forced herself up and went to the window in the corner. She watched as Red poked the fire back to life and took her black book out of a suitcase like she had at the ritual. It was like the one Grandma Mama used for her recipes, and like the brand-new one she had given her just a few months ago. Dreama had been eager to learn; she'd felt the power of the land bubbling up inside of her for weeks before Grandma Mama said she was ready. But her mother had taken it away from her and forbidden Grandma Mama from teaching Dreama anything about her work. It had enraged her, especially when she found her mother's secret love charms.

Now, as she watched Red place her hand on the book and then push it into the flames, something sparked within Dreama. Here was her chance. For vengeance. For power. If she was an evil little thing, then she would embrace it.

She snuck out the front door as Red came in through the back, and without concern for her body, she thrust her bare arms into the fire, pulled out the book, and beat it against the lawn to extinguish its embered edges. When it had cooled, she opened it to the first page and read about the power Red had discovered, and the spark ignited and became a blaze inside of Dreama.

Everything went black, and Lee felt the layers of her gradually returning until she could feel her head and body again. Then she opened her eyes
to find she was back in Ruby Jo's house. The same young Dreama stood
over her with a concerned expression, until she saw that Lee was fine, and
she bared her teeth once more.

"How dare you!" She launched at Lee again, and Lee tried to fight her
off without hurting her.

"Dreama, I'm sorry. That must have been so hard. Blaming yourself for
your mother's death"

At the mention of Ruby Jo, Dreama thrashed even harder in Lee's grip
and attempted to slash her face with her small jagged fingernails. Lee held
her down and allowed her to tire herself out, and eventually she slowed
and then stopped. She moved away from Lee and leaned against the wall,
breathing hard from a teary-eyed grimace.

Lee sat down at a safe distance. "I would have been angry, too. She
was going to leave you and Earl all by yourselves." Lee paused. "I know
what it's like to feel like your mom doesn't care about you. It made me
feel worthless when I was younger. I had to get angry just so the sadness
wouldn't pull me under."

Dreama let the tears trickle down her face and collect in the folds
of her neck while she stared at a spot in the middle of the floor. "I
wish I could take it all back. That was the first spell I looked for in
Aunt Red's book. One that could turn back time so that I could save
her." Her voice cracked, and she took a deep breath. "I would have
forgiven her for wanting to leave. Now that I'm older, I understand it
a bit more. Not that I think it was okay, but I understand it. Wanting
to escape."

"Me too. I've spent most of my life wanting to escape."

"I just wish I could see her again, so I could tell her I'm sorry."

Lee went to open her mouth, but then stopped. There was a smell of
bread browning in the oven that she hadn't noticed before. They both went

quiet and sniffed the air. Lee trailed it to the kitchen with Dreama following closely behind her.

Ruby Jo was hunched over the counter with her back to them. While
the bread rose and crusted in the oven, she chopped plant bits and added
them to a rich stew.

Dreama stood behind her mother and stared, as if she was afraid
to touch her. When Ruby Jo turned around, she yelped in surprise and
wrapped her arms around Dreama's shoulders and pulled her in against
her chest. Dreama's body trembled, and Ruby Jo held her out so she could
see her face.

"What's wrong, baby?"

Dreama could barely speak above a brittle whisper. "I'm so sorry,
Mama. I'm so sorry I didn't warn you."

Ruby Jo smoothed Dreama's hair, and the tenderness of the gesture
undid her; she put her face into her mother's shoulder and allowed it all to
flow out of her, untempered, in racking, hysterical sobs.

When she quieted, Ruby lifted Dreama's head from her shoulder and
held her face in front of hers. "No, baby, I'm the one who's sorry. I don't
know what I was thinking. You and your brother were my whole world.
Hank was just another man passing through." Ruby Jo smiled tearily at
Dreama. "I don't think I woulda gotten more than a few hours down the
road before I turned back. But I guess we'll never know." She wiped under
Dreama's eyes and then her own. "Do you think you can forgive me? I'd
understand if you couldn't. It's the worst thing a mother can do to her
children. In all honesty, it shouldn't be forgiven." She tried to smile again.
"But it ain't for me. It's for you, baby. I want you to have a little peace in
this life."

"I can forgive you, Mama. I've already forgiven you. What I can't do is
forgive myself. It's not just your blood that's on my hands. I've hurt other
people."

"No one is beyond forgiveness, my love."

Lee thought of her own mother back at the clearing, lying unconscious. If they made it out of this, and Lee finally, truly forgave her, maybe
Redbud would disappoint her. Maybe she'd relapse and hurt her and the
cycle would start all over again. But even if she did, could Lee be free of
the weight of it if she forgave? Could she finally forgive herself? They'd
never get back to that time before, when everything felt like magic. But
maybe they could have something else, something real and honest.

Ruby Jo took Dreama's chin between her fingertips and brought her
face up to hers. "But you have to atone for what you've done. Don't just
say you're sorry like that does a damn thing. Atonement means action.
Sacrifice." She made sure Dreama was looking her in the eye. "Can you
do that?"

Dreama cut her eyes at Lee.

"Dreama, I asked you a question."

She turned back toward her mother.

Ruby Jo continued, "You know how good it feels when you make
things right. Like a weight is being lifted off your shoulders, and you're
light enough to drift up to Heaven."

A serenity settled over Dreama as she contemplated this. "Okay,
Mama. I'll do it."

Ruby Jo smiled. "I knew you would. You're my good, strong girl. Now
run along now. I'll be here if you need me."

Dreama lingered in the kitchen staring at her mother's back as she
stirred the stew, unwilling to leave her presence yet. Then she inhaled
deeply and forced herself to turn away.

Lee followed Dreama back into the bedroom. The small fire still crackled coldly in the middle of the floor. They both crouched and stared into
its flames.

"When you moved back, I dreamt you would continue the tradition
like I said, but I also dreamt y'all would be a family again—you, Redbud, Belva, your kids. I was so angry." Dreama clenched her fists at the
memory. "It wasn't fair. I have lost everyone who's ever truly loved me. I

couldn't let y'all be happy like that." Her face drooped. "It was easier to blame your mama and channel all my rage toward y'all than to confront my own shame." Her voice cracked. "I don't know if I can really forgive myself, and I don't know if I should. But I can try to make it right."

Lee rubbed Dreama's back and wrapped her arms around her bony frame. Dreama buried her face in Lee's shoulder, and they crouched there together. For a moment, they were just two lost girls comforting each other.

Then Dreama turned back to the flames. "I don't think I can put it out. I need you to do it."

"Okay."

Dreama got up and turned toward the wall, keeping her back to Lee. "I can't watch."

Lee went into the now-empty kitchen and filled a dirty pitcher with brown sulfuric water. She positioned it over the flames. "Are you ready?"

"Goddamn, just do it."

Lee emptied the pitcher onto the flames, and a cloud of smoke filled the room. When it cleared, the fire was still burning brightly.

She found a dusty blanket on the couch and tossed it onto the flames, but the fire seemed to repel it, and the blanket ended up on the other side of the room.

Lee studied the fire and noticed again that it wasn't giving off any heat. She swiped a finger through the flames and felt only a slight chill. Lee brought her bare hands down to smother it, but a strong force resisted her from within. She pushed down with all of her might, but it wouldn't yield.

"Dreama, I need your help. I think it has to be you."

Dreama exhaled in a way that reminded Lee of Meredith and turned around from the wall. She crouched down next to Lee and put her hands above the fire, then brought them back to her lap.

"Do we really gotta do this? I promise I'll be good from now on."

"Can you make that promise?"

Dreama's eyes glinted with mischief. "I guess not." She put her hands back up, and they both brought their palms down on the fire. It resisted again, the blue seeping through their fingers and curling up around the sides.

Dreama bore down harder and screamed as if she was giving birth. Blood vessels broke in her face, and water streamed from her eyes and forehead. Lee felt the fire give way beneath her hands.

And then there was nothing.

# THIRTY-SIX

## MEREDITH

Meredith was the only one awake when Cooper knocked on the door the next morning. She'd never gone to sleep.

She had come to in the clearing last night with Redbud and Belva crouched above her, looking faint and haggard but mercifully alive. Her mother was still unconscious, but Belva assured her she would be fine. Dreama was gone, and Belva said they wouldn't have to worry about her any longer. They carried Mom between the three of them up to the house in the early-morning darkness. There was no spirit of victory among them; Dreama had been one of their own.

After they put Mom to bed, Meredith watched the sun come up from the porch swing, her body a lantern with the land's energy still blazing inside her, meeting the dawn.

She went out to greet her father on the front grass. He was bent over a makeshift fire pit and fingering a charred remnant of sleeve. "Hey, Dad."

He looked up at her, startled. "What is this?"

"Last night we had to burn our clothes." They hadn't used the ritual clearing for fear of tainting it with the powerful, vengeful magic they'd been exposed to. She wasn't interested in explaining this to him. "So, what are you doing here?"

"I'm here to take you home." He smiled expectantly.

"What are you talking about?"

His mouth flattened. "Your mom said you guys were coming back to California."

"Oh, right. There's been a change of plans. We're staying here."

"If she's changed her mind, then she can stay here. You guys are coming with me."

"Mom won't let that happen."

"She can't stop me. I didn't bring the police this time, but if she wants to involve them, I will. She didn't show up for court. I have the right to assume custody."

Meredith was struck by how petty he seemed with his talk of police and courts; these institutions that knew nothing of their lives. Did he know what their family could do? To think that he could wield any power over them was absurd.

"Dad. We're not going with you."

"I know your mom won't be happy, but she's made her decision. If she came with us, you guys could be together. This is not my fault. I'm just trying to protect you."

"You're not listening. Cliff and I are not going back to California. We are staying here. This is where we belong."

He balked. "You can't be serious. This place is . . . a nightmare. How could you ever want to live here?"

She felt sorry for him. His worldview was so limited, and it hadn't necessarily been his fault. He was a victim of his upbringing. "I don't expect you to understand. But you can respect what we want and drop all of this legal stuff. No one cares about it. No one's paying attention to you. It's why Mom hasn't come to court. We have more important things to tend to."

He seemed to realize he'd lost control of the conversation, and he groped around to take it back. "You're still a child, Meredith. You don't get to make these decisions."

"Dad. Is this what you really want? To be in a house alone with me and Cliff? It would be so weird and awkward. You know it. I know it. So please, just let us be happy here. We'll all be so much happier if we admit what we want and allow each other to have it."

Cooper sighed and chewed on the end of his sunglasses. He looked around at the property as if surveying the place, but she knew he was just avoiding eye contact. "Fine. If that's what you and Cliff really want." He put a hand up to the back of his head. "I love you guys, no matter what she's been saying to you. I'm still your father."

Her face softened, and she put her arms out for a hug. "I know, Dad. I love you, too." He put his arms around her, and she could smell his cologne, like spicy, deep-hued oranges. He was such a fragile man at his core, and she started to write a spell in her head for his protection.

*Corn silk wrapped around an abandoned turtle shell until you can't see it. Must be kept in breast pocket of coat for storage against the heart. Words said while wrapping, "This man is a soft by-product of insulated privilege. He does not have the armor for this world. Give him this shell and protect him from harm."*

# THIRTY-SEVEN

## LEE

Lee came to in the milky light of morning.

Her mother sat sleeping in a chair pulled up to the bed. She wasn't the wretched addict, and she wasn't the glowing witch. She was something in between, or maybe she was neither of those things. Lee thought it was a special talent to be inscrutable, even to those closest to you. It didn't have to mean that you were emotionally deficient. It could mean that you were constantly changing, and that you had a rich inner life that was like a world unto itself.

Lee reached out for Redbud's wrist hanging over the arm of the chair, and she felt her rich inner life opening for her.

It had the wispy watercolor quality of a dream. Rocks rose up on either side of the wide lazy river, sparkling mud-colored in the sun. Daddy rowed in the back of the small boat, looking sober and wily in his blue jeans with a cigarette clenched between his lips. Redbud sat in the front facing him, her vibrance startling—hair like lacquered wood, skin undented, clean hazel eyes. She got on her knees next to a young Lee, and they both leaned over and trailed their hands in the water. A dragonfly landed on Lee's small arm, and she and her mother cooed at its iridescence. A look passed between them, something unknowable and charged with an amber light.

Lee lingered on the fairy-tale tableau, trying to soak up the feeling. Then it started to dissolve at the edges, and slowly, the light at its center went out, and she returned to the bedroom.

Redbud was watching her from the chair, and Lee let go of her wrist.

"You got your memories back."

"Some of them." Redbud sighed. "If only we could go back and do it all over."

"It wasn't all romantic river floats, Mama." She smirked at her mother, and they both chuckled.

"I know. It just hurts to remember what I used to be. I wasn't perfect, but I was powerful. And I'm the one who threw it all away. No one took it from me. I got no one else to blame." Her eyebrows raised and her eyes filled. "And what I did to you. And us. I'll never forgive myself. I understand if you and I can't have a real relationship. I don't deserve it. As someone who can hold a grudge, believe you me, I understand."

Lee gestured for Redbud to join her on the bed, and she obeyed. They sat there against the headboard with their legs crossed at the ankle in the same way. "We'll never get back to the way things were. I was only a kid back then, and things are more complicated now. But I want a real relationship. I want to give you another chance. That's all I've ever really wanted. I was just afraid you would hurt me again if I gave it to you."

Redbud clutched at Lee and wrapped her arms around her, and Lee let herself fall into it, as scary as it still was. She fell into a tender, pink feeling of their love.

Then Lee gently pulled away, and Redbud settled back against the headboard and entwined her arm with Lee's. "I'll try as hard as I can to deserve it, baby, I promise. That's the fun of grandkids, ain't it? You can do things right this time. They can know a better version of me than you did."

Lee smiled. "There's just one version of you, Mama. All of that power is still in you. I can feel it."

Redbud smiled gratefully and wiped a tear away.

Meredith came into the room and stood in front of the bed, and they made a space between them for her.

Redbud gripped Meredith's hand. "I've been meaning to apologize for lying to you, honey. I was trying to keep you from making my same mistakes." She smiled. "But I don't have to worry about that with you. You're a better person than I ever was."

Meredith smiled and leaned into Redbud's shoulder. "Thank you for saying that." She paused. "Will you teach me for real now?"

Redbud raised an eyebrow. "We'll see."

They heard footsteps, and Cliff timidly entered the room before leaping onto the bed. Meredith pulled him into their pile, and his giggles were infectious, spreading through their bodies.

"What's going on in here?" Kimmie appeared in the doorway, looking put out. "How dare y'all cuddle without me!" She launched herself at the pile, and the bed groaned beneath them.

Sausage vapors wafted into the room, and Meredith's stomach grumbled audibly. They all laughed at the demonic sound and filed out of the room to the kitchen.

Billy was stirring sausage gravy in the skillet, and Belva was pulling fresh biscuits out of the oven. Luann came in from outside with a bowl of apples from the tree.

Meredith and Cliff pushed the tables together and covered them in a tablecloth like Belva liked. Then they all sat down to eat together, devouring the food like wild animals until the plates and pans were clean. As they sat there with their hearts and bellies full, Belva slapped her thighs and looked around at her family. "Okay, y'all. Let's go to the creek."

•  •  •

They were some kind of procession as they walked down to the water: Cliff and Meredith skipping ahead with Kimmie, Billy and Lee supporting Belva between them, Redbud and Luann linking arms like teenagers. Lee felt like she was attending a reverse baptism, a group of people restored to themselves, unsaved.

When they reached the bank, Belva tried tugging off her sweater, and Lee helped her pull it over her head. Then came her T-shirt and pants and her shoes. Billy and Lee held one arm each as she lowered herself into the water and sighed.

Meredith was the first to follow suit, stripping down to her underwear and wading in, followed by Luann, Cliff, Billy, Kimmie, and Redbud. Meredith and Cliff splashed around in the sun, and Luann and Belva floated on their backs like lilies.

Lee just wanted to sit and take it all in from the bank. She swept her fingers through the water, warm as a bathtub in the autumn chill. It was like a hot spring, but she wasn't sure what the energy source could be. She imagined something warm and pulsing below them, like a giant heart made of fat roots.

The peach seeped back into Belva's pale cheeks and hair, and the violet bags disappeared from Luann's eyes as they giggled on their backs. Billy rose from the creek with Cliff standing on his shoulders, and he shrieked before diving off. Redbud glinted with the water as she swam strokes. Meredith and Kimmie jumped in holding hands, and when they came up for air, Kimmie's quiet sadness had washed away.

Lee allowed herself to lean back onto the bank and listen to the sounds of her family. The wild grasses cocooned her, and she could smell the wet split of their broken stalks. She brought her face up to the sunshine dappling through the canopy.

She wondered at how she had overlooked such nourishment. Elsewhere, people were trying to re-create this feeling in many different ways and often coming up short. Here, she only needed to stop moving and unfold herself to it.

# EPILOGUE

## Six months later

The sun was still out as they made their way to the clearing.

Cliff pulled his hand free from Lee's and ran ahead to Kimmie, who placed her flower crown on his head. They skipped through the throngs of people coming down the path.

Once the investigations into TJ and Mr. Hall went cold and the memory of the Bucks' involvement was buried under the frost and snow, the town returned to Belva's booth at Peeper's and resumed shaking their hands in church. No matter what happened, the community always came back together. They had no choice; they were all they had.

At the clearing, the townspeople greeted one another and gossiped in clusters and held each other after the long, harsh winter. They were like cave creatures poking their heads out after a lonely hibernation and drinking up the sunshine. They were all blasted off its rays.

Billy and Luann tended to the fire. The flames took on a different quality in the sunlight, light meeting light and becoming a joyous, unfamiliar element. Beverly and Linda handed out flower necklaces and wove the leftover blooms in their hair, so that every encounter was filled with wild perfume.

Redbud stood off to the side, away from the crowd. She had known most of these people her whole life, but she was self-conscious that they still saw the addict. She'd yet to relapse, and Lee was grateful for the time, however brief it might be.

Belva sat in the corner on an old wooden chair, her skin and hair bleached, more sun than blood now. She was fading, and they all knew it.

Meredith spent hours with Belva every day, watching as she went about her daily business, sometimes with Cliff when he was interested. Lee liked to sit in just to hear Belva speak.

It was clear that Meredith was special. Extraordinary, like Redbud had been. A conjurer.

And then there was Cliff. The first seer in the family in five generations. He could see snatches of the future, but also people's emotions and the hidden qualities of things.

They, not Lee, would be the ones to perpetuate the tradition and continue Belva's work. Lee would always be there to support them and to spend a day or a night around the fire. But she didn't want to dedicate her life to it.

Lee had started looking at the counseling graduate program at the university a few hours away. She may not be powerful like her mother or Meredith, but she could roam around a person's internal landscape. She wanted to help people like her mother. She knew how seemingly impossible it was to treat addiction, and that was a challenge she wanted to meet. The quest for knowledge was where she'd thrived all those years ago, and she wanted to return to it. That was where she belonged. And now she would use it to serve her community, as generations of Bucks had done before her.

Lee had only seen Dreama from afar since that night, roaming the back roads in a daze. Her hair had thinned close to the skull, and her features were puffed but frail like balloon skin. She looked like a husk of a person, hollowed out and fading into the gray around her.

She and her husband were forced to file for bankruptcy after failing to sell enough plots in their subdivision development. Their restaurant chain had also failed to draw the right investment, and the crowds had slowed to a trickle, annoyed with the high prices and the forced versions of their grandma's favorites. They could taste the pretense, and it would close soon as well. Her husband had already left town to return to the Northeast without her, and he'd taken his strapping sons with him.

Lee imagined Dreama wandering the woods for the rest of her days and slowly fading into the scenery. Lee couldn't feel pure empathy for her after what she'd done to Otis, but she could lament the ruin of it, that such degradation could exist inside a person, and she had witnessed it.

A band began to play off to the side, and she noticed they were the same musicians from the bonfire when she first returned to Craw Valley.

Lee thought of drinking, and the way it had made that bonfire transcendent. She could feel that there was magic happening here, even without the booze, and she tried not to grip the feeling too hard. She'd started going to meetings with Redbud, and while she felt like a fraud with her stories of suburban boredom and late-night benders that paled in comparison to the depravity of the others, she found kinship and fortitude against the temptation there. Her addiction story extended beyond the boundaries of her own experience and radiated out around her in the community and behind her for generations, like the healing and magic that was also a part of her blood.

The smell of wild blueberries filled her nose, as if materializing out of the memory of the bonfire. A hand touched her shoulder, and she turned around.

There he was. Haloed in sunlight and wearing a garland of blossoms over his flannel. Otis ran a hand through her hair, and she kissed him on the wrist. They would have their time together later, and she burned at the promise of it.

Otis had woken from the coma the morning after they met Dreama in the woods. He still had a few minor neurological and motor issues, but it was undeniably *him*. He'd returned to her.

Meredith began to hum in the middle of the crowd, and gradually, the rest joined her unquestioningly, caught up in the moment. The sound was not as harmonious as usual, but it was beautiful for its slipshod form, like a cocoon made of sticks, feathers, and metallic ribbons of old chip bags.

When the hum reached a crescendo, Meredith let it resolve into a scream that she lobbed up toward the sky. In that scream, Lee could feel her daughter's love for Belva and her fear of losing her that had stored up all winter like snowdrifts. The energy of it released into the air like invisible fireworks.

From Redbud's place at the edge, Lee heard a painful, guttural holler shoot up like a rocket. Something shifted in her mother's face, and then her shoulders relaxed, and Lee watched her finally join the crowd.

Lee imagined all of her old regrets combining into a small sticky ball inside of her. She lit it on fire, and it burned a trail through her as it exited in a scream, sailing up and disappearing into the raw sunlight.

Others joined in, and their energy shot up in plumes among the treetops. The land would absorb this energy, this pain and elation, and channel it toward growing new things.

The band kicked up, and she watched as Kimmie pulled Cliff into a feral, twisting dance. Then Billy and Otis joined, moving their shoulders and shuffling their feet. Meredith leaped into the fray with Redbud, who swept her around the floor in a gleeful two-step.

Others joined in, inspired by the rough-edged movements of her family. Luann dragged Belva's chair to the center and danced around her as she clapped her hands. The dark flowers were innocent and emerald in the sun, curling around the dancing throng like wedding decorations.

For a while, Lee watched from the outside. There was so much joy and beauty in it.

Meredith came toward her with her arm outstretched and mischief in her eyes. Lee looked at her daughter, her heart pounding and the air fluttering in her throat. Then Lee took her hand, and she was pulled into the twisting, writhing tangle—

And she became one of them, their bodies moving together under the redbud branches flowering in the new sun—the first sign of spring.

# ACKNOWLEDGMENTS

First off, thank you to the ancestors, both distant and recently departed. To Peggy Shockley, the original "Grandma Mama," you were a special woman. I wish we had more time to know each other. To Lowangie Buck, a historian, a naturalist, an autodidact, a figure of elegance. This book is neither of your stories, but little pieces of you live within it.

To my former editor, Natalie Hallak, for helping me locate the organs of this book, especially the ones that feel. I have learned so much from working with you. To my new editor, Laura Brown, I'm excited to start this journey with you. To Elizabeth Hitti for your thoughtful suggestions and continued support—I am so happy to have you on my team. To Lindsay Sagnette and the rest of the exceptional team at Atria—I can't imagine a better place for this story.

To my agent, Alexandra Machinist, for reading this book in the middle of the night and deciding to take a chance on it. You are a force, and I am grateful to have your power in my corner. To Katherine Flitsch for everything you do behind the scenes—it is not taken for granted. To Michelle Weiner, Sarah Harvey, Karolina Sutton, and the rest of the team at CAA for your hard work.

To Clare Beams, who ran an online workshop for the Center for Fiction in the fall of 2020 where I wrote the first chapters of this book. Your enthusiasm helped me finally begin something I'd been working toward my whole life. Thank you to the writing group that grew out of that workshop—Tim Wojcik, Jason Baum, Rosa del Duca—for your invaluable feedback.

To the writing professors at UVA for my first undergrad workshops and to my fellow writers for reading and commenting on my early work.

To my friends at WME and Temple Hill for teaching me about books and stories, and to all the authors I've worked with for teaching me about writing.

To Kate Ringo for being my first reader and sounding board for all things. To Alex Addison for reading and offering guidance every step of the way. To Kaleigh Oleynik and Sarah Dougherty for reading early drafts. To Audrey Terrell for reading my first stories when we were kids. To all the friends who encouraged me to write and supported me over the years.

To Mark Dyer for giving me opportunities for a good life. To Amy Dyer and Lamont Ingalls, who showed me a life devoted to ideas and books. To Neile Minette, an avid reader and a loving mother; I wanted to write a book that you would read. To Jen Murphy for all that you do for us.

To John Dyer for your magic, and to Zach Hudgins for your attitude and tenderness. To Doug Hudgins for showing me what nature could offer. To Cindy Cates for your wildness. You all make up the strange little world that inspired this book.

To Lyca and Kingsley, my familiars.

To AJ Minette, my love, who made me believe I could do this.

To my mother, Cathy Hudgins, for everything. As usual, your contributions are too vital and overwhelming to capture.

And to the land—thank you for allowing me to draw from your power.

# ABOUT THE AUTHOR

Alli Dyer grew up in the Blue Ridge Mountains of Southwest Virginia, where her family has lived for generations. For the last decade, she has worked in entertainment and book publishing and now lives in Los Angeles. This is her first novel.